THE DROP

THE DROP

KRIS SWALES

A catalogue record for this book is available from the National Library of Australia

ISBN: 978 0 6489332 0 5 (paperback)
ISBN: 978 0 6489332 1 2 (eBook)
Cover design by Damian Wheeler
Cover illustration by Pete Georgiou
Waveform illustrations by D-Ko
Author photo by Rakhi Swales

Printed by IngramSpark

Lyrics to 'ABC', written by Adam Routh and Pete Gooding, used with permission.
Lyrics to 'Hands up for Detroit', written by Matthew Dear and David Shayman, used with permission.

CONTENTS

BREAKDOWN

BUILD-UP

THE DROP

OUTRO

ACKNOWLEDGEMENTS

To the scene I loved, and all those who made it.

Underground will live forever, baby.
We just like roaches, never dyin', always livin'.
Gang Starr (via Trancesetters)

C is for consciousness . . . L is for love.
Drax & Gooding feat. Taariq

PRELUDE

| 1.01 |

June 1, 2025

A chill westerly wind gusted up behind Kai Ishii, blowing in from the mountains bordering his corner of suburban Sydney across the endless hectares of bitumen and cement and megamalls in between. Summers that melted tarmac; winters that turned the household deep-fryer into an ice-skating rink for German cockroaches; bushfire smoke and dust storms semi-permanently blanketing the city. Even at thirteen, Kai understood the seasons were becoming more extreme; that the axis he'd learnt the world turns on seemed increasingly askew. He knew the Earth was dying, no matter how much his mother tried to deny it, and that one day he would too. His insides hollowed out, right on cue.

'Get out of your head, *noroma!*' Kai cursed himself out loud, plumping for the Japanese word for dunce. (He reserved his more colourful insults for Toca when his twin was at her most unbearable.) Kai smashed his left fist against his thigh, as if self-flagellation would banish the thought of his own mortality forever. As if the only real escape from any of his woes wasn't inside the thin Perspex lens wrapped around his eyes.

HeadBand, show me everything.

At Kai's thought command, dialogue box after dialogue box began to materialise in the viewfinder of his HeadBand. Countless translucent white boxes – some within swiping distance, others beyond his reach – competed for Kai's attention, each adding a layer of context to the world outside his head. In an instant the boxes were populated with data tables and tiny rows of crisp, deep blue digital text, presenting phrases and numbers about every facet of the distant cityscape: the height of Sydney Tower (Skywalk platform – 279 m; Top of spire – 305 m), its white and gold turret keeping watch above the skyscrapers on the horizon; the chance of rainfall on this gloomy first Sunday of winter (0%, though after being reliably informed his whole life by his father that 'the weatherman's a *noroma*', Kai didn't put much faith in this forecast either); the passenger load on each jumbo jet preparing to land at Sydney Airport.

Nothing of interest to him existed in the soulless expanse he looked out upon from the rooftop terrace of his family's apartment block in boring old Doonside. None of what surrounded him mattered. Twenty apartment towers, identical to theirs, all the way down to the dull textured-cement finish. Housing estates swallowing up the last remaining patches of green he'd played in as a kid. School bullies. Hate-tagging. HeadBand gossip groups. If you didn't skate or shoot hoops or big-up yourself over who you wanted to shank, Western Sydney was worse than a teenage wasteland. It was life as a death row inmate.

Yet the sinking feeling in Kai's stomach had begun to slink away, carrying the intrusive thoughts of his own mortality with it. 'Like when you've got a fever and Mum puts a cold towel on your forehead' was how Toca described the HeadBand's knack for putting everything in its right place. Except his HeadBand didn't just make Kai forget – it made him feel more alive.

Endless streams of data danced out of Kai's HeadBand processor and across his field of vision. Everything he could ever want to know, about the scene laid out before him or anything else besides, was but a thought command away. But there were only two things worth knowing: that he wanted to be over *there*, in the CBD, where everyone moved at an urgent pace and the apartment towers and their inhabitants positively sparkled; and that the only dialogue box that interested him on this first afternoon of winter was the one that would soon serve him up the highlights from Juanita's One World set in Singapore from the night before.

Toca teased Kai incessantly about his Juanita crush (among many other things), but about this one his twin sister was bang on target, for a change. ('Ewwww, brotato, she's as old as Mum,' Toca reminded him, often. As if Cosmo, her One World DJ crush of choice, wasn't comfortably into his thirties as well.) He'd been obsessed with Juanita from the mid-December morning he'd laid eyes on her, six months earlier. The afternoon before he'd come home from school wearing the HeadBand he was stuck with, to stop the spread of COVID-23, for the rest of his life.

That early summer dawn was the first time Kai had braved the lift to the Nurragingy Towers roof, to escape the snoring offensive being waged from the other side of the bedroom he shared with his twin. The skies, for a change, had been clear of dust and smoke, a rare event that summer (and spring for that matter) and for any of the five summers before it. Flipping through video feeds of everything from crocodile racing to profiles of Earth's most compassionate dictators, Kai had chanced upon the One World festival and his first crush – a DJ called Juanita, honey-voiced and immaculately tanned and manoeuvring her hips and torso in ways he couldn't quite comprehend. In one of the cavernous abandoned sports stadiums of Europe she had bounced behind a robust metal table, a single finger raised tauntingly to the sky. The late afternoon sky above Juanita morphed stealthily into night. Every time she made a move, the vast crowd spread before her mimicked. Kai felt a giddiness he'd experienced just once before, on his birthday ten months earlier when the Luna Park roller-coaster neared the top of its climb. This, though, had been something else entirely. Never before had a twelve-year-old boy been so happy to be awake before 7 am.

'Are you feeling the love?' Juanita had demanded of her audience before leaping off the stage into a gigantic bubble – of what Kai couldn't be certain, but it clearly wasn't soap and water. Her body, tranquil amid the chaos, seemed to float above a sea of hands leaping up and down as one, in sync with the music blaring all around them. Her soundtrack thundered through Kai's speaker cups at breakneck speed: tuneless synthesisers screamed for attention left and right while repetitive kick drums pounded down the centre. One almost identical song segued seamlessly into the next. Kai had heard EDM before, but never like this; beats so fast they left you gasping for breath, silly melodies that sounded naggingly familiar, like something his mother, Stefanie, had listened to around the house when he was a child.

'Juanita's been playing EDM just like this since I was young and cool enough to be on the Olympic Stadium dancefloor right in front of her,' Stefanie Ishii had explained to him matter-of-factly once he'd gone back down for breakfast on that morning in December. 'I've met her, you know,' Stefanie continued, absentmindedly flipping rashers of bacon. She'd swerved instinctively to the right as fat spat towards her face, but not quickly enough. With a wry smile, she'd wiped two round blotches off her HeadBand lens, leaving long streaks like tyre marks across sand. 'Well, I saw her up close, inside the Love Inn foyer when I was window shopping on Oxford Street just before Christmas.'

On the roof six months later, Kai stared longingly towards the city, his glimmer of hope. He reached out to the horizon, clutched a chunk of thin air in each hand like he was grabbing his winter blanket and pulled the cityscape towards him. The jumbo jets, lined up across the Inner West in one direction and Botany Bay in the other, grew to the size of the Lego spaceships he'd built as a much younger child from the tiny insects they'd resembled moments ago. If only HeadBands had access to passenger manifests so Kai could track Juanita's return flight from Singapore this afternoon all the way to the tarmac. At least he could narrow things down by zooming in further on the jets' tail-fin decals, to try and spot the one bearing Halcyon Industries' distinctive logo – a vinyl record with corrugated edges, representing a small (musical) cog in a larger machine, with an ideogram of two hands pressed together to form a heart on the white circular label at the record's centre. The heart-hands symbol that Juanita had been spreading around the world for a decade or more.

'Do you think Juanita could rock a crowd the way she does if she didn't know the basics?' Kai's mother had teased him ten minutes earlier, issuing her standard challenge to her eldest son any time he was dispatched to his room to practise his scales.

Toca had mockingly played air piano at him from across the dining-room table. Standard. So far as Kai could tell, his twin's primary role was to be a mirror image of himself that he had to resist popping right in the nose for its incessant sass. Air piano he could handle, especially when the skin-tight bodysuit he'd taken to wearing on weekends, in tribute to Juanita's standard One World attire, was her preferred object of ridicule.

No matter how much his HeadBand's KeyRoll emulator made playing piano feel like a video game, practising scales was the worst. A thirteen-year-old boy wasn't supposed to spend so much time locked away in solitude unless he'd locked himself in there of his own volition. Why couldn't he just skip past the rigmarole of rehearsal and fast-forward straight to the stadiums and the crowds and the glory?

Satoshi Ishii's clenched fist had thumped the dining-room table, jolting his favourite tea cup – an ornate antique Japanese design which Kai and his twin dared not touch – from its perch atop its matching saucer, also trimmed in gold. At the foot of the table Kai's kid brother and their father's enabler, Kentaro, squealed with delight.

'These fascists in Canberra and their bullshit!' Satoshi thundered, his eyes focused two feet in front of him on something only he could see.

Kai and Toca locked eyes across the table, daring each other to be first to laugh at their father's latest out-of-context outburst. Satoshi Ishii had waged a long and determined campaign to keep HeadBands out of the Ishii home, and especially off Kentaro, the golden child and wannabe football prodigy. But even Satoshi's protests against the 'fascist' imposition of it all ('Did the Privacy Rioters die for nothing?') had dried up once he'd found the *Akira* soundtrack in the database on his first night of installation, just a few days after Halcyon's mobile surgeries had done the rounds of Doonside's schools. And there he was, just over six months after the Transglobal Union's HeadBand Accord had made wearing them compulsory for all persons over six, paying more attention to what was happening inside his viewfinder than on the faces of the people seated around him at the table. One rule for the man of the house and one for the rest the family, who were banned by Stefanie from swiping through dialogue boxes at mealtimes.

'*Such* a double standard, Mum,' Toca had complained after Satoshi spent Christmas lunch, smelling of sake, swiping through a private reel of every goal Keisuke Honda had scored for the Japan national football team, long before the first pandemic had put an end to international competition.

'Goalllll!' Satoshi shouted. 'Can you say that, Kenny?'

Kentaro, synced up to the same video feed, nodded eagerly. '*Goalllll!*'

'Just let your father have this one, dear,' Stefanie had countered. 'He can be as frustrated with the world as he wants in there if it means we get the best of him out here.'

(Kai had quickly discovered a workaround to the meal-time ban – assign all of the HeadBand's default tactile commands to your thoughts before sitting down to eat and you could swipe away to your heart's content without the grown-ups being any the wiser.)

Satoshi raised his right hand, now unclenched, and angrily back-handed the air in front of him as if swatting aside a particularly persistent fly.

'Blow up one politician and more of the bastards crawl out of the gutters, looking to take their place. And nothing changes for us honest working folk. Not for the better, anyways.'

Stefanie Ishii rinsed her plate at the kitchen island, a bemused smile edging out from the side of her lips. 'That's right, dear,' Stefanie said. Kai's mother had a knack for perfectly balancing her tone somewhere between patronising and accommodating, which Kai had only recognised as quiet genius now that he'd moved into his teens. 'But I think we've seen enough since Valentine's Day to realise this country's not going to run itself forever.'

The twins' younger brother, Kentaro – such a short, round six-year-old facsimile of his father that Kai was eternally grateful he'd received a generous portion of his mother's genes – kicked his heels against his chair's legs, bored of the traditional Sunday lunch from the second he'd devoured the last crumbs of his ham and cheese toastie.

Poor little Kenny, Kai thought. *Doesn't know what to do with himself when he's not the centre of Dad's attention.*

The installers had told Kai he would grow into his HeadBand eventually, but Kentaro's was so disproportionate to his face it was like he'd been fitted with an adult diving mask.

Stefanie ran the frypan under the tap while Satoshi continued. 'As if corporations haven't been running the lot for decades,' he mumbled beneath his breath, animatedly swiping the air.

Kai had a good idea which two video feeds his father would be scrolling through inside his HeadBand – Sky Tokyo and CNN Japan. Both were running the same *The World Votes* coverage Australia's two remaining broadcast news feeds had begun spewing forth once the dust had settled on the V-Day massacre, when a missile blast had hit the Transglobal Union's annual conference in Moscow, killing most of the world's key leaders in one hit.

With the exception of the night the breaking news broadcast had overridden his HeadBand commands, Kai had paid scant attention to the mass political assassination or any of the other horrors clogging up his news feeds: more mass fish kills in the Murray, fields of oil in the Middle East desert set permanently ablaze. Doonside was depressing enough, why make it worse? The only broadcast he cared about came from Juanita and her fellow One World DJs. He didn't need reminding the world wasn't a happy place. All he wanted was a place to escape.

'So, if you could go vote for whichever candidate seems the least likely to have foreign invaders fired the next time unemployment spikes, that would be grand. I already voted at the polling booth this morning while you slept off the graveyard shift,' Stefanie continued as she surveyed the inside of the fridge. 'And you better take Toca to pick up what we need for miso soup tonight.'

Suck it, sister, Kai mouthed to the caustic carbon copy seated across from him.

'But *Muuuum,* how come Kai gets to stay here and ogle Juanita—'

'Your brother will be practising scales for the rest of the afternoon, which should knock that smug look off his face,' Stefanie interjected. 'Then we'll all sit down to watch Juanita's birthday homecoming tonight – together, as a family, the way Tito said One World broadcasts should be.'

Toca's eyes narrowed triumphantly behind her HeadBand's orange-tinted lens. Kai could almost hear her saying '*Toosh,* brother, *toosh!*', mangling their favourite French cliché in true western Sydney bogan style. Not that it was a stretch for the twins to put the accent on – Japanese-Portuguese their heritage may have been, but the Ishii family dialect was as western Sydney bogan as it got.

'As for you, Bubsy'—Stefanie ruffled Kentaro's hair as she collected his plate—'go downstairs and play now or you'll miss your chance.' She squinted through her HeadBand's clear lens and out the window. Narrow shafts of darkening sky were visible between their own Block 19 and the adjacent Nurragingy Towers apartment blocks.

'*Goalllll,* Ishii scores!'

Kentaro kicked his chair back and sprinted towards the front door, slamming it behind him.

'Energy to burn, that boy of yours,' Satoshi grumbled in Stefanie's ear. He kissed her cheek and swiped his keys off the kitchen island in one motion. 'Don't just sit there, Toca!'

'He's his father's son, after all,' Stefanie retorted. She stole a worried glance over Satoshi's broad shoulders. 'Be quick, Satty – looks like another nasty one rolling in.'

Toca poked her tongue out at Kai, who wasn't quick enough to snatch it between his fingertips.

'Sorry, brotato, gotta shuttle – hands to shake, babies to kiss, you know how it goes,' Toca quipped. She followed their father through the lounge room towards the front door before spinning to taunt Kai some more. Shuffle-skipping backwards, nimbly weaving past furniture without so much as clipping it, she poked her tongue at Kai again through the narrowing crack in the doorway. The data-readout on the right side of Kai's HeadBand viewfinder showed his vital signs – heart rate, blood pressure – tick briskly upwards.

But his sister had left the front door ajar. His mother's head was buried deep in the pantry.

Now's my chance.

'Thanks for lunch, Mum,' Kai said, dumping his plate in the kitchen island's sink. If he wanted to escape sight unseen, he couldn't even risk stopping to slip on his sneakers. 'I'll be in my room doing scales until dinner time.'

Kai had slipped out the front door and into the lift to escape to his safe place: the rooftop of Nurragingy Towers Block 19. Now, his previously uninterrupted view of the skyscrapers and queued up passenger planes was obscured by a flickering array of dialogue boxes, so haphazardly arranged he couldn't distinguish one from the next.

HeadBand, hide all.

His viewfinder decluttered. Kai heard rather than felt the westerly wind increase in strength, so wide was the windbreak of the lift's enclosed engine room at his back. There were no stainless-steel barbecues nor terrace gardens up here, like Kai imagined covered the rooftops of the nearby metropolis, so close yet so tantalisingly out of reach; no futsal pitches, tennis courts nor infinity pools. Up here, almost every square metre of space was covered with solar panels, each of them, like his HeadBand's speaker cups, bearing a tiny Halcyon Industries stamp on their underside. (Kai's pleas for a Halcyon shirt for his birthday had copped a typically off-hand dismissal from his father: 'You're a teenage boy, not a billboard.') A smattering of air-conditioning units – barely a year old, like the apartment tower itself, yet already covered with a thick layer of silt from that summer's bushfire smoke and dust storms – stood dormant between them.

Apart from the huddle of small satellite dishes in the south-east corner, jerry-rigged to a metal umbrella stand by Kai's neighbour Mr

Banerjee (when Kai asked his father why he would need them when Halcyon's 10G internet was everywhere, 'probably match-fixing some Mickey Mouse T20 league' was the grunted reply), the only other fitting on the roof was Stefanie Ishii's makeshift clothesline – three strands of twisted cable stretching across the five metres separating the nearest air-con unit and the lift shaft against Kai's back. As the westerly found its voice, the items of clothing on it whipped back and forth: his mother's activewear, his little brother's Doonside United soccer kit (bearing Keisuke Honda's famous No 4, at Satoshi's insistence), two of Toca's hopelessly optimistic training bras, and six brown, button-up short-sleeved shirts Kai's father insisted on wearing when on ride-share driving duties, even though he answered to no one but himself. Kai knew he'd regret it when looking for fresh underwear before school tomorrow, but his dirty clothes were piled up in a corner of the bedroom floor, where they belonged.

And Kai was where he belonged, in his safe space, or at least what passed for one now that the Ishii family home was shared with 142 other families. After Satoshi had lost his shift manager job at the hydraulics warehouse, the cubbyhouse Kai had sought refuge in behind their house on Birdwood Avenue had, for twelve months now, been the refuge of some other kids he'd never know. But he'd finally found a new place he could be on his own, among the softly humming panels that powered his building. He'd found Juanita here, as well.

BZZZZT!

The ping of his HeadBand's message notification system interrupted Kai's daydream with all the finesse of a drill bit about to tunnel into his skull. He instinctively felt for the stainless-steel MIDI disc connecting his HeadBand's technofibre side straps to the implant in his left temple. ('Musical Instrument Digital Interface might be 1980s tech,' Matthias 'Tito' van Dijk, Halcyon's charismatic founder, had explained in one of the HeadBand's many video tutorials. 'But it remains so perfect for helping computers send commands to synthesisers that I knew it could help us talk to our HeadBands as well.')

The HeadBand's straps felt like no other substance Kai had touched. Sitting somewhere between plastic and neoprene, each length of technofibre was composed of precisely forty strands of thin cable, rigid yet able to expand as his skull dawdled its way towards full maturity. Despite being the hub via which Kai's thought commands were distributed through his HeadBand, the MIDI disc always felt ice cold, even as torrents of data coursed with such urgency through the rippled straps that they pulsed like external arteries. The straps ran from the edges of Kai's viewfinder to his speaker cups – big, cumbersome things more akin to what he'd seen Juanita wearing while DJing in her old photo galleries than any earplugs the cool kids of Doonside would've been caught dead in, back when they'd still had a choice in the matter. These headphones didn't shut out the real world so much as amplify it, turning something as nondescript as Satoshi's brown shirts, flapping in the breeze with slightly more vigour now, into a binaural masterpiece all of their own if Kai thought-commanded his HeadBand to zero in on it.

Kai was still coming to terms with the sheer deluge of information spat at him by the viewfinder, most of it unbidden. At least the MK4 viewfinders, mass-produced once the Accord was signed, were closer in size and shape to regular speed-dealer sunnies – the MK1s the Doonside soccer mums had been flashing around in late 2023, soon after it was discovered COVID-23 spread via tear ducts, had more in common with welding goggles than what HeadBands had become. The upper frame of the MK4 pressed tightly across his eyebrow line, the underside vacuum-sealed to his cheekbones and affixed to his nose with a black rubber clip. Six months since installation and his HeadBand almost felt like an extension of his face, although he was still adjusting to its near-constant hectoring. Even the hourly interruptions of the moisture control system misting up his viewfinder were more tolerable than the alerts, and he'd never been troubled by dry-eye syndrome – a common complaint for wearers, even with moisture control dialled up to eleven – inside his HeadBand or otherwise.

BZZZZT!

Toca's avatar blinked on and off at the left of his screen next to an icon of an ancient telephone receiver. (Kai didn't understand why they still used this icon when he hadn't seen a phone in years.)

'Not now, Tokes.'

HeadBand, dismiss incoming call.

Within a nanosecond of Kai issuing the thought command, the pinging in his temples stopped. Zero-latency response to thought commands was, as Satoshi Ishii described it, perhaps man's greatest accomplishment since the invention of the vuvuzela; to Kai, anything slower than an instantaneous response would've been unacceptable.

He lifted his hands into the space before his eyes, obscuring the magnificent city view on the far side of the far-less impressive urban sprawl. So far as Kai could ascertain, his viewfinder's workspace had a default setting of three parts: essential apps pinned to a virtual tabletop along the lowest point of his vision, which he could reach with his arms half extended; to his right a column of essential data, including weather conditions and his own vital signs readout; opposite on the left, a column of identical proportions with a constantly updating dataflow of newsflashes, video dumps and incoming messages.

Every icon across the three-sided frame was touch-sensitive and translucent, augmenting the real world as Kai now saw it. 'Every colour saturated and enhanced, every megapixel zoomable', as Juanita had explained in another of his HeadBand's tutorial videos.

Kai pressed the icon pinned to the top of the left-hand column, its thumbnail photo shot from behind Juanita in her signature pose – frozen mid-leap, hands forming the shape of a heart above her head, straight blue locks shooting out either side like wings, thousands upon thousands of hands in the crowd throwing their own heart-hands right back at her.

HeadBand, waveform and human-movement analysis of Juanita, One World, 31-5-25.

And this is why you can go shove your scales, Mum.

Practising scales was for amateurs when your onboard computer could parse Juanita's secrets for you. The status bar across Kai's tabletop began counting down from forty-seven seconds. He screwed up his mouth. *Slower than yesterday!* The clock below his vital signs box ticked over to 15:04. Keeping time with the dots marking each passing second, Kai tried to blink away the tiredness in his eyes, which were still adjusting to the constant stimuli of his viewfinder's digital readout. It wasn't just his eyes that ached. The growing pains wracking his lower calves were in lockstep with the throb beating away inside both temples.

BZZZZT!

The Ishii family reminder rumble, again. It may have been designed as a gentle nudge, but to Kai it was as subtle as one of his father's barked orders across the apartment. He'd switched off his HeadBand's auto-answer functionality shortly after Kentaro had realised he could pop up in Kai's viewfinder at any time – which he did, with an uncanny knack of picking the exact moment Kai assumed the position on the toilet. Nonetheless, Stefanie Ishii had insisted that notifications of some form were compulsory for all intra-family messaging as a 'safety precaution'. Vibrating alerts was a compromise Kai had grudgingly accepted.

HeadBand, ignore all calls from Toca Ishii for five minutes.

Toca's avatar zoomed off to the left of Kai's viewfinder dashboard, a tiny icon of an envelope beside it (*What even is an envelope?*), just as a rotund figure barrelled out of the lift, almost tripping over Kai's outstretched legs as it rounded the corner. Mr Banerjee had his young daughter, Sanya, flung over his left shoulder like a beach towel, her dark, disoriented little eyes made to look even darker by lids outlined thick with black kajal to keep evil spirits away. Tucked under his right armpit was the widest Hong Kong shopping bag Kai had ever seen, still so neatly folded that its red, white and blue chequered polypropylene looked like it'd come hot off the press. Sanya's hands gripped her father's white cotton kurta for dear life as his body careened past Kai and towards the tangle of satellite dishes and cables crammed into the nearest corner of the rooftop.

'What's the hurry, Mr Banerjee?' Kai cried out. His meek little boy's voice was overpowered by the wind, rapidly shifting up through the gears from gusting to howling.

In one motion, the Bengali deposited his daughter on the ground, opened the bag to its full expanse and began to tear wildly at wiring and DIY cotton cable-ties with the reckless abandon of the two year 9 girls Kai had snuck into the girls' toilets to watch fight during his first week at Doonside Tech. Without losing momentum, Mr Banerjee stamped his foot on the base of the bag so it didn't get swept over the edge and off towards the CBD. Red satellite dishes and rusted clamps and clumps of green-coated wire were shoved into the bag in a matter of seconds. Fingernail-shaped slivers of the metal discs and loose ends of cable spewed out of the bag's mouth like sliced tomato and shredded lettuce from a badly packed kebab.

Collecting Sanya – under his arm this time – and slinging the bag's flimsy straps over his shoulder, Mr Banerjee turned back towards the lift, only to leap back with a start when his eyes met Kai's. Little Sanya's eyes, still unburdened by a HeadBand because she was well below kindergarten age, just looked confused, while terror popped through her father's sepia-tinted HeadBand lens. Wind swirled around Kai's speaker cups with such ferocity it seemed the sky was about to open up and unleash a comic-book movie army of alien marauders on the citizens of Doonside, though it wasn't fierce enough to disturb Mr Banerjee's impressively thick combover.

Rapid-fire buzzing rumbled through Kai's entire HeadBand. The download of Juanita's set analysis froze with three seconds remaining as a dialogue box flashed on and off inside Kai's viewfinder, bold red text on white background flanked by two swirling storm cells.

** WARNING **

CATEGORY 5 DUST STORM APPROACHING

SEEK SHELTER IMMEDIATELY

** WARNING **

Kai turned his hands counter-clockwise, sending his HeadBand's menu bars into an unseen recess to declutter his view, and looked up to the sky. The red alert held its position in front of a sky which had suddenly transformed from overcast to ominous, clouds smashing up against each other in a whirlpool of rage: red and yellow and grey colliding in furious anger to produce a vibrant orange haze, emitting a glow so eerie it seemed the entire sky had been set ablaze. Kai sensed his technofibre straps heating up, even without any visible data read-outs to power.

Their father had lectured Kai and Toca long and hard on why so many dust storms were now blowing in from far-western New South Wales. 'Hopefully the great drought of 2025 is the worst you kids will ever see,' he'd whispered, tears welling inside his viewfinder in a rare show of emotion other than frustration, anger, or gushing admiration for Keisuke Honda's running game. 'Hopefully whoever we vote in will put the planet ahead of their donors this time.'

Still, Kai couldn't remember a storm this fierce creeping up unnoticed, despite looking for all the world as if it had blown in from the surface of Mars. Goosebumps prickled beneath his bodysuit. These goosebumps had nothing to do with the wind, although his naked feet were freezing. These goosebumps were all fear. This storm wasn't like the dust storms Kai had come to know, all fierce winds and dull grey haze with the occasional crackle of lightning above the distant hills; this storm's sickly orange glow and violently clashing clouds placed it far, far beyond normal.

Mr Banerjee snapped back into action. '*Kai ji, chalo, chalo!*' he blurted as he trundled past Kai towards the lift. Kai understood that much in Hindi from the Doonside Tech schoolyard. *Kai sir, come on, let's go!* Sanya reached both hands out to Kai and giggled on their way past. 'You don't want to get caught out in the storm itself!'

The lift doors swallowed them up as the fire escape door burst open. 'Kaiiiii!'

Mum. Shit!

Stefanie Ishii clattered out of the fire escape entrance straight to Kai's secret spot, which was clearly a little less secret than he thought. *Toca, you little snitch.*

'I need you to get down to the playground and find Kentaro right now!' she cried, her face pale with panic. 'Have you heard from Toca? Your father must be driving.'

'I was practising and put her on mute,' Kai lied apologetically, twirling his right arm in a clockwise direction to bring his dashboard menus back into view.

He grabbed the flashing envelope icon next to Toca's name, then threw it towards Stefanie's HeadBand so they could watch the message simultaneously. As Kai leapt to his feet, Toca appeared in their viewfinders as seen through the dashcam of Satoshi Ishii's taxicab – the green Mitsubishi Mirage he'd bought to celebrate his short-lived job at the hydraulics shop. Satoshi's deeply lined face wore an extra layer of worry. Toca's face was flushed. Kai hadn't seen her so distressed, not even watching movies in which a dog died.

'Kai, Dad says tell Mum right away that we're on our way home from the polling booth.'

'Get Kentaro inside, quickly!' Satoshi rasped.

'It's scary as bro, even worse than the Anzac Day storm,' Toca spluttered. 'See you s—'

Stefanie swung a forehand at Kai's bottom the instant the message was cut short.

'Ow, what was that for?'

'Fuck me dead, Kai, this is exactly why we keep family notifications on.'

Kai had never heard his Mum use the f-word before so he knew he was in seriously deep shit.

'I'm getting the washing off the line,' Stefanie fumed, still catching her breath from the sprint up twenty flights of stairs in her less-than-athletic state.

Until now, Kai had never thought to ponder why his mother had quit her touch football competition shortly after the twins' twelfth birthday, when they'd been forced to sell their perfect little house and spacious backyard just around the corner after his dad lost his job – had it stolen from him, Stefanie had said, when the ruling came down that only Australian-born citizens could hold middle-management roles. It had been right in front of Kai all along, flapping away on the clothesline between the activewear and the training bras. She hadn't wanted to stop playing touch footy, or even to downsize; she hadn't had a choice. They were poor people now and when hard choices had to be made, golden child Kentaro's dreams of soccer stardom, which no one had the heart to tell him didn't exist now that professional contact sport was banned, had come first.

Stefanie wrapped her hand around Kai's wrist and stormed towards the lift, dragging Kai in her wake. 'Go get your brother from the playground,' she said, pushing the down arrow, 'and we'll work out how to deal with you when your father gets home.'

Kai's mother shoved him into the lift the second the doors opened. No fists on hips. No playful head tilt. Not even one of her withering *now I'm really mad* looks. *Deep, deep shit.*

In the lift, soothing muzak piped gently through a pair of tinny speakers, each instrument slathered generously in emotion-deadening compression. The bandleader's saxophone solo was delivered with dispassionate precision, despite quite obviously being played by human hands. Kai often whiled away the seconds of his daily downward journey trying to put himself in the sax player's no doubt pointy shoes. What message was he trying to deliver while his fingers danced nimbly across the valves? Where was his imagination taking him? Whatever his intention, the melody was as lifeless as the speakers delivering the muzak to its captive audience.

Today, the music barely registered. Muffled screams from the apartments buttressing the shaft cut through the lift's mirrored walls. Kai focused on the floor numbers counting down, praying he'd get past the eleventh floor without other passengers joining. No one got on. ('Different lifts to service the top and bottom halves of the building,' Satoshi had sales-pitched his unconvinced family when he signed the lease a year earlier. 'Genius!')

Trembling, Kai tapped out rhythms on his thighs as the lift cruised towards the ground floor. The screams grew louder, more condensed.

Three . . . Two . . . One . . .

Ding!

Panic-stricken people forced their way into the lift before Kai had a chance to step out. He sidestepped left and slid past a deluge of mothers and children – some, like Mr Banerjee's Sanya, so young they'd yet to reach legal HeadBand age. They howled buckets of crocodile tears as the hysteria engulfing their parents infected them as well.

Kai sprinted through the automatic sliding-glass front doors of Nurragingy Towers Block 19 into a swirling bedlam of red and yellow, day and night. Under the storm-front surging towards the city from the west, eucalyptus saplings bowed to Kai as he ran by. A semi-crushed soft-drink can scraped across the cement footpath beneath him.

Tiny stones rebounded off Kai's viewfinder like bugs off a windscreen. To his left, the basketball court's chain-link gate swung violently. He put his head down and ploughed into the onslaught, which despite its visual ferocity was doing little to slow Kai down; his body felt so detached from his mind, the ground beneath him so unsteady, it was like he was trying to escape from another person's dream. He swerved his way past the basketball court, recoiling as a green shopping bag zipped past his face a little too close for comfort, then abruptly vanished.

The footpath curled around to Kai's left, leading him to the small array of children's play equipment his mother had got up a petition to be erected for the Nurragingy complex's youngest inhabitants, not long after the Ishiis had moved in.

'Kentaro!' Kai's voice cut cleanly through the surrounding chaos. No response. *Fuck fuck fuck,* Kai thought. *If he's not here I am screwed.*

Both of Kai's temples were jolted by the forceful buzz of his Head-Band's breaking news override system. Dust, leaves and cigarette butts swirled around him. A woman's face materialised in his viewfinder, hovering serenely as if impervious to nature's fury. Her face was backed by the headrest of a passenger plane's seat. The rim of her sky-blue-tinted HeadBand lens glowed an even more brilliant green. But Juanita's hair was a wavy mouse brown, not bright blue and perfectly straight. Her cheeks sagged; her lips had lost their glisten; behind her viewfinder, crow's feet as deep as Stefanie Ishii's showed. Kai couldn't decide whether Juanita had just woken up or hadn't slept at all, but he knew he'd never seen his idol looking quite as unglamorous as this, like she'd been called upon to perform at short notice.

'Greetings, my beautiful people,' Juanita said, game face restored, her delivery as cold and controlled as Kai's tutor bot. 'The catastrophic storms striking your area are being experienced simultaneously across the world. Py-ro . . .' she stuttered, as if momentarily confused, before ever-so-slightly nodding her head. 'Pyrocumulus cloud fronts are generating lightning strikes unlike anything Halcyon's scientists have previously encountered. Please seek safety inside and await further instruction. Children aged two and up should be fitted with the emergency HeadBands you've been provided.'

Juanita's face usually radiated joy, her voice typically an abundant source of energy that welcomed all who heard it to join her for the ride. Today, her face was ashen, her voice shaky and tense, like Toca when she'd just woken up from a nightmare.

For the first time, Kai saw his teenage crush as human. *She's as scared as I am.*

'I'm about to touch down safely in Sydney and can't wait to perform for you all again soon.' Juanita's projection blew a kiss down the lens before her face was swallowed by static.

'Kenny!' Kai roared, unlatching the safety gate and racing onto the play area's spongy green and gold flooring. From the opening at the bottom of the spiral tube slide Kentaro spent most of his afternoon playtime riding, Kai heard an anguished whimper. Kai slid to a halt. His kid brother crouched in the darkness, just above where the slide coiled towards its exit tube. Kentaro's wide eyes were lit up by his viewfinder's darkness-sensing LEDs.

'Kai, Kai, what's wrong with the sky?'

'C'mon, bubsy, I've got you,' Kai urged his brother towards the lip of the plastic tube.

Kentaro shook his head. Kai was going to have to bring out the big guns.

'We're going to play Keisuke Honda all the way to the lift, okay?' Kai extended his hand. 'The fastest we've ever played it.'

Kentaro looked doubtful. His entire body shivered. But he latched onto Kai's little finger.

'Winner gets Toca's dessert tonight.'

Kentaro suddenly leapt out of the tube, squealing with delight. His mini-Satoshi body (spindly legs, round girth) somehow curled around, then through, the open security gate at breakneck speed, despite appearing as aerodynamic as Mr Banerjee's beach-ball face. Kai pirouetted into step three metres behind him and sprinted with everything he had, ducking and miraculously avoiding the tidal surge of debris overhead – palm leaves, moulded plastic chairs, a kids' slimline metal scooter – watching as it collided with the tower wall to his left, spraying chips of concrete against the nearest bedroom window.

Kentaro passed through the sliding-door entrance and had disappeared amid the surging waves of humanity by the time Kai crashed into the foyer.

'Kenny!'

'Kai, Kai, quick!'

A tiny hand poked out between two adult thighs, clutching the air as it was sucked through the lift doors. Kai sprinted across the tiles, swerving through bodies moving every which way, and slid on his knees into the unclaimed space in the lift before its doors shut on desperate fingers behind him. He manoeuvred his hand around an overweight man's putrid, sweat-drenched rear to press the button marked 11. For a second time, he fully appreciated why his father sang the praises of two lifts dedicated to each set of ten floors in their twenty-storey tower – and that their floor was always the first this lift stopped on. The cabin was filled with a panting, uneasy near-silence. A woman openly wept. The sax player, failing to read the room, wailed on.

The lift's bell tolled. As the door opened. Kai was forcibly ejected from the rocking cradle of sweat and despair, sprawling onto the hallway's polished concrete floor. Kentaro crawled out between a pair of bowlegs, thick with matted black hair, and raced through the open door of their apartment to his right. Kai half-crawled, half-walked through the entrance and pulled the door closed behind them.

'Bubsy!' Stefanie blubbered, turning away from the horror movie showing on the other side of the balcony's glass sliding doors.

Kentaro lunged towards his mother, latching on like a koala to a gum tree. Kai slid across the tiles on his knees, a move perfected across six months of parent-infuriating practice. No comparisons with a Keisuke Honda goal celebration could ever convince his father to approve. Nor his mother, given how quickly Kai burned through bodysuits.

Stefanie held Kai and Kentaro close. Through the living room window, they watched unidentified objects flying through the gloom. Forks of red lightning crackled urgently from the sides of ill-tempered clouds, as if licking their lips expectantly while awaiting the signal to strike downwards instead of sideways. Greater Doonside was gone, obscured by clouds of dust. The CBD backdrop was but a memory. There was only their balcony and the other blocks of Nurragingy Towers. Beyond that, mayhemic destruction.

Minutes passed. The storm's severity built and built until Kai's weather readout was maxed out (although the chance of rain still sat at 0%).

Then the front door burst in as if smashed by a battering ram. Kai jumped. Kentaro squealed. Exhausted, Satoshi Ishii fell onto the lounge room floor, Toca clutched to his chest. Mother, father and youngest son gravitated to each other. A bawling Toca wrapped herself around her twin, sobbing uncontrollably into his shoulder.

Shadows of black and gold and red danced across Kai's face and perfectly straight black hair, strangely unruffled by the maelstrom he'd just encountered. He was lost, adrift in his own secret confusion, while the rest of his family found comfort in each other's presence.

Something caught Kai's attention inside his HeadBand – the 10G icon on the lower, tabletop-style menu bar, lit up green instead of red. *Excellent.* He peeled away from Toca and moved towards the balcony's sliding glass door on the pretext of taking a closer look at the carnage outside.

HeadBand, complete analysis and launch One World player.

The afternoon wasn't a total write-off after all. Juanita was waiting.

INTRO

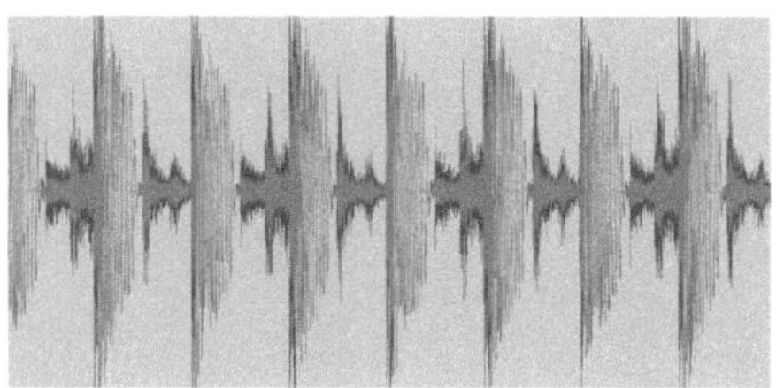

| 2.01 |

Something Good

Kai hustled and bustled along the underground tunnel connecting Nurragingy Towers to Doonside Station, swerving past sluggish pedestrians with more enthusiasm than he'd mustered in months. Cosmo's warm-up set, coming in hot from his studio in Valencia, thundered through Kai's speaker cups. The Virtuoso moved through Love Buzz anthems, from the uplifting 'Don't You Worry, Slippy Children' to the punishing 'Aftermath of Del Mar's Sandstorm', so effortlessly it was as if the set had been recorded in advance. Kai's heart pumped in double-time – ticking towards 170 beats per minute, according to his Head-Band's vital signs readout – as if racing to catch up to the souped-up tempo. Default layout aside, his HeadBand display had been cleared of unwanted distractions.

Kai had been waiting for this night since before the Storm; since the dust-choked, brown rain-sodden days of his thirteenth summer, when One World had sowed the seeds for Love Buzz, the non-stop EDM party that had brought the broken planet back together – or as together as it could be when each Survivor was stuck in the city they happened to be in on 1-6-25, the day the Storm struck. Then along came Love Buzz, four days later: the world's twenty-four best DJs playing round the clock, beaming the biggest EDM bangers ever made direct from their living rooms into your HeadBand. By September 1, 2025,

Halcyon's Trancentral stadium network had been fortified against the Storm, ready to take real-life crowds. In the just short of three years since, Kai had campaigned so fervently to attend a Love Buzz festival in person once he and Toca reached legal age that his father had finally relented his hardline stance against any of the Ishiis leaving the safe-and-sound Doonside Cluster, the self-contained neighbourhood they shared with 30,000 Survivors and counting. ('It's not a suburb any more,' Toca joked. 'It's a breeding ground.')

Ever the pragmatist, Stefanie Ishii had suggested the nearby old Olympic Stadium as the most suitable Love Buzz live venue for her son and daughter.

'Too much riff-raff there; I don't care if it's closer,' Satoshi Ishii had barked from the parental bedroom. 'Safer at the old SFS in the city so they're going there or not at all!' And what Satoshi said, went.

At last, Kai's special day had arrived – his sixteenth birthday! his first live Love Buzz! – and it seemed most of Doonside had conspired to dawdle along his path to destiny. His frustration bubbled ever closer to anger. Juanita's set time was less than an hour from beginning. Missing even a second of his idol's performance was *not* an option.

'Toca, let's shuttle!' he screamed over his shoulder, wincing. The muscles running from his upper back to the base of his skull felt like they'd been tied in a double knot. Kai shook away the twinge in his neck and broke into a jog. His white jumpsuit and sneakers combo may have been subjected to the usual mockery in the Ishii household, but he'd at least dressed himself with the urgency of their last-minute dash (standard fare for any outing involving his sister) in mind. Toca had different priorities, putting more thought into her outfit than making sure her brother was on time to see Juanita in the virtual flesh.

Kai squinted at the tunnel opening, half a football field ahead of him. 'Juanita's countdown ticker is all over the big screens already!' he shouted, up towards the tunnel's cement ceiling this time, as if the words would bounce back to Toca with more urgency. Though knowing the volume of the music Toca always had exploding through her speaker cups, he'd be surprised if she could hear anything else at all.

A convoy of industrial light fixtures, zipping past him like road markings indicating it was safe to overtake, were just out of reach above. Kai leapt excitedly for the ceiling then continued apace.

HeadBand, how long to Trancentral Sydney, LOT 49, Section 45:33?

A countdown timer appeared in the right-hand column of Kai's HeadBand viewfinder, automatically shuffling his vital signs and weather readouts down towards the essential apps toolbar along the base.

'You will reach your destination in forty-three minutes, twenty-six seconds,' his female tutor bot's voice – simultaneously warm and cordial, cold and clinical – filled his speaker cups.

Then the roar of Love Buzz – repetitive kick drums and hyperactive synthesisers and rasping, off-beat basslines; core tenets of the EDM sound Kai had found irresistible almost from the second he'd heard Juanita performing it – burst back into the foreground inside his Head-Band. Cosmo's skills were serviceable enough to Kai's ears by normal Virtuoso standards, but no match for his hero's. Cosmo's music made Kai grin; hearing the same tracks played by Juanita made him soar.

The time readout above the ticker read 18:13. *Come on, Tokes, we're cutting it fine.*

Something suddenly smashed into Kai's right hip, sending a flash of silver streaking across his peripheral vision like a comet. Kai spun around, poised to unleash a torrent of Japanese insults on the culprit, only to find himself facing off against a rotund Indian man with a face like a burst beach ball. In his right hand, the unidentified silver streak – a stainless-steel tiffin carrier – swung on its handle. In his other was the tiny paw of a six-year-old girl, peering at Kai through a clear HeadBand lens that appeared even more oversized than when Kentaro's was first fitted.

Inside Kai's viewfinder, hexagon-shaped holographic boxes filled with data danced above the pair's heads, but he didn't need the identifiers. Kai had done this dance before – on the Nurragingy Towers rooftop on 1-6-25, before he'd raced to rescue Kentaro from the mounting chaos outside.

'Kai ji, get your proximity sensors checked,' blustered Mr Banerjee, the Ishii family's busybody neighbour. ('If I fart while showering before work,' Kai had overheard his mother telling a giggling Toca recently, 'the whole building will know what key it was in before I've finish drying my hair.')

'Sorry, uncle!' he said, motioning to touch Mr Banerjee's feet as a sign of respect.

Little Sanya looked as bewildered as she did in the moment etched in Kai's memory, when Mr Banerjee had almost wiped them all out on that frenzied afternoon the Storm struck. Kai was bewildered, then and now, by the fact this future heartbreaker had been fathered by a man whose jowls flapped around his neck like a baby elephant's ears. Mr Banerjee's combover, wispier and thickened with more wax than ever, reached forlornly across his light brown scalp, resolute in the face of its increasingly futile task. Toca was still nowhere to be seen in the tunnel behind them.

Kai cocked an apologetic thumb over his shoulder, in the general direction of the Doonside Station roundabout. Within a week of being opened two-and-a-half years earlier, the underground hub had been nicknamed the Three-Way by the older kids at Kai's school – for reasons his thirteen-year-old self had been too naïve too grasp.

'Today's our swinging sixteen,' he explained breathlessly, before spinning back towards his destination, 'and the countdown is *on!*'

Mr Banerjee's muttered response – something about Kai being an 'incorrigible *balaka*' (*Sorry, Mr Banerjee, but I will NOT be corriged!*) – disappeared from Kai's mind the instant he turned back towards his destination.

On each side at three-metre intervals the tunnel walls were dotted with speakers shaped like the Halcyon Industries logo, spewing forth Love Buzz's continuous aural assault on all who walked past, day and night – not that there was much discernible difference between the two anymore. As each kick-drum struck, the heart-hands speakers pulsed as bright red as the lava lightning that ruled the skies outside. Kai marvelled at how the speaker fittings were free of the cobwebs that clung to the lights stretching along the apex of the arched tunnel. Somehow, no cobwebs, no signs of dust, no water stains or other assorted filth coating this stretch of the tunnel were able to penetrate a five-centimetre radius around each cog-shaped speaker. Runoff from the raging Storm above trickled down to the rugged tunnel floor, but circled the speakers, as if a forcefield (Anti-pollution magnets? 10G? Something else?) was keeping the encroaching muck at bay.

The speakers' Love Buzz broadcast added a low-end throb to Cosmo's synths and cymbals, snapping and crackling away in the speaker cups wrapped around Kai's ears. He reached for his left temple, where his HeadBand's MIDI implant had been fighting a running battle with his skull for much of the month leading up to his sixteenth birthday. One night of fitful sleep on his lumpy pillow and his neck had joined the party, growing stiffer and more painful with each subsequent night.

Squinting the pain away, Kai pushed on. He'd grown quite accustomed to the privileges of HeadBand life being interspersed with regular visits from an invisible fist, tap-tap-tapping away inside of his skull like it was looking for a solid piece of wall to hammer a nail into. In Kai's memories, not the video playback generated by his HeadBand, the final stage of the HeadBand installation process always felt like a padlock clicking permanently shut. These growing pains made that sensation feel about as menacing as one of his mother's head massages, which always made the pain go away.

Kai careered out of the tunnel and into the Three-Way, an open plaza some thirty metres in diameter where the tunnels from the apartment towers and schools skirting the station intersected. On a regular day he could see the hustlers, the spruikers and street-food vendors, crowded around the HeadBand scanner that let you pass through the station's gates, but not today. The collision of corridors outside Doonside Station's underground (and only operational) entrance was even more frenetic than usual, packed with people much taller than Kai's puny five-foot-five frame. And the human traffic was all clamouring to catch the Stadium Loop to Sydney's twin Trancentral stadiums; to watch Juanita, the undisputed queen of Love Buzz, strut her stuff.

Swarms of Doonsiders emerged from the tunnel to Kai's left, which he walked six days a week to Doonside Tech. Hundreds more surged in from the tunnel to his right, which passed Kentaro's school, Doonside Public, on its way to Bungarribee Towers, the housing complex that dwarfed every other building in the Doonside Cluster: Kai's apartment block, the schools, the various food factories, and especially the skeletal remains of the housing estates that just three years ago seemed like they'd been beamed in from a future filled with bright lights and Dutch angles. Bungarribee's towering immensity was visible only on the rare occasions there was some let-up from the thick soup of dust and debris which had swirled around Sydney since 1-6-25 – and around the whole planet, as seen on Halcyon's broadcasts – keeping everyone underground or sealed inside.

A technicolour rainbow of bodies merged into a giant, indistinguishable paint spatter; moving together in perfect motion, synchronised by the music pumping through every speaker cup. All but Kai were resplendent in Love Buzz's dress code of hippie iconography: afro wigs and tie-dyed shirts and peace sign pendants, rainbow flares and faux-leather tan moccasins. ('What's the point of dressing up,' Kai had argued with Stefanie Ishii earlier, 'if you just end up looking like everyone else?') The Gen Zs and Gen Xs, the Millennials and Alphas, and he and Toca's fellow Stormers – and one lone, stooped Boomer grandma pushing her way through the crowd like her Zimmer frame was a steamroller – circled the Three-Way's central hub like dirty water around a drain.

Kai felt his ribcage begin to flutter. Waves of robophobia (or technofear as Toca preferred to call it) rippled across his limbs like a fight or flight response. *Sentry drones.* Kai shuddered. He always felt them before he saw them.

Then he saw them: metre-high silver robots, suspended at head height either side of the tunnel mouth he'd just been spat from, their red 'eye'-slits surveilling the Love Buzzers. The sentry drones always reminded him of the ideograms of human bodies on the walls outside the toilets at Doonside Tech, only minus the legs and triangular dresses. Kai clocked a pair of sentries flanking each of the tunnels opening into the Three-Way, as they had every day since the tunnel system beneath Doonside opened, exactly three months after the Storm stuck. They were such a constant fixture in these corridors that it was as if they'd always been part of Kai's world, just like lava lightning and syntho-shakes and the flavourless rice crackers his parents spent their work days making. But, for reasons that he'd not yet been able to put into words, the sentry drones were utterly terrifying to Kai and he felt the familiar queasiness of robophobia invade his stomach.

He resisted the temptation to touch the Halcyon logo-shaped button on the side of the drone to his left. This was not the time for satisfying his morbid curiosity. Instead, he stepped forward to let the current of humanity sweep him towards the station entrance.

The smell of charcoaled meat substitute and stale deep-fryer fat from the Three-Way kiosks was only rivalled by an eye-watering cock-tail of sweat so toxic Kai wondered if spraying it on the tunnel walls would strip away the years of decay and restore them to their original polished concrete state. His fellow Doonside dwellers had barely known their way around a can of deodorant before the Storm. They clearly weren't using their monthly ration allowance on soap.

The mob circling the Three-Way swelled as it revolved its way to-wards the station's scanner gates. Kai's head was able to lock into the tempo of the crowd, bobbing to the 4/4 rhythm of Love Buzz in their speaker cups, the drone-induced nausea gone. His eyes were locked not on his destination on the far side of the Three-Way but at the cen-tre of the hub, on the hexagonal, wrought-metal support structure that sprung from the ground like a twisted tree reaching up and out to keep the roof from collapsing. Affixed to the structure were dozens of shoe-box-sized screens, cycling through the Love Buzz colour palette of yel-low, red and green as they flashed a recurring sequence of slogans: 'Go with the flow'; 'It is what it is'; 'What's done is done'.

Kai craned his neck to see over the adult heads surrounding him, his gaze fixed on the jumbo screen at the centre of the slogans. The picture of perfection on the screen smiled benevolently down on them all. Her azure-blue hair, normally straight and hanging halfway down her back, today swirled behind her head in slow motion as if tickled by a gentle breeze. Her lips were pursed tantalisingly. Her skin was tanned and blemish-free. From beneath the sky-blue tint of her HeadBand's viewfinder, the ageless woman's mysterious, spiderweb-patterned eyes sparkled golden green.

Below her face, which glowed in radiant high-definition, a digital clock face beside a *COUNTDOWN TO JUANITA* graphic confirmed how fine Kai was cutting it.

45:00. 44:59. 44:58. The ticker counted down in sync with the read-out in the lower left-hand corner of his viewfinder. None of the other readouts cluttering up his view even registered. Echoes of a Love Buzz breakdown danced, almost unnoticed, across his speaker cups' stereo field like a passing car. The colour wheel of humanity came to a stand-still, as if heeding a silent command.

Kai silently cursed Toca's unparalleled knack for wasting hours of his life he'd never get back picking an outfit that made her blend into the crowd. *Where is the annoying little gro-bot?*

In Kai's viewfinder a speech bubble popped up above the Juanita ticker.

RIGHT BEHIND YOU BROTATO <]

Kai swivelled but couldn't see his sister through the crowd.

His mother's parting words lingered in his ears. 'Keep an eye on your sister, and don't forget your scales,' Stefanie's best nagging voice had commanded from the kitchen as Kai had scampered through the front door. 'Do you think Juanita could do what she does if she hadn't perfected the basics first?'

HeadBand, tell Toca: That's not how you do a <3

Thunderous drums gave the signal. The breakdown was over. At Cosmo's bidding, the whirlpool of unwashed Doonsiders swirled back to life. Kai held his nostrils shut. As the human tide pulled him towards the station, he cursed Toca again, and his mother for insisting he take her along.

| 2.02 |

I Feel Love

'My minutes have become hours have become days.' Juanita mouthed the words to no one in particular. Helpless, pointless. Endless, nameless. *Ladies and gentlemen, I am floating in space.*

Distant sheets of red lit up the crumbling corpses of empty office buildings littering the back blocks of Oxford Street, directly across from Juanita's apartment. During those first frightening days after 1-6-25, Juanita had spent hours at a time transfixed by lava-lightning strikes as she looked out on the death and destruction littering the road outside her suite in the Love Inn – littering everywhere, according to the images beamed into her HeadBand from Halcyon's emergency news channel, the only video feed still broadcasting.

If Tito hadn't stepped up so quickly to marshal the recovery effort, Juanita didn't know how she'd have found the strength to go on. He'd had Halcyon's food-delivery drones reprogrammed and put to work fortifying every city that still stood on the morning after 1-6-25. There was no scope for pedestrian tunnels here, on the edge of Sydney's CBD, where the soil beneath the city streets was eaten up by drains, sewers and railway lines, both operational and abandoned. Instead, footpaths and awnings on the now-desolate glitter strip were enclosed in slabs of cement to keep the Storm at bay so Sydney's VIPs could safely make their way between apartment towers.

Leave the rat runs to the rats, Juanita reasoned to herself on Day Zero as she'd reached for the cool, comforting touch of her speaker cups. She'd adjusted her viewfinder's nose clip, bearing down a little too heavily on her face. *I've got everything I need right here.*

The boutique owners and barkeeps who'd been rostered on that fateful Sunday had no option but to hunker down and survive on what meagre rations they had on them. Juanita, sequestered inside Love Inn with Halcyon's syntho-food stockpiles to sustain her, had been luckier than most. Once accustomed, Juanita found the snap and crackle of lava lightning over the Sydney cityscape had its own hypnotic beauty. But the billowing black clouds that buffeted her apartment window with dust, pebbles and garbage over those first seventy-two hours channelled every apocalyptic blockbuster movie cliché she'd ever scoffed at – all rolled into one. And her memories of the afternoon of 1-6-25 had tormented her restless nights: her four-man security detail barrelling men, women and children out of the way on the dash through Sydney Airport's Terminal 1 to the car; a westerly wind that breathed fire buffeting her driver's Tesla Cybertruck as it sped along the freeway from Mascot to Darlinghurst; the crunch of metal on bone as pedestrians, screaming incoherently in their frantic scramble for safe havens, were collected by the Cybertruck's bumper, smashed skulls emptying their contents across the bitumen like dropped bowls of beef bolognaise.

The following morning, Tito had reassured her the worst would blow over soon. 'We already had something even better than One World coming,' he'd said, bunkered in Halcyon's Rotterdam headquarters, 'and it's going to make you an even bigger star than ever.'

She'd watched the bodies, piled up outside the fresh-built tunnel walls that lined the road below, become withered carcasses, then skeletons draped in fluttering cloth. Then one morning they were gone, carried away by a drone squadron or nuked by an overnight lava-lightning strike, any sign that they'd existed removed from the planet. And the Storm overhead thundered on and on and on.

But Juanita could not forget – not then, not now – no matter how hard she tried to drown the unwanted flashbacks in synthetic single malt, tried to lose herself in increasingly elaborate sexual de-viancy. *Neets, we've been through this before*, she reminded herself. *You know there's no point replaying those tapes again.* Juanita slowly nodded in agreement. She was right, as she usually was. She didn't need to look outside any more. She didn't need to look any further in front of her than her HeadBand's screen. The Storm was horrific and all but she was Juanita: superstar Virtuoso, Love Buzz queen. Paying attention to the bloodbath outside her window was a waste of energy when she had an EDM habit to support.

Beneath her MIDI implants, Juanita's entire skull seemed to throb. Since Friday night's post-set kick-on had exploded to a halt, Juanita had lain supine for almost twenty-three hours on her plush violet recliner, naked but for the white knickers she'd pulled on before the last set and her Virtuoso utility belt. Velour gently tickled forearm skin, which was threatening to ignite from the inside out. She was hanging out for her nightly hit of new tunes. *Ooh baby, and how.* What felt like litres of comedown sweat had oozed from her palms while she slept, leaving a damp outline where her wrinkled palms had clutched her recliner's armrests; her fingertips, capped in phosphorescent latex, were more wrinkled still, like she'd spent the entire day passed out in the bath. A hot bath, Juanita remembered those. *I'd even snort some bath salts right now.* The damp cushion cradling her behind was drenched in sweat and cum and spilt shots of synthetic single malt and who knew what else. She squeezed her eyelids shut more tightly still, pressing the back of her head deep into the groove she'd moulded in the spongy chair.

Juanita knew what was next, as regular as restless nights followed her equally dire days. And there it was, ladies and gentlemen, boys and girls – her inner jukebox, right on queue!

Random song fragments from before the Storm started spinning around her brain while a particularly nasty case of the DTs, along with an ordinary, everyday case of deep-seated self-loathing, got to work on the rest of her. The tracks vacillated from the sublime to the utterly ridiculous: *Look around, everywhere you turn is heartache/It's everywhere *that you go* from the song that was number one the week Juanita was born; mouthing *It's Britney, bitch* and dancing round her bedroom 'til the world ends over an endless coda of Auto-Tuned *Woah-oh-ohs*; *I'm wicked and I'm lazy, don't you want to save me* danced side-by-side with *Put your hands up for Detroit, a lovely city.* Her inner jukebox ran the full spectrum from the deep to the desperate; from profound insight into the human condition to mindless sloganeering in the space of a single kick drum.

The all-star cast of earworms played on and Juanita, as always, found zero comfort in the toplines her subconscious sucked out of her fragmented memory banks. Triumphant singalongs were few and far between at this nightly solo show in her recliner, which played out like a tragic party for one in a long-abandoned karaoke bar. No camaraderie. No applause. Not even a bouncing ball on the lyrics to jog her memory if she lost her place.

On a good night, Juanita could at least distract herself from her misery by pondering the imponderables. What did Lou Bega do with his life after finding perfection on his fifth 'Mambo'? Why didn't ABBA sing *You can dance, you can die* to give 'Dancing Queen' more emotional heft? And what did any of it matter anyway?

Juanita's inner jukebox resumed, skipping the endless supply of guilty pleasures at the top of the stack to unfurl the inevitable closing track: DJ Tito's 'Singularity' and its eternal runout groove, not silent like the inner circle of every other record Juanita had ever played but looping on and on and on like it was all end and no start. Triggered again, Juanita was back in the Cave – the dark-and-dirty side room of Chinese Laundry, the nightclub secreted away in the bowels of Sydney's Slip Inn. She and her four besties had snuck into the club as guests of an older-sister's DJ boyfriend. It was the first day of winter, 2006. Juanita's sweet sixteen.

The excitement and confusion (the labyrinthine layout; flashing lights distending hundreds of ecstatic faces; the enormous Polynesian bouncer, whose eyes always seemed to be scrutinising her) had merged into a blur of thousands of barely distinguishable nights since. But for Juanita – even this barely functioning incarnation of February 28, 2028 – the wall of sound Tito unleashed from the Cave's DJ booth that night was not so easily forgotten.

'*He saved my life, I nearly drowned.*' On her recliner, Juanita whisper-sang to herself between sniggers dripping with pain. '*I showed off, splashing around.*'

Juanita's karaoke skills wowed her captive audience of one and then she was back in the Cave, always the Cave, and the night she first experienced the sonic pop and fizz of 'Singularity', Tito's timeless mega-bomb. From his battle station in the shadowy far corner of the dancefloor, Tito's battery of beats had bombarded her young brain as if hammering away at a castle wall, looking for a breach in its defences. She'd fought to stay steady on her feet as the cavernous club bent and twisted all round. It was a feeling she'd eventually spend the summer of 2010 trying to recreate, hosing bags of horse tranquiliser in her quest to slide into the ultimate K-hole void. But this sixteen-year-old, less-seasoned incarnation of Juanita felt like she was fuck-dancing in quicksand. Juanita sunk deeper the harder she fought to stay afloat. Keeping her besties' pledge to party substance-free (the last thing they'd wanted was security to call their parents if things went sideways) wasn't protection enough. Tito's wall of percussion had lured her onto the dancefloor, caressed her, found her vulnerabilities. Then came the time to exploit them.

A clandestine pedal note, like the dissonant drone of an untuned church organ, soared across the top of Tito's unrelenting tribal groove. Juanita was mesmerised by the wall of Latin and African hand drums, which to her ears fell progressively more out of tune with the surrounding rhythm track from one 4/4 bar to the next, then from one-shot to one-shot, then within each singular snap of the duelling djembes and congas themselves. The sound of each drum hit oscillated through the musical scale, from *do-re-mi* through the register up to *do* and back again in a millisecond.

Sinking into her recliner, twenty-two years removed, a familiar feeling of dread overcame her. The hum of tinnitus in her ears reached fever pitch. Then she was back in the Cave, always the Cave, where 'Singularity' climaxed with the orchestral synth stab that had laid waste to the Cave's dancefloor, and Juanita with it, all those years ago. One second, Juanita was reaching for the ceiling in ecstasy; the next, her lights went out. The memory, as always, made her soul vibrate.

The details were still so vivid: returning to consciousness on the cold concrete floor, bathed in the echoes of her besties' disembodied cries of panic, like Juanita was in a parallel universe, or maybe they were. Her top row of teeth ached. She could taste the blood that had trickled across the floor from her flattened nose. A discarded baggie stuck to her spilt bourbon-streaked cheek. She felt a firm hand on her shoulder, then another, before being rolled onto her back.

Everlasting black became a head surrounded by swirling lights. The eyes of Juanita's future stared down at her, stunned, as if she were the solution to a puzzle he never thought he'd complete. After composing himself, his hands formed the shape of a heart in front of his chest.

In the Dutch-American accent that had lured her to the club across internet radio waves, Matthias 'Tito' van Dijk, for the first time, addressed her directly: 'Are you feeling the love?'

| 2.03 |

Never Gonna Come Back Down

From his ready room, deep inside the golden basket of Halcyon Tower, beneath the sky needle transmitting Love Buzz from Sydney's CBD to the remote suburban clusters that sustained the Harbour city's Survivors, Tito watched a video feed of Juanita tossing and turning on her recliner. The spectral analysis of her brain activity on display inside his viewfinder was depressingly familiar. *Only the worst of memories for my darling protégée.* The guilt of what he'd put her through over the past twenty-two years had long since passed. He accepted what he'd subjected her to was a necessary evil – any rational human being would. And he enjoyed reliving that night as much as she despaired of it. One more time, he was right back there as well.

HeadBand, mute Love Buzz.

Cosmo's warm-up set was silenced. Tito's cochleae contracted sharply and he was back in the Cave, always the Cave – the underground nightclub space that well and truly lived up to its name – buried deep, like a secret too big to contain otherwise, beneath the courtyard of Sydney's Slip Inn. The vibe was dark and dirty and debauched as always. Flashing lights of red and gold swirled recklessly across the ceiling and walls. Every face was pointed in Tito's direction, though not all of their eyes were open. Some of the faces were struggling to focus on anything at all.

Arcane rhythms rolled out of a sound system the equal of any Tito had encountered in any other small club in the world, and he'd played them all. He reached his arms forward and struck poses – kung-fu or tai chi or some bastardised equivalent of them both – for the benefit of the faces peering, hypnotised, over the chest-high barrier in front of him.

He looked down at a small platform in front of him, covered entirely by artefacts from another age, his standard rider at the time: an Allen & Heath DJ mixer; two Technics vinyl turntables; two Pioneer CDJ-1000s, turntables designed for compact discs. He leant forward to check the time display on the CDJ at his right. It ticked up towards the four-minute mark. He nodded to himself.

Let's see if this fucking thing works this time.

The kick-drum stopped for a bar. Strings and horns and brass and white-noise swelled then collided as the beat resumed. The resultant orchestral stab struck with the force of the Big Bang. Sampled tribal drummers, layered so thickly atop each other they wouldn't recognise their own contribution without a thorough forensic examination, ratcheted up their assault.

Tito felt it anew, that surge of empathy as the rush comes, felt it echoing across the years; a surge of compassion and love and the understanding that this moment made everything else worthwhile – the hustle and the struggle and the nagging suspicion he was a lone voice, shouting into the void a message no one wanted to hear. But inside those four walls, in that secret club for kith and kin, you could forget about your pain. Back then, it was all about the music: the spaciousness of the breakdown once the beat and bassline cut; the synthesisers sweeping across the room as the white-noise built up and up and up; and then boom! After the expectation came the pay-off – the drop – when the beat and bassline kicked back in and you danced until the next breakdown, and the next and the next until there was sweat on the walls and you dropped from exhaustion – or the club closed and you kicked the party on someplace else.

Back in the Cave, always the Cave, where a young female voice screamed from the middle of the room, then another and another, each brimming with terror. Somewhere on the floor in front of him something heinous was going down. People pushed towards the DJ booth. Behind them, the sea of gurn on the dancefloor began to part.

Tito took a nervous swig on a bottle of Coopers Pale Ale. 'No fucking way!'

He gulped down another mouthful of beer – lukewarm and metallic and altogether too dense for his more refined palate of 2028 – before swinging into action. Headphones were discarded on the empty turntable. The beer bottle was slammed down on the other empty vinyl platter. A CD wallet tumbled off the DJ console and onto the concrete floor, scattering silver discs scrawled with Tito's intentionally indecipherable handwriting (so no prying eyes in the front row could ID the exclusive tracks in his collection).

Tito recited Ken Loi's directions, simple and precise: 'Hit Hot Cue C to trigger the loop. Make sure yours is the first face they see. Show them the heart-hands symbol, then speak.'

Head nodding, running the numbers through to the end of a 16 count. And, go! Tito slammed his finger down on the CDJ button marked C. The tribal drums ceased. A 4/4 rhythm of kick and clap and off-beat hi-hat linked fingers with a triplet base stab, holding the root note. A low-slung alien voice repeated its mantra: 'When times becomes a loop. When times becomes a loop.'

Tito slipped out the side of the DJ booth. The Cave's booth was slightly less salubrious than he'd become accustomed to on the global superclub circuit – less altar of worship than thin Perspex wall, barely marking the divide between performer and crowd. Tito's crowd navigation skills, honed on the dancefloors of England's early-'90s warehouse raves, were no match for these dancers – heads down, hands up – hips sideswiping his, throwing him off his golden path. This dancefloor's collective minds had left the room, left the planet maybe. Dr Loi had told him 'Singularity' would be big; all it needed was one person who was ready to truly hear it.

Tito reached the middle of the floor, between two brick pylons keeping the Slip Inn's outdoor terrace from collapsing into the Cave. A group of four underage girls – a cursory glance was all he required to know they were trying way too hard to look old enough to be night-clubbing legally – were rubbernecking in horseshoe formation around a fifth girl, splayed face-down on the dirty, sticky floor.

'Let me through, girls, let me through!' Tito shouted, abruptly, urgently. If they'd been listening, if they'd been cognisant of anything outside of the music and lights and their own fear of being grounded, they would've heard the nervousness in his voice, fairly dripping from every syllable. Nearly twenty years of planning how he was going to change the world and it all suddenly revolved around this moment.

Brushing the cordon of hysterical girls aside, Tito crouched down beside the girl and slowly rolled her onto her back. She was young like the others, possibly even younger if her face, a picture of naïve innocence, was to be believed. He let his gaze slip to the breasts threatening to burst out of her lace-trimmed singlet top.

Not now, Tito. He cleared his throat. *Keep your eye on the prize.*

The girl opened her eyes – cobweb-patterned saucers of sparkling green full of fear and wonder. Struck dumb, Tito's script abandoned him. When Ken Loi had talked him through the plan, it had seemed so simple. 'When my boy Peter's secret weapon finds its target,' Loi had assured him, 'instinct will take over and you'll know what to do.' The head of Halcyon's nascent Artificial Intelligence team clearly hadn't factored in the possibility that the golden ticket would go to the most beautiful creature Tito had ever laid eyes on.

Tito composed himself, flashing his most sympathetic smile. He brought his hands together before his chest, forming the shape of a heart. Satisfied the girl's eyes were his alone, Tito spoke.

'Are you feeling the love?'

| 2.04 |

I Feel Space

The Stadium Loop train rocked and rolled its way towards Trancentral Sydney and Kai Ishii's destiny. Toca looked mischievously across at him from the opposite bench seat, having edged her way through the Three-Way crowd and joined Kai to race through the Stadium Loop's sliding doors and up to the top deck. The two young, square-jawed Lebanese men sharing Toca's seat had boarded the train with the twins at Doonside but looked unfamiliar to Kai. From the moment they sat down they'd been lost inside their own HeadBands, intently focused on something a foot in front of their respective faces, their hands manipulating data streams or puzzle pieces or some other form of time-pass stimulus only they could see.

It was high time Kai joined them. Whatever sass Toca was brewing could wait.

HeadBand, launch VizWave and queue The Watson Beat's* Space *playlist.

At Kai's command, his visor went opaque and his sister faded to black, mouthing something about 'no swiping at mealtimes, brotato!' that he chose to ignore. *Practise time > family time.* His rationale was simple and he knew he had their mother's support. And what Stefanie said, Satoshi backed up, no matter how much noise he made for his own amusement.

The data readouts competing for Kai's attention inside his viewfinder – Juanita's countdown ticker, his vital signs data, the identifiers hovering above each of the rainbow-garbed masses crammed into the train carriage – folded in on themselves like transforming robots and disappeared into the peripheries.

HeadBand, play the Watson Beat's 'Space 1' from zero seconds – audio only.

Kai closed his eyes, inhaled deeply and the piano melodies swept him out of his surroundings, as if summoned into someone else's daydream. From some unknown point of origin – one of Juanita's wordflows, maybe, although it was a little more long-winded than your typical Love Buzz fare – a now-familiar mantra slid into Kai's thoughts and played on repeat: *Let resistance go and the energy will flow right through your soul like a river of gold.*

Kai had always found something unnerving about the way each of the *Space* playlist's nine songs voyaged outwards from their respective starting points. Each distinct movement of the composition seemed to make way for the next before it had properly resolved, the conflicting chord structures and random tempo changes often rendering Kai off-balance, like he was struggling to stay upright on top of Kentaro's beloved soccer ball. It was as if the internal logic of all the music Kai had immersed himself in before the Storm, and in the slow crawl of time since, didn't exist in the Watson Beat's song sheet. And if those accepted rules and conventions of composition were enforced here, they would feel out of place.

Matthias van Dijk – 'the world's most unlikely saviour,' Kai's mother Stefanie often quipped of the multimedia mogul who'd never bothered to shake off his stage name of Tito – had once boasted that 'every piece of music ever recorded by humans or processed by machines' existed inside the HeadBand network's sound libraries. After diving headfirst into the library every day for the past three years and more, Kai had no reason to doubt his claim.

Though he was almost certain that vast cross-sections of the world's back catalogue were disappearing from the Halcyon streaming database on a daily basis. Toca would no longer entertain his theories on where the music had gone. ('Your conspiracy theories about the Storm are bad enough, little brother' was her last word on the subject, before adding a reminder that she'd entered the world fifteen minutes before him, as if those additional fifteen minutes had blessed her with insight he lacked.) And not that it mattered anyway. All that mattered was that his Head-Band's access to the database had introduced him to *Space* and, more importantly, Juanita's back catalogue of EDM greats.

That first morning on the Nurragingy Towers rooftop, Kai hadn't heard anything like Juanita's take on EDM and never intended to again. He'd tuned in again, to watch Juanita with no sound, but found the experience to be sorely lacking until he turned the volume up loud enough that each beat moved the air inside his speaker-cup chambers. Then it made sense. Then he understood. And soon enough he couldn't get enough of Juanita and her music's barely contained violence.

Almost four years later and EDM was inescapable, as essential to life on Earth as OxyPure air filters and Vitamin D supplements, but it was still the Watson Beat's *Space* playlist that entranced Kai most. From early on, he suspected that neither *Space* nor the music Juanita performed to was created by humans. The longer he immersed himself in the ultra-sonic discord, the more somersaults his queasy stomach turned. But the more he listened to it, the better he felt. Every night he lay in bed with his HeadBand running *Space* on repeat – from the moment he lay down for the night to the moment his mother's reminder rumble jolted him awake in the morning. He likened the sensation of listening to the Watson Beat's compositions to a feeling from his earliest memories, of being rocked in the arms of Nana, Stefanie's mother, who'd died before the twins reached school age.

In his temples, the growing pains marched to the beat of their own drum. The HeadBand installer assigned to Doonside Tech had warned the Ishii twins to expect some mild discomfort whenever the four plates of the skull surrounding their MIDI implants expanded to accommodate a growth spurt. As it turned out, 'mild' was an understatement.

Memories of that afternoon just before school finished in the summer of '24 came back to Kai: of lining up outside the silver-shelled Halcyon Industries caravan with Toca, growing pains wracking his calves then as they did now, with no real understanding of the magnitude of what was going on inside the mobile operating-theatre's walls; of the blinding white sterility of the caravan's interior; of how just one breath of nitrous oxide made the world's edges blur; of the sound of the metal MIDI implants being pushed through his skin, the unnerving sensation of their microfibre cables piercing his pterion to connect with his brain; of the wiry silver strands springing out of the otherwise orderly black of the installer's eyebrows – the last thing Kai saw with his own eyes before the HeadBand's viewfinder and speaker cups were lowered into position. Then the slow grind of each implant's five pins, tightening their grip on the MIDI discs attached to his HeadBand's technofibre temple straps, before snapping into place.

Minutes later, he'd brought his first thought to life. But activating the tiny rail of LED flashlights along the top of his HeadBand's viewfinder on that distant mid-December afternoon seemed positively quaint given what he'd learnt in the three years since – not just via Tito and Juanita's in-lens tutorials, but through his own intuition.

He forced his idle mind to focus. *Earth to Kai, it's time for lift-off.* Scales, now, or his mother would never let him hear the end of it.

HeadBand, activate KeyRoll in weighted mode.

Kai attempted to issue the thought command in a monotone that would do his HeadBand's tutor bot proud, although he wasn't entirely certain whether thoughts could convey tone or, for that matter, whether artificial intelligence understood the concept of pride. His eyes flicked open to a thirty-seven-note piano keyboard materialising just above his legs. He spaced his hands evenly across the black and white keys, then ceded control of his hands to the sound.

HeadBand, activate VizWave live transcription mode.

The darkness inside Kai's viewfinder took form and he found himself surrounded by ringed planets and kaleidoscopic nebulas and unfathomably far-flung galaxies of stars. His fingers effortlessly tapped out a melody in sync with the staggered array of digital cubes zooming towards the keys. With each correct key strike, the corresponding coloured cube burst into a puff of stardust as Kai progressed elegantly through the sequence.

Since finding the *Space* playlist in Halcyon's sound library, he'd practiced 'Space 1' daily to reach this point – fingers working on muscle memory, instinct guiding him through the unpredictable notation with such precision he could switch off his mind and enjoy the spacewalk that had unlocked once he'd perfected the eleven-minute piece.

Sometimes he felt something else, too; a 'presence' that watched over him until his scales were done. (He didn't dare tell his mother, lest Toca get wind of it – she'd only just let up on him over his fear of the boogeyman under their Birdwood Avenue home, and he hadn't spoken of that in a decade or more.) That indefinable presence felt as strong in the carriage of the Stadium Loop as it did in his bedroom at home; a nagging feeling that he was sharing his cockpit with a proud teacher, watching over Kai's shoulder as he piloted their starship safely home.

| **2.05** |

Let the Good Times Roll

And there he goes again, my little brother, the pride of Doonside. Toca eyed Kai with bemusement as his fingers danced nimbly across his air piano, eyes glazed over, mouth contorted into a variety of shapes as his concentration deepened. *Taking centre stage halfway between the gutter and the stars.* Wasting his life away on something so frivolous when he could be like her – learning everything she could about COVID-23, putting every spare second she had into her quest to find a cure so she could be free of this HeadBand for good. Her brother's only ambition was to entertain the world. Toca wanted to save it.

Inside her speaker cups, Cosmo's set galloped past the halfway mark and set a collision course with its explosive conclusion. The video feed from Trancentral Valencia showed her Virtuoso heartthrob's hologram, dancing like a giant marionette between two speaker arrays dangling from the stadium ceiling, conducting a capacity crowd. Billions more would be tuned in from the cities that still stood: some in person across the Trancentral stadium network, where Toca and Kai would soon join them; the rest from inside their HeadBands, at work or at home, or in the tunnel or rat run that linked the two.

Some life this is, Toca thought. *But better than the alternative.*

She looked around the crowded carriage. Like Kai, every other passenger was lost in a little world of their HeadBand's making. On the bench seat behind Kai, Toca caught a man staring intently at her – mid-forties, perhaps, with an unusually tanned olive complexion for someone who hadn't seen the sun in years, beneath what she assumed was a wig of thick black dreadlocks. But when she smiled at him, she drew a blank. He wasn't staring at her at all; he was seeing something else, something she couldn't see, a HeadBand viewfinder treat for his eyes only. To disguise her embarrassment, she self-consciously brushed at the heart-shaped fringe of her own, blonde wig – a tribute to some Japanese cult figure that her father considered the height of pop culture – which tickled her forehead where it met the viewfinder's frame.

A banner ad for Love Buzz 1000 streaked across her field of vision. Cosmo's set thundered on. Nine-hundred and ninety-nine consecutive days of this music, distorting its way out of her speaker cups, only stopping to catch its breath when she drifted off to sleep and her Head-Band powered down for the night. Though Toca loved Cosmo as a performer – not a patch on Kai's blind devotion to Juanita, but she could admit to herself it was love all the same – there was nothing about his music to set him apart from Kayce-E's hour of power out of Trancentral Chelsea before him, nor from Juanita and Rakh-E, Kam-E and Usura and Ralf-E and the rest of the 24/7 cycle of Virtuosos to come. Was another day of the same really something to celebrate, with so much about the world so very wrong? After all the hype from her schoolmates who'd already turned sixteen and raved about the Trancentral experience, Toca was excited to finally experience Love Buzz in person. But as much as the prospect of seeing Cosmo perform (if they made it in time) made her giddy, what she craved in this moment more than anything was some respite.

HeadBand, mute Love Buzz.

Toca felt her cochleae contract at the microsecond of silence, then scream again as the Halcyon History video feed took over her Head-Band viewfinder, pumping a different EDM track – 'Big Groovy Xpandernova' if she wasn't mistaken – through her speaker cups. The train carriage was gone and she was suddenly Outside, in the thick of the wind and the dust and the angry pyrocumulus clouds, like she had been the day the Storm struck, when the baby lava lightning had merely hinted at its building power. Here, inside the 360-degree video feed Toca was sucked into, was the Storm's aftermath across the shattered cityscape of Canberra – Parliament House blown open, Lake Burley Griffin sucked dry, cars piled up where they'd crashed on that mad race for safety on 1-6-25, bodies dotting the wide streets and oversized roundabouts at regular intervals.

Tito's voice spoke over the devastating scene, pushing the music deep into the background. It wasn't quite the respite Toca was looking for – there was no full respite, as she'd learned on the other occasion she'd issued a mute command, only for the order to be overridden by Halcyon History in exactly the same way – but her tender ears were grateful all the same. 'Tragically, for the billions of people trapped outside the big cities, our salvage effort came too late – our resources were so few, and Halcyon's food-delivery services only extended only so far,' Tito said, his voice betraying just the slightest hint of emotion about the partial elimination of mankind. Toca found something reassuring about the gentle lilt of his delivery and the unusual accent, sitting somewhere at the point where Dutch, English and Australian meet.

'That's how those of us who remained became known as Survivors, and honouring our fallen friends and family members' memory – their sacrifice – became my life's work.'

The scene switched to another city, this one not destroyed beyond all recognition. A handful of modest high-rises surrounded a tiny harbour, its northern and southern sides connected by a cable bridge with a bent pylon at one end. Toca recognised the city from History lessons at school: Rotterdam, Tito's hometown, the birthplace of Halcyon Industries. The camera suddenly swept across the harbour to an enormous football stadium, its roof covered with construction drones. Lava-lightning strikes thrust their way through the surrounding clouds like jagged, burning spears.

'By necessity, we would have to make this new civilisation 100 per cent sustainable.'

The vision switched to time-lapse, showing the roof across De Kuip expand from covering just the terrace seating to the grandstands and playing surface in its entirety. Like flowers suddenly in bloom, an array of wind turbines sprung from the rooftop's surface, their blades spinning in time with the quadruple-time build-up of 'BGX', its kick drums fluttering like Kentaro's lips blowing raspberries.

'We knew we had the food production essentials in place to sustain Survivors' bodies, but that would not be enough – we would also have to sustain their minds.'

As if by magic, the camera passed through the roof and into the stadium – fully enclosed and empty.

'And with no football, no television, nothing to watch on your widescreen TVs, we would have to come up with a new form of entertainment to bring us all together for society to thrive.'

The camera flew through the southern end of the stadium seating and arrived in a tiny apartment, sparsely furnished, Juanita standing tall and proud on her Silo performance platform at its centre.

'The Love Buzz experience is about triggering a universal feeling of empathy for all – Peace, Love, Unity and Respect, as we said back in the day – and sharing that love with your fellow man,' Tito continued, his voice rising to the occasion.

Beneath her HeadBand lens, Juanita's eyes began to sparkle. Her long blue locks emitted a supernatural glow. On the black bodysuit that sculpted her body like a high-tech leotard, parallel lines running the length and breadth gushed with light, like she was living, breathing circuitry.

'After years of seeing her headline One World, of seeing her blossom from the moment she debuted at the tender age of sixteen, we believed Juanita was the uniting force this new world needed,' Tito continued, no longer a nurturing teacher but a preacher, sharing his religion with his followers.

The camera pulled back and Toca was again inside De Kuip, a digital readout across the top of the southern end displaying its new name: TRANCENTRAL ONE. Beneath the sign stood Juanita, towering above the stadium floor, each shake of her hips deploying rippling waves of stardust across the exultant crowd that filled every seat in the Premium grandstands, glitter bombs detonating above the reaching hands of the robot-masked Survivors dancing atop their Silos on the VIP Floor.

'With all of our old choices taken away, we believed Juanita and her fellow Virtuosos could bring this broken world we share back together.'

The camera zoomed through Juanita's sky-blue viewfinder and emerged in the Ultraworld – Tito's virtual reality playground, a simulated universe filled not just with red but blue and yellow and green, the ultimate escape from reality for teachers and doctors, scientists and engineers, the key workers Halcyon had decreed as VIPs. Sceptical though she was about Love Buzz and its music, Toca felt herself submitting to its power as the trance-inducing synthesiser sounds of 'BGX' filled her heart with joy.

'We don't have fresh meat and we don't have travel and we don't have the smell of the beach or mountain air, but we've got music, all day and all night long.'

'Big Groovy Xpandernova' climaxed, synths and swooshes and machine-gun kick drums zooming up and up and up into a dissonant symphony, collapsing on top of itself.

'We've got each other. Love will bring us back together.'

And then blackness, and silence. Toca's cochleae contracted again. It was just her, in the Ultraworld, alone with a glowing ideogram of a heart.

'And in the end,' Tito declared, solemnly. 'Love is all you need.'

| 2.06 |

Beautiful Burnout

A gentle buzz on Juanita's temple jolted her weary eyes open. She couldn't tell if she'd drifted off for a minute or an hour. Dusk was taking hold outside her apartment, though the only discernible difference between night and day since the Storm had set in was the deepening shade of red enveloping her apartment once the sun set. She was still tilted back in her favourite velour recliner, a welcome gift from Tito when he'd installed her as the first permanent tenant of the Love Inn in the summer of 2025. As soon as the Storm struck six months later, Tito had her apartment merged with the adjacent one and specced out with Love Buzz broadcast facilities. Otherwise she'd have been fortified against the apocalypse in a glorified shoebox.

'The queen of One World finally gets her throne room,' Tito said on the day she'd moved in.

A little more than three years later, it felt more like her final resting place.

Juanita's apartment overlooked the derelict party district of Oxford Street, on the fringe of Sydney's once-bustling CBD. The old Parkridge had been bought by Tito and rebranded as the Love Inn several years before the Storm, to accommodate Halcyon's growing roster of globe-trotting performers, promoters and handlers.

When Juanita had questioned why he'd chosen such modest digs for his stars, when the far grander Oaks and Pullman overlooked Hyde Park just around the corner, Tito gave her cheek a patronising pinch. 'All the better to keep you safe and secure, my dear. Only one door in and out.'

Yet she'd kept dancing to Tito's tune from the first moment they'd locked eyes, through the Love Inn honeymoon and beyond the Storm, and in this double-wide luxe apartment he'd finally caged her – literally. Eat, sleep, rave, repeat. (Steps one and two were optional.) She worked, she played, she sunk into despair. What she'd give to be whisked away, by anyone, to anywhere at all, if there was anywhere still worth being whisked to.

Juanita's eyes remained fixed in a thousand-mile stare, looking out upon her open-plan living room, trying to find the will to get ready for work. Clutching tight to her armrests, her forearms still shuddered, pining for a hit of the music that gave her life. Her HeadBand's frosted-metal frames felt like slabs of ice pressed against her temples. The skin above and below was flaking like dandruff onto her bare shoulders, but still nowhere near as badly as when she'd worn the MK 4. (Her skin had reacted so badly to the warm pulse of its technofibre straps that she'd insisted Tito have a HeadBand custom made to her specs, for her use only.) Juanita longed to scratch the itch beneath the frames, which connected the speaker cups to the broad lens enclosing her eye sockets and the bridge of her nose; a thin layer of Perspex that filtered Juanita's view of the world through a sky-blue hue. Beneath each speaker cup, her ringing ears cried out like it was morning tea time at a school with seven bells.

The television she hadn't wanted, sunken into the feature wall in front of her, remained blank as always. The only show she ever watched was the Storm, as the crimson lightning sheets crackling outside reflected off the screen. On the wall above, a half sphere of dark-tinted plastic no bigger than a snow dome housed her motion-capture camera. Below the television monitor, an OxyPure-5000 unit sent periodic gusts of breathable air into the apartment.

The square, silvery-white retroreflective sensors – which always reminded Juanita of motorcycle tail lights – were dotted across the walls, floor and ceiling at half-metre intervals to capture her real-world performance for transmission into Love Buzz and the Ultraworld. The only other fixture within her line of sight took pride of place at her living room's centre: her Silo performance platform. A black circular podium the size of a mini trampoline, one step up from the floor, with an intricate white honeycomb grid pattern across its slightly spongy top. In the centre sat a sleek, matte-blank helmet with a pull-down visor like a traffic cop might wear.

Sensing her brain was active again, Juanita's HeadBand powered itself up for another night of feeding on her thoughts. ('If we're ever to be a sustainable society,' Tito had explained to Juanita on using the human brain's electricity generation as a power source, 'change starts at home.') As she re-entered the land of the living, her viewfinder began bustling with activity. Cosmo's warm-up set, delivered from an apartment set-up identical to Juanita's but in Valencia, screamed the ringing in her ears into submission. She knew the song, 'One More Time to Burn Saltwater', as inside out as she knew every Love Buzz staple. If her setlist for February to date was any guide she'd be playing it herself in the coming hour. And her choreography, her intrinsic understanding of what empowering slogans Survivors needed to hear and when, would elevate the track to a level Cosmo could only dream of.

Juanita's control panels formed a virtual frame around the apartment's television screen: incoming dataflow from Love Buzz to the left, personal data to the right, essential apps pinned to a console along the base. Reams of meaningless data spewing forth in miniscule white text clamoured for space inside the semi-opaque lens. A thumbnail-sized silver 3D briefcase with a flip-top lid blinked insistently in the lower-right corner of her field of vision.

And not before fucking time, Juanita cursed Tito and his set-generating robots, as if they were the only thing delaying her getting her nightly hit when she was well aware their daily track top-up dropped as regular as her 6:30 pm shake-and-bakes. Her viewfinder's digital display confirmed the virtual record crate had been refreshed for Love Buzz 999 and returned to her console by Halcyon on schedule, as always.

It was official. 6:50 pm. Ten minutes 'til showtime.

HeadBand, unpack record box and cascade.

As Juanita's mind sent the command through her MIDI implants, her mouth stifled a yawn.

Computer-generated vinyl records in immaculate white sleeves leapt out of the matte-silver box and arranged themselves in an orderly manner, twenty-deep, in the darkness between Juanita and her living room's unloved television screen. To give her record crate priority, her vital signs data-readout and the raw video feed of Cosmo's performance, as seen from his own apartment's motion-capture camera, automatically minimised.

HeadBand, scroll through playlist – two-second intervals.

Juanita brushed a dirty clump of honey-blonde fringe from the front of her viewfinder, giving her unobscured access to the virtual workspace laid out before her. She'd been meaning to trim and touch up her dishevelled ombré for weeks. Not that it really mattered how much she let herself go; the Virtuoso avatar of Juanita that Love Buzz attendees saw was her as she had been over twenty years ago, forever young and fit and flawless.

Four records in, Juanita interrupted the scroll command with a forward thrust of her right hand. *You've got to be fucking kidding me.* With growing impatience, she manually flicked through the remainder of her Love Buzz playlist. Each record sleeve lit up as it reached the front of the selection in her viewfinder, track titles radiating above the round label at each record's centre. Next: 'Don't You Worry, Slippy Children'. Next: 'Safe from Block Rockin' Freaks'. Next: 'One More Time to Burn Saltwater'. *So predictable.* The same tracks she'd been playing for the past twenty-seven days. The same tracks Cosmo had been flogging all month as well. The same tracks her old Virtuoso buddy DCR had been pumping out of Liverpool all through 2027 until he'd vanished from the Love Buzz line-up and Juanita's life.

Jesus, Tito, this is some pile of reheated shit you're asking me to polish.

Love Buzz anthem after Love Buzz anthem, and not a hint of anything new among them. There was a time when she'd found amusement in the names of Halcyon's AI-composed anthems, titles of the tracks they'd mined for inspiration smashed together in a way that paid lip service but made zero sense. But the classics didn't touch the sides any more. Only the freshest drops gave her that first-time feeling, the ultimate buzz. And there was still a bonus day of February to endure before her March playlist rotation kicked in.

Juanita pushed on through, masking her contempt for the night's meagre offering of tunes. This particular performance – the feigned excitement at tonight's setlist – was for the benefit of her most important audience, analysing her every move from Halcyon HQ through the motion-capture camera that never switched off.

Her insides turned on themselves once more. 6:52 pm. Juanita stifled a groan. Eight more minutes and the pain would be gone. Before the Storm, the music made by Halcyon's machines made Juanita feel nauseous. Now, she felt sick without it.

Every night after her set she would party with her devoted boy-toys, Davide and Roberto, provided by Halcyon to keep her happy – or as close to happy as the increasingly depraved sexual acts she subjected them to could get her once the rush of Love Buzz had worn off. Robbie, the sensitive, generous lover; Dav, who fucked her like he had somewhere else to be until she was spent, or too drunk on syntho-malt to stand. Sleep the bender off all day then as soon as she awoke, the withdrawal pangs would begin again.

As her 7 pm set-time approached, the 'stomach feeling' would return, the twitching sensation tap-dancing up from her core and down her arms. As an aspiring Penrith party girl, teenage Juanita used to froth at the thought of downing her Saturday night potion – a staple diet of bourbon and Coke and poorly cut trucker's speed – before cutting sick on the dancefloor as eargasms rained down from above. That giddy feeling of anticipation of an epic night ahead was now a distant memory; in its place, a world of pain.

Juanita's tolerance to the power of the Drop grew stronger by the day. 'Like nangs, amyl and two green Mitsubishis, all coming on at once, for eternity', was how she would describe the Drop to anyone who asked. The same every time and with no comedown, at least in the beginning anyway. She hated it and she loved it. She wanted it to end and she dared not stop.

Juanita's hazel eyes, which had once bewitched all comers with their sparkle, were now a clouded, lifeless brown. On the rare occasions she faced off with her bathroom mirror, the haggard reflection staring back at her dragged her further into the mire. Every day felt like history repeating the same mistakes, only worse. Even through the sky-blue filter of her HeadBand's viewfinder, Juanita was an avatar of a memory of herself.

Going AWOL from Love Buzz was a fantasy she'd been mulling over since her NYE syntho-malt bender had come to an unforeseen end (who knew syntho rations could run out?), but the lure of each set's new closing tune, the incomparable bliss of the Drop's embrace, kept her from trying to leave. And there was Halcyon Industries to consider. Tito and his high-powered cronies wouldn't reveal what had happened to Juanita's Liverpool-based pal DCR, who'd bunked Virtuoso duties one night, and was never seen on – or off – his performance platform again.

'Maybe they fed him to the Brainfeeders?' Juanita speculated to her Italian counterpart Usura on Vid-Link a few weeks after his disappearance.

'Bella!' Usura gasped. 'You know the Brainfeeders is . . . how you say . . . fake news.'

Newcomer Kayce-E had taken DCR's place in the Love Buzz rotation, and the friend for life she'd made the night they'd shared the booth at Liverpool club Circus five years earlier was never mentioned again. The prospect of meeting a similar fate kept Juanita on the right track.

'Neets!'

Juanita's thoughts were interrupted by a familiar face, a holographic model of blue-eyed western European supremacy, pushing the cascaded record sleeves aside to fill the entire left side of her viewfinder.

'Time to rise and shine my queen!'

Juanita groaned inwardly. *And just as I was starting to get it together.*

'Cosmo is absolutely *killing it* out of Valencia tonight!' declared Juanita's virtual assistant, Abbie, in an accent that straddled the Atlantic.

Abbie was far from the worst handler Tito had foisted upon her. Although she had entrenched herself in Juanita's Top Ten Most Annoying Things list and was pushing hard for top spot, the undisputed title of Worst Assistant Ever went to Chloe Jay. Poor, pathetic little Chloe Jay, who'd ended most shifts in her seventeen days of undistinguished service weeping beneath a flurry of Juanita's choicest insults, for everything from the crooked angle of her fringe to her inability to begin a sentence with anything but 'Like, totally'.

'Full-on flower-power vibes, baby,' Abbie said brightly. 'The afterglow will be *truly* cosmic.' Not even the distance between Abbie's cubicle in Rotterdam and Juanita's Oxford Street, Sydney apartment could dim Abbie's boundless fake enthusiasm, a character trait the Halcyon HR department seemed to insist upon as a prerequisite for its stooges.

Juanita rolled her eyes. *Cosmo truthers are the worst.* She knew her warm-up DJ's finale would be little more than a primer for the power she'd unleash in an hour's time. She also knew Abbie's shtick well enough to know what was coming next – an effortless switch from slogan-heavy sales pitch to supercilious bitch, so predictable it was as if she'd been programmed that way.

'Hope you're ready to bring it home strong tonight to set us up for tomorrow's big one?'

'Chill, Abbie,' Juanita snapped. She hoped she didn't look as broken as she felt. Love Buzz 1000 was just a number when every Virtuoso set looked and felt the same as the last. And besides, she had to get through her 999th straight day of work first.

Juanita moved her hands into the virtual workspace before her. Her left hand gently, but pointedly, backhanded Abbie's holographic head to the side, bringing the record collection back front and centre. Her right index finger flicked anxiously through the remaining record sleeves.

'You've seen me play enough by now to know I've got the beautiful people covered.'

| 2.07 |

Age of Love

A horn blast caused Kai to strike a false note on his KeyRoll. The animated cube cruising towards the key on which his left ring finger was poised transformed into a big, bold red X. The success rate readout rolled downwards to 99.987%.

Kai smashed his hands down on the keyboard simulator, restoring his HeadBand to its default real-world setting. He was furious. Moments of solitude were few and far between in the crowded Ishii household, even within his HeadBand. Now the Stadium Loop's driver had chimed in uninvited, blemishing Kai's hitherto perfect, peerless KeyRoll stats in the process.

Ignoring the multi-coloured masses crowded into the carriage around him, Kai turned to the window. The bottom dropped out of his stomach. The Stadium Loop had temporarily exited the tunnel, making its way past the platform of what was once Circular Quay Station and its breathtaking view of Sydney Harbour. Since that long-ago birthday party at Luna Park, this idyllic view of the harbour to his left was one he'd seen only in photos. Blue skies were dotted with the faintest smattering of what he remembered from year four science as cumulus clouds. A lone, shapeshifting white giant soared kilometres above a vast expanse of water. Multi-storey homes crowded the shoreline on the opposite side of the harbour. Intermittent white caps broke up the water's dark, flat surface, flowing beneath a magnificent coat hanger-shaped bridge completely devoid of traffic.

This view was not right. This view had died on 1-6-25.

Swaths of static swept across the train window, restoring Sydney Harbour to its proper grim state. Kai's *hāfu* features remained unmoved in the face of the unexpected change in programming outside. Red lava lightning bolts lashed the Opera House. Dust, plant-based detritus and green fabric bags were whipped about by a fierce wind, gusting under a sky filled with fire-breathing pyrocumulus clouds. The miserable scenario repeated itself as far as Kai could see, from above Circular Quay to the mansion ghettos of Kirribilli and far into infinity on the horizon beyond.

'*Attention, Premium passengers,*' an impossibly polite female voice, like Kai's tutor bot with a personality simulator installed, rudely interrupted the Love Buzz broadcast that had resumed in Kai's speaker cups. '*You may have been unintentionally exposed to a visual display from our VIP carriages. We apologise for any inconvenience caused.*'

If Kai and Toca had shared the psychic connection of other twins he'd read about, he knew just how the silent exchange about the big-screen malfunction would play out.

Kai, exasperated look, pleading: *I'm telling you, something's not right.*

Toca, raised eyebrow, dismissive: *No one likes a Paranoid Jack.*

The red lightning crackled down towards Circular Quay's abandoned ferry terminals, tantalisingly out of view from Kai's position on the upper deck of the Stadium Loop. Kai's irritation at muffing his Key-Roll stats was superseded by fear, of seeing lava-lightning strikes up close. Since the Storm, he'd not ventured out of the Doonside Cluster – just as no one needed to venture out of Chatswood or Macarthur or Green Square, or any of the other pockets of humanity in which work, school and home had been combined into mixed-use precincts for Survivors by Halcyon, unless they were going to Love Buzz. From his family's eleventh-floor living room – its glass sliding doors, like every other glass surface in Nurragingy Towers, double-glazed by Halcyon construction drones within days of the Storm taking hold – Kai could just make out the lightning flashing above Sydney's CBD as a dim red glow, forty kilometres in the distance. Only Trancentral Olympic, which had been lit up 24/7 since Survivors had been invited to attend Love Buzz in person and experience the Drop in all its augmented reality glory, shone through the morass.

A fork of lava sent sparks flying off one of the empty flagpoles atop the Harbour Bridge as Kai's carriage descended once more into the darkness of the rail tunnel. The butterflies in his stomach were colliding more frequently now; more urgently. Feelings of nervousness and excitement were new territory for a boy who'd cultivated a disciplined, detached demeanour since the Storm had struck. Losing control usually agitated Kai, but he knew this new 'stomach feeling' was one to savour. All his KeyRoll practice, his persistence in wearing his belligerent father down, his sister's endless barbs about his bodysuit – it was all about to be worthwhile. It had all been a build-up to this.

Toca's hand clasped down on his left knee from the opposite bench seat. Kai gazed into a more excitable image of his five-foot-five self. Her almond eyes locked onto his from inside her HeadBand, her mouth flapping silently.

'What now?' Kai mouthed, annoyed at his twin's interruption. *Headband, re-engage voice receptors.*

'Get out of your head and look around, brotato,' urged Toca, eyes so wide they seemed to be plotting escape from her tangerine-tinted viewfinder.

The Stadium Loop's horn sounded again as it disappeared into the tunnel at the eastern end of the platform taking the iconic Sydney Harbour views, old and new, with it.

Neither the horn nor Toca's restless enthusiasm could stir the two muscly young Lebanese men, so devoted to whatever their HeadBand was showing them that Kai wondered if that was how he looked when he worked his way through *Space.*

Toca, as oblivious to her surroundings as the randoms, bit down on her bottom lip to rein her excitement in. Her eyes grew wider still, as if she'd held her breath to bursting point. 'After all those years watching from home'—she leaned in—'it's *really* happening.'

Toca was right – it *was* really happening, except it meant something vastly different to each of them. Kai's twin was like the rest of the Premium serfs ram-jammed into the carriage, all dressed in outfits that appeared to have been vomited onto them by a dozen stylists. Toca had teamed their mother's vintage Andromeda Galaxy leggings with a long-line men's T-shirt tie-dyed yellow, green and black. One thick, fake gold chain hung between the faintest outline of breasts. ('They're about as impressive as mine,' Kai had teased his twin as he slipped into his chest-hugging white jumpsuit in tribute to his idol.) Toca capped off her costume with row upon row of fluorescent yellow and pink Kandi bracelets, variously inscribed with her catchphrases – GROOVY, BE-IN, and the ubiquitous alternating LOVE and BUZZ.

All that separated Toca from the Stadium Loop's other Premium drones was her wig – long, golden blonde and perfectly straight, with a heart-shaped part in the fringe bordering the top of her HeadBand viewfinder. At their mother's insistence, Kai's own close-cropped hair was covered by the same wig in tribute to Sailor Moon, another of his father's anime idols. ('It will make your father a little less reluctant to let you go alone,' Stefanie Ishii had reasoned. 'Even old grumps like him can't fight nostalgia.')

'If you blended in any better, Tokes, you'd disappear altogether,' Kai said drily, regarding his fellow passengers with an air of superiority.

His sister clutched at her heart in mock agony, as if trying to remove a stake that'd been thrust deep then twisted. 'Well I hoped you'd go to a little more effort for our special day,' Toca retorted, 'but this "dress for comfort" vibe is so, so you. You're the male clone Juanita never knew she had.'

Kai snorted. Unlike his sister, he wasn't content to celebrate his uniqueness with cookie-cutter technicolour fashion. He'd settled upon an iridescent white inversion of the black bodysuit he'd worn on the regular since first seeing HeadBand highlights of his Virtuoso hero. From the second he'd slipped into his black sneakers and had Toca zip up his back, the form-fitting spandex made Kai feel powerful – and a little more confident he could cope with the long, blonde wig's affront to his manhood.

Kai's speaker cups suddenly spewed forth a barrage of beats and uplifting synthesiser riffs, striking his eardrums like a coward punch. A pop-up advertisement for Love Buzz took over Kai's HeadBand. The outside world disappeared.

'Feel the love the way Tito intended at your nearest Trancentral stadium!'

Kai closed his eyes to shut out the commercial break filling his viewfinder. He didn't want any spoilers when he was so close to finally experiencing the real thing.

'See your favourite Virtuoso's visuals come to life in three dimensions from our magnificent Premium grandstands!'

Kai realised it was the same voice as the train's public address system, only sounding enthusiastic about life, like his mother before and after her morning coffee.

'Bank your monthly credits to upgrade to the VIP Floor, where you can Robot Rock away on an adventure beyond the Ultraworld!'

Kai resisted the temptation to peek at the VIP Floor, a sensory overload he'd never experience in person, unless his dream to become a Virtuoso miraculously came true.

'Come together with the world at Love Buzz – where it's peak time, all the time, every time.'

The horn sounded three times, signalling the train had reached its destination. A gently glowing, three-dimensional outline of Trancentral Sydney – which Satoshi Ishii still stubbornly referred to as the Sydney Football Stadium – appeared across each of the carriage's windows under the words *'YOU. HAVE. ARRIVED.'*

Kai's 'stomach feeling' butterflies fluttered their wings. He took a deep breath before rising to his feet. Toca's eyes found his again, blinking daintily, doing their best to coax her tension-riddled brother into a smile. Kai held firm. Toca could have her Kandi and her communal individuality and her embarrassment at being identical to Kai, flat chest and close-cropped hair and western Sydney bogan accent and all.

All Kai cared about in this moment was finally getting to show Juanita his heart.

| 2.08 |

Energy Flash

The hyperspeed build-up of the Drop at the end of Cosmo's set raced to its conclusion in Juanita's speaker cups. In the middle-distance of her viewfinder record sleeves stood tall, megapixels twinkling, in anticipation of her next command. Halcyon had designed the icons of their fresh drops distinctively – the animated sleeve, the unmistakeable heart-hands label – to enable a harried Virtuoso to quickly identify new tracks in their setlists at a glance. In her peripheral vision, she sensed rather than saw Abbie's idiotic blonde head bouncing to Cosmo's remote soundtrack, its apogee almost within reach. Beneath her viewfinder, the signature green, red and yellow colours of Love Buzz flickered and flared across Abbie's vacant eyes, the uncovered portion of her face ghostly pale. Robotically dancing like someone's watching, and not daring to stop.

She is clearly not feeling the love, Juanita thought, *but bless the young petal for trying.*

'What's the plan for tonight, Abs?' she asked, in the same way she used to ask her fans on the Outside what they'd thought of her set – with no genuine interest in the answer, which rarely deviated far beyond 'Fully sick', 'Fucking lit' or whatever that year's variation on the theme was. She'd not bothered to ask Abbie or any of her predecessors about themselves before, but hoped the distraction would at least press pause on her stop-start two-step routine. Juanita was having a hard-enough time focusing as it was. 'Hope the boyf is treating you to dinner at a hot new teppanyaki restaurant or something after work?'

'Hah! Tito told me you were hilarious, but I didn't believe him 'til now!' Abbie laughed. Her head was close enough to stationary not to raise Juanita's hackles. 'There's no restaurants left in Rotterdam either, so Joris won't be taking me anywhere unless street food counts.'

Raise right index finger. Swipe left. The penultimate record sleeve swung to the back and Juanita's closing track shuffled forward to the front of her queue. The square sleeve, pulsing gently, consumed Juanita's entire field of vision and her anxiety dialled down a little, allayed by the record sleeve's slow-motion throb.

'I'm meeting him at Trancentral One later to watch Kam-E's set from the VIP Floor. But I've got to get you on stage first.'

Kam-E this, Kam-E that. It was bad enough hearing about the young Brazilian thing on the rare occasions Tito graced her with his virtual presence without Abbie joining the PR blitz as well.

'Why party with the rest when you already work for the best?' Juanita quipped offhandedly. Not that she cared now she'd found the record in her crate worth looking for.

'I *always* watch your sets, Juanita, but there's just *so* much hype on Kam-E, and the Brazilian stadium scene in general,' Abbie gushed. 'I'd kill to be on the dancefloor in Trancentral São Paulo when her avatar beams in there.'

Juanita ignored Abbie as she studied her setlist's glowing new addition. The track's title, 'Rabbit Warrior', was etched in apologetically small type on the top right corner of the sleeve. Nonsensical word soup like this had become the norm since Halcyon had upgraded their track-title generator a few months earlier. Juanita figured that with each track now sucking inspiration from thousands of AI-generated productions, on top of Halcyon's database of manmade timeless mega-bombs, the time for compound track titles like 'Big Groovy Xpandernova' was over.

'Glad she'll never set foot in my city though,' Abbie droned on. 'She's just so tall and dark and, like, Amazonian! I've never seen a boy crush on a Virtuoso like Joris does on Kam-E – not even my older brother on you in your pri—' Abbie stopped herself short, oblivious to Juanita's complete lack of interest. 'Well, you're still in your prime, of course . . . but it was a little bit gross how obsessed he was.'

Abbie's social life interested Juanita about as much as the title of her new closing track, tucked away in a corner like the afterthought it was. All that interested her was the giant pixelated heart-hands icon, beating in time with Abbie's bobbing head, on the label at the centre of the record sleeve. The light at the end of Juanita's tunnel switched on. The Drop she'd discharge with this track in an hour was all the motivation she needed to get herself up for the treadmill grind.

'That new track is *sooooo* groovy,' Abbie cooed into Juanita's Head-Band. '*Feed your headdddd, feed your headdddd.*'

Jefferson Airplane – 'White Rabbit'. Juanita recognised the hook immediately and briefly tossed up whether to ask Abbie for her thoughts on the group's pre-Starship oeuvre. She thought better of it – Abbie would likely regurgitate some unrelated soundbite, possibly endorsing the post-Storm ban on air travel, like the good little Tito shill that she was, conveniently ignoring the fact that Tito and the Halcyon board zipped around the world on their private jets at will.

Juanita's jet-setting glory days had ended the afternoon she flew into Sydney from Singapore as the skies outside the Dreamliner's tinted windows turned red. She'd rewatched the video of the final moments of that terrifying flight, of the address in which she'd broken the news of the Storm to the world, more often than any performance from Outside. She saw something in this video that her audience did not – her frightened gulping, her terror-stricken face, just before she began reciting a script fed to her through her HeadBand's speaker cups by Tito, in his ready room at Halcyon HQ, Rotterdam.

'Greetings, my beautiful people,' Juanita had said robotically. She was so terrified by the mounting hell outside the plane her usual charm deserted her, and her cold, controlled voice mimicked Tito's own delivery to perfection. 'The catastrophic storms striking your area are being experienced simultaneously across the world. Py-ro . . .' she stuttered, confused, before ever-so-slightly nodding as her brain caught up. 'Pyrocumulus cloud fronts are generating lightning strikes unlike anything Halcyon's scientists have previously encountered. Please seek safety inside and await further instruction. Children aged two and up should be fitted with the emergency HeadBands you've been provided.'

The voice she heard on the video was brittle and taut, like her throat was caught in a vice. The face that stared back at her was ashen – worse even than in the deepest depths of her GHB phase.

The beginning of the end, Juanita often reminded herself during her frequent rewatchings. Or, as Tito sometimes said with a bitter smirk, 'The end of the beginning'.

Spinning her index finger in a clockwise semi-circle, Juanita sent 'Rabbit Warrior' back to the back of the stack. She dragged Abbie's expectant face into her field of vision. There'd be ample opportunity in the nights ahead to play games with the young fool. For now, she had a set to fake her way through.

Flashing Abbie her toothiest faux smile, Juanita swung into action.

HeadBand, cue opening track and repack record box.

Nineteen record sleeves leapt back into the silver briefcase icon. Its lid slammed shut as the twentieth sleeve launched a record onto a spinning platter at the centre of the control panel along the base of Juanita's viewfinder. The turntable's Auto-Mix function was switched on, as always. Mixing tunes had died with the DJs of the old world. Virtuosos like Juanita didn't mix. They *performed.*

'So, umm, are you going to put on some clothes?'

Juanita looked down at her near-naked frame, still tanned and lithe despite not being worked out in direct sunlight since the morning of her thirty-fifth birthday, the day the Storm struck. She touched her index fingers to her nipples. The e-motion gel covering her fingerprints came to life with a dim, grape-green glow. Oozing from her fingertips like creamy moisturiser, the phosphorescent liquid propagated itself until the circles of her smooth, light-pink areolae were concealed. She hurriedly repeated the process, pressing her fingertips onto her torso and limbs at irregular intervals to create a network of luminous dots across her body. She'd worn enough of Halcyon's motion-capture suits since the Storm to know where her apartment's retroreflective sensors would be focused.

Juanita rocked her recliner forward and rose. She removed last night's underwear and retrieved a pair of fresh, white cotton knickers from a pile beside her chair, pulled the briefs up and tucked the waistband under the utility belt – as permanent a fixture as the HeadBand on her face. She reached around to grip a frisbee-like disc, the size of a 7-inch record, sitting snugly in a technofibre pouch on the back of her belt. Juanita tapped it twice for luck. If not for her Drop Disc's reassuring ballast, she sometimes feared she'd float away like a bunch of NOS balloons.

Juanita picked the helmet up off the lightly glowing circular podium in the centre of her living room. With the visor open, she pulled the helmet down tight over her head, felt its insides shapeshifting around her skull and HeadBand frame until all but her nose and mouth were airtight.

Whenever Juanita slipped inside her performance headpiece, she imagined she looked to others like the leader of a bikie gang – hard and cool and unflappable and invincible. In her heart of hearts, the queen of Love Buzz knew she was anything but. Until she got into character. Until she stepped into the Ultraworld.

'Is my rider on its way?' Juanita asked, turning left and then right to cover her back with more of the motion-capture markers from her fingertips. Her skin squirmed beneath each dot, wet and abrasive like she was being licked by a litter of kittens, until the e-motion gel settled into place.

'Of course, and they'll have your fresh supply of Vitamin D blotters as well.'

'Then let our boy Tito know I'm ready to party.'

'*Grooooo-vy!*' Abbie squealed. 'Can't wait for the Drop!'

Juanita clapped her hands once and held the tips together tightly. She sensed the helmet's visor slide down over her eyes. Abbie's face and Juanita's record box disappeared, replaced by a three-sixty-degree vision of her apartment rendered in crisp, three-dimensional lines glowing green. Juanita was no longer naked but covered neck to toe in a black cyber-leotard, the tiny rivulets of light which began at her solar plexus and flowed out towards her extremities emitting an expectant white glow. She separated her hands, each now clutching the centre of a glowstaff – like broomsticks with fluorescent light tubes of radioactive green on each end. She twisted her right hand slowly clockwise, pushing her helmet's volume dial from its lowest reaches up past eighty per cent. From a muted rumble, the sonic discord of Love Buzz reverberated around her skull at near full power.

'Oh yes, oh yes!' Cosmo's voice shouted over the chaos; his accent the same cosmopolitan American twang as Abbie's. 'That's the end of tonight's journey through the Cosmos.'

Juanita had never known stage fright, from her early teens as a competitive gymnast, where her stag leap took her to the brink of the Athens Olympics, to holding 27,000 nocturnal beach bunnies in thrall at her last set on the Outside. The blissful calm that only performing could provide returned to her body. Preparing to face her fans, she waited alone in Love Buzz's virtual green room, floating in a universe of falling stars. She'd not noticed the climactic Drop which had brought Cosmo's set to a close, but the sonic supernova he'd detonated from his Valencia apartment had cleansed Juanita's troubled soul. The devils dancing up and down her limbs were gone, chased away by a succession of gently tingling aftershocks.

'Love Buzz Nine-Nine-Nine, please make some noise for the Virtuoso who started it all!'

Juanita tapped her right staff downwards, opening an additional channel of audio inside her helmet. The gesture summoned the binaural adulation of billions of voices crying out as one.

'Your headliner now and forever . . . Juanita!'

As Juanita stepped onto the podium in the centre of her living room, her helmet's visor snap-locked shut. She set her legs in her favourite floor routine starting position across the metre-wide Silo platform – left foot and body turned outwards; right leg forward, knee bent, toes just touching the platform; head twisted right and to the front; glow-staff held across her avatar's face like a shield, as if trying to conceal her identity from her adoring fans. The goddess of Love Buzz was no Aphrodite. This was the pose of a warrior.

Juanita initiated her Silo platform's performance mode with an infinitesimal flick of her index finger. The opening orchestral strains of her intro music pumped more life into her listless body. The line drawing of her apartment's walls vanished and she stood alone at the centre of an endless expanse. Crystal castles burst out of the ground around her. A million ribbons of every colour raced across the sky, rippling as if in a fierce breeze. Billions of voices roared.

'*You're a superstar,*' Juanita mouthed the words. '*Yes, that's what you are, you know it.*'

Juanita was home, at last, in her virtual reality playground. A surge of power coursed through her limbs, heart and lungs as her mind became one with the Ultraworld.

| 2.09 |

Temple of Dreams

Trancentral Sydney's cement concourse rattled with an intensity Kai hadn't anticipated, each throb lining up precisely with Cosmo's warm-up set, the sound of violence, sprinting towards a climax inside his speaker cups. Tie-dyed Love Buzz acolytes scurried past the twins in both directions, some tittering excitedly to each other, most lost inside the sneak peak of Love Buzz their HeadBand was serving up to them.

The vibrations from the stadium dislodged a shard of dead skin and wax from Kai's right ear, tickling his ear canal as it rattled around inside. Kai felt for the button on the underside of his right speaker cup and held it down for a second. Love Buzz's fierce roar was temporarily usurped by the hiss of rapidly escaping air. The chunk of debris was sucked from Kai's eardrum then spat from the speaker cup's rear outlet valve as fine dust. Kai supressed a satisfied grin, maintaining his cool mask. Of all the things HeadBands had made better, dispatching gunk from his earholes was one of his favourites.

'Bro, how groovy is this!' Toca cried with glee. 'Stand still for a minute.' She grabbed Kai's arm. 'Can you see it?'

He could. Cosmo's kick drums thudded so powerfully the stadium – the entire world – was shaking.

'This is nothing!' Kai shouted to be heard over the din. 'Wait until Juanita starts!'

Round LEDs dotted the ceiling of the interminable stairwell that led the twins and their fellow nosebleed seat dwellers to the top tier of Trancentral Sydney. The cement walls were a mishmash of neutral colours – faded whitewash and cement in all shades of grey, with mottled black and blue streaks left by leaking rainwater. If the stairwells were claustrophobic, encouraging partygoers to navigate them swiftly, the wide-open corridors wrapped around the back of the stadium's heaving grandstands were oppressive in a different way. The atmosphere was steamy and Kai felt like he was in a locker room draped in sweat-drenched playing kits which had begun to cool.

Must stick all the Doonsiders together so they don't stink out the rest of the stadium.

He'd expected the entrance to Love Buzz to be cleaner, grander, but this was no different to when the Ishiis had climbed these same stairs to watch the football, in another life. Entirely adequate then, but hardly the appropriate welcome mat for his long-awaited date with destiny.

'Don't stress, bro,' Toca reassured him. 'The smell's gotta thin out once we get inside.'

As they exited the stairwell at the top level of the grandstand, a giant TV screen flashed a simple message:

LOVE BUZZ 1000

*FEBRUARY 29, 2028**

ONE MORE SLEEP!

And in small print tucked into the bottom-right corner.

**guestlist subject to Halcyon Industries discretion*

Not that Kai and Toca could've done it all again the next day anyway – Sundays for them meant a full day on childcare duties at Doonside Public, as if spending six days a week with the Doonside Tech bitches and bullies wasn't already punishment enough. The twins marched along the murky concourse, intermittent explosions of colour from inside the stadium escaping through the entry gates. Kai appreciated the tease, however brief. They were so close he could almost touch it.

A whirring siren screamed to life inside Kai's HeadBand, shunting the sounds of Love Buzz deep into the background. A flashing red light zoomed towards the twins from the darkness ahead.

'*Medical emergency, medical emergency,*' an urgent robotic voice blared in Kai's speaker cups.

Toca and a short, heavyset man draped in long dreadlocks just ahead of her backed up against each side of the corridor's walls.

'*Step aside and remain still while you hear this warning.*'

Kai covered the ten metres to his sister in a sprint. He slid in beside her, holding her hand tightly. The older man grimly looked across the aisle at the twins. Toca's warm hand shivered inside Kai's, whose eyes remained fixed on a seismic crack in the opposite wall. The repetitive thud from inside the stadium continued, each strike dispatching flecks of cement from the crack towards the floor.

The robot's voice drilled into their ears on loop. '*Medical emergency, medical emergency. Step aside and remain still while you hear this warning.*'

An egg-shaped medical drone, about the size of the deflated Steeden football wasting away at the bottom of Kentaro's toy box, flew past just above Kai and Toca's head height, all lit up in red. Two distraught men in their late twenties followed, carrying another young man, his feet dragging along behind them like anchors. The third man's babyface appeared almost frozen in a state of incomparable bliss. Beneath his HeadBand's viewfinder, his eyes were locked on the middle-distance. To Kai's untrained eyes, Babyface's only obvious sign of distress was his jaw, chomping away with such ruthless determination that he appeared hellbent on devouring his own mouth.

The robot voice cut off the instant the trio passed Kai and Toca, replaced by the annihilating rhythms of Love Buzz as Cosmo's set swirled upwards to its peak.

'What happened to him?' Toca asked the man opposite – the same man who'd stared through her on the Stadium Loop, whose dreadlocks, she realised now, were as authentic as Kai and Toca's own blonde wigs. Up close it was also clear there was nothing synthetic about that skin pigment, so deep and rich he must've been the proud owner of a Vitamin D blotter that never ran out.

The man turned his gaze to the twins after the emergency convoy disappeared down the stairwell they'd just climbed. 'They call it Total Euphoria,' he said.

Kai's viewfinder identified the man across the aisle – Ian, 52, maintenance supervisor, Chatswood Cluster. While Ian had the shoulders of someone accustomed to physical labour, the hands emerging from his long-sleeved tie-dyed shirt were smooth and uncalloused.

'There's a reason you're not supposed to consume more than three Drops a day, especially not at Trancentral where it's so intense, and rookies like that triple-Dropping fool are the unfortunate result.'

'Will he be OK mate . . . umm, mister?' Kai asked.

'Ian will do just fine, Kai . . . unless you'd prefer Sailor Moon?' the man said, reaching up to pop the collar of his rainbow-striped polo shirt.

Kai squeezed down on Toca's hand, which she understood as, *Just the slightest snicker from you and these little piggies of yours are done for.*

'As for old mate,' Ian continued when he had the twins' full attention, 'they'll hook him up to one of Halcyon's anti-euphoria playlists for a few hours until he snaps out of it. Once he can stand on his own they'll send him back to his Cluster, where he'll likely do it all again tomorrow and the next day until he eventually burns himself out'—Ian shook his dreadlock-wigged head in disgust—'Drop after Drop until he can barely string enough words together to sweep floors at a food factory, if some of my mates are any guide. Sometimes you get the feeling these idiots want to become Brainfeeders, honestly.'

He looked Kai's outfit up and down and flashed an affable grin. 'Looks like one of you knows how to stand out in a crowd even better than that poor bugger,' he said. 'First timers, I assume?'

'It's our swinging sixteen today,' Kai replied.

'And Juanita's little clone here is her biggest fan,' Toca quipped.

Kai elbowed his sister playfully in the ribs. *You know you won't be laughing when I'm a star.* Toca elbowed him back with a giggle.

'Aren't we all!' Ian laughed. 'She's come a long way since I met her in '07, that's for sure.'

'You met her?!' the twins gasped in unison.

'Oh yes, oh yes!' Cosmo's voice yelled in their ears. The hectic, galloping beats of a minute earlier were gone, blissed-out echoes of the climactic Drop they'd built up to floating languidly in their place. 'That's the end of tonight's journey through the Cosmos.'

'At ease, sailors!' Ian shouted over Cosmo's end-of-set hype, booming through their respective earpieces while echoing out of the stadium and ricocheting through the corridor around them. 'My only advice is to have the best birthday ever, play hard but fair, and keep an eye out for each other.' He brought his hands up from his sides to the front of his chest, joining his fingers together in the shape of a love heart. 'I'm heading in to see Juanita for the millionth time, but don't worry'—Ian winked at them—'I'll keep a lazy eye on you both.'

He turned before the twins had a chance to return his heart-hands salute and walked through the nearest gate, swallowed up by the stadium's lights.

'Time to shuttle, brotato, our lot is the next one down.'

Bugged out by something Ian had said, Kai shuttled along halfheartedly beside his sister. It wasn't just jealousy of meeting Juanita that consumed him. *Brainfeeders?* Surely they were just boogeymen, used by parents to keep their kids in line – as if the nightmare Outside wasn't incentive enough. The tall stories that did the rounds of the Three-Way tunnel system made his school's rumour mill seem second-rate. Rory O'Flaherty, his former piano teacher's son, whisked away by collection drones for removing his HeadBand in the weeks following the Storm – or so the story went. Tromping through the Three-Way on his way to Doonside Tech or to pick up a deep-fried satay chicken stick for his father, Kai had eavesdropped on dozens of accounts of alleged collection drone sightings: cracking down on street-food vendors who broke 9 pm Lockdown (or beat the 7 am Unlock alarm), or rounding up kids for tagging the derelict cars beneath each tower block. The only consistency in the stories was that the drones' appearance changed dramatically from one telling to the next – one week the 'bots looked like metallic baby sharks, the next like chrome pigs on the wing. But if Brainfeeders were real, like Ian said, Kai could no longer rule out the existence of collection drones either.

A neon sign reading '*LOT49*' hung above the entryway at the end of the cement concourse. Beside the gate to Kai and Toca's nosebleed seats worked a male cleaner, Koori in appearance, who seemed as ancient to Kai as his paternal grandparents stranded in the north of Japan. Using an extendable high-pressure spray nozzle, attached via coiled steel hose to twin gas cylinders on his back, the cleaner directed a fine spray of mist across a five-word slogan, splashed in faint phosphorescent paint across a five-metre expanse of the concourse wall. His airy, hooded white suit rippled under the current thrown off by a pair of sentry drones, hovering to form a perimeter around the cleaner. The drones' once shiny silver bodies, cylinders which hung in the air like floating salt and pepper grinders, appeared to have been dulled by the dents of past skirmishes.

Kai was taken aback by the intimidating presence of the drones, which were half as big again as those that patrolled the Doonside Three-Way hub. The robophobia emitted by these drones, sending a feeling of subservient awe through any person passing within a three-metre radius, was for Kai counteracted by the comforting smell of the cleaning agent – tangy and fresh, like the synthesised citrus protein shakes his mother slurped down for breakfast daily. But what intrigued Kai most was the slogan, THE STORM IS A FRONT, visible only in the brief moments of darkness between the Love Buzz light explosions.

Toca interlocked fingers with her brother, dragging him towards their gate. 'There's graff like that everywhere these days.' She tugged insistently on his arm. 'Kai, Juanita's waiting, come on!'

'Love Buzz Nine-Nine-Nine,' Cosmo gasped, his voice near breaking point. 'Please make some noise for the Virtuoso who started it all!'

Kai let Toca pull him through the LOT49 entryway. The light show engulfed him. The hairs on his neck stood to attention like cactus spines and he was shaken by an off-kilter sensation, like when the ground had seemed to shift beneath his feet when he ran into the Storm; an uneasy feeling that the grave he'd just walked over was his own. As quickly as the words were disappearing from the wall, the slogan disappeared from Kai's mind.

'Your headliner now and forever . . . Juanita!'

Toca raced down the stairs towards their seats the second the twins entered the arena.

Kai remained frozen at the entrance. He stared into a distant kaleidoscope, oscillating above where Juanita's avatar would soon appear at the far end of the Trancentral Sydney dancefloor. A tingling sensation beginning at the base of his skull swept across his scalp in waves, the first hint of euphoria taking hold – even more intense than the Drop as he'd experienced it through his HeadBand watching Love Buzz transmissions from his bedroom in boring old Doonside. Kai felt the past few minutes – the faulty train window-screens, the burnt-out Babyface, the sentry drones' sweeping dread – coalesce into a speeding montage of images, then a swirling fractal of coloured light, merging with the kaleidoscope above the dancefloor. Kai laughed aloud in delight. Nothing else mattered.

His special day had finally arrived.

| 2.10 |

Injected with a Poison

Outside Juanita's apartment window, nature's ceaseless red fury raged on. Lava-lightning bursts greeted the onset of another black, baleful night. The last of dusk's light crept through her window, throwing a faint shadow of Juanita, arms held out like a dancing human crucifix, across her TV feature wall.

Like an aerobics instructor in private rehearsal mode Juanita went through her Love Buzz routines, the OxyPure unit firing intermittent gusts of fresh air at her knees. The only other sounds in the room were locked in almost perfect sync: her laboured breathing; her left heel keeping the beat; the drip of her kitchen tap, drifting in and out of time on the off-beat.

After nearly three years as the face of Love Buzz, her movement through virtual space was so fluid that each choreographed step looked improvised. The music may have controlled her but the grandeur of her movements controlled the people, whether with her in the Ultraworld, in the 600-plus Trancentral stadiums dotting the planet, or watching inside their HeadBands from home. The effortlessness of her performance, the ease with which she held the entire population at her command, came from somewhere deeper, though; from lessons learned across twenty-two years of ruling the global underground. Juanita had seen dancefloors from every possible angle. She'd spearheaded Halcyon's mega-festival assault on Australia's capitals across the early 2010s, orgies of flag-cape wearing nationalism that devoured every other event, great and small, in their path. Then, with the might of Tito's promotional machine behind her, she'd taken EDM global. Her grasp of this sound was so complete that each beat, each bassline, felt like an extension of her soul.

Inside the Ultraworld, Juanita held her arms aloft in a Jesus Christ pose, upward palms summoning a virtual universe of stars. Her body shimmied, slave to the rhythm of a thumping kick drum, thundering away beneath a swirling filter sweep. The intensity built and built again as an increasingly harsh blanket of white-noise coiled around her helmet's full-surround speaker system like a snake charmer's pet. With each shimmy her fingers motioned inward more dramatically. The swooshing sound around her soared towards its high-pitched peak. ('Whenever you get lost, just listen to the hiss,' Tito had instructed Juanita on that first Asian tour in 2006, when she could barely tell when one track ended and the next began. 'When the pitch starts to rise, you know the beat's about to return.') Juanita's global audience of billions feasted on the illusion that her movements were summoning these sounds, out of subspace or somewhere deeper still, to create the head-caving crescendos they craved.

The devil dance on her arms of an hour earlier was gone, replaced by the relentless adrenaline rush Juanita had been dealing out her entire adult life – across the dancefloors of Sydney sex clubs; chasing the sun across Singapore beaches and Nevada deserts; inside the DJ booths of superclubs and cruise ships and failed galactic passenger planes. She'd conquered both sides of the real-world DJ – dancefloor divide, but performing as a Virtuoso, her home the Ultraworld, made her feel more alive than life itself.

Fuck the sickness, fuck the planet, hang the consequences.

This was life, this was all that mattered, this one hour of every day that was hers to control. The world's citizen ravers were mere passengers on her nightly ride, as transient as any crowd she'd encountered at her first residency, at a swingers' club, in a terrace house not far from where she'd been trapped for the past thousand days and change. She fed on Survivors' need for escape as they fed on her love. That was the only positive of the Storm, so far as Juanita could tell – with Love Buzz the only form of entertainment, it had made EDM fiends of an entire planet whether they were clubbers, caners or didn't know the difference between a breakdown and a build-up until the Storm had struck.

Juanita filled her lungs with chill-filtered oxygen in preparation for the next kick-in.

'*Arrgghh!*' she roared, bellowing all she had into her helmet's airflow vents. The huskiness of her voice, a recent battle scar of hard-living that she'd taken to wearing with pride, masked her exhaustion. Her eyelids drooped shut.

'We're all in this together, Love Buzz, can you feel the burn?'

Juanita opened her eyes to an elaborate fractal spanning the entire Ultraworld, zooming endlessly into the vast emptiness beyond. Patterns of red, yellow and green curled up, around and behind her avatar, its perpetual body sculpted – at Tito's behest – in the form of her illegal, club-hopping sixteen-year-old self. A wall of sub-audible buzz-saw bass mobilised behind her, slowly filtering up until the whisper became a scream.

She ramped up the force of each beckoning motion. With a tap of her right middle finger on her palm, a semi-opaque layer of real-world visuals appeared inside Halcyon's psychedelic oasis. Each subsequent tap took her one spin further around the carousel of former sporting cathedrals – the global Trancentral stadium network – that her avatar held residence in, every night, all at once.

Tap.

In the middle-distance of the Ultraworld, Soweto's Soccer City coliseum materialised, packed with glistening, semi-naked black male perfection. Tens of thousands of vuvuzelas were raised to mouths, readying a horn blast to signal the end of yet another epic breakdown, build and drop.

Tap.

Next the humid hellhole that was once the Wankhede in Mumbai, which still refused to fall despite Shiv Sena extremists finding ever cleverer ways to smuggle mortars into the bleachers, determined to blow up the heathens who'd abandoned Shiva to worship Juanita and her fellow false gods.

Tap, tap, tap.

On and on and on through Old Trafford, the Maracanã and the MCG, the Melbourne stadium boasting an inhouse lightshow that dwarfed its sister Trancentral stadiums. It dwarfed any real-world set-up Juanita had ever encountered, almost matching the virtual pyro controlled by Juanita herself.

Tap.

Juanita settled, as always, on her 'home ground' of Trancentral Sydney. During her early days as a Darlinghurst resident, when stepping out for fresh air without being mobbed was theoretically still possible, the Sydney Football Stadium was just fifteen minutes' walk from her doorstep. Now, the only way Juanita could safely reach Trancentral in the real world involved a phalanx of security – human and drone – rushing her past the rat-run foot traffic to the relative safety of the Stadium Loop's VIP carriages.

On the lone occasion Chole Jay, her dearly departed and completely unlamented former handler, had suggested doing a meet-and-greet backstage at Trancentral Sydney, her response had been emphatic: 'Fuck. That.' Pulling herself off the recliner to perform every night was enough of a battle; having to deal with other humans was inconceivable. That was the last Juanita had seen of poor Chloe, and Abbie had wisely left the topic of Juanita leaving her apartment closed ever since.

'We're on the home stretch now, my fabulous freaks,' Juanita purred.

'Don't You Worry, Slippy Children' was almost through. *Thank fuck.* After twenty-seven days in a row of this track – same time, same place, same absolute butchering of the songs it sucked the life out of

– Juanita didn't even have to think about the choreography. The steps danced themselves.

A fresh influx of silver orbs had mobilised across the Ultraworld. She could see them as her audience could, hanging above the rear corners of each Trancentral stadium's dancefloor, lined up like pinballs, ready to launch as soon as she gave the signal.

Juanita, ever the conductor, brought her arms across her chest then opened them out with a dramatic flourish. Cymbals crashed. The world roared. The end of 'Slippy Children' was nigh.

Rushing forward on a bed of white noise, the first pulsating Love Buzz party favour flew towards her head from the rear of Trancentral Sydney. She swung her right arm across her chest as the orb neared its target. Juanita's fierce backhand collected the orb, sending showers of fireworks across tens of thousands crammed into the eastern grandstand of the old SFS, across the millions more in its sister stadiums around the world. The collision triggered a sonic boom, pleasurably rattling Juanita's ribcage. On the count of four her left hand disintegrated a second orb, then joined her right above her head to form a V, as if she were readying for a star-jumps workout. She dispatched a third orb from below her right ribs on another four-count; count to four then a fourth, down to the left.

All too easy. Orbs dispatched and sonic booms deployed, Juanita felt herself warming to the challenge of the home stretch. A serpent's head hovered above her, barely restraining the flames flaring out of its nostrils. Rhythms and melodies raced around her like a cacophony of warring dragon armies, shooting fire and ice and venom as their screams pierced the night. The BPM was rising, almost too hard and fast too think.

Double-ended glowstaffs of luminescent green materialised in Juanita's hands.

Finally, she thought, twirling the glowstaffs with the expertise learnt across five years of rhythmic gymnastics training. Appropriately, her specialty apparatus had been the clubs. *The fun part.*

The beat dropped again. Juanita swung her glowstaffs in tandem, left and right, knocking incoming pairs of orbs off their course and into the elated crowd. The orb assault picked up pace, arriving and disappearing in shades of gold, purple and green as Juanita propelled them across a 180-degree axis in front of her. The number of orbs per attack-run doubled, then doubled again after four bars. Sixty-four down, infinity to go – at this speed, there was no point counting.

No matter how quickly the visuals flew towards her, Juanita countered the lift in intensity with consummate ease. Each hit she made to repel the virtual baubles corresponded with a sampled clapping sound. The digital claps her movements conjured up didn't clap like human hands so much as crack like whips, resonating through the Ultraworld with enough clinical precision to slice a cement slab clean in half.

The digital clock on Juanita's Virtuoso console flipped over to 19:54.

Six more minutes, her internal monologue encouraged her. *Come on, Neets, push!*

Exhausted, Juanita battled towards her set's conclusion on muscle memory alone. Every sinew in her arms, legs and neck screamed in agony. Worse still, her most loathed of Halcyon's musical creations had begun: 'Aftermath of Del Mar's Sandstorm', her now signature penultimate record. Whatever sorcery Halcyon's machines had performed on the source material before spitting out this abomination had removed all the depth, all the nuance and subtlety Juanita had grown to love since the tracks had been force-fed to her from the moment Tito took her on as his apprentice. Only the bare bones of the anthems she'd cut her teeth on remained: the hypnotically repetitive minimalism of Pryda's 'Aftermath'; the slow-burning arpeggiated synthesisers of Nalin & Kane's 'Café Del Mar' remix; the obnoxious synth riff that transformed Darude's 'Sandstorm' from banger to meme by the time Juanita reached her mid-twenties.

Tito had explained it to her, early one morning, at some far-flung kick-on a decade ago or more. 'It's the Theory of Cycles, darling,' he'd said, sipping a Long Island iced tea out of one hand while his other stroked Juanita's natural hair, dark blonde and draped across his lap, as she stretched out on the day bed beside him. 'Take something they love, give it a twist, blend in hints of other music they know and EDM basically writes itself. And twenty years' later, once you've gone full cycle, everything old will be new again.' But the next time Juanita had brought it up, he offered only a shrug of confusion before walking way.

'Let me see those hands, people!'

Sixty thousand Sydneysiders touched the sky. She felt the weight of expectation of billions more across the planet, sensed the dead souls of the billions more again, trapped Outside on 1-6-25, left to burn in the lava lightning of the Storm.

Juanita coasted towards her grand finale on autopilot. She amused herself by mentally identifying the track's fault lines, seeking out what had been secreted away beneath its ultra-compressed digital sheen and layers of abrasive rage. There was something big missing at the core of 'Del Mar's Aftermath' (she refused to acknowledge its whole name), an absence typical of Halcyon's early post-Storm output – the heart and soul and sense of purpose which made the original tracks so essential. In the place of the big missing thing was nothing at all; a vacant lot that had yet to be filled, an empty, meaningless void.

The last time Juanita and Cosmo had Vid-Linked, only a few months ago after her thirty-seventh birthday, the mere thought of articulating her fears to her friend – 'What's missing from the music, Cossie? What's the story behind the sound?' – made her anxious. Paranoid and confused, she'd ceased contact with her Virtuoso peers from that moment forth. One slip and the newcomers who coveted her crown would be giving Tito much more than a stamp on his United Nations of nubiles passport.

No, Juanita would *not* be going the way of DCR, the adorable Scouser who took a sickie, that much was certain. Juanita *was* Love Buzz. Billions of beat junkies needed her. And she needed the round-the-clock tension and release of EDM even more.

Fuck the sickness, fuck the planet, fuck you, Tito – fuck you all.

Juanita swung her glowstaffs up to star-jump formation, bracing for impact.

'You know what comes next!'

A single kick drum. An echo from the Big Bang. A nanosecond of silence.

'Make some motherfucking noiiiiise!'

| 2.11 |

Higher Than a Skyscraper

If Kai and Toca were perched any further up Trancentral Sydney's bleachers and the stadium wasn't fully enclosed, they could've raised their hands above the roofline to catch forks of lava lightning. A colossal air-purification turbine silently whirred directly above their section. Identical machines clung to each corner of the enclosed roof, covered in enormous hexagonal speakers that butted together in a honeycomb array.

Between two speaker arrays suspended from the southern end's roof, a holographic Juanita strutted her stuff on the world's only remaining stage. Kai's eyes were glued to the flickering avatar of his hero, towering fifty metres above the VIP Floor. The Virtuoso's hologram sported an arm span so great Kai imagined her lazily peeling the roof back like she was opening a sardine tin from the inside out, then casually flicking a purification turbine into the sky. At home inside Kai's HeadBand, Juanita appeared merely as a conductor; at Trancentral she was a towering totem of hypersexual femininity, holding three billion Survivors in her thrall.

Tens of thousands of revellers worshipped their goddess from the 270-degree terrace; the lucky thousands of Halcyon's 'key workers' spread across the VIP Floor writhed and wailed together, united, as if Juanita pulled their strings. Beside him, Toca screamed the scream of sixteen-year-old girls immemorial when confronted with a pop idol in person. Kai, a solitary beacon of calm, stood resolute. For him, the purpose of this pilgrimage was equal parts pleasure and study tour. Yes, he was here to lose himself to Juanita's power, eventually, but not at the expense of learning how to lead Love Buzz himself.

'*Woooot!*' Toca shrieked, closed eyes turned skyward. Like a child pining for her mother's warm embrace, his sister's hands reached out to the pyrotechnics, virtual and actual, exploding across the arena. Toca's rapture was repeated around the Premium bleachers and across the entire VIP Floor below.

Kai took in the full majesty of Trancentral Sydney, its innards simultaneously familiar and foreign to him. The Ishii family had been regulars here until 2023, when the Public Order Act kicked in.

'These Transglobal Union bastards,' Satoshi Ishii had bristled on the night Sydney's 9 pm Lockdown was formally invoked, to stop COVID-23's rampant spread. 'Keeping us all locked up inside so they can wage their Oil War in peace.' As the twins' father waved his arms in the general direction of the TV newsreader, their mother had quietly wept, again.

Before tonight, to Kai the stadium had represented a far simpler time, when most school weeks ended in a family trip to the football. Even though he hated the game, there was something to be said for the allure of the familiar, the crass chants and the putrid toilets and the overcooked meat pies. His nostalgic melancholia was wiped from his mind the minute he'd stepped inside LOT49 five years after he'd last visited. Gone was the manicured grass playing-surface dotted with twenty-two athletes scurrying after a slippery white ball. Now the stadium floor was polished cement. Thousands of fauxbots, robot-like human figures, danced in sync atop Silo platforms arranged in diagonal rows, surrounded by tiers of standing terraces crammed with rainbow-outfitted dancers reaching for the stars. In front of Juanita's 'stage' stood a platform, twenty metres from the far end of the VIP Floor. Atop the platform a pair of silhouettes – the front-of-house tech crew – diligently worked a console lit up by spectrum analysers and empathy regulators and orb counters, and other displays Kai couldn't see now, from so far away, but had examined while dissecting Juanita's broadcasts from home.

The beat dropped, kicking Juanita's avatar back into action. Kai mimicked her every movement, note-perfect, from the subtle backwards tilt of her neck right down to the beckoning flicks of her hands, palms up either side of her hips. The hologram guiding him was clad in a skin-tight black catsuit, near identical to Kai's replica in all ways but colour. Kai's iridescent white jumpsuit was somewhat dull compared to Juanita's; hers was covered in thin, parallel lines which began at her core and stretched out to her extremities. Pulsing rivulets of light flowed from the centre of her chest, shifting constantly across the colour spectrum on their journey towards her fingers and toes.

'Arrgghh!'

Juanita's honey-coated roar sent Trancentral Sydney into a chorus of delirium. Juanita drew her right arm back over her shoulder then emphatically slung it forward. A computer-generated spear whizzed straight down the middle of the ground towards the giant video screen to Kai's right, leaving a trail of stardust in its wake. Screams of terror from the dancers in the firing line turned to joy as the spear became a torrent of falling stars, disintegrating above the stadium floor mid-journey.

I'll never be her, Kai lamented as the beats rolled on, hammering his torso with such intensity he'd have to ask Toca to check him for bruises later. *She's just too good.*

Ferocious synth melodies continued to rain down from the enormous hexagonal speakers, as if soundtracking Satan's army of fallen angels as they massed outside the Gates of Hell. Kai had analysed every permutation of Juanita's set a hundred times over, parsing her playlists for clues on how each track complemented the last. But across all those late-night deep dives inside his HeadBand, he'd never suspected Love Buzz could be as visceral – the vibrating bones, the bruised ears, the lumpy throat, the tear-streaked cheeks – as it was in Juanita's presence, in Trancentral Sydney, in the flesh.

What's she doing now? Kai tapped his MIDI connectors, convinced his HeadBand was glitching out. The MK 4 had never let him down before, but it had never had to deal with Love Buzz in all its three-dimensional, augmented-reality glory before either. It was three-year-old tech, after all. Given how quickly the OS in his old smartphones had slowed to a crawl before HeadBands superseded them, it was a minor miracle his tired old MK 4 still worked at all.

But what he thought he saw was really there – unexpected cracks in his Virtuoso hero's perfect façade. Patches of Juanita's skin, much paler than her immaculately bronzed face, revealed themselves through her jet-black bodysuit, then disappeared just as quickly. Basketball-sized beads of sweat rolled down from the edges of her viewfinder to her jaw, before disappearing into thin air. All set long, he'd noticed Juanita's windmill-sized eyes switching from focused to disinterested and back again. They were now somewhere in between; the windows to a soul on the brink of collapse, just as he remembered them looking on the emergency broadcast on 1-6-25. But she was Juanita, Love Buzz queen . . .

What could she possibly be afraid of?

'Love Buzz Nine-Nine-Nine, how good does it feel?' Juanita's voice echoed around the arena, its huskiness standing the hairs at the nape of Kai's neck to attention.

Every voice in the immense arena roared in the affirmative. Whatever had troubled Juanita was gone. Kai's misgivings washed away as his eyes welled with tears.

'The whole world is on this journey together, man,' Juanita spoke, her eyes focused again and darting across something inside her Head-Band's lens.

All around her beguiling voice, bubbling acid synths bounced across echoes of silence.

'The Outside world, it is what it is. Can you dig it?'

On either side of Juanita's face appeared a monarch butterfly, golden wings ten metres across, rimmed with black dividing lines and stark white spots and gently flapping in slow motion. The back of Kai's head went numb, then his entire skull, engulfed by a wave of empathy which swept over him by stealth. Every body in Trancentral Sydney was still, mesmerised. The VIP Floor's fauxbots were frozen atop their Silo platforms. Toca's face – eyes squashed shut, lips forming a silent shout – had contorted into an almost unrecognisable expression of ecstasy.

Relaxed at last, Kai was ready to follow her lead.

'But inside us, what we all hold here.' Juanita paused, tapping her right hand just above the giant dome of her left breast, as large and symmetrical as an igloo. 'As long as we have this, our HeadBands and this wonderful space, we have everything we need to make Inside a better place.'

Every lightbulb in Trancentral Sydney blinked out. All that was left was the eerie glow of Juanita's suit and her face, flanked by the swish of ghostly butterfly wings. Kai felt his head gently nod up and down, accepting Juanita's statement as irrefutable fact.

'Kai!' a man's voice hissed inside his speaker cups, overriding Juanita's homily.

Kai's trance was broken by a hand lightly tugging the crook of his right elbow. He ripped his arm from the stranger's touch and turned to face him, an immaculately groomed man in his mid-twenties with stubble so carefully sculpted he looked like an avatar come to life. Deep blue eyes twinkled beneath a lime-green viewfinder lens, which Kai hadn't seen since HeadBands first appeared outside Doonside Public School in fourth grade.

'I know you're feeling the love right now, brotato.' What was this guy's accent – Yank? Aussie? Euro? It crossed more borders than all of Nurragingy Towers combined. 'But we need to talk.'

The man's presence was cold but somehow familiar, like Kai had met him before. Kai's ID sensors scanned his face but failed to get a lock for the first time since his HeadBand had been installed (*Maybe it is glitching out?*), which made the fact he knew Kai's name even more disconcerting.

As if sensing Kai's discomfort, a smirk crept out from the side of the stranger's lips. The man's face was otherwise inscrutable. His thick shadow of facial hair disappeared below the neckline of a white T-shirt bearing the Love Buzz logo – two hands, held together to form the shape of a heart.

'How would you like to feel the Buzz like the one-per-cent do?'

The man Kai guessed must be a Love Buzz rep was flanked by two muscle-headed Polynesians (Siliva and Sia, according to the identifiers generated by Kai's HeadBand), dressed head-to-toe in black with the Halcyon cog and heart-hands plastered across the front of their T-shirts in white. Kai couldn't decide whether they were unmoved by proceedings or in a higher state of consciousness than everyone else in the stadium. The pair were as expressionless as Easter Island statues, and almost as broad.

Kai scolded himself. His father would be furious if he found out he'd been caught off guard, having drummed into Kai that as the male half the twins' safety was his responsibility. ('No matter how much Tokes gives you that "little brother" nonsense.') He looked uneasily at Toca, still staring blissfully into some unknown time and place, transfixed by Juanita and her butterfly sentinels. On the terraces around the twins, mesmerised spectators swayed from side to side like metronomes running at half-speed.

Kai understood, now. He'd almost been there himself. All the times he'd experienced Love Buzz through his HeadBand at home were just a teaser. The older kids at Nurragingy had tried to tell him what he was missing out on, the true depth of the Buzz, and here, in Juanita's virtual presence, he finally understood what being a Virtuoso was really about: control. Once the fizzing fireworks, the sonic spears, the slow-mo flutter of monarch butterfly wings took over, the real world existed only in soft focus. Inside Trancentral they stood on the precipice of paradise, the Ultraworld, where happiness and empathy reigned.

Beside him, Toca was still oblivious to her surroundings. Kai and the new arrivals may as well have been conducting their business in a different dimension. But on the adjacent terrace, Kai saw that one set of watchful eyes had clocked the new arrivals – Ian, the dreadlocked maintenance supervisor from the Chatswood Cluster. Ian's head tipped forward ever so slightly, telling Kai: *Go. I've got her.*

The newcomer reached his hand out to Kai again. Kai warily shook it.

'I'm Maarten. Come.'

Kai hesitated, looking at his twin, wide open and vulnerable.

'Don't worry about Toca,' Maarten said reassuringly. 'Sia.' At a tilt of Maarten's head, one of the goons assumed Kai's position on the terrace.

Kai met Ian's gaze, who nodded his approval.

Kai stepped into the aisle, leaving Toca alone in her euphoria.

'Come, quickly.'

Maarten put a guiding hand on Kai's shoulder and started down the concrete stairs.

'The Ultraworld awaits.'

Adventures Beyond the Ultraworld

From her apartment overlooking Oxford Street Juanita conducted a spellbound dancefloor: on solo Silo platforms and loaded Trancentral terraces; inside HeadBands tuned to Love Buzz from Cluster colonies and Halcyon factory floors around what remained of the world. Her glowstaffs cut vapour trails across the length and breadth of the Ultraworld. Shooting stars streaked past her avatar at warp speed.

'We're in this together, Love Buzz, this is what we live for!'

You're a superstar, Juanita reminded herself, *Yes, that's what you are, you know it!*

She was the conduit. She was the focal point. She was invincible. No longer did Juanita crave those ephemeral moments of eye contact between dancefloor denizen and DJ; the returned smile, the raised eyebrow, the nod of silent understanding; those unspoken encounters which left both punter and performer secure in the knowledge that this here and now they were existing in was the only here and now that mattered. These fleeting memories were from another time, deep-sixed by the impenetrable barriers put between DJs and crowds at the mega-festivals she circumnavigated the globe headlining a decade and a half before. And impossible to emulate in the Love Buzz era, now that the project to separate Virtuosos from viewers, VIPs from mere spectators, was finally complete.

Love Buzz, the Drop, the Ultraworld – Survivors thought she did it all for them, but in Juanita's mind it was all about her. All in this together? Hardly. Juanita was in her home, and hers alone, alone and lost inside the dance. Everything the world had ever offered before and ever would again was irrelevant.

Emerging from the hyperspace tunnel into the Ultraworld's everlasting night, Juanita almost stumbled on her Silo platform. A single kick-drum drenched in space echo wafted through every HeadBand, every Silo helmet, every retrofitted sporting arena of the world. Juanita spiked her throbbing glowstaffs down either side of her, planted like flags on a conquered planet. She reached around for the Drop Disc tucked into her belt and held it overhead, like a trophy from her gymnastics career more than half a lifetime ago.

'This is what we live for!' Juanita repeated. Her thighs shook like jelly, atop calves stretched like the truth. She searched for a point in the furthest reaches of the Ultraworld to lock on to, and found it – nine yellow neutron stars orbiting a larger green dwarf, against the backdrop of a red giant, the formation looking less like a science-fiction special effect than a bloodshot, all-seeing eye.

And then it began: a single phrase, weighty and plaintive, looping over and over in the deepest depths of her performance helmet's speakers. *Feed your headdddd. Feed your headdddd.* It crept slowly into focus, building in intensity from mumble to wail.

Juanita released her Drop Disc, which revolved, unaided, above her head, in her apartment and the Ultraworld alike. She lowered her hands until they reached her chest. She pressed her thumb and forefingers together, bringing her fingertips down to form the shape of a heart.

'This has been Love Buzz Nine-Nine-Nine!' Juanita shouted.

Around her, the '*Feed your headdddd*' mantra unfurled with ever-increasing fervour.

'I'll be back tomorrow when Love Buzz makes history – for the thousandth time!'

Juanita slowly raised her hands up from her chest, in increments, keeping time with the snare drum beating over the vocal loop.

'Right now I'm going to take you out with something you've never heard before . . .'

The Drop Disc began to spin above Juanita's head. Three concentric circles appeared on its surface, emitting a blinding yellow glow. As the disc's speed picked up, the circles became one until the entire disc lit up like the sun. White petals sprung from either side and the disc was now a daisy. Petals shot out in all directions behind Juanita and the disc was the sun, then petals, then the sun, then a daisy once more.

'The one you've been waiting for . . .'

Half a billion pairs of hands shaping hearts raised inside her visor, from every Trancentral stadium in every broken city all at once. Every sound of every song from the previous fifty-nine minutes collided and collapsed around her.

'Wait for the Drop!'

As the glorious build-up reached its pinnacle, Juanita's hands lined up with her disc, not the sun nor a daisy but now a star going super-nova.

'It's time to feel the love!'

Her heart-hands exploded across the Ultraworld, leaving a blood-red trail in their wake, before Juanita and the denizens of Love Buzz were consumed by a blast wave of white light.

| 2.13 |

Digital Love

Maarten led Kai down into the old football stadium's players' tunnel. Plucking two scuffed-up, robot-like helmets from a near-empty wall rack, he thrust one at Kai's chest.

Finally, Kai had a story that would divert his father's attention from golden child Kentaro – that he'd walked the same race as Satoshi's hero, Keisuke Honda, the emperor of Japanese football.

Although calling it a shared experience, Kai conceded to himself, *is like saying classical pianists and rock drummers are both musicians.*

His father's hero had run onto the playing field in the navy blue, white and silver of the Melbourne Victory, illuminated by the Sydney Football Stadium's floodlights or perhaps the sun itself. Kai bumbled his way onto Trancentral Sydney's once-hallowed turf, now a concrete playground, with none of Emperor Honda's confidence. He stared not into a sunlit sky, but a lightshow from another dimension: waterfalls of light cascading from the top tier of each grandstand; fireworks showering down from above; sterling-silver helmets, as much as seven feet above the stadium surface, twinkling in unison, like a blanket of dancing stars.

'Make some motherfucking noiiiiise!'

Kai gasped, unable to respond, overwhelmed by the enormity of the holographic figure towering above. ('I bet we'll hear Juanita swearing now we're legal age,' he'd confidently told Toca while waiting for his mother to fit his Sailor Moon wig. He couldn't wait to gloat. He loved being right.)

Caught off guard by Kai's swift halt, 120 kilograms of islander body ploughed into his back, knocking most of the wind from his lungs. If Siliva hadn't latched on to the shoulder of Kai's bodysuit, the momentum would have skittled him into at least one of the helmeted VIPs dancing, oblivious, atop metre-wide mini podiums.

'All good?' Maarten asked, more out of obligation than any real duty of care, tugging Kai's elbow.

Kai nodded eagerly.

'The Silo platforms keep people's bodies contained inside a force-field, so they don't wander off chasing pretty lights in the Ultraworld,' Maarten yelled inside Kai's speaker cups, straining to be heard over the speaker array hanging either side of Juanita's avatar. He expertly ducked and weaved them through Juanita's VIP Floor, with Siliva nipping clumsily at Kai's heels.

'The Silos keep you in suspended animation once the Drop hits, so you don't collapse in a heap, because in the Ultraworld the Drop is much more powerful than you've ever felt it out here.'

They shuttled through the epicentre of the sound system's sweet spot, only thirty metres from the front, the music buffeting Kai from all sides like bumper cars. The closing stretch of 'Aftermath of Del Mar's Sandstorm', or 'Del Mar's Aftermath' as Kai called it. (Juanita's music meant too much to too many people for it to be sullied with something as ludicrous as Darude.)

Maarten brought them to a halt in front of a vacant, cordoned-off viewing platform twenty metres from the stage. On another platform directly behind it stood two men, the silhouettes Kai had spotted earlier. Juanita's tech support team were dressed in hooded coveralls so black they seemed to create a schism in space. Their faces glowing like moons inside their hoods, Juanita's reflection danced across their viewfinders. Somehow ignoring the majestic holographic woman towering above them, the men's hands busily tweaked dials visible only to themselves.

Roused by a fresh wave of *um-tz-um-tz* beats, all three sides of the Premium bleachers erupted in a roar. But the VIP Floor danced in synchronised silence, like a troupe of cybernetic mime artists rehearsing the same three choreographed moves: single-finger point to the sky; double-fist pump to the chest; pirouette and repeat. Maarten's eyes narrowed inside his HeadBand. Kai sensed his growing impatience, and understood why. 'Del Mar's Aftermath' meant the Drop was almost here.

'Quickly, put these on,' Maarten hissed at Kai, thrusting a pair of black gloves at him.

Kai almost dropped his helmet as he hurriedly pulled the oversized gloves on.

Maarten stepped into the centre of an empty Silo platform and pointed Kai to the spare one adjacent. 'Now slip your helmet on, like this.' Maarten pulled on his helmet; a curved lens of obsidian Perspex flanked by tiny, golden ear nubs. 'And don't forget to flick the switch.' He felt behind the right earpiece until his thumb landed on a cog-shaped button, which he pushed theatrically for Kai's benefit.

Kai recognised his headgear – a glimmering silver-coated facsimile of the second robot's helmet from retro-rave icons Daft Punk, part of a two-piece set with Maarten's. Kai took a moment to appreciate its construction: the bulbous earpieces; the visor, stretching from ear to ear like a darker, wider HeadBand; the narrow inch-long slit of a mouth, seemingly designed to allow the bare minimum of oxygen in, while not permitting a peep of sound to escape.

Time to do the Robot Rock.

Discarding his Sailor Moon wig on the floor (what Satoshi Ishii didn't know couldn't come back to bite him), Kai took a deep breath for luck and slipped his head inside. Love Buzz stopped. The world was black and silent and terrifying. He felt around for the Halcyon cog and pressed it. His helmet's interior bubbled around his skull like a bowl of half-set jelly, forming a seal around his HeadBand's viewfinder and speaker cups once it had remoulded itself to the shape of Kai's head. The viewfinder and helmet visor synchronised, transforming the robot heads of the VIPs dancing around him into radiating spheres of light. The music of Love Buzz returned with fresh dimensions, coming at Kai not just through his ears but the entire surface of his skull. *Feeling the Buzz like the one-per-cent do.* The stadium's grandstands vanished as Kai entered the Ultraworld, a starburst canvas shooting into an endless expanse of black space. And towering above him, Juanita raved on, not flickering but three-dimensional, fully realised.

Unbidden, Kai felt his head begin tilting almost imperceptibly from side to side. His feet shuffled forward and back in time with the beat, as if compelled. His hips gyrated in a way they hadn't before. Each footfall Juanita planted down in the infinite space of the Ultraworld sent ripples of energy through the light spheres dancing around him. Her melodies flew in every direction – not just straight down the middle but left and right, up and down, all around Kai's Daft Punk helmet – leaving trails across the Ultraworld like jet streams across a cold night sky.

A single kick drum sounded then stopped and Kai lost his bearings, cast adrift in an endless void. All that oriented him, all that kept him upright, was Juanita's majestic avatar, his guiding light, the lone source of heat at the core of this strange new solar system. Kai saw alarm cross Juanita's face, as if she'd lost her balance. And then it was gone, so quickly he must've imagined it, replaced by a benevolent smile.

Juanita planted her glowstaffs firmly either side of her legs. She reached behind her for her Drop Disc and lifted it to the sky in the salute that had become her end-of-set trademark.

Kai had waited for this moment from that first morning on the roof of Nurragingy Towers Block 19, when he'd chosen to be in his Head-Band, drinking in Juanita's beauty, over watching one perfect sunrise. But he never dreamed his first experience of Juanita unleashing the Drop live at Love Buzz would be like this – his swinging sixteen on the VIP Floor, every inch of his body succumbing to his hero from inside the Ultraworld.

'This has been Love Buzz Nine-Nine-Nine,' Juanita shouted.

An ominous vocal loop curled around the inside of Kai's helmet. The hyper-compressed voice Juanita had summoned felt somehow distant – like it was coming from another place and time, but with a message Survivors should heed right now.

Feed your head? Kai wrapped his mind around the words. *That's all I've ever done, Juanita, and I've done it all for you.*

'I'll be back tomorrow night when Love Buzz makes history – for the thousandth time! Right now, I'm going to take you out with something you've never heard before . . .'

Kai reached his arms out and up, only just able to bring his fingertips together in heart-hands over a helmet too big and heavy for his slight frame.

'The one you've been waiting for . . .'

Hundreds of ruby-red heart emojis appeared above the VIP Floor's starburst formation.

'Wait for the Drop!'

Kai's head and chest numbed as every track of Juanita's set layered on top of this climactic breakdown and rebuild. The spinning flower above Juanita's head burst back into a sun.

'It's time to feel the love!'

Juanita's hands lined up with the Drop Disc, sending a heart-shaped shockwave through the never. Kai caught the briefest glimpse of Juanita's face, lighting up with glee as energy surged from her fingertips across the Ultraworld. A bright white dome of light built up around her then exploded, sweeping Kai and Love Buzz towards the outer limits of existence.

Kai was a celestial body disguised as a human. A tingling sensation shot down from his head, bristling over his back, shoulders and arms like static. The final track Juanita dropped was but a memory, its place taken by a tinkling digital piano melody, which Kai dreamily thought might have escaped from some obscure foreign nursery rhyme.

Kai surrendered to the intense euphoria washing over him, a feeling of universal love and understanding that had Kai reaching out to his twin across the Ultraworld.

This is what we live for, Tokes, I love you so much.

As Kai flitted between the Ultraworld and oblivion, Toca's anxious voice reached back.

The Storm is a front, you were right from the start.

BREAKDOWN

For What You Dream of

Bonnie Stapleton's body floats limply in a universe of twinkling stars. Her head is a frantic fever dream of short quests: of collecting a rare compilation of early-noughties Brisbane breakbeat producers from a street-side second-hand CD seller, whose pop-up stall collapses into the catacombs below as she walks past; of rescuing school friends from drug-induced reveries beneath festival tent-poles covered with shirtless, selfish, long-haired surfer boys; of taking the stage behind broken turntables that slip every time she drops a slab of 12-inch vinyl on either platter.

Then she's back in the Cave on that first night, always the Cave, before re-entering her body on the observation deck of the old Sydney Tower thirty-six hours later.

'Everything in this view from up here,' Bonnie Stapleton muses dreamily, through cracked lips that will peel right off if she doesn't soon get back to Tito's hotel room and her tub of lip balm. 'From the city below until you get to those blurry bits right on the edge.' She sweeps a floppy arm in the general direction of Sydney's north shore. 'One day it will all be mine.'

Another part of her brain is ruminating over what would best take the edge off the end of this long, lost weekend – a Macca's cheeseburger or another half a pinger. Getting ready to go out with her besties on

Friday night seems a lifetime ago. She's not slept since and is pushing fifty-eight hours old.

'It looks cold out there now.' Bonnie feels the shiver of her young life's first punishing comedown. Regaining her train of thought, she motions towards the windows and across the city. 'The horizon's as far as my parents can see, you know? And my besties as well. I love them to bits and everything, but all they think about is which boys they like and where the party's at this weekend and how cool it's going to be when we're all going to Sydney Uni and have our own house and can party with whoever we want, any time we like.'

Bonnie steps back from the deck's coin-operated binoculars pointing across Sydney Harbour towards Manly. Once she's squinted the inside of the observation deck back into focus, Tito's charming, salt-and-pepper-stubbled face gazes serenely back at her from behind the cover of his shades. She senses Tito's eyes running the rule over her, as many men had in the three years since she'd quit gymnastics and her body had initiated a sprint towards womanhood. Bonnie self-consciously adjusts her breasts beneath the plunging lace-trimmed singlet which is struggling to contain them. She eyes her outfit up and down: skin-tight black pants, thigh-high black vinyl boots, a corset-suspender combo, which is midway through consuming the aqua singlet beneath it. The look was on-point in the all-encompassing darkness of the Cave, a little less so here with gawking Asian tourists all around. She brushes awkwardly at her midriff to remove lint that isn't there.

Bonnie skips back across the walkway towards her weekend-long spiritual guide, tourists and day trippers side-stepping to get out of her way. The swollen egg on her forehead is almost forgotten now, the pain of her faceplant on the Cave's floor buried beneath copious hits of MDMA, cocaine and crystal meth, laid out by Tito on the desk of his Harbour-side hotel room. Even the dull ache of the anal-sex marathon he had insisted on is beginning to subside; the pain as inconsequential as the loosened row of top teeth and the gnawing sense of loss in her stomach.

'Sorry sweetheart, no regular sex on the road,' Tito had declared while unrolling a condom onto a cock crisscrossed by a river delta of veins as Bonnie watched on, head reeling from the potent drug cocktail, temporarily (or so she'd hoped) speechless. He'd shoved the mortarboard back under her nose before taking another bump himself and turning a bewildered Bonnie onto her hands and knees. 'For the sake of both our careers.'

It hurt until it didn't, and then it was done, and now it was irrelevant. For little Bonnie Stapleton feels for the first time like she's finally flying – flying away from a life of outer-suburban Sydney drudgery and soaring towards her lifelong dream.

'I've always wanted more than this little world, babe,' she gushes, gripping Tito by the cheeks and smacking a forceful, loved-up kiss on his lips and deep into his mouth.

Tito recoils ever so slightly onto the guardrail of the wheelchair ramp he's perched on, pulling away from Bonnie's cracked lips with a congenial smile.

'I want to *be* the party, just like you,' she says. 'I want to travel the world starting it. The way you bring a group of people who've never met each other together for the . . . what did you call it?'

'A celebration of the—'

'A celebration of the purity of music and dance, that's it,' Bonnie completes Tito's sentence with him, enunciating every syllable to help the phrase sink into her brain. 'It's like a secret world just for us.'

'A safe haven for outsiders, is how I like to think of it,' Tito adds. 'An escape from a world that wants to grind your individuality into dust, where the symbiosis between DJ and dancefloor is all that matters.'

'In the club is the only place where I can just be myself,' Bonnie says wistfully, trying not to let on that she has no idea what symbiosis means.

'For some of us, that safe haven is everything,' Tito says, his voice barely above a whisper.

'Exactly,' Bonnie says, pressing a finger, its nail scuffed with green and purple glitter, on the tip of Tito's nose. 'You get it, dude, and you're the only grown-up that does.'

Tito raises a quizzical eyebrow at the 'grown-up' gibe but shakes it off.

'What if I told you,' Tito posits, 'that I've spent the past four years of touring life looking for a girl just like you? That orchestral climax in the track that laid you out two nights ago was a test I've been running through all my DJ sets for months now.'

Bonnie blinks the first warning signs of irresistible tiredness from her eyes. It's 4:43 pm Sunday and, like the sun, she's suddenly fading fast.

'You see, in January my ghost producers at Halcyon handed me a CD-R marked *Weapon 101* – if you've seen the Willy Wonka movie, it's kind of like his golden ticket. It took me five months of performing around the world, but I've finally found my chosen one.' Tito presses an index finger on Bonnie's nose, as if turning a lamp switch on. 'What if I told you that we're on the brink of a new age of electronic dance music consumption, where the technical skills of the DJs won't even matter anymore? A time when a natural-born performer like you, who is already looking beyond this little city, can become more than a superstar.' He pauses. 'We can make you the face of a new movement, Bonnie. A symbol of hope for a world that's lost its way. You've got the looks, you've got the brains, you've got everything. All you need now is the right soundtrack and some showbiz magic.'

'I'd love that.' Bonnie blushes. 'I love you so much and I'd do anything to make you proud.'

Tito takes Bonnie's hands and focuses intently on her eyes. To Bonnie, the rest of the world has become little more than moving shadows in his Wayfarers' reflection.

'It's going to be much easier than you think,' Tito says, gently running his thumbs along Bonnie's palms. 'I fly out for my Asian tour Tuesday morning. You will join me as my official warm-up DJ for the three dates there and carry on with me through the European summer.'

Bonnie's bottom lip quivers.

'What's wrong?' Tito asks, gently reaching for her cheek.

'I . . . I don't think I'm ready.'

'Why not?'

'Well, I've never even tried to DJ.'

'A mere technicality!' Tito laughs. 'I'll have my production team upload a premixed set to my server for you. All you'll have to do is dance.'

'And I don't even have a proper DJ name,' Bonnie whimpers. 'I mean, Bonnie Stapleton? It doesn't exactly scream International Party Girl, does it?'

'I guess not.' Tito strokes his bristled chin. 'Short for Bonita, no?'

Bonnie shakes her head. 'Nope,' she says, a little sheepishly. 'Just plain old Bonnie.'

'It doesn't matter. It's close, but Bonita doesn't quite do it for me either,' Tito says. 'But you know what does?'

Bonnie shrugs.

'Have you heard of Underworld?'

'The movie?'

'The band.' Tito pokes her nose again. 'Surely you know "Born Slippy"?'

Juanita reaches for imaginary lasers.

'*Laaa-ger, laaa-ger, laaa-ger!*

'Keep it down!' a woman no older than Juanita's mother turns around and hisses from behind another set of high-powered binoculars.

Juanita giggles. *Fuck her.* She doesn't care about anything in this world except the words currently oozing out of Tito's mouth.

'That's not even their best song,' Tito says, 'but I've always liked "Juanita".' Tito sees his smile reflected on his young protégée's face. 'That's the name of a DJ superstar.'

| 3.02 |

In White Rooms

Kai faceplanted out of unconsciousness onto a smooth white surface. He was sprawled across a single bed on a satin sheet, cool and comforting to a head once more wracked by MIDI implant growing pains. Overcome by a serious case of the bed spins, as if he'd just leapt off a merry-go-ground at full speed, he clung desperately to the sheet, dirty fingernails doing all they could to pierce the tightly woven fabric. His already reed-thin body felt completely insubstantial, as if consumed by an emptiness from deep within. Kai held the sheets tighter, afraid that if he released his grip he'd be sucked through a portal into another, more frightening realm; a nightmare Ultraworld where there were no stars, no love, no Juanita – just black nothingness.

Sentient but uncharacteristically perplexed, Kai lifted his chin. He could see pristine white wall meet crumpled pillow, wrapped in satin like the bed. His surroundings were bathed in a harsh fluorescent light, reflecting off every stark white surface. More spacious than the bedroom he shared with Toca, the sterile room was devoid of anything in the way of a human touch. It reminded him of the sick bay at his old primary school, Doonside Public – functional, spartan, smelling overwhelmingly of pine-flavoured disinfectant – except instead of being built to offer relief to its occupant, it felt more like a holding cell.

Feeling slowly returned to his hands. His body felt light and tingly, as if he were treading water in lemonade, a mysterious feeling of dread bubbling just below the surface.

'There was a time not so long ago when the first thing you'd hear waking up in a room like this was my voice saying you could put your clothes back on if you felt uncomfortable,' a calm, reassuring voice ricocheted off the white cement walls.

Kai rolled over with a start and sat on the edge of the bed, instinctively shielding his crotch from the intruder's gaze. He needn't have worried – his skin-tight white jumpsuit clung to his body precisely as he'd left it. Nonetheless, he snatched his Sailor Moon wig from the bed beside him and placed it in his lap for insurance.

The man sat two metres from Kai in the room's centre, perched on a tall, timber circular stool of immaculate brilliant white. 'Those days, though, are long behind me now,' the man, who Kai placed somewhere in his sixties, continued.

Behind him stood Maarten, to the left of the only colour in the room, a green door draped in black curtains. Maarten stared, trance-like, both directly into his HeadBand lens and straight through it, while his arms motioned through the air before him.

Probably controlling those hired goons of his from afar, Kai figured. Or more likely, making sure Rakh-E had the opening set of Love Buzz 1000 – slowly increasing in volume inside Kai's HeadBand as his brain activity powered it back up – on lock from her Mumbai studio.

Above the doorway whirred a shiny new pair of OxyPure units – from the latest, high-end 10K range, offering 'a decade of filtration in every breath', according to the commercials currently bookending every day of the Love Buzz broadcast. All was silent apart from intermittent mechanical rumblings from behind the door, Kai's only possible escape route.

The older man smiled sadly at Kai from beneath silver hair, cut short with occasional stylised tufts standing casually to attention, framing his clean-shaven face like a Roman helmet. Kai was shocked to discover his eyes were near identical to Maarten's glazed-over ones, and more shocked when he realised the deep blue eyes were looking back at him without the protective cover of a HeadBand lens.

He knew who this was. He was in the presence of the head of Halcyon Industries, the creator of Love Buzz, the self-appointed saviour of Earth's three billion Survivors. He sat across from Kai with his face HeadBand-free except for the pair of circular MIDI implants on his temples, just like the ones which so tormented Kai. Adding to Kai's confusion were his HeadBand's identifiers, which skirted around Matthias van Dijk's face as if the leader of the free world wasn't in the room at all.

'And you're a far more complex proposition than every other Virtuoso in the Halcyon stable combined,' Tito said.

But I'm not a Virtuoso at all, Kai thought. He couldn't tell if his host, whose face had appeared inside Kai's HeadBand almost as often as Juanita's, was being sincere.

Atop a single shelf on the wall to Kai's left sat a HeadBand, its viewfinder devoid of light, the speaker cups on the end of its loose technofibre straps emitting not a skerrick of sound. The last time Kai had seen a HeadBand in this state there'd been rows of them, hanging expectantly in Halcyon's mobile surgery van, waiting to meet the young faces they'd be attached to forever.

Enigmatic and exuding effortless cool, Tito wore a perfectly pressed long-sleeved T-shirt printed with inch-wide hoops in black and white, neatly tucked into faded black skinny jeans. The deep-red foxing stripes on his navy-blue deck shoes looked like they'd glow if the lights went out.

'You're probably wondering why your HeadBand's ID scanner can't get a lock on me,' Tito said, leaning forward. He pressed his fingertips together in front of his mouth. 'When the Transglobal Union banned facial-recognition software after the Privacy Riots, you see, we recalibrated our HeadBands to scan users' biometric data, not the faces inside them.'

Kai nervously reached around his back and gripped his zipper's dangling pull tab, only now registering Tito's first words to him. One tug was enough to confirm the line of metal teeth along his spine remained closed tight.

'Here, let me help you with that.' Tito leapt from his seat with a swiftness belying his old-man frame, startling Kai. He'd barely enough time to brace for impact before Tito's arms swung towards either side of his head. Like a monkey with a miniature cymbal, Tito's hands clapped down on Kai's speaker cups.

The dull ache that had been creeping back into Kai's temples disappeared in an instant, as if Tito had pulled the plug from the power point. Cautiously, Kai opened his eyes to see his HeadBand resting on Tito's right palm, speaker cups dangling from their technofibre straps. He reached for his temples, running his fingers around the metal implants' circumference, over the five tiny pins which connected his thoughts with his world. Love Buzz was gone, replaced by an interminable high-pitched ringing sound emanating from inside his head and pulsating in time with the beat that wasn't there for the first time in a thousand days. No vital signs readout, no menu bars, no identifier floating adjacent to Maarten's distracted head. Just the cold, harsh light of this sick bay, or whatever the hell it was. And a strange sensation flowing through him, like an outer-body experience. And on the periphery, the faintest memory of the disappearing slogan, of Toca's final words.

Back on his stool, eyebrow cocked, Tito awaited something, anything in the way of a response. Kai met his gaze defiantly, trembling not out of fear but fascination.

'Those tingles flowing through you will stop soon enough, my boy,' Tito said. With a grin, he straightened up on his stool. 'Magnificent, the Drop, is it not? I'd give anything to be in your place right now, trying for the first time to understand what it is that you've just experienced.'

Maarten chuckled, though whether at Tito or something in his viewfinder was unclear.

There were no windows in the room. Kai had no idea how he'd even gotten here, let alone where he was. Yet instead of the anxiety which usually wracked his body when he awoke, disoriented, in the dead of night, he felt only a delightful, lingering buzz.

'It's a roller-coaster to be enjoyed, my boy – don't fight it, feel it,' Tito urged Kai, his own voice trembling in the same rhythm as the trills washing over Kai's body. 'Revel in every last second of the Drop's afterglow. It only gets better – until it gets worse, regrettably – but there's nothing quite like your first time.'

'Where is my sister?' Kai asked, shocked by the meek little boy's voice that squeaked out. He dropped his voice as low as it would go. 'And where are we?'

'She's perfectly okay,' Tito said, brushing off the question. 'Sia is one of Maarten's finest men and he'll have Toca safely back in Doonside before Lockdown.' Tito glanced down at his wristwatch, a plain gold timepiece with analogue hands displaying multiple time zones. 'As for where we are? This is one of my ready rooms, like hundreds of others in Halcyon properties around the world. And Maarten needs to get you home before 9 pm as well, which is why I need you to hold any more questions until the end so we can complete our business quickly and get you on the last train home.'

Kai's eyes darted around the room, seeking an escape route. He wondered if his HeadBand's Personal Safety protocols could be set off against their maker. *Not when he's holding it in his hand, brotato,* Toca's most mocking tone reminded him.

Sensing Kai's unease, Tito sat slowly upright on his stool, attempting to look unthreatening. 'Don't worry, my boy,' Tito assured him, 'you'll be back inside your comfort zone with your KeyRoll soon enough.' He regarded Kai's HeadBand with pity. 'Though once you try out the new tech we're about to send worldwide, you'll wonder why I've let you suffer inside these old rags for so long.' Tito chuckled wryly, tossing Kai's HeadBand onto the shelf beside his own.

The Tito of HeadBand tutorials, the post-Storm broadcasts, exuded an air of nobility, of reassuring calm. Kai couldn't decide whether the old man in front of him was repulsive or amazing. Either way, he had to concede that hitting the shelf from that distance was impressive.

'The thing with a quest like mine, Kai, is that it needs constant re-generation,' he continued. Kai noticed Tito's shoes moving atop the stool's foot rests, tapping out the rhythm to a beat only he heard. 'One of the first promoters I worked with here in Sydney had a slogan – "Never Stand Still". He, of course, torpedoed his own grand vision with a lethal combination of naiveté and hubris, which I'm sure you'll agree is the magic formula when it comes to us creative types sabotaging our-selves into irrelevance ... This is the part where you're supposed to nod in silent agreement, though this particular worldview does assume a certain amount of life experience that you're only half a lifetime to-wards accumulating.'

As predicted, Kai didn't know how to respond. *What does any of that have to do with me?*

'But I digress,' Tito went on, clearing his throat. 'Are you familiar with the concept of ASMR?'

Kai shook his head warily.

'A truly wonderful thing.' Tito sighed. 'A beautiful and random and indefinable experience that's been with me since I was old enough to remember. Then somebody thought to give it a name – autonomous sensory meridian response. Doesn't it just roll off the tongue?'

Sensing he had a part to play in this performance, Kai issued a cautious nod. There was something about the way Tito spoke – the carefully paced rhythm of his phrasing, the cadence of each perfectly re-solved idea – that made every sentence seem like part of a longer incan-tation. Tito's voice had at first felt creepy to Kai; now it felt irresistible.

'This special feeling was tarnished by a bunch of glory-hunting YouTubers, all whispering into a mic to try spin a buck out of some-thing they didn't truly understand.'

Kai remembered YouTube from before the Storm, when his father used to show him Keisuke Honda highlight videos on his smartphone. Otherwise, he had no idea what Tito was on about. The Drop's after-glow, switching his brain between intensely focused and as insubstan-tial as fairy floss at random intervals, wasn't helping matters.

'The ASMR feeling I grew up with wasn't something you could force,' Tito said. His eyes never left Kai's. Behind him Maarten's arms moved in a series of dramatic flourishes, as if he were conducting an orchestra that only he could see. 'It would come unexpectedly, when reading a list of important songs someone had compiled – not very exciting, right?' Kai obediently shook his head. 'Or playing Bert and Ernie with the mentally handicapped kid from down the street—' Tito cut himself short. 'You do know Bert and Ernie, right?'

'*Sesame Street?*' Kai cracked a smile. 'Toca and I used to watch it with Mum all the time.'

'Yes, yes, those late-sixties ideals of inclusion and equality really did cut across generational lines,' Tito said. 'But again, I digress. The true ASMR feeling is an organic surge, almost like an eruption from an untapped quadrant of your brain – a sugar-rush of the "warm fuzzies", I guess you could call it, which begins at the base of your skull—'

'I felt that!' Kai said. 'As soon as I saw Juanita inside Trancentral.'

'Just as we designed it,' Tito interjected, holding up a hand to signal he still had the floor. 'The teaser before the Drop proper hits you. And I know that as we speak, you're still feeling it gushing down your body from head to toe.'

Kai nodded. Goosebumps rippled across his neck and torso. Although his eyes strained against the first unfiltered light he'd seen in over three years, the clouds around his head were beginning to clear for longer periods. His skin felt the foreign touch of cool air where his HeadBand's technofibre straps usually rested. Another surge, and another. Kai felt his arm hair trying to pierce the tight weave of his bodysuit.

'Now that you've felt the true power of Love Buzz, in person and from within the Ultraworld, you're beginning to understand the full depth of our mission here at Halcyon. It's about symbiosis, Kai ji.' Tito moved his hands towards each other until his upright index fingers met in the middle. 'The shared moment I once craved as a DJ, now shared by everyone on Earth, all at once.'

He relaxed his posture, as if satisfied Kai was intrigued enough not to try anything rash.

'But all the peace and love in the world mean nothing if you don't have the delivery right.' Tito clicked his fingers in Maarten's direction. 'I've been watching you, Kai, for a long time.' He leaned forward again. 'I sensed the love flow through your fingers from the very first moment I watched you tapping out our EDM experiments on your KeyRoll.'

The shudder that crept across Kai's shoulders this time was decidedly unpleasant. He'd always disregarded the feeling that an invisible presence was watching over his shoulder while doing his scales, writing it off as the twin connection he and Toca didn't otherwise have – or hadn't, at least, until the Drop unleashed by Juanita had consumed them minutes earlier. (And why would she say that? *You were right from the start.* She'd always refused to entertain his conspiracy theories – what happened while they were apart?)

'I was right there with you on the train this evening when you turned every note of *Space* but the last into stardust. Do you know how rare it is for someone to get the rhythm *and* the melody, to intuit how all the puzzle pieces create the perfect whole? That's what I've come to expect from Halcyon's machines, not the humans who feed on their creations.'

Just behind Tito's shoulder, Maarten stopped moving and Kai noticed the similarity in their bearing, relaxed yet oozing confidence. His father's son, of that there was no doubt, though Tito had somehow managed to keep his existence a secret from the world.

Tito flashed him a generous grin. 'Which is why you've been chosen to undertake our training and become the youngest Virtuoso in Love Buzz history.'

Kai was incapable of any response beyond the biggest smile to ever grace his face.

'And because the only possible answer to that statement is "yes, Tito",' Tito said, wrapping his arm loosely around Maarten's waist, 'do you have any questions for us?'

'Can Toca come too?' were the only words Kai could string together from the thoughts tumbling through his brain. *This is it!* Love Buzz stardom was all he'd ever wanted. But not like this. The pine-smelling ready room. The speech patterns that felt like a magic spell. Something about it all wasn't right. Had Toca come around to his thinking as well?

'This is a journey only you can take,' Maarten replied, 'though your family will be well compensated for their gift to Survivors.'

'What about Love Buzz?' Kai asked.

'What about it?' Tito deadpanned.

'The name and the costumes,' Kai shrugged. 'It doesn't really seem to fit the music.'

'I'd think the name Love Buzz pretty much speaks for itself after you've experienced the Drop in person for the first time, no?' Tito gently rebuffed him. 'Before the Storm struck, One World was all about bringing the planet together after the pandemic and the protests and the Privacy Riots. After the Storm we knew people needed something more than mere hope, which is why Love Buzz enhances the feeling of being alive. And the costumes are a personal conceit of sorts, since I share my date of birth with the Beatles releasing *Sgt Pepper* on the eve of the Summer of Love.'

'The hippie-dippie dress code came down to what we could salvage from Outside as well,' Maarten cut in. 'All the new clothes collected by our drones have been warehoused for periodic distribution until we can spare Survivors to make anything except syntho rations. Tie-dye had made a comeback the year before the Storm hit and the two-dollar shops were overloaded with this crud, so it was out of practicality as much as anything.'

'But really, it was about touching as many people as we could,' Tito said, after flashing Maarten a look which Kai placed somewhere between righteous anger and resigned disappointment. 'For the older generations, the hippie era reminds them of a time when a utopian existence seemed possible. We figured if we could get older Survivors to buy in to what we're doing, the young ones would do whatever it takes to finally have some fun.'

Maarten shifted weight and awkwardly cleared his throat.

'Anything else?' Tito prodded, as if Maarten hadn't called attention to himself.

Kai stopped himself before the next question could cross his lips.

'No limits,' Tito assured him. 'Even those questions you're too scared to ask yourself.'

'One thing I've wondered is, what happened to all the old songs?' Kai said cautiously. 'HeadBands used to have every song ever made but now most of them are gone.'

'What you're really asking me is, "Why did the Watson Beat's music survive the cull?" Am I right?' Tito responded.

Kai nodded.

'*Space* was just an experiment, some of the most primitive early machine music. You know that Watson was actually the IBM computer purpose-built to beat human game show champions, no?'

'I did not.'

'That's just an irrelevant factoid, really, like your father's Keisuke Honda stories,' Tito continued. He was pleased to see the mention of Kai's father drew the desired look of surprise. 'I know that you find solace in it and I enjoy watching you pilot a course through *Space* with your KeyRoll, so I asked my content managers to preserve it. As for the rest? Surplus to requirements. Terabyte upon terabyte of inconsequential music has been nuked from our servers, as has anything but the essential rhythm and melody data of the Beatles and Nirvana and Beyoncé and—'

'Drake?' Kai said hopefully.

'Oh, I'm sure he's in there somewhere.' Tito laughed. 'Though it's been some time since I've consulted our programmers about what source material they're feeding our song generators.'

'But seriously,' Maarten's voice startled Kai. '*Fuck* Drake.'

So engrossed was Kai in the words rolling out of Tito's mouth that he hadn't noticed his son creep up beside him. Kai was beginning to realise that Maarten's ability to glide silently across any room was a key part of his skillset. Maarten helped Kai off the bed and led him to stand directly before Tito. Kai felt Maarten put his HeadBand's tangerine viewfinder back in position over his eyes. The technofibre straps gripped the MIDI implants like magnets, sending a familiar stab of pain through Kai's skull. Tito flashed Kai a kindly smile before completing the installation with a sharp thud to Kai's speaker cups, locking them back in place around his ears. Slowly, Kai's implants firmed their grip on the straps, each tightening motion feeling like the final wind of a winch.

'That's enough questions for now,' Tito said.

Maarten took Kai's full weight on his right arm as he walked unsteadily towards the green door and freedom.

'There is much work for you to do for us, and very little time to prepare you. Love Buzz 1000 is going to change everything, Kai – the music, the delivery, the lot – so get yourself home to a nice, hot shower and get some rest. Maarten will collect you tomorrow morning at nine o'clock sharp and we need our new star to be at his absolute best.'

Maarten pushed through the black curtains and opened the door into a dimly lit cavern. As Kai crossed the threshold, he saw he was back in Trancentral Sydney's subway station. The platforms, which had bustled with Love Buzzers just over an hour earlier, were now deserted.

'And if you're worried about what to tell your parents, it's probably best you don't say a thing.'

Kai turned to find Tito still facing the bed. Halcyon's figurehead stood up and reached for his own HeadBand, discarded on the room's single shelf. He began slowly walking towards Kai and Maarten. With a whack of each palm, like slamming down on a deck of cards during a game of Snap, Tito reattached a speaker cup to his left ear, then his right, before lowering the HeadBand's viewfinder and straps into place.

'There's a reason I've told your hero Juanita barely any of the secrets I've shared with you today,' Tito said, his bronzed, wrinkle-free face gleaming through the part in the curtains. His HeadBand's straps found his MIDI implants and clicked into position. 'People with small minds are seldom ready to hear the truth.'

Tito turned his attention to something inside his HeadBand.

Kai, still stunned (Juanita wasn't included? He was to be the youngest Virtuoso in *history*?), couldn't turn away.

Another warm rush engulfed him, this time from the outside as a blast of hot air preceded a train click-clacking into the station. The holding cell's door swung inward, blending seamlessly with the train station's tiled white façade the instant it clicked shut.

| 3.03 |

Aftermath

Juanita lurched out of unconsciousness for the second time in a little over an hour. Eat, sleep, rave, repeat, minus the eat and with nowhere near enough sleep. She was spreadeagled across her velour recliner, covered in a thin layer of cold sweat and drowning in creaky thoughts. (Not a good sign, so soon after the Drop. *I shouldn't be this paranoid already.*) She anxiously felt for her face, finding her HeadBand where her performance helmet should've been. Her throat felt dry and raspy, like someone had shoved several balls of steel wool down it as she slept. Her tinnitus chimed ad nauseam.

But your set was another triumph, my darling. Juanita could almost hear the words roll off Tito's silver tongue. *So when the boys get here tonight you should celebrate in style.*

She could only hide in the darkness for so long. Time to make herself pretty.

HeadBand, engage night-vision mode.

At Juanita's command, her apartment and its few fixtures glowed green inside her viewfinder: the mirror and small console table to her left; the bell-shaped lamp shade, tucked into the corner where her living room's feature wall met the kitchen bench. Juanita spotted her helmet on her Silo platform and figured she must've dropped it there after

Love Buzz, though she'd as little memory of this Drop as any in the past year or more. From the moment Juanita donned her helmet, no Virtuoso set distinguished itself from the last. Smash the orbs. Raise your hands. 'We're all in this together.' Going through the motions without ever really feeling the love.

What had Lawrence, her bespectacled best-friend-forever-for-one-night-only, enthused to her at the tail end of her first summer of love? *It's about the journey, not the destination.* It was in the early months of 2007 that she'd met him – Harry Potter glasses, Mediterranean tan, a computer programmer and DJ who boasted of the beginnings of a real-estate empire – on the staircase down to the Candy's Apartment basement. The summer festival season had begun its inevitable wind-down into the party-killing dead zone of Australia's early autumn. The Habit boys in the booth rained down a blitzkrieg of prog bombs – prog short for progressive house, which attracted a breed of clubber who self-identified as 'discerning', like her bookish new DJ friend Lawrence. Dawn broke and they'd emerged, amid throngs of their fellow face-chewers, lurching and laughing uncontrollably through dark alleys until they'd found wherever the Spice crew were dishing out, whatever flavour of trippy shit they were vibing on that month.

The night had ended as most of the best nights out inevitably did – in unfamiliar surroundings, offered up by a clubbing acquaintance who regretted his generosity under the harsh early afternoon light, once he'd plummeted from his ecstasy-fuelled high. Punters had massed shoulder to shoulder, Juanita and Lawrence nestled among them, wrist-deep in dust bunnies on a timber-floored kitchen in a grotty Art Deco apartment.

'It's like, when I'm up there and I'm playing those records I'm the conductor, you know?' Lawrence had announced. 'I'm the Phat-mother-fucking-Controller. "Phat" with a P-H, yeah?'

Juanita felt his right shoulder involuntarily twitching beneath her left cheek. *Fucking gurner.*

Across the kitchen sat Sven Alexander, another DJ she'd seen behind the decks in some side room or other. He'd just double-dropped

Versaces for the second time in an hour and his face was wracked by spasms, like a rubber mask being manipulated by a cruel puppeteer. A perimeter of seventeen recovering partygoers in varying states of lucidity leaned against cupboards, walls and balcony doors, everyone speaking at once in the misguided belief they'd just stumbled upon some earth-shattering insight into the human condition that the world needed to hear. A beat thumped out of the lounge room at the other end of the hallway, where Juanita knew a similar scene played out.

'That's why I don't pay much attention to randoms at kick-ons,' Tito had warned Juanita in the early days of that first Asian tour, eight months prior. 'Plenty to talk about, nothing to say.'

'But we can't all be glamours like you, Neets,' Lawrence chuckled nervously. Juanita took the compliment as it was intended – not as the start of a line to lure her back to his pleasure palace, but as a statement of fact with no underlying motives. It may have been the E talking, but twenty-one years later she still remembered that rare sense of feeling safe in his company. Like Lawrence had looked at her as a person, not a commodity to mine for profit like any other natural resource. In her short time on the scene, Lawrence was one of the few men she'd met who hadn't wanted a piece of her, sexual or otherwise.

'So if you're not the centre of attention you've got to gently guide the dancefloor in the right direction, stealth-like.'

Sven, the gurning DJ with the scarlet complexion, abruptly fell back and across in slow motion, toppling into a recess littered with empty Coopers Pale Ale bottles. The buttons of his shirt tore open, revealing a crusty riverbed of sweat and hair from neck to navel. Sven was done.

'But it's not just my journey,' Lawrence continued.

Three of the other four conversations in the kitchen dissolved into hysterical laughter. The couple beside them crawled across the floor to the garbage alcove to check on the semi-foetal man.

After seeing Sven lick dried flecks of disco foam from his lips, Juanita relaxed and snuggled deep into Lawrence's shoulder.

'It's about everybody moving in the same direction at once, right? Fucking . . . I dunno, it's like we're all, fucking, symbiotic fucking organisms or something!'

Symbiosis. Lawrence was reading straight from Tito's 'club culture philosophy' playbook. *Yawn.*

'The point is, we're all just people with problems out there in the real world too big to deal with . . . or, fucking maybe the problem is so big we won't even admit to ourselves that it exists, so we come to this place, right, this place where if all the ducks line up – the googs, the tunes, all of it – then before you know it we're all moving towards this uncertain future together.' Lawrence pressed on, the words shooting from his mouth in rapid-fire bursts of friendly fire as quickly as his brain could reload the chamber. 'Where not even the DJ knows how their own set is going to end, let alone what note the party will finish up on.'

Lawrence fidgeted with his glasses before replacing them in the same position. In profile, his facial features reminded Juanita of an ancient Greek statue, only in glorious tanned colour rather than faded marble. He'd have almost been hot if he could open his mouth without unleashing a river of absolute cod-shit.

'That's why it's about the journey, not the destination. Always has been, always will be.' Lawrence paused for breath. Beneath Juanita's cheekbone, his shoulder twitched again. 'I know that sounds like some doe-eyed PLUR shit, Neets, but trust me when I say this – it's the only truth, in this godforsaken scene of ours, that is always 100 per cent real.'

PLUR? Tito spruiked Peace, Love, Unity and Respect as some sort of four-pronged holy trinity of the '90s rave scene. In quoting it, Lawrence may as well have handed Juanita his birth certificate and confessed he wasn't far from the scrapheap. The only acronym any of Juanita's age group were spraying around that summer was 'YOLO', during that brief window where it was an ethos to live by, before marketers caught a whiff and packaged it up for mainstream consumption.

PLUR, YOLO, ROFLMAO. By the time Lawrence had delivered his sermon Juanita had heard it all before, from the mouth of Tito as he paraded her through the DJ booths of the Northern Hemisphere. Even in those first nine months of her apprenticeship under Tito, Juanita was playing bigger clubs and festivals than Lawrence could ever had dreamed of.

Over the years since that night turned to day in 2007, Juanita thought on more than one occasion she'd glimpsed Lawrence lurking in the back-right corner of some dancefloor she was commanding, only for his doppelganger to be gone by the time she'd cut through the crowd. (*Seeing ghosts again, you fucking gurner*, she'd always chided herself with a giggle.) Given she'd never seen his name in any of the club listings when flicking through the pages of *3D World*, Lawrence's journey must've taken him from the Sydney club scene not long after that epic night-morning-early afternoon on that filthy polished timber floor.

Maybe his name had disappeared from the gig listings because he'd left Sydney, but if he hadn't landed up in any of the nation's capitals but Canberra – which had been wiped out the instant the Storm struck, just like all of those other regional Australian shitholes Tito had made her play to build her 'brand' – he was dead now, just like the rest of them.

A piercing shriek in Juanita's speaker cups snapped Juanita out of her reverie. Rakh-E, conjuring up party favours from her Mumbai compound, kicking off Love Buzz 1000 with 'Safe from Block Rockin' Freaks' for anyone unlucky enough to have missed Juanita land the Drop with a perfect dismount for the 999th time in succession.

Juanita's Silo platform, the centre of the world's attention just minutes before, was empty but for her discarded performance helmet. To the right of the circular podium, Juanita's kitchen was spotlessly clean. No great achievement, really, given she'd abandoned food prep entirely once she'd learned to subsist on a diet of EDM, synthetic single malt, Vitamin D blotters and the occasional bowl of tinned Alphabetti spaghetti.

Juanita peeked back over the top of her recliner's headrest, through the window above her empty dining table. She was relieved to see the worst of the lava lightning seemed to have passed, though the world Outside still occasionally crackled blood-red.

Juanita let her head flop back on the recliner.

HeadBand, open chat channel – Abbie Vinke at Halcyon HQ.

A red dialogue box flashed on and off in the left lens of Juanita's viewfinder.

'*This user has temporarily suspended communications,*' a disembodied fembot informed her. '*Please try again later.*'

'For fuck's sake, Abbie!' Juanita cried, collapsing back in her recliner. 'Where the fuck are Dav and Robbie!'

Machines Work

Matthias van Dijk was sinking into the cool white depths of the ready-room bed. A pounding tension headache spread further down his neck with each grind of his teeth. Lactic acid burned his limbs, tense and powerless, like they'd just been removed from cold storage and reattached to his torso. His back ached in a way it hadn't since the morning after he played his first and only game of rugby league, when his King's College classmates had shown him there was more to late 1980s London than football riots and raving.

With each passing second, the mattress recently vacated by Kai seemed to absorb a little more of his unease. Comfort was the last thing on Tito's mind when he'd drawn up plans for the Trancentral station network's ready rooms. He'd had them built in the event Storm truthers or other anti-Love Buzz dissidents needed to be hidden from view. Maarten's insistence that beds be installed in case any Halcyon crew copped a hit of Total Euphoria had seemed an unnecessary expense at the time. Yet Tito had found himself increasingly seeking solace in them: in Rotterdam, in Toronto (as close as he dared travel to the US since its pre-Storm slide into permanent disarray), here in Sydney.

You can't retire yet, old man, Tito reminded himself. *The job's barely half done.* As his mother had been fond of saying whenever she was exhausted, he was walking on his gums. And the hardest part, the part he'd long dreaded, had finally come. He battled an urge to climb beneath the satin sheets and cover his head until the next twenty-four hours had blown over.

'Peak time, all the time, brother,' Tito said ruefully, repeating the DJing mantra he'd turned into a way of life. The words rang hollow in his heart – hollower than the cocksure younger man who coined them would ever have believed possible.

Tito felt around on the mattress beside his head until he found his HeadBand. There would come a time early next century, long after Halcyon's endgame had been played out – *Once the piglet has been washed,* his father would've said – when no human alive would have known any other form of communication.

Sometimes, Tito admitted to himself in his most vulnerable moments, he craved the simplicity of his childhood landline phone. The long, coiled brown cord he used to wind out of the kitchen and into his bedroom for privacy (though his mother, God rest her sticky-beak soul, still knew all his secrets) would've weighed more than the device now permanently attached to Survivors' eyes and ears. Yet this piece of wearable tech he'd foisted upon the world, with the help of his programmers and the venture capitalists brave enough to buy in, weighed down on him like a lifetime of accumulated possessions. He felt a different burden to his parents, whose plethora of 'stuff' kept them forever rooted in his childhood home on what was once the outskirts of Rotterdam until they passed – years before Tito transitioned from worldwide superstar to global saviour. The migraines were never going to stop, he accepted that; but in these brief moments of solitude, released from his HeadBand's grip, Tito, for a time at least, felt freed from the burden of the truth.

He sat up on his elbows and slipped his HeadBand viewfinder back over his eyes. With a defiant grunt, he slapped his speaker cups into their locked position.

'*Godverdomme!*' Tito barked.

When he'd rolled out the HeadBands before Christmas 2024, of the myriad factors he'd not accounted for, the lifelong growth of ear cartilage was the one he most regretted overlooking. The speaker cups clung to him too tightly these days, rendering the small pleasure of his daily ear vacuum ineffectual. Ken Loi had been trying to schedule Tito in for a refitting for months, maybe even years now. 'Remind me again at cucumber time,' Tito replied every time Dr Loi reached out, knowing full well the 'quiet period' was a myth. And besides, the ViZar's time had almost come.

'One lens for life!' was the slogan dreamt up by Halcyon's marketing bootlickers to trumpet the imminent arrival of the ViZar-1000, the next generation of HeadBand; one giant leap in keeping Love Buzz fresh after the big step soon to come, the step he knew he had to take.

As Tito fiddled in vain with his left earpiece, clamped to the lowest reach of his ear lobe, he thought, *And not a moment too soon.* He climbed off the bed and trundled, hunched over, towards his white stool in the middle of the room.

HeadBand, open Vid-Link channel – Abbie Vinke at Halcyon HQ.

Once seated, he lined himself up with a small camera lens embedded in the wall just above the ready room's solitary shelf.

Abbie's cheerful face, backed by a cubicle as starkly white as Tito's own, appeared in his viewfinder. 'Good morning, sir!' Abbie greeted him with a smile set to stun.

Her enthusiasm would've startled Tito if every conversation with Abbie, whether Vid-Linked or in person, didn't kick off in the same excitable fashion.

'Or should I say good evening?'

'Either is fine, my dear. And so is calling me Tito, if you can remember.'

'Sure, Tito,' Abbie blushed. 'How was your flight?'

'Long and uneventful, thanks for asking,' Tito said. He'd lost interest in exchanging all but the barest of pleasantries long ago, but recognised their importance to the boffins helming Halcyon's research into Abbie and her ilk. 'Have I missed much in Rotterdam?'

'Blizzards all night made the Storm worse than usual today,' Abbie replied. 'For a while there, the engineers were worried that later on Ajax wouldn't be able to beam into Love Buzz from his studio, and his apartment is practically next door to Trancentral One.'

Tito congratulated himself. *So I did the board a favour inviting them to Sydney instead of Rotterdam.*

'My best men and women are in engineering, young lady, so I'm sure they'll work it out,' Tito said through a stifled grin. 'How did our girl go tonight?'

'Juanita?' Abbie paused for dramatic impact, catching Tito off guard. 'She's cooked, sir,' Abbie said with an apologetic smile. 'Lethargic, distracted, disinterested, you name it – all the symptoms of advanced isolation sickness.'

'And you think this is something to smile about?'

'All reports about Virtuosos are to be filed in a positive manner,' Abbie said. She was positively beaming now. 'Is that right?'

'This is one of those occasions where you might dial it back, lest your colleagues start to think you lack basic humanity,' Tito said sternly. 'Anything else to report?'

'All of her biometric levels are down slightly on last night's set, repeating the trend we've been seeing since her thirty-seventh birthday last June,' Abbie reported. 'Something interesting did occur towards the end of her performance, though – in the lead-up to the Drop we tracked a significant spike of activity in both her motor cortex and the left hemisphere of her cerebral cortex.'

'Meaning?'

'Meaning she was completing some other complex analytical task while her body was going through the motions in the Ultraworld – almost like she was performing on automatic pilot,' Abbie said. 'We've noticed similar activity whenever she's performed to "Aftermath of Del Mar's Sandstorm" recently, but never this extreme.'

Tito sighed the sigh of a man who'd just had his worst fears confirmed. After twenty-two years under his spell, the puppet was showing signs of self-awareness. Not that the Setlist Generation team were helping his cause. *Playing 'Sandstorm' every night for months on end would be enough to make anyone crack.* If the idiots in Set Gen truly had the system under their knee – if they were thinking carefully about how they structured a Virtuoso's performance, dropping subtle variations from one night to the next to keep them on their toes rather than lazily rolling out the same twenty bangers in a row – Tito wouldn't be in this uncomfortable position in the first place.

'This is excellent work, Abbie, thank you,' Tito said.

'You're welcome, Tito,' Abbie said, chest puffing with pride.

'Please ensure Production has "Del Mar's Aftermath" analysed and re-pressed before it's returned to the Set-Gen team for circulation.'

Abbie nodded, stroking her thick blonde hair. Over months of interacting, it was the closest behaviour to a nervous tic Tito had observed in Abbie.

'Is there something else?' Tito asked.

The words of Dr Loi, the mathematical genius who'd proven the difference between Halcyon and the erstwhile tech giants in the AI arms race, had always stayed with Tito: 'Body language, Matthias. Words are meaningless if the body tells a different truth.' With a gesture of Tito's right hand, Abbie's video feed expanded to take in his entire viewfinder.

'Well,' Abbie began cautiously. The bubbly smile had departed, but her hands continued to play with her hair. 'Juanita asked me about my life for the first time.'

'Very good!' Tito said. His HeadBand frame concealed the involuntary arch of his eyebrow. 'What did you tell her?'

'She was "taking the piss out of me", like you said Aussies do,' Abbie said flatly. 'But I told her about my new boyfriend and how we're heading to De Kuip to watch Kam-E's set from the VIP Floor tonight.'

Tito nodded his approval.

'But that's not going to happen, is it, sir?' Abbie asked solemnly.

'No, my dear, it is not,' Tito replied. 'But your recognition of the difference between illusion and reality means we'll be seeing a lot more of each other in the future.'

'I'd like that, sir,' Abbie said, a sly smile curling her lips. She took a deep breath before bursting into song. '*What a beautiful life, what a beautiful world.*'

'Beautiful Life' by Gui Boratto – one of Tito's favourite set closers from the northern summer of 2007. Only through personal touches like this, Tito had long argued, will our AI handlers ever be accepted as part of the team; as true citizens of this world. *Ken Loi, take a bow.* The attention to detail in the programming of this latest batch of Prodigies was truly astounding.

'You've done some excellent work with Juanita, but it's time to go into standby mode until we assign you a new Virtuoso,' Tito said. 'It'll be our pleasure to welcome you back.'

'As you wish, sir,' Abbie said. 'Enjoy your stay Down Under. I hear it's pleasant there?'

'Always pleasant in Sydney, my dear.'

Abbie's head flickered and faded away. Tito tapped the blank box, hovering one foot in front of his face, where Abbie's head had been. The square of grey pixels disintegrated.

HeadBand, open chat channel – Maarten van Dijk.

He scratched at the patchy stubble where sideburns had always refused to grow. The 'facial carpet' gene had leapfrogged from his father over he and his brother's generation and straight to the golden grandchild, his son, Maarten. Tito made a mental note to tidy himself up back at Halcyon Tower before tomorrow's extraordinary general meeting lest he cop some good-natured heckling from the fossils on the Halcyon board.

'We're almost back to Doonside on the last Loop, Father,' Maarten's voice crackled in Tito's earpieces.

We can send a satellite past Pluto, Tito lamented, *but I still can't get decent 10G signal in this city.*

'I can Vid-Link from the Doonside Station ready room within the half hour.'

'This can't wait, Maarten,' Tito said, irritated by the implication his call wasn't urgent.

'If things are so urgent, I can think of a quicker way to get out here than by train.'

'Not now, son,' Tito snapped. 'It's time.'

'I figured as much,' Maarten replied after a pause just long enough to get under Tito's skin. 'And I think he's up to it.'

'He has to be,' Tito said. 'Let's get Kai on the fast track tomorrow morning.'

'Understood. Anything else?'

'Call our girl in from the field,' Tito said. 'She's got all the data we need for the big reveal.'

'On it.'

'And send the collection drones for Juanita once she's been worn out by her boys.' Tito felt a spike of pain behind his left eyebrow, as if his HeadBand was constricting his eyes as well as his ears. 'It's been one hell of a journey, but her work here is done.'

| 3.05 |

Kid Dynamite

Maarten van Dijk looked down at Kai Ishii on the seat beside him, hard at work inside his HeadBand, conscientiously doing his scales. *Careful what you wish for kid.*

The Stadium Loop sped through Trancentral Olympic Station, its platform already deserted, without stopping. But for Maarten and Kai, the lower deck of the VIP Carriage they were seated in would've been deserted as well. 'That's why Australians barely raised a peep when the 9 pm Lockdown came in,' his father reminded him, often and always. 'Their rights were slowly stripped away for so long that for them staying in is a way of life.'

My father, the saviour. Maarten grunted. *Saving the world at arm's length from the evidence.*

But Maarten had never forgotten what Tito had made him do in the Halcyon HQ ready room that Valentine's Day, three years ago. Never could he forgive himself for what he'd done. Never would.

'Maarten, my boy, our worst fears have been realised.'

Maarten's father, seething with self-righteous fury, had been seated across from him along the long sides of a white desk the size of a ping-pong table. Maarten's jaw clenched shut beneath a thick covering of facial hair. White walls. White floors. White desk. White chairs. Versatile décor that could soothe or intimidate, depending on the mood.

Tito's interior design specialists, who'd lobbied for their own wing at Halcyon's Rotterdam base, clearly knew their way around the human psyche. One man's ready room was another's Room 101. The single bed tucked against the far wall couldn't help Maarten now.

'Someone here has let the monkey out of the sleeve and the Transglobal Union are onto us.'

Maarten's eyes barely twitched beneath his HeadBand's lens. He had to play this cool – with a straight bat, in the cricket parlance he'd learned over Australia's once glorious summers, no matter how many absurd Dutch idioms his father used to try and pierce his defences. Given he too wore a MK 5 HeadBand, he knew what he was up against: Tito's HeadBand sensors working overtime, analysing blood pressure fluctuations, the slightest deviation in his speech-pattern soundwaves, probing for a stray bead of sweat, trying to glean some insight from the signals around his son's implacable stare. One misstep and the monkey would be well and truly out of the sleeve.

'Onto us?'

'The Union knows about HeadBands, the EDM, the works,' Tito explained. 'I dialled in to the Moscow summit through that cretin from Canberra's HeadBand as he was telling the other right-wing nutjobs the lot.'

'Will it impact our plans?' Maarten asked evasively. The vital signs readouts (increased heart rate, dilated pupils) inside his own viewfinder confirmed the worst – if Tito hadn't seen through his lies yet, he can't have been looking too hard.

'Nothing will ever "impact our plans", my boy,' Tito hissed. 'The Public Order Act would've wiped us out forever if I didn't get One World exempted. When the Privacy Riots peaked and the militant right joined the activists, they threatened everything Halcyon's machine learning had been geared towards achieving.'

'I know all this already, Dad,' Maarten interrupted, knowing how much it'd piss his father off. 'I've been right here beside you the whole way, remember?'

'Well then, as you know, the TGU and I negotiated a deal,' Tito pushed on, undeterred. When Tito was on a roll, Maarten had worked out as a child, he loved the sound of his own voice more than any music in the world. 'They pushed the HeadBand Accord through and in return they got their access to more info on their citizens by last Christmas than smartphones could eavesdrop on in a lifetime. But now, my boy, they think they've harvested all the info they'll ever need, so why not cut and run? Surprisingly clever for a bunch of populist buffoons, really.'

Another thing Maarten had learned about his father: in politics and technology, in sniffing the winds of change around music trends to how it was consumed and beyond, he was always two steps ahead. His old man. The crafty old bastard.

'I'm sorry to disappoint you,' Tito added, 'but we'll just have to go early on our backup plan.'

Tito fixed his son with a cold, hard glare.

'In five minutes, our UXO drones will strike the TGU summit in Moscow and wipe that ship of fools and their Oil War out for good,' Tito said. 'Moreover, you'll be the one to pull the trigger.'

Maarten squirmed in his seat.

'And June 1st is unavoidable, my boy, because all of our science is clear.' Tito paused, his fingers interlinked to form a fist beneath his chin. 'If we're serious about saving the world,' he declared. 'Half of us must die.'

Enough! Maarten knew the repressed memory of what happened next would lurk forever, just below the surface, until he wiped the slate clean. Quivering lips. Watery eyes. *Just like your mother,* Tito would've taunted him. *A pretty face with a weak little heart.* Maarten pulled himself together, in case the Ishii boy pulled himself away from his scales for long enough to notice him quietly falling apart.

HeadBand, encrypted voice message – Lottie Gardner.

The empty seats of the carriage rattled around him. Kai's hands danced across the invisible KeyRoll. *Tito's right, this kid is good.* Maarten gritted his teeth. *We must act fast.*

'Lottie, get up top, it's time . . .' The words almost caught in his throat. 'It's time to burn.'

| 3.06 |

We Come One

'*Nine pm Lockdown will commence in five minutes.*' A female voice over-rode Toca's speaker cups. '*Repeat: nine pm Lockdown will commence in five minutes. Any Survivors found outside their apartment towers will be subject to collection under the Public Order Act 2023.*'

The unmistakeable buzz of a Virtuoso set racing towards its conclusion – Rakh-E opening Love Buzz 1000 from Mumbai, according to the readout in Toca's HeadBand, twenty-three hours before Juanita would do it all again to bring the show home – roared back into the foreground. Toca was exhausted – by this music, by this day, by this life and having to sass her way through it to stay sane. The Drop was everything it'd been hyped up to be but its afterglow had faded. *Could really use that mute function right about now.*

Through the semi-circular entryway carved into the car park wall, Toca could see Survivors decked out in Love Buzz finery scurrying along the tunnel linking the Three-Way to Nurragingy and the other tower blocks on the Doonside Cluster's outer rim. Amid the rapidly thinning trickle of tie-dyed wigs and free-flowing silver arm tassels, Kai's white jumpsuit was nowhere to be seen.

Toca couldn't believe her brother had abandoned her at their first Love Buzz, even if Tito had come calling – even if Juanita had coquettishly beckoned him from the Ultraworld, for that matter. She'd woken up after the Drop, disoriented with pins-and-needles top to toe, to find herself being cradled by a totem pole with arms, legs and lungs.

'Tito just has some business with your brother, sis,' Sia had said – the only sentence he'd uttered with more than a handful of syllables. Though she wasn't ruling out the possibility that this was the chattiest moment of Sia's entire life given he was more the 'communicate with a raised eyebrow' than conversational type.

Beyond a cursory introduction, the burly Samoan hadn't been one for sparkling repartee (nor much of a reader, either – Toca's question about whether his parents were Ents had gone right over the walking tree trunk's head). He'd ushered Toca onto the Doonside Loop, responded to her questions with a grunt when absolutely necessary, then at the end of the line walked her to the Block 19 access point. Shortly after 8:30 pm he headed back in the direction they'd came, with a raised eyebrow and mumbled assurance that Kai wouldn't be too far behind, before lighting a cigarette and loping towards the Nurragingy tunnel.

That was twenty-five minutes ago. If the twins weren't inside their apartment building in the next five minutes, collection drones would be the least of their troubles. The wrath of Stefanie Ishii would rain down upon them both – maybe even worse than the time Toca, aged seven, had almost drowned Kai at the bottom of a water slide.

'Always the good twin,' Toca fumed under her breath. 'Always covering up whenever this selfish *kusogaki* goes rogue on me like the Storm never happened.'

Toca could almost hear Kai's response. *Sooking again, Tokes?*

It's just not fair, Toca fumed to herself.

Simmering resentment of her brother never sank far from the surface. She studied her biology texts until her head hurt, desperate to join Halcyon's medical guild and spend her adult life saving others. All that work was just enough for her to scrape by, getting her high Bs and low As. Meanwhile, Kai racked up VIP-worthy marks at school with so little effort that he received minimal scrutiny from their parents. It was typical that he was getting special treatment from Halcyon already.

'And he couldn't even be bothered dressing up,' Toca grumbled.

Toca paced back and forth in front of the lift doors on the lower-basement level of Block 19. The old car park smelled of rusted metal and rotting upholstery, ravaged by damp and dust. Away from the OxyPure-1000 units, which hummed constantly in their eleventh-floor apartment, the air around her was dense, semi-opaque. Every morning on the Ishii kids' walk to school, from their lift to the archway opening on to Doonside's main thoroughfare, Toca always felt like she was seeing her surroundings through a fine mosquito-net canopy. When winter was at its deepest, the light mist became a thin sheet of fog. She liked holding her hands in front of her face as she walked so she could watch her fingers cut trails through it.

Toca's eyes darted around the automobile graveyard, matching the wreckage to the families who lived on in the tower above. The population of Block 19 had plummeted in that punishing first winter after 1-6-25. Toca hated thinking about those dark days of almost three years ago; huddled in the lounge room, weathering the barrage of Kentaro's non-stop howling while their parents assured the children that they'd all survive; of the poor souls who couldn't adjust to this new reality. A brigade of bold teenage boys had made a run for it out of Block 19's sliding glass doors, in search of answers, never to return. Something had happened to the adult son of Kai's old piano teacher, though the accepted wisdom that 'collection drones' had got him was too far-fetched for Toca to take seriously. ('I only believe in myself and what I can see,' Toca often told Kai – a motto she lived by.)

'Shuttle, brotato, come on!' Toca urged, shaking the memories from her thoughts. Her voice eerily bounced off the car park walls. 'Three minutes or we're on permanent probation until our tower placement comes through.' The prospect of a two-year wait until her next trip out of the Cluster made her feel sicker than any HeadBand tension headache.

Cars sat on rusted metal wheel rims where they had been abandoned three years earlier. Around the rims, deflated tyres disintegrated into mounds of rubber resembling black rock salt. The Ishiis' car, a green, early-2010s Mitsubishi Mirage parked snugly in an alcove on the opposite side of the lift, had been smashed into a barely recognisable state by the bored teenagers of Doonside only a month after the world changed. The Mirage's carcass, and the rusted Kias and HAVALs and Great Walls in the Block 19 car park, bore the same spray-painted slogan – words Toca had never seen outside the basement until Trancentral Sydney.

THE STORM IS A FRONT

Either Kai's got a secret life as a tagger, Toca thought, *or he's not the only Paranoid Jack doing the rounds.*

She'd been caught in the Storm the day it struck. She'd tasted its fury firsthand. From the morning following, Halcyon's talking heads had appeared in HeadBand bulletins three times a day, urging patience and calm. Juanita and Cosmo (Toca's personal favourite), and Tito himself for the most important announcements, kept the people of the world – immediately dubbed Survivors – up to date on which cities had crumbled, which were being rebuilt, and how their trust in their HeadBands' capabilities would give mankind the strength to thrive.

Kai had taken their advice to heart. Fortified inside his HeadBand, Toca's brother had whiled entire nights away at the controls of his Key-Roll piano simulator. He'd immersed himself in the complete archive of Juanita's performances, poring over her setlists, gliding through every song's notation over and over until he could perform each note verbatim. Music was his escape from the family home. Toca didn't get his obsession. To her Love Buzz was just a silly distraction, but she'd been jealous Kai had found an easy escape. She'd known what her escape would be as soon as the first coronavirus tore through Doonside, though she knew even then that saving lives was a more difficult path. She'd been obsessed with the search for a cure for COVID-23, even after the rest of the world had strapped on their HeadBands and moved on. Kai wanted to help the world forget its troubles; Toca's mission in life was to take the world back to how it was.

Inside her speaker cups, Rakh-E's beats pounded ever faster as the Drop neared. Toca pivoted on her feet, swiping imaginary bliss bombs out of the air with invisible glowstaffs, pirouetting before landing in Juanita's statuesque starting position; eyes wide, panting heavily, weapons at the ready for the commence of another assault. She grinned to herself. *Maybe Halcyon took the wrong Ishii?*

Relaxing her stance, Toca grabbed the map of Sydney tucked into the corner of her viewfinder and scaled it up to full size. The throbbing red pinprick representing Kai was still stuck where it had been since 8:48 pm – somewhere in the spaghetti junction of rail tunnels beneath Trancentral, where the underground rail from Macarthur, Richmond, Hornsby and Doonside collided. Kai was either too far below ground to make Vid-Link contact or had his HeadBand comms switched off altogether.

Her speaker cups picked up footsteps, from the hole in the wall that linked the car park to the Doonside tunnel network. A tiny figure clad in white was sprinting towards her, bursting through the map display like a runner breaking the tape at the finish line.

'Kai!'

'I'm shuttling, calm down!' Kai laughed.

A man slipped back into the shadows of the central tunnel behind him, too swiftly for Toca's HeadBand to register his ID.

'Come on, *adlay!*' Toca screamed Kai's least favourite insult. (The only thing he hated more than kicking the football with Kentaro was hearing his twin dish out Western Sydney lad slang.) 'Mum is gonna lose her shit.'

Kai took a flying leap and wrapped his limbs around Toca's torso, almost sending the pair of them barrelling onto the ground.

'What the—'

'Carry me into the lift, quickly,' Kai hissed in his sister's ear.

Toca could feel Kai's fingers trembling as they dug deep into her shoulder blades. She turned one-eighty degrees and lumbered towards the middle set of lift doors, servicing floors 11 through 19. To her relief, her finger found the Up button first go and the metal doors slid open.

'Lucky you haven't had that growth spurt yet, bro.'

Toca carried them both inside. Kai released his grip on his sister's waist and near silently dropped onto the floor of the cabin. His left finger covered his lips in a *Shhhhh* signal as his right instinctively reached for the position on the panel where, after almost seven years riding this lift morning and night, he knew the 11 would be.

The lift doors slid shut. They were surrounded by the unremitting refrain of the saxophone solo which had long fascinated Kai. Kai held his palms just outside the ears of his HeadBand. Mimicking Matthias van Dijk's movements, he popped both speaker cups towards his head with a snapping motion. A jolt of stabbing pain shook both sides of his skull as the suction cups he'd thought immovable forty-five minutes prior released from his head. Pushing through the pain, he gripped each technofibre strap at the point it fused with his MIDI implants and tore them free. He carefully lifted the HeadBand's lens from the bridge of his nose and tucked it under his right armpit.

'Bro, have you lost your—'

'I'm sorry, Tokes.'

Kai reached both arms across the lift and popped Toca's speaker cups as well.

'Arrgghh!' Toca screamed.

With the earpieces loosened, Kai wrenched Toca's viewfinder until it dislodged, cutting it off from its power source, her overactive brain.

'You almost tore my ears off, you *manuke*!'

'Shut up and listen!' Kai screamed back, stuffing his sister's viewfinder under his other armpit. He glanced up at the indicator as it ticked through level 1. 'Do you remember, after the Drop tonight, what you said to me?'

'What are you talking about?' Toca said. 'You were gone when—'

'"The Storm is a front, you were right from the start",' Kai interrupted her again.

'What?! That's written all over the cars!'

'That's what you said when we reached out to each other in the afterglow.' He shook the HeadBands hanging in his hands. 'And it's got something to do with these.'

'Kai, what the hell is going on?'

'Put this back on.' Kai passed Toca a HeadBand. 'Just line the straps up with your MIDIs and pop the speaker cups like I did and they'll lock back into place.'

Dubious, Toca attempted to cajole her earpieces into position.

'Quickly!' Kai hissed. 'Tito wants me to start Virtuoso training tomorrow.' He held a finger up to his lips. *But I think I've come up with a better idea.*

Kai lined his HeadBand viewfinder up with his eyebrows. With a nod, Toca signalled that hers was also good to go. The lift dinged its arrival at the eleventh floor. The twins cracked their speaker cups in tandem. As the lift doors slid open, Kai and Toca's MIDI implants locked them back inside their HeadBands.

| 3.07 |

Last Rhythm

The silence Juanita had grown to love in her apartment was sliced open by the shrill holler of her doorbell, tuned to resemble the opening synth stabs from 'Sandstorm' – Tito's idea of a housewarming joke, which she was stuck with forever.

'*Je*-sus *Christ*, that *fuck*-ing *tune*,' Juanita whined. 'Can't these fucking fucks just knock?'

Using all the strength left in her shattered body, she peeled herself off the recliner.

'Dav, Robbie, the steam room is on, so you boys better be ready to put on a good show for me tonight,' she crowed and strutted towards the door.

Davide and Roberto had been her boys since shortly after Love Buzz kicked off, her Halcyon-appointed rider for any post-set activity she cared to dream up. Nearly four years ago while traversing the Ultraworld en route to her usual home-ground destination of Trancentral Sydney, Juanita had spotted their unmistakeable forms (she'd always been partial to barrel-chested black Adonises) just as she was about to flick past the dancefloor of Trancentral Marseille. As soon as she'd torn herself from her helmet after the Drop, Juanita had dialled in Fleur, Abbie's even more moronic predecessor in Rotterdam (but a rocket scientist in comparison to Chloe Jay), and insisted she track them down.

Dav and Robbie had been with her, in person, every night since – for just seven seconds or seven days and one week or however long a night kicked on. What was certain is they were the closest thing Juanita had left to friends, though she knew little more about them than their names and willingness to submit to her sexual whims.

Juanita stopped briefly at the mirror adjacent to the entryway to preen and purr. Her utility belt was still in position. The elastic trim of her underwear was lined with sweat. Hardened discs of e-motion gel dotted her sweaty torso. She tore the discs off her stomach, flicking them onto the console table beneath the mirror. The nanotech-liquid circles scattered themselves between her belongings: a single-use canister of toilet seat sanitiser spray; an assortment of hair elastics, bobby pins and scrunchies, which Tito had proudly hand-delivered to her before Love Buzz launched as if they'd never gone out of style; the photo taken minutes after Bonnie Stapleton became Juanita. Embracing, young-ish Tito and younger Juanita were rocking the crazy eyes of an epic drug binge, cradled in the arms of a super-sized koala, gripping the side of Sydney Tower like a cuter, furrier King Kong.

Tito had affixed the photo to Juanita's mirror on the evening they'd christened her apartment-cum-performance space.

'Every day I hope you see this photo as a reminder,' Tito had said, gently caressing the straight blue locks hanging halfway down Juanita's back from her azure-blue wig. 'I want it to take you back to where it all began for us, and remind you how much further the journey still has to go.'

She'd moved in to the Love Inn six months before the Storm but Tito was touring her so hard at the time she'd barely set foot in her apartment until 1-6-25. The entire planet had been in the iron grip of the Transglobal Union's 9 pm Lockdown, yet Juanita's DJ schedule had escalated – sunset slots in every corner of the world, on any night of the week – courtesy of Halcyon's One World festivals and the HeadBand rollout that connected them. 'Hashtag blessed,' was Tito's explanation for the final stage of her ascent to household name, and Juanita knew she was. Careers were obliterated in an instant when the Public Order

Act 2023 passed. DJs who Juanita had partied with on the global circuit disappeared overnight. Safe spaces for Sydney's vagabonds and miscreants were permanently shuttered closed. On top of all that, the Oil War had ground all but the most affluent cities to a standstill. COVID-23 had rolled on, wave after wave, making a mockery of the 'unprecedented' Public Order Act the TGU had activated as a means to combat it.

And through it all Juanita's runaway success could not be stopped. For her and Tito's stable of DJs, 'Peak time, all the time' just kept on kicking on until the Storm changed everything in the space of an afternoon.

Juanita shuffled some discarded serviettes over the wrinkled photograph. Even though she'd been born in the echoes of the tribal-drum battalion that still rang in her ears, Matthias van Dijk would not control her destiny tonight, as he had ever since she'd abandoned her friends at the Cave. Juanita pulled her sweat-mangled hair into a ponytail through a polka-dotted black and white scrunchie. The face staring back at her from the mirror was unusually lively, a hint of satisfaction from tonight's Love Buzz performance visible in the lines around her weary smile. She adjusted the scrunchie until her two-tone hair flared in a manner that could be interpreted as fashion-forward. *Pretty enough.*

HeadBand, disengage night-vision mode.

Juanita's apartment reassumed its regular dull, lifeless appearance as the surreal shades of luminescent green melted away. She turned and lined her HeadBand up with the door's security lock scanner.

The door slid sideways to reveal two towering, muscle-bound black men standing shoulder to shoulder. Dav and Robbie's chests strained against their white polypropylene bodysuits, threatening to burst out. Robbie's hair, freshly bleached, looked like tiny tufts of blond cactus.

Spray-painter's suits don't do you boys justice, Juanita thought. At her request, she'd grown accustomed to them arriving in boots, pants and suspenders only, for easy access.

In front of Dav and Robbie stood a tiny white woman, her full moon of a face so anaemic she made Juanita look positively Latino. She was much younger than Juanita, mid-twenties at most, but the steely confidence in those eyes was something she recognised. *This is a woman who's used to getting her own way.* At five-foot-nine Juanita was no giantess but this woman's head barely reached her chin, let alone the pectorals of the perfect specimens flanking her. Her own spray-painting coverall's hood was pulled tight around her face, lightly freckled, her brown eyes flecked with ambition and mischief, her fixed smile trapped somewhere between grief and contempt.

'Who the fuck are you?' Juanita snapped, stepping back. Dazed she may have been, but her grip on reality was solid enough to know the ID profile generated by her HeadBand – Jeremiah, 72, maintenance technician, Macarthur Cluster – wasn't accurate. 'And why have you dressed my beautiful boys up like common cleaners?'

The petite young thing looked Juanita up and down, appraising her dejectedly, as if she'd finally tracked down a valuable artefact only to find the passing years and poor maintenance had made it worthless.

'Jesus H. Christ,' the woman drawled. 'She's in even worse shape than you let on.'

Juanita placed this young upstart as being from deep rural Queensland, or worse, some long-abandoned community of inbreeders on the outskirts of Bumfuck, Tasmania.

'Have you looked in the mirror lately, you cheeky little bint?' Juanita blustered. She held firm in her doorway. 'Double-drop Vitamin D for a month and get back to me.'

'Juanita, this is our friend, Lottie,' Dav almost whispered, coolly, as if reciting lines from a script. Juanita had always adored Dav's voice, several semitones deeper than Robbie's and enhanced by a whistle created by the gap between his top-front teeth. But his current preference for slow-motion whispers was really starting to creep her out.

Roberto looked at Juanita like her pathetic condition had destroyed all hope. 'She's here to help, miss,' he said – not in the singsong African-

French accent the boys had always shared, but in something more suited to the streets of south London.

'What the fuck is that accent about?'

'This ain't no accent, it's me real voice, miss.'

'And we need you to calm down and pull yourself together,' Lottie chimed in.

'And I need *you* to back the fuck up and remember who you're talking to, sweetie,' Juanita spat in the unwelcome visitor's face, prodding Lottie's chest with the heel of her right hand. 'Or I'll get my boys to throw you back into the rat runs you crawled out of.'

Lottie sighed. Staring into her eyes, Juanita was shocked to see neither fear nor awe in her antagonist's gaze. Instead, she saw a hint of pity.

'Juanita, I adore you, but I need you to shut the fuck up and trust me,' she said soothingly. 'I need you to talc up and slip into your favourite catsuit so we can get you the fuck out of here before Lockdown. If you won't listen to me, just ask Dav and Robbie.'

No no no. Juanita looked to her boys. *Not now, not like this.*

'Your worst fear is coming true, ma'am,' Dav said. Something about his voice – it may have been the subtle undercurrent of disdain – always gave her the jitters, even with its newfound cockney edge. 'You must've knew it would happen soon.'

Juanita shook her head in denial. Dav looked to his bleached-blond associate for support.

'It's true, miss,' said Robbie. 'The collection drones are coming.' He put a sympathetic hand on Juanita's shoulder. 'Tito's in town, and he's having you replaced.'

BUILD-UP

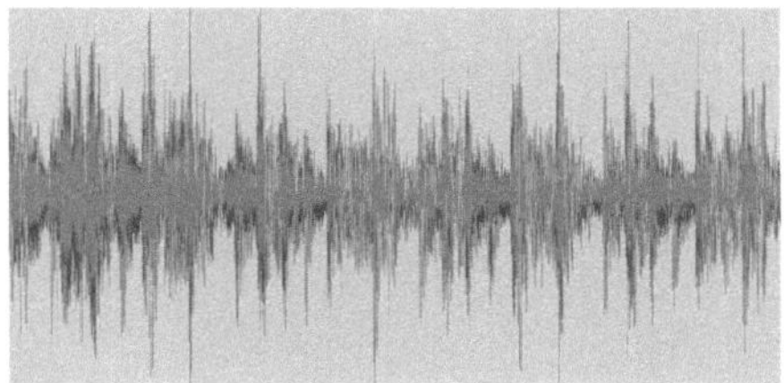

| 4.01 |

Spin Spin Sugar

'*Ground floor*,' recited a perfect robot impression of a woman who'd never known what it was to love. '*Enjoy your stay at Love Inn*.'

'Mind the gap,' Dav cautioned Juanita. He hauled her into a long, thin rectangular room.

It took Juanita a moment to clock her locale, so unfamiliar did it look without warm bodies draped across every square metre. The Love Inn's foyer was once a veritable zoo of Halcyon superstars, each peacocking their way through the assembled attendants and fame whores and other assorted hangers-on, all of whom had landed up in search of some rubbed-off celebrity status of their own. Now, even the powered down heart-hands symbol above the front desk was unrecognisable – an inscrutable tangle of thin white tubing, without the neon glow that helped it take shape.

Juanita had treasured the feeling of connectedness here, to her friends and fellow Halcyon DJs, however short-lived it had been. This was where she'd first seen Cosmo tucked under Tito's protective wing as he held a throng of screaming fans and paparazzi at bay. Three seconds of eye contact with the emerging heartthrob was all Juanita had needed to sense the scale of his ambition, but what had struck Juanita most was the ennui beneath the painted-on smile; like everything he'd worked for had finally come to fruition, only to find out his dream job was predicated on a lie. *Not just a fox, but a kindred spirit.*

Years later (or had it been months?), on New Year's Day 2025, Juanita and Usura had crept through the foyer arm in arm, giggling like underage clubbers who'd just pulled the wool over a door bitch's eyes. The Italian starlet had been Juanita's unofficial apprentice until she became a genuine competitor for Tito's attention. ('She'll never be a patch on my number one,' Tito assured Juanita whenever her sulking jealousy threatened to boil over.) After a renegade recovery party held in an abandoned underground whisky bar, protected from the HeadBand network's sensors by a jerry-rigged scrambling system, they'd braved Lockdown to sneak across the CBD back to Love Inn. In the rooftop pool they'd soaked up the new year's first rays – for the last time. Within months, the Storm had brought life's great party to a shuddering halt.

How Juanita longed to dive into that pool; to break the surface and clear the water from her eyes; to see the sky turn violet as dusk fell behind the nearby skyscrapers; to feel the overgenerous chlorine burn away days of baked-in filth and grime; to strip away the horror her life had become.

'Shit, Lottie, wait up a minute,' Dav's voice broke through Juanita's dark cloud. With his free hand, he summoned his companions back through the fortified glass sliding doors that opened onto the Oxford Street rat run. 'She's vagueing out on us already.'

'Calling el-vague-o, do you read me?' Robbie chattered away in Juanita's face. 'Yeah, Lotts, this is no good, like.'

Lottie raced back across the tiled floor to Dav, who held Juanita's buckled body upright.

'She usually gases out about twenty minutes into me 'n' Dav's show,' Robbie added, anxiously scanning the scene for signs of trouble. 'But she's worse than usual tonight.'

Lottie motioned for Robbie to cross the floor and keep watch at the door. If she'd been properly conscious, Juanita could've told her the chances of any foot traffic in this part of the rat-run network were low.

Most of the VIP apartment towers in the CBD Cluster were centred on Pitt and George Streets, in the shadows of Tito's beloved Halcyon Tower headquarters. Rather than rubbing shoulders with the 'here to be seen' types on the VIP Floor, CBD dwellers would be more likely to be enjoying Love Buzz at home, from the comfort of their Robot Rock helmets.

'I must say I expected a little more from Bonnie Stapleton, International Party Girl extraordinaire,' Lottie sighed.

Juanita's head lolled on Dav's biceps, but her drooping eyelids couldn't mask her surprise.

'Oh yes, sweetie, we know a lot more about you than Matthias van Dijk would be happy about,' Lottie continued.

Juanita's eyes sprung to life beneath her sky-blue viewfinder, darting around the foyer, searching for any sign of the security detail Tito had assured her would be a permanent fixture beneath her studio. Lottie took hold of Juanita's chin. She smirked, shaking her head dismissively in response to Juanita's pleading eyes.

Sorry to be the bearer of bad news, sister, Lottie's face seemed to say, *but Tito's sentry drones can't help you now.*

'Gymnastics prodigy, Olympic dreams, blah blah blah, until you quit and wouldn't tell your parents why. Superstar DJ, touring treadmill, blah blah blah, thrashing out your inner turmoil in the gym every day without fail, no matter how long and hard you'd kicked on into the night. So I'm pretty sure that under this catsuit, which is a good look for you, by the way'—Lottie pinched the elbow join of shiny black latex between thumb and forefinger, raising an impressed eyebrow at the outfit Junita had hurriedly slipped into before being dragged out her front door for the first time since the rat runs had opened, three months after the Storm—'really showing the young moppets what body confidence is all about . . .' Juanita slapped Lottie's hand away. 'Under all this is that fit and tenacious and intelligent woman I fell in love with.'

Juanita's attempt to fix Lottie with a blazing glare was futile when her own eyes felt seared by the Ultraworld's visual assault and wouldn't focus. Inside her speaker cups, her tinnitus reached for the high notes.

'We're racing against the clock here, sister.' Lottie stared Juanita down again. 'So, if someone resembling the old Juanita could join us soon, we can all get ourselves to safety before Tito's collection drones snap us up. Can you dig it?'

Overwhelmed by it all – this strange girl, Tito's betrayal, the simple act of walking out her front door – Juanita pulled herself to attention using Dav's arm as a brace, and nodded. 'I can dig it,' she wheezed.

'Good for you.' Lottie smiled. 'Cos it's Lockdown in seven minutes, and this will be fuckloads easier if we don't have to explain to anyone why a VIP and three worker-bees are roaming the rat runs when we're supposed to be tucked away inside, like the rest of this sad joke of a city.'

Juanita hesitated at the double doors leading into the rat run. She was scattered by her lack of sleep and sustenance. She was confused by Lottie's long-winded ways of saying the simplest things. She knew even less about Dav and Robbie than she'd thought. *But they're my beautiful boys, and I trust them.* They'd proven themselves across many torrid post-set sessions, succumbing to her increasingly dark desires for years without uttering a word of protest. Robbie had even warned her of the chat bouncing around Halcyon Tower; of how Juanita's increasingly erratic performances hadn't gone unnoticed by those monitoring Love Buzz from the turret and beyond. Dav had only shrugged helplessly at Robbie's revelation, though whether through ignorance or disinterest wasn't clear.

Reluctantly, Juanita trudged through the automatic doors. *If the boys trust her, so be it.*

Lottie and Davide exited the Love Inn foyer behind her. Her mood-generated synthesiser app restarted, filling Juanita's ears with a gentle bed of electronic percussion. On the far side of the rat run, Robbie's silhouette played hide and seek beneath a malfunctioning fluorescent tube.

'Pretty sketchy out here, Lotts,' Robbie said. 'Let's shuttle before the Brainfeeders get a whiff.'

'C'mon, Neets,' Lottie extended her hand. 'Time to feel the buzz like the one-per-cent do.'

Break & Enter

Lottie briskly led the group through the flickering darkness. Juanita had sleepwalked her way through more Virtuoso sets than a tech-house DJ who'd just discovered the sync button on Serato, but no amount of aerobic exercise on her Silo could have prepared her weary hips for the simple act of walking down the Darlinghurst rat run. The path from her recliner to her bathroom to her front door was crystal clear, even with lava-lightning strikes outside the front window distorting her perspective. Outside, every shadow seemed a threat, every step a risk.

The old shopfronts beneath Love Inn – a jewellery repair shop, a HeadBand accessory dealer, Juanita's favourite laser hair-removal clinic – had been trashed beyond recognition. The Burdekin Hotel stood vacant and lonesome, as it had since the 9 pm Lockdown had seen off what remained of its clientele. Everything already hurt, but seeing her shattered neighbourhood up close ramped up Juanita's latent guilt for rising so far above it, as if she had it in her power to command Mother Nature, the power to make the Storm go away.

A violent clash of repugnant odours had her pining for the gentle hum of her apartment's OxyPure-5000. The rat-run reeked of every offence that enclosed public thoroughfares misused by humans had always reeked of: vomit, piss, spilt drinks, acrid sweat, rotting garbage.

Past the Oxford Street strip, it was all concrete – no awning overhead, three-metre slabs of cement to all three sides. Embedded in the concrete dividing wall to their left, miniature purification turbines spun forlornly against the torrent of unpleasantries. Speakers shaped like Halcyon logos interspersed the strip lighting along the tunnel wall, ensuring the sounds of Love Buzz 1000 were piped through every cubic metre of the network.

Juanita's Gucci mini backpack, housing a spare scrunchie and the discarded serviettes, bounced against her back. Her utility belt sat loose above her hips. (Even a catsuit needed accessories.)

HeadBand, engage night-vision mode.

She gagged as the group crossed the bitumen of what had once been bustling College Street. When Oxford Street was still in its debaucherous prime, she'd hauled her chopped eyeballs across this intersection at sunrise on a hundred different Sundays. She and her besties had always imagined they'd come of age, albeit illegally, during Peak Sydney – those glorious nights and days when you could dance through the Star-fuckers-Habit-Spice holy trinity and still have the stamina to kick on with Lawrence the Phat Controller ('"Phat" with a P-H, yeah') and the other weather-beaten old clubbers trying to keep the dream alive.

It wasn't until years later, on the other side of the DJ booth, that Juanita realised one punter's peak was another's decline. Sydney had bubbled away at more or less the same level until the state government-enabled real-estate barons finally wrapped their tentacles around Darlinghurst and Kings Cross, successfully crushing the life out of the night economy by the time the 2010s lurched to a close. By then, Juanita was so firmly ensconced at the pointy end of Tito's roster that she was immune to the petty politics of her home town. 'Peak time, all the time' was Tito's philosophy. And she'd been living that life since before she was old enough to know any different.

Juanita tripped on the kerb as she attempted to mount the College Street footpath. Where once she'd gazed in wonder down Hyde Park's fig-lined avenues – past the Anzac Memorial towards the needle of Sydney Tower, gleaming in the distance like a rocket readying for take-off

– she now saw only walls of water-stained grey. Beyond the rat-run walls the famous sky needle was now Halcyon Tower, the southern base of Tito's operations since he'd claimed it post-1-6-25. Gone were those smells she remembered so fondly, coffee beans and dew-covered grass and buses spewing fumes as they lurched up Liverpool Street. Instead, she battled through a cocktail of human waste; each breath of OxyPure-filtered air supply infused with trace elements of decay.

'I couldn't even tell you,' Juanita mumbled.

'What's that, sister?' Lottie's anxious eyes appeared in close-up. Her look of alarm was amplified by Juanita's HeadBand in night-vision mode.

With a gesture of her thumb, Juanita eased back the volume of her mood-sensor synthesiser. The syncopated percussion was bubbling a little too darkly for comfort given her current predicament; a little too close to *The Terminator* when what she really needed was *Blade Runner*.

'I couldn't tell you the last time I came Outside,' Juanita continued.

'This isn't quite "Outside", miss,' Robbie said from over her shoulder.

'You know what I mean.'

Robbie's hands on Juanita's shoulders brought her to a halt beside Museum Station. Dav lifted a section of green fence palings attached to the entry's brick façade. Robbie motioned Juanita through and Lottie pointed her towards a window frame emptied of glass. A folded-up packing blanket lined the base of the frame, protecting Juanita's hands as she clambered through and took a leap of faith into darkness.

As his feet hit the floor, the frame at the top of Dav's viewfinder lit up like a fluorescent tube. Dav tagged Robbie's hand on his way past and his partner's torch strip also activated as he took the baton and led the group into the bowels of the station.

'The rat runs were lit from end-to-end back then and looked like they ran on forever,' Juanita said. 'And the entryways at Museum and St James had all been polished like new.'

'Well, you definitely need to get out more, sister; it's been a jungle out here for at least two years,' Lottie laughed. 'With all the Brainfeeders around these days, the rat runs around these parts are *not* for the faint of heart. That's why most of the VIPs that aren't in the Cross moved from Oxford Street down to the CBD.'

They skipped down the stairwell two steps at a time, Roberto almost tearing the rickety metal railing from the beige wall tiles as he rounded the final corner onto the platform. Under the moderate arch of the platform's ceiling, the dank was even stronger than in the confines of the rat run. Still, Juanita breathed a little easier – the smell here was more still air and rotting vegetation than human waste. The platform itself looked like it hadn't seen any notable foot traffic in years.

'Town Hall is the only other station in the CBD that the trains stop at anymore,' Lottie explained. 'And they made it the access point for the CBD Cluster, which means our boys, the rat-run crews, can walk the tunnels to and from their barracks in Barangaroo. Otherwise all rail lines lead to Love Buzz, baby, just as your boy Tito decreed.'

The group hurried towards the platform's northern end, past vintage billboards advertising tea and haberdashery and other quaint bygones of a long-forgotten Peak Sydney. Dav leapt onto the tracks at the edge of the platform and grasped Juanita under her arms to help her down. Lottie and Robbie lowered themselves over the ledge. Once her footing was firm, Lottie sharply slapped her speaker cups. Dav and Robbie slapped theirs in tandem.

'But it's time to leave your world behind for now, sister.' Lottie smiled. She knelt beside a cavity in the underside of the platform and hooked her HeadBand – a standard-issue MK 4, with none of Juanita's custom mod cons – on an unseen attachment in its upper reaches. Robbie followed suit. 'Where we're going, you won't need your HeadBand.'

'Fuck right off!' Juanita snapped, backing into Dav's chest. She gripped the hard casings encircling her ears. 'This is the only thing keeping my shit together.'

'You need to trust Lottie, miss,' Dav said. He gently massaged her shoulders. 'You two are more alike than you know.'

'What about COVID?'

'Eradicated last year,' Lottie said matter-of-factly. 'Can't believe Tito didn't tell you.'

The light from Dav's HeadBand shone out above Juanita until it didn't. He crouched down behind her and Juanita heard him feel around beneath the platform before he stood behind her again. Dav pried her fingers from her HeadBand. He popped her speaker cups, less forcefully than Tito had when she'd road-tested his new ViZar headset the last time he'd visited – sometime between her thirty-seventh birthday and Christmas.

Lottie and Robbie's footsteps echoed from down the tunnel. Juanita awaited the sound of her own HeadBand being deposited in the secret chamber, but Dav instead dropped it onto her fists. She clutched it anxiously to her chest.

'Shhhhh,' Dav hissed into her right ear, patting her butt gently to propel her in the direction of the departed duo. 'This is our little secret.'

Tucking the HeadBand into her Gucci and slinging it over her shoulders, Juanita gripped the back of Dav's coverall and stumbled blindly down the railway track.

| 4.03 |

Curfew Time

Juanita could make out body-shaped patches of bright white fabric moving through the darkness. Above Robbie's outline, knots of bleached hair bounced about like a lumpy beanie. After what felt to Juanita like an eternity in pitch darkness, the tunnel widened. St James Station. Juanita clambered onto the derelict platform and followed Lottie away from the tracks and around a white-tiled wall. Robbie was there already, opening a green door tucked into the base of a staircase. He waved the group through and onto another platform, running parallel to the one outside but only half its length.

Juanita's jaw unclenched a little at the welcome sight of lights, however dim, lining the cavern wall to her left. The string of half-interested bulbs led towards a rail tunnel opening which, instead of snaking off into the distance, had been stopped in its tracks by the construction of a brick wall. If Juanita had her bearings correct, it would have continued on past where they'd just entered the rail system. Her HeadBand would have the definitive answer, but this wasn't the time to invoke Lottie's wrath.

At either end of the platform was a pair of demountable dilapidated office units, their remaining windows rattling rhythmically. Juanita saw no sign of the vibration's source. As far as she could tell, it was a primordial throb radiating from Earth's core itself.

'Finally, we can lose these ridiculous things,' Dav said in disgust. His voice briefly echoed through the tunnel before being consumed by the distorted heartbeat beyond.

Juanita cautiously eyed off her 'guardian angels', as she had decided to designate them until she could determine exactly what she was being lured into, and where and why. Although she trusted Dav and Robbie, their new companion – who'd never been mentioned by her boys – remained a mystery. Whoever Lottie was, wherever she'd come from and whatever her intentions were, she was clearly skilled in the dark arts of making herself appear inscrutable.

Looks like we're settling in for the long game, then, Juanita surmised.

She recalled another lesson Tito had imparted once their first Asian tour had moved onto the summer festival frenzy of Europe. 'It doesn't matter what corner of the world you land in that afternoon,' Tito had told her as they lazed by the pool outside his Ibiza villa. 'You can be sure that no random who bails you up for a chat immediately after a headline set will reveal their true character until the new day's sun shows its face.'

All too easy. She'd patiently wait her new 'friend' out of hiding.

Dav and Robbie kicked and twisted themselves out of their street-cleaner suits and hung them on hooks behind the green door. Each had been concealing a pair of Rasta-themed Cross Colours pants, held up by suspenders over white shirts that bore the goofy yellow visage of the smiley face. The matching outfits were completed by bright white Adidas hi-tops with side stripes alternating blue and red. Her Halcyon-issued groupies had never looked so circumspect, though in fairness Juanita rarely let them wear clothes. She couldn't suppress a weary smile.

Out of the spray-painting suit, Lottie's true colours shone through. Curly red hair sprouted from her head in two short and snappy pigtails, which would've looked out of place on her mid-twenty-something face if they weren't complemented by cut-off Day-Glo overalls and mud-flecked Dunlop Volley sneakers.

'At least the disguises make more sense now,' Juanita scoffed at Lottie, eyebrow raised as she looked the escapee from Toytown up and down. 'No one would've believed you'd just left Love Buzz dressed like that.'

'Well, would you look at that, boys,' Lottie fired back. 'I've just been stitch-shamed by a chick who thinks a belt, some underwear and a few dabs of paint constitutes an outfit.'

Juanita hastily changed the subject, not liking the harsh (but fair) reminder of just how far she'd let herself go. 'Where'd you get this stuff?'

'All the original Summer of Love threads had been warehoused for Love Buzz, so we dug deep to find something better, miss,' Robbie said. He pushed his cockney geezer accent a little further towards the mean streets of Brixton, placed his hands on his hips and slid fluidly from side to side; his body dipping towards the ground in time with the rattling windows, his Cheshire smile sending joy through Juanita's dead heart like only he could. 'And the steez in our little scene is more Second Summer of Love stylee, aight?'

Juanita remembered more about the Second Summer of Love than most of the people who'd been there, having lost herself in Tito's many late-night tales of navigating London at the back end of the '80s. 'I was just a twenty-year-old atmospheric scientist on a break from his mission to save the world' was how Tito habitually opened this chapter of his memoirs. From there he'd ramble through the importance of the Harmonic Convergence and the arrival of acid house to his generation, then wrap things up by railing against the horrors of Margaret Thatcher's England.

And you're doing it again, Juanita scolded herself. She shook Tito's old-man stories away and surveyed the hidden platform. 'Where *are* we?'

'Come,' Lottie said, taking Juanita's hand, leading her towards the throb that seemed to distort the air. 'We don't want to miss a second of the best warm-up crew in the biz.'

They stepped down a small ladder onto the track floor.

'This is the train line that never was,' Lottie explained, her voice getting louder as they turned left, then right past the tunnel opening, then through a towering metal gate. 'Dav, let's switch padlocks when we lock it up, this one's been on far too long.'

'On it, miss.'

Lottie pushed ahead into a tunnel twice the width of the one they'd just left.

'These tunnels were supposed to connect St James to Bondi and Randwick, until the Great Depression and then the Second World War basically crippled the city,' Lottie continued, her voice growing louder still as they neared the source of the progressively less muffled thudding sound. 'They set it up as an air-raid shelter for 20,000 people but never needed it. As far as I know, it got used for counter-terrorism training and emergency rescue exercises around the turn of the century. Keanu Reeves filmed some scenes for *The Matrix* here, and all sorts of urban myths about séances and the like have done the rounds.'

The group was surrounded by knee-high piles of decomposing soil, broken bricks and crumbling cement barriers. The throb grew clearer with each turn through the convoluted tunnel system. In the low-end, warbled frequencies found their voice; on top, the repetitive snap of a hi-hat cymbal cut through.

Juanita's tour guide fished a small flashlight from the front of her overalls and held it under her chin as if telling horror stories on a camping trip. The source of the nearby din was clear to Juanita now. Even after all these years ensconced inside her HeadBand's virtual world, she recognised the unmistakeable sounds of a party going down.

'Y'all ready for this?' Lottie handed her torch to Roberto. Cackling, she turned on her heel and pushed through a green door identical to the one at the start of the tunnel.

'*It's curfew time!*'

Dull throb begat rolling thunder. The music, which had teased from afar over their fifteen-minute journey through the tunnels, slammed into Juanita with such clarity she struggled to push through. The distorted snippet of speech that had heralded their arrival was more than just an announcement: it was a call to arms.

This new tunnel was enormous – the same width as the two-track platform of Museum Station, with a ceiling at least twice as high. A cornucopia of lights crept down the walls from an origin point that Juanita guessed was close to a kilometre away. Juanita took in her immediate surroundings. A generous growth of moss had worked up the sidewalls, stopping just short of where the arched ceiling began. About fifteen metres above the rugged flooring below, bricks curved up and in to meet in the centre. The ceiling's white paint was mottled, pockmarked with mould. Even more so than in the earlier passages, the surrounding brickwork was a patchwork of shapes, sizes and colours. Juanita got the feeling the original tunnellers had left this part of the tunnel system half-finished, and just used whatever was close at hand to roughly finish the walls, shore up their dig and get the hell back up to fresh air.

'Welcome to the St James Lake rave cave!' Lottie beamed.

Soil loosened by the beats rumbling from the far end of the cave tumbled down from between the arched ceiling's brickwork, littering Juanita's eyes.

'Sydney's home of the underground, for one night only.'

Juanita heard cheers erupt as the beat kicked in hundreds of metres ahead. Two things were clear: the people on the dancefloor were up for it, and there were a lot of them.

'Let's get you to the cloakroom,' Lottie shouted. She interlaced her fingers with Juanita's left hand and tugged her in the direction of the right-side wall. 'And into something a little more appropriate.'

Juanita shuffled along behind Lottie, blinking the dirt from her lashes and again fighting the temptation to slip her HeadBand safely into place. Through watery eyes she could make out the outline of the cloakroom, though calling it a room was overstating its majesty. A man and woman stood behind a waist-high sideboard not unlike the one in the Love Inn's foyer.

Neither of them wore HeadBands. Juanita looked around to confirm – no one down here was.

The male attendant wore a tiny fluorescent orange cap with the brim turned up, dark sunglasses dangling on a yellow cord over a shirt bearing Ken Done's Sydney Opera House painting. The woman sported a copy of Jenny Kee's garish, knitted Luna Park dress.

Juanita was impressed; these vintage fashionistas were seriously on-point.

A pair of mobile clothes racks, overflowing with bright shirts and dresses and elaborate coats, stood either side of what Juanita recognised as an IKEA Expedit unit – the very same design which dominated Tito's Rotterdam apartment, but filled with pants and footwear instead of twelve-inch vinyl records. Tucked behind the Expedit were two sets of three height-adjustable metal clothes racks, each over six feet in height with black curtains dangling from the crossbar. Arranged in square formation with the wall, Juanita guessed they were the cloakroom's pop-up fitting booths.

'Something light and airy for our guest, Leo,' Lottie barked across the counter, which had been positioned, perhaps intentionally, in the deepest trenches of a river of bass. 'And some comfortable dancing shoes.'

'Back to basics is so hot right now,' Leo agreed, stroking his greying goatee. 'Mary!' Leo's co-worker tilted an ear in his direction. 'Something a little bit loose and about the same size as you.'

Mary tucked a dangling lock of black hair behind her ear and winked at Juanita. 'Take her out back, Lottie, and I'll pass some things through.'

Beneath Juanita's catsuit, a thin film of sweat lightly stimulated her all over, but she knew the second skin would begin to rub strips of flesh away from her heels and inner thighs if the night escalated. Lottie led her towards the nearest change room. Once the curtain was pulled closed, Juanita unfastened her utility belt and hung it over the crossbar. After double-checking the zip was secure, she hung the Gucci backpack beside it.

'These should fit!' Mary thrust some clothes through the gap in the curtain. 'And these shoes are always on trend.' She flung a pair of sneakers, laces tied, over the top rail.

'Really?' Juanita asked, eyebrow cocked. She held up the pile: cut-off Day-Glo overalls, purple sports bra, white ankle socks and Dunlop Volleys.

Lottie grinned mischievously. Turning Juanita around, she unzipped her catsuit with a flourish.

| 4.04 |

ABC

'Where will you be at the end?' Mary asked Juanita. Elaborate patterns of silver and gold paint, like painted-on fairy wings, blended seamlessly with her MIDI implants. Enthusiasm brimmed from her dark-green eyes. In her primary-coloured short slip dress and hanging black hair, the cloakroom attendant looked like an android – an unusually tall and slender one – who'd simply torn a mask-shaped strip of skin from her face to ready herself for the masquerade.

Juanita passed Mary her catsuit. 'That's a pretty deep question to ask someone you've just met!'

'She means at the end of the night, you caner!' Leo said. 'I'll just hang this up back here.'

Juanita leaned over the counter. 'To tell you the truth,' she yelled in Mary's ear, 'I've got no fucking clue where I am right now, let alone where I'll end up!'

'Well I'll be here if you fancy coming back for a boogie,' Mary said. She grabbed Juanita's hand before she could take off. 'And I know the only place you can go to the toilet without the smell making you want to puke.'

Even down here the door bitch is the best person to know. Juanita blew a thank-you kiss at Mary.

Leo was deep in the zone, swaying his head side to side as the beat ricocheted down the chamber, arms motioning ahead of him at half-speed like the Wiggles pointing the fingers after chasing a dose of morphine with a bump of Special K. He mouthed the words, 'How good'. Juanita agreed. She remembered what this felt like now. The unspoken connection. The silent understanding. The small wonder of those ephemeral shared moments. Then Leo and Mary were dancing together, creating a shared moment all their own.

Juanita turned to re-join the others, huddled tight in conversation.

Robbie tapped Lottie's shoulder and motioned behind her with a tip of his head when he saw Juanita coming.

Lottie turned and spread her arms wide, greeting Juanita with a smile. 'Can't you feel it?'

Lottie motioned Juanita to follow her down the middle lane of the rave cave. Due to its slipshod construction, this hangar-like space seemed more vulnerable to the shifting earth below than any of the tunnels prior. Juanita's Volleys gripped the sturdy central corridor of the uneven surface with ease. In fact, Juanita was impressed with the way the entire ragged ensemble fit her body, although she'd not be giving Lottie the satisfaction of telling her just yet.

'Feel what?' Juanita shouted back.

'That indefinable special something,' Lottie said, spinning to face Juanita. 'Don't you remember walking into a party for the first time and sensing magic in the air?'

'Like something momentous was about to happen tonight,' Juanita shouted.

'Exactly!' Lottie cried. 'It's why we all fell in love with this music in the first place.'

Lottie pushed ahead into the milling crowd. Robbie put a reassuring hand on Juanita's shoulder and nudged her gently forward. Lottie expertly swerved the group through small puddles dotting the tunnel floor. By the entrance, people had been gathered in small groups along the cavern's perimeter; several hundred metres in, the sprinklings of humanity began thickening into a more united crowd, their attention on the huge, ever-growing, pulsating cocktail of sound and light emanating from the far end of the room. Bodies gravitated towards the party's centrepiece like caners to a kick-on's final plate of racked-up lines. Party people were decked out in a variety of recurring themes: spray-painting suits complemented by the tattered surgical masks that had been distributed during the first coronavirus pandemic; tracksuit pants, seemingly held in place around jutted-out hips by bumbags; knee-length stonewash denim shorts, mostly hidden by tailored long-line button-up shirts with eclectic prints; hot pants and swimming goggles; the ubiquitous smiley face shirts; the equally ubiquitous no shirt at all. Some danced atop blue water-storage barrels, spaced intermittently along the rave cave's walls near its entrance. Closer to the stage, the barrels had been grouped together to form makeshift terraces either side of the main dancefloor.

'Everything's connected!' cried a man whose face was hidden behind a raggedy red beard, so wild and wispy it made the face below impossible to carbon date. He weaved erratically through the dancing throng past Juanita, his eyeballs turning cartwheels in their sockets with each repeat of his chant.

Bounding behind him like a sprite, an ageless woman of eastern European descent tied a rainbow-coloured band to Juanita's wrist, solemnly informed her 'I think you need this', then allowed herself to be absorbed by the crowd.

An elderly lady not much taller than Lottie – her long white hair in a ponytail, flicking away at the rear of her loose black cotton dress – spun around and around, oblivious to the respectful perimeter forming around her, marking out a private patch of dancefloor.

Lottie grabbed Juanita's arm to keep her moving towards the front. 'If Spinny Lady's here spinning,' Lottie shouted to be heard, 'you know you're in the right place.'

All around Juanita, the party was catching fire. Thousands of revellers heaved together as one. The room was so thick with moisture it seemed to form its own atmosphere. Juanita could imagine storm clouds brewing overhead and showering one last late-summer storm down on the carefree thousands, washing the hedonism and the decadence away like another great flood.

'*A . . . B . . . C . . .*'

A man's impossibly deep voice – deeper even than Dav's baritone – rang out from the party's sound system, its gravitas at odds with the chaotically joyful scene all around.

Juanita and her spirit guides were close enough to the front to see what passed for the St James Lake rave cave's stage. Fashioned from milk crates crammed tightly to support timber shipping pallets cable-tied together, it supported two DJs and a trestle table covered with two turntables, a DJ mixer and a small desk lamp. About ten years older than Juanita, the duo manning the decks were flanked by a hodgepodge of speakers and oozed the unmistakeable confidence of experience and trust.

Lottie brought the trio to a stop in the middle of the crowd. A kick-drum punched its way deep into Juanita's solar plexus, reminding her of how Mandy had dragged them into the Cave's 'sweet spot' on the night DJ Tito headlined her sixteenth birthday party, as she liked to think of it. Tito had 'discovered' her on the floor just a few hours later. In the twenty-two years since, she'd rarely had to jockey for prime position on any dancefloor on the planet. Juanita couldn't recall the last time she'd witnessed a party in full flight from outside the exclusive sanctity of the DJ booth, each designed more elaborately than the last as the barrier between performer and punter became more clearly defined.

'*A . . . B . . . C . . .*'

Reappearing behind them, Dav screamed something unintelligible before throwing a high-five at Robbie above Juanita's head. A sinewy synthesiser riff entered the scene, wrapping around the kick drum, melting in and out of focus. In front of Juanita, Lottie's tiny body began to shimmy and shake in time, her head rocking, her sync with the music so perfect that Juanita wanted to film it for Abbie and make her study it so Juanita wouldn't have to endure her off-beat head-bobbing anymore. The elasticised synth sound twisted and turned so subtly that it was impossible to define with any great certainty where one note ended and the next began. It was fluid and it was slippery and it was sexier than any sound Juanita had encountered in decades.

'*C is for Consciousness-s-s-s-s . . .*'

Artificial hi-hat cymbals and cowbells joined the cacophony, providing counterpoint to the rolling bassline that simultaneously entered the fray. Another synthesiser called and responded to itself, its high-pitched *dinna-dinna-dinna* answered by *dinna-dinna,* an octave lower. The frantic elements of the track suddenly retreated; the bassline settled into an insistent groove, its steady hand wrapped protectively around the dancefloor's core.

'*A is for Awareness – the awareness of others that takes a man and makes him a human.*'

The monologue by the man with the impossibly deep voice continued on. The air reeked of 'sweaty wet, dirty damp', a non-sequitur Juanita vaguely remembered a trio of trashy electro-pop upstarts spitting across the Club 77 dancefloor during that brief window of 2007 when upper-middle-class white Australians dressed like they were backup dancers in a Madonna film clip from 1983 – all puffy tropical jackets and bouncing curly perms and shiny satin pants. More than two decades later Juanita finally understood what 'sweaty wet, dirty damp' was – the muggy atmosphere being created in this long-forgotten cavern as warm bodies kicked up dust and collided with their new best friends. She felt it and smelt it and hungered to taste it.

'*B is for Beauty – that obscure object of desire that begins where hunger ends.*'

The room hung heavy with something outside the smell of unwashed bodies, drenched in the fumes of the roaming fire-dancing troupe's turpentine. Juanita was surrounded by a collective euphoria, thousands of strangers suddenly optimistic at the mere promise of a beautiful future. She felt what everyone else felt: it could all go up in flames any minute now and that would be okay because *it is what it is.* And in this room at least, Juanita knew it really was what it was.

'C is for Consciousness – the consciousness of the world and of others that lights up the darkness so that no one is alone.'

The wall of sound thundered with such energy, the stage lights swung so quickly past Juanita's eyes, that the speaker casing, cones and tweeters seemed to spring to life. She saw robot faces form inside the inanimate boxes of metal and cable, their expressions as chilling as Halcyon's faceless sentry drones.

'D is for Desire-ire-ire-ire-ire-ire . . .'

Juanita studied the DJ duo. Standing stage right was the technical marvel, lips curled in concentration beneath a devilish goatee, eyes focused on some point only he could see, hips locked in so tightly to the groove he seemed to have been assimilated by his workstation. To his left, his partner assessed the damage being wrought before him, his bald white dome seemingly impervious to sweat. Juanita knew the type on sight – a more visceral deployer of sound, more understated than his counterpart yet partial to dishing out more primal rhythms and melodies. These were two individuals with their own unique skills and sounds, and as a DJ team they were more powerful than the sum of their parts.

As the previous track finished its long, seamless segue into this one, the stage-left DJ's eyes gleamed. Juanita remembered that satisfaction; of digging through Tito's Expedits to find the right record, the next piece in the puzzle; of working the EQs, subtly tweaking the mids before snapping between the lows; of it all coming together when she'd nailed the perfect mix.

Or maybe it's all going down on a deeper level than mixing the next track into the last, she pondered, remembering one of Tito's more esoteric soapbox lectures on how a 'DJ's DJ', like him in his prime, works a ravenous crowd. *Maybe these guys are so deep in the zone that the next track is anticipating the one they just dropped.*

A single green laser shot a pinprick of light between the DJs' bobbing heads, straight down the middle of the cavernous dancefloor. Smoke billowed from beneath the stage.

'E is for Equality – that beautiful dream that will become reality.'

The beam of light unfurled and expanded in tandem with a barrelling snare drum build-up. It formed a tunnel that cut through the rising fog, as dense as the mid-winter Penrith dawns of Juanita's childhood. There was no blind worship of the odd couple manning the controls, no mindless exaltation to the cult of celebrity as Juanita had always experienced the art of DJing. Here, there was only the sound, the lights, and the self as part of an even more important whole.

Tito had barely bothered to teach Juanita the skills of a 'real DJ', accounting for the sneers she copped from older heads on the circuit when she first stepped up to the decks. Her honey-coated voice alone had been enough to have dancefloors waving their hands in the air at her command.

This rave cave's dancefloor swayed, too, but its movements were far more random. Arms swirled sinuously above heads to herald the impending arrival of the next barrage. Howls of approval and shrieking whistles pierced the air. Beside Juanita, Dav and Robbie embraced.

'F is for the eternal flame of Freedom – burning in each of our hearts.'

But there was something more elemental at play; an understanding between performer and participant of the energy loop between them that was making this moment happen. So *this* was what Tito had meant. Symbiosis. The records were the fuel and the DJs were the fire, but the dancefloor was the star of the show and the spotlight was on everyone.

'J is for the Joy – that springs from the triumphs of the good, giving us hope and inspiration.'

Juanita didn't notice the narrator skipping from G to J. So overwhelming were the music, the smoke and the lights that she'd lost herself in the dance without realising.

Juanita thought she had seen it all, from nightclub dancefloors being reduced to background wallpaper for carbon-copy Insta stories to DJs adding pedestal fans to their festival main-stage tech riders so that their hair would float gracefully behind them (when they weren't firing confetti cannons into the first fifteen rows of barely legal 'VIPs', the next generation of fodder for Tito to assimilate, before the VIP acronym had its meaning restored in the wake of the Storm). She'd assumed Peak Sydney was over for everyone, but this expression of sensuality and joy was another Peak Sydney entirely. She couldn't tell whether it was from a time before or a time to come, or all of Sydney's historic peaks going off at once.

'K is for the certain Knowledge – that one day we will all live in peaceful understanding.'

'Now that you've seen how the one-per-cent party,' Lottie shouted in Juanita's ear, eyes threatening to pinwheel out of her skull as the snare roll clattered its way towards another a crescendo, 'are you sure you'd ever want it any other way?'

Juanita took Lottie's hands and gave them an enthusiastic squeeze. *You and me, babe*, she was trying to tell Lottie. *Where you go, I go too.*

'L is for Love . . .'

Hurriedly shaking the younger woman away (their time to bond would come), Juanita reached her fingers towards the laser-formed tunnel of love. The lights flashed even more rapidly as the build-up reached its peak, the precious moment when they all became strobe-light queens. Juanita's hands appeared to melt.

'L is for Love . . .'

Juanita closed her eyes and felt her soul vibrate in a way it had just once before, mere moments before DJ Tito's 'Singularity' sent her crashing face-first into the Cave's concrete floor.

| 4.05 |

Rapture

Lottie crouched on her haunches in the rave cave's ad hoc green room, poring over the contents of an aluminium record crate. A tattered hessian curtain, hanging from above the entryway to her right, trembled with each strike of the adjoining chamber's bottom-heavy bass drum. She peered past the curtain, down the short, narrow corridor, secreted away in the shadows of the stage-right speaker stacks. Strobe lights ricocheted off the hallway's blotchy brick walls. Lottie adjusted her moulded earplugs, a gift from her DJ mentor before he'd sent her out into clubs on her own. After all these years the left plug still sat in her ear too snugly, though she'd come to accept that as the reason her left ear remained her sharpest. There was a trade-off, though, to preserving her most precious organs. Once her plugs were in position, the musical elements that Lottie loved most – the spiralling synth melodies, the intoxicating clatter and crack of cymbals and tribal percussion that propelled a dancefloor along – became pale, low-pass filtered imitations of themselves.

Then she was back in Tito's lair, always Tito lair, putting the final pieces of the underground resistance's long, long game in place.

'We both knew this part of the journey was coming, lover.'

Lottie tilted her head playfully towards Tito – not the silver fox she'd opened her eyes to see staring down at her as a sixteen-year-old but the old man he'd turned into within five short years, the fate of the world baked into the lines around his eyes, incredibly sharp and focused but tinged with sorrow. She twirled her index finger in his hair, twisting and turning away in his thick matted curls. Below her collarbones, a white sheet protected whatever remained of her modesty.

'The last few months have just been one long bridging track – a bridging track, *haaaa*, haven't I learned my lessons well?' Lottie giggled. 'A holding pattern at the end of all that's come before, until the bomb is dropped and the party explodes.' She flicked the switch on a cheeky grin. 'The calm before the storm, so to speak.'

'Or literally.' Tito laughed. He cupped a hand to her cheek. 'Biblically, even.'

'I'm just glad that you finally accepted the reality of the situation, lover,' she whispered.

'That Lottie Gardner was always going to be too headstrong for me to successfully turn?' Tito asked. 'Sorry to break it to you, but that sixteen-year-old I met strutting around in an AC/DC logo shirt spelling out ACID didn't exactly scream "counter-revolutionary".'

'I'm a woman who'll fight for what she believes in,' Lottie countered, 'but I'll never compromise myself to get it.'

'Yet here you are,' Tito said.

'Come now,' Lottie said, condescendingly pinching Tito's cheek. 'This is exactly where I want to be, in the middle of all the action. I might be a headstrong bitch—'

'A "batshit cray eight" is the technical term, I believe,' Tito interrupted.

'Oh, puh-*lease*,' Lottie scoffed. 'High seven, at best. So I've had to rely on my wiles to compete with the vacuous nines and perfect tens throwing themselves at you.'

Tito shrugged, as if to say, *What's a man to do?*

'Anyway, I'm a hundred per cent in on the Halcyon cause, because I can see the genius behind it,' Lottie continued. 'You've channelled your imperfections into something that might just be perfect. I mean, the whole "when I'm on tour it's anal sex only" thing is a bit off, but I get it – the ultimate system of control, right?'

'It was never enough to control you, though,' Tito said ruefully.

'Oh, Tito, you silly old sausage,' Lottie smiled upon him pityingly. She pressed an index finger into his chest. 'I love anal so much I used *it* to control *you.*'

Lottie rolled out from underneath the covers and strode naked towards Tito's en suite.

'And I think I made it pretty clear from the start how much I hate that music you created,' she called over her shoulder. 'I was never going to be happy jumping up and down, pointing a finger skywards after every drop, let alone doing it with a smile on my face. As for that blue-wig fetish of yours, the less said the better.'

'Did you ever hear me playing those tunes at home?' Tito shot back. 'One World has never been about the music for me. It's just a tool to unlock people's minds.'

'Unlock their minds?' Lottie snorted. 'More like slam them shut.'

She danced back from the mirror, turning 180 degrees to glide towards Tito, her hips swaying seductively from side to side. She lowered herself into child's pose on the foot of the bed. Doubled over, her hands reached tantalisingly towards Tito's before snatching back just out of his reach.

Lottie sat back on her knees, her expression briefly betraying the only hint of uncertainty she'd ever let Tito see. 'Are you sure it's going to work?'

Tito sat up against the bedhead, unlatching the top sheet from the prickly regrowth on his muscled chest. 'It has to.' He sighed. 'The few populist idiots who survived the assassination are still quibbling over oil fields and Paris targets and—'

'Not that,' Lottie interrupted.

'What, then?'

'My part in it all,' she said, pretending to be tentative, reeling him in. 'I'm going to be out there in the thick of it working off little more than a hunch.'

'Think of it not so much as a hunch as an educated guess based on a large sample-size of historical precedent,' Tito said reassuringly, not content to say five words when he could just as easily say twenty-two. 'The bigger the mainstream gets, the deeper the underground goes. It's one of the only two certainties in this game, as sure as brutal comedown follows glorious high.'

Lottie nodded, just enough to give Tito the impression she remained unconvinced.

'Maarten's intel is solid, my dear ginge,' Tito continues. 'We know that some of my old Superstar DJ rivals have been holding renegade parties since the Public Order Act came in. Your hero Juanita even dragged young Usura along to one of them, which I pretended to turn a blind eye to, but her HeadBand was the window on the scene that we needed.

'The underground's idealism is commendable, and their music too, but there's enough space between those particular grooves to foster free thought, and—'

An urgent buzz rattled Tito's HeadBand, tossed casually aside on the chair at his bedside.

'Looks like it's official,' Tito said, mildly annoyed at the interruption.

Lottie could barely contain her relief, knowing the old 'progressive house is the music they play in heaven' monologue had been just about to hit its stride. (If there was anything she hated more than Tito, it was the rare moments she agreed with him.)

Tito slapped his speaker cups back into place around his ears. '1-6-25 is on.'

He leaned in towards Lottie and took her hands.

'Trust my son with your life,' Tito said. 'Keep your HeadBand on until he tells you to do otherwise. Earn the underground's trust and learn their music's secrets – if EDM ever grows tired, the people will need a new soundtrack.'

Lottie nodded her understanding.

'Once Juanita has been introduced to her playthings, they'll be yours outside of Lockdown hours. After that, we're playing the long game until your mission is complete and her successor emerges.' Tito gulped at the tightness in his throat. 'Out of everything in the world from before, I'm going to miss you most.'

'Oh Tito, you old softie.' Lottie beamed at him. 'I always told you falling for me would be the end of you.'

| **4.06** |

You Are Sleeping

'I'd forgotten what it felt like, you know?' a female voice, on the brink of exhaustion, panted from behind Lottie, lost in her record crate and her guilt – her complicity in what Juanita and the world had become.

She half-turned to regard the broken figure over her shoulder.

Juanita was sprawled across a tattered, filthy futon mattress, folded in half so that the surface moisture of the green room's floor didn't soak through. Her eyes flitted across the ceiling's brickwork. With each boom of the kick drum on the other side of the curtain, specks of dirt and grout dislodged from the cracks and fell to the floor separating the pair.

'I've been insulated from it all,' Juanita continued. She attempted to regulate her shallow, laboured breathing then surrendered, letting her lungs do as they pleased, deciding she deserved to ride the high of her exhaustion. 'Dancing on my own, inside my Silo, all these years.'

'Making us dance alone is the general idea, sister,' Lottie said dismissively, turning back to flick through her records. She took a swig from a military-style canteen and placed it beside the crate. 'Your master might market the Ultraworld as the ultimate VR playground and the Silos as a safety device, but in the end they're just another wall between us all.'

'I wouldn't expect you to understand,' Juanita scoffed. She read the stickers covering Lottie's dilapidated record crate – *'ZERO TOLER-*

ANCE', 'DESTROY THE EGO', 'FUTURE CLASSIC' – and wondered which of Halcyon's releases those catchphrases had been assigned to, and how she'd missed them. 'The high inside the Ultraworld is just so . . . I don't know, so much *cleaner* than out here, you know? When the heart-hands go up it's like hugging a stranger at the end of a "best night ever", except you're hugging billions of strangers and never want to let go. But as a Virtuoso you give up so much . . .'

'Control?' Lottie filled the dead air at the end of Juanita's musings.

'No, that's not it,' Juanita said snippily. Lottie had not only interrupted her stream of consciousness, her smackdown of Virtuoso culture was bang on target.

'I was thinking more of what you said about the electricity in the air,' Juanita said wistfully. 'That "indefinable special something". I mean, I've seen it all, Lotts, before the Storm and now – played to crowds you could only dream of, smoked, swallowed and inhaled things that didn't even exist when I started. And this new ViZar headset Tito showed me – fuck me, just a game changer.'

Lottie allowed herself a smirk. *Thanks for the news flash, Scoop Dogg.* She continued flicking through record sleeves, more out of habit than anything. She knew exactly what was in her crate. Unless someone had come across a stash of 12s they weren't telling her about, no one in the underground had added any fresh wax to their collections in years.

'But being anonymous out there, man,' Juanita continued, waving an arm at the curtain. 'Even if people recognised me they weren't watching my every move, looking for some little flaw in my character to troll me over on the *Inthemix* forums. There's a freedom out there just like when I perform, you know. Time stops and you just express yourself.'

'Fucking "perform"! Can you even hear yourself?' Lottie snapped, pulling her crate closed with a fearsome thud. 'None of that *Dance Dance Revolution* shit you do in the Ultraworld is *real!*'

The unexpected *thwack* shocked Juanita out of her reverie. She dragged herself into a sitting position to match Lottie, who was storming across the room to confront her. Juanita felt the brick wall's soothing cool on her back where the overalls ended, before the clammy heat of Lottie's fingers wrapped around her chin.

'Didn't you see what the boys were doing behind the decks out there, Neets?' Lottie asked. She was crouched beside the misshapen mattress, holding Juanita's sagging head upright. 'That understanding of the room and of each other. When to lift the energy and when to hold it and when to ease back. How sometimes two tracks can blend to create something new and beautiful, and another two can be so discordant when they overlap that you need to mix the old track out before it sucks the whole room out of the moment – and that's okay as well.'

Juanita realised that Lottie's eyes, which appeared black under the rave cave's flashing lights, were a deep brown, focused and persuasive. There wasn't much to Lottie physically – Juanita didn't feel threatened by her like she did by the rise of Kam-E, the 'Brazilian bombshell' Virtuoso, all legs and long dark hair and Lockdown-defying tan – but whatever 'indefinable special something' she possessed was impressing Juanita more as this strange night wore on.

'Everything out there,' Lottie said, releasing Juanita's chin and pointing down the narrow corridor behind her, 'is what people used to spend a lifetime chasing, trying to recapture that same elusive high. These tunes the boys have been dropping aren't just a collection of waveforms, patched together by robots and pumped into the Ultraworld for you to preach empty slogans over. There's real emotion, human sweat and tears and piss and all the rest of it at their core. And even if Halcyon harvests the DNA of every bar of music we've ever produced, that's something their production bots and set-gen algos will never be able to synthesise.'

'But Tito has done more to unify the world—'

'You still don't get it, do you?' Lottie laughed incredulously. She pushed herself up off Juanita's knees and prowled the room. 'Everything that Tito has ever done has been for one cause – making Head-Bands indispensable and increasing his grip on power. And anyone who spends their entire life inside one of his pleasure machines is as blind as the idiots who allowed Tito to get inside our brains'—Lottie tapped her right MIDI implant for emphasis—'in the first place.'

'So what, you bring me down to this party to *save* me, but it's really about ramming some anti-Love Buzz propaganda down my throat?' Juanita asked. The impish redhead was revealing herself, alright, as a sanctimonious cow, much to Juanita's disappointment. They'd shared so many dancefloor moments over the course of the night that she hadn't been merely impressed – she'd begun to like her. 'Please, tell me more about Tito's agenda since you're such a fucking expert on how the world works.'

Lottie crouched again, holding a finger of silence across Juanita's lips. 'Stop me if you've heard this one before, sister,' Lottie said, resuming her sardonic drawl. 'A sixteen-year-old girl goes out dancing with her girls for the first time ever, ready to have the time of their lives on the dancefloor in front of the DJ they all adore. Except one of them gets so sideways she's separated from her friends at some stage, and then she comes to in a strange room with a strange older man. There's a voice in her head saying this is where she's meant to be but a nagging feeling deep inside that something's horribly wrong.'

'How do you know about—'

'Uh!' Lottie clasped Juanita's lips closed. 'You need to hear all of this.'

Juanita nervously tugged the sweat-drenched ponytail resting on her shoulder.

'This girl is whisked away from her home, shown the rudimentals of DJing and sent out onto the circuit. Every week the scene bears less and less resemblance to what drew her to it in the first place as EDM grows more and more dominant.' Lottie paused for breath as a chorus of cheers greeted a breakdown in the adjoining rave cave. She clamped Juanita's opening lips shut between her thumb and forefinger. 'Carbon-copy setlists are ripped straight from the Halcyon streaming platform's Top 10 hit parade and the kids in the crowd don't know that it's all a sham, and even if they did, even if they thought to question why a certain Superstar DJ's star-maker move was throwing cake into the crowd while his DJ set mixed itself in the background, what would it matter?'

The invective leapt from Lottie's tongue. 'They knew they were inheriting a world that'd be cooked by the time their kids were adults, so, in the grand scheme of the universe, why should they give a fuck about something so inconsequential?'

Lottie unbuckled Juanita's lips. The collagen she'd had pumped into them as a thirtieth birthday gift to herself automatically reset them into duckface form.

'That's our job, isn't it?' Juanita asked. She shrugged. 'Helping them not think?'

'Our job is to open their minds, not bolt them shut, but I digress,' Lottie raged. 'Remember how pro sport was banned after HeadBands started detecting brain damage symptoms in wearers? Next minute, the One World festival is filling the empty stadiums every weekend of the year. Then the man who has changed your life says there is more change coming – that you're about to enter a wonderful world of Drop Discs and starburst waterfalls and glowstaffs that swat silver orbs out of the virtual sky. Then one Sunday afternoon the sky rains fire, and you think escaping to the Ultraworld is the only hope you've got left.'

'How do you know all that?' Juanita demanded through gritted teeth. 'I've never t—'

'It's not all about you, Juanita, even if that's exactly what Tito wants you to think . . . wants *everyone* to think,' Lottie said furiously, her pigtails shaking.

She gripped Juanita's shoulders. Tiny chunks of ceiling grit fell through Juanita's eyelashes. She blinked the dirt away. Lottie's eyes were locked on hers.

'That sixteen-year-old girl's DJ hero was you, and that girl was me.'

'*What?*'

'I was picked up off the floor of Centennial Park by Tito just like you were, to spread this disease disguised as music, and just before the Storm I was supposed to team up with you—'

'Bullshit! Tito knows Juanita only plays alone.'

'He also knows the power of a good partnership. Think about it – Sasha and Digweed, Kemistry and Storm, Kenobi and Shureshock . . .'

'The Stafford Brothers and Timmy Trumpet?' Juanita interjected.

'Sure, if that's what it takes to get you on board,' Lottie sighed with exasperation. 'But it's just like the boys warming up out there – apart they're amazing but as a team, they're invincible.'

'Lottie!' Robbie called.

Juanita heard his footfalls pounding down the corridor before she saw him, sliding to a stop at the entrance. His smiley face shirt was soaked through, gripping the pectoral muscles she knew so well. His bleached-blond knots had been striped with lashings of red and blue hair spray. Juanita thought he looked more like himself now than he had on any of the endless nights she'd set Dav to work on him. 'Lottie! It's nearly 4 am, miss. You're up.'

Lottie stood up swiftly, grabbing Juanita's arms and hauling her to her feet. The smaller girl's strength stunned her, particularly given they'd spent most of the past seven hours heads down, hands up between the rave cave's moss-covered walls. Juanita willed her third wind to kick in.

'It's bigger than that and it's bigger than us,' Lottie shouted, putting Juanita into Roberto's waiting hands and grabbing her crate's top handle. 'And now another kid needs our help before it becomes too big for any of us to do anything about it, if it's not too big already.'

Lottie wrapped a pair of flimsy headphones around her neck. Their circular silver earpieces clung to the black head-strap courtesy of several generations of white cloth tape.

'But there's still three hours until Lockdown is over up top, so until then,' Lottie shouted, punching the curtain off its rails as she entered the rave-cave corridor, *let's get loose!*

| 4.07 |

Hugs 'N Kisses

From Juanita's vantage point behind the rave cave's makeshift booth, the DJ duo's bodies appeared only as silhouettes. She peered through their legs, past the tangle of audio and power cables dangling down from their workstation. Layer upon layer of dry ice obscured the faces gathered before them. Rapid-fire strobes gave the illusion the dance-floor was trapped in a slow-motion instant replay. The people raised hopeful spirit fingers, cutting shapes through the laser fanning out from directly above Juanita's head. The laser's green ray cast itself wide across the cavern's expanse, gradually tilting upwards until it formed a false ceiling running parallel with the railway-tunnel-to-nowhere's semicircular roof.

The kick drum's uncompromising assault suddenly subsided. The gentlest murmur, a barely audible pulse of sub-bass, pushed the laser-kissed masses through the fatigue they surely shared with Juanita, whose hip flexors and lower back ached under a form of RSI she'd forgotten existed.

Lottie took Juanita's hand and climbed up to the stage via a step fashioned from a pile of bricks. Sampled found sounds chimed in around the synthesised ones, giving Juanita the impression she'd walked into a primary school at playtime. The undercurrent of school-yard noises – footsteps down echo-chamber hallways, the excited titter of conversations, the occasional jarring shriek of a budding attention-seeker – settled comfortably into a frequency spectrum well above the filtered bass pulse. Gusts of white noise (*listen to the hiss*) gathered around a searing three-note synth lead – unsettling, foreboding, bordering on prescient. A dark, arpeggiated synthesiser melody rolled up the centre, unfurling like a missive from the Grim Reaper.

Even before Love Buzz, Juanita's sets had always ended with an uplifting message to the world. This closing track felt more like a warning, a distress signal from a distant galaxy whose inhabitants feared a strike.

The bald DJ turned to Lottie, his face radiating the same glee Juanita had seen when she entered the cave seven hours earlier. 'Hugs n' kisses, baby!' he gushed, wrapping a sticky arm around Lottie's shoulders. His T-shirt had started the night grey. Now, drenched in sweat, the distressed cotton hung off him in shades of black.

His counterpart couldn't break himself free of the track's spellbinding breakdown. Each flick of the DJ mixer's controls sent a jolt through his jiggling hips, as if he weren't throwing down other people's records but generating the sounds himself. His fingers recoiled from the console's knobs and sliders with each tweak. 'Playing with hot knobs,' Usura had called it. 'When the DJ isn't actually doing anything but wants it to look like they are.' Except this guy actually was, the sound manipulated subtly each time the unseen shock jolted his hands skyward.

Lottie surveyed the scene, nodding tacit approval, her record crate in hand. 'The old classics have still got it, hey?'

'Nothing but bombs all night long and the caners have lapped them up like it was 2006 again – when bombs were bombs and gurns were gurns, baby.' He laughed, flashing a knowing smile and a quick 'Hello' at Juanita. 'Closing slamfest is all set up for you now.'

'Three hours of power in the temple of chug, crony,' Lottie squawked in his ear, losing her footing on the rear edge of the stage and instinctively reaching an arm out to Juanita.

'The only way I know—'

A sudden blast of drumfire reverberated down the rave cave from the far entrance. Distant screams somehow cut through the PA's wall of sound.

Juanita's mouth formed words – *What the fuck?* – but no sound came out.

The green laser's sweeping eye caught a ripple of dust and dirt surging towards them, as if the white noise build-up coming out of the speakers had invited the tunnel's century of surface grime to the party. Punters at the far end of the tunnel started sprinting towards the stage; just a few, at first, and then the sprint became a stampede.

Juanita glimpsed something – no, *some things* – flying smoothly, stealthily under the camouflage of the slow-moving haze. Adult screams joined the innocent childish shrieks already ricocheting around the rave cave from the sound system's distant schoolyard.

A dozen beams of red light cut through the smog, like theatre followspots. The floating things revealed themselves as drones, cobalt-coloured and shaped like miniature sharks. The shafts of light weren't solid and singular, but made up of hundreds of tiny, red pinpricks, fired from the eye-shaped recesses either side of the drones' sleek fuselages. Each of their light beams combined to form the shape of a featureless human face, like a neutral theatre mask, which the drones traced across the mounting chaos in search of prey. Countless red beams, two dozen or more, swept the room. The wingspan of the lead drone expanded half a metre either side of its shell and its fins sprouted skeletal claws.

'Collection drones!' the bearded DJ turned on Lottie, spitting desperation in her face, his music's spell on himself finally broken. He nodded in Juanita's direction. 'And this is why I told you not to bring this glorified mime in the first place!'

The lead drone's facial-recognition projector crept down the tunnel wall to their right. From several hundred metres away, it locked onto the face of a woman near the stage and lifted her, frozen, until she hung limply from the wall, like a coat on a clothes hook.

'We took all the right precautions,' Lottie hissed. 'Someone's sold us out again.'

'This might have something to do with it,' Juanita said. She slung the Gucci from her back and meekly offered up the HeadBand she'd stuffed inside. 'Dav said to hold onto it.'

Long crimson levers cut across the rave cave in search of prey. Body after body was lifted skyward from the dust cloud enveloping the dancefloor and thrust towards the stage. Seven ravers dangled from the wall of speakers flanking the DJ booth. Their lifeless figures rattled like chains, shaken by the kick drums thundering through the bass bins behind them. Juanita watched the dancefloor's remaining population swirl chaotically before her, frantically searching for an escape route that wasn't there. The shafts of light seemed to become tractor beams, slowly drawing the seven drones towards their respective captives. Smoke poured from the crosshatched faces; Koori and Caucasian, Indian and Asian, all barbecued black like well-done steaks. The skin on the nearest captive's face was pouring down her neck like melting chocolate ice-cream. Juanita recognised the flowing black dress, and that long shock of white hair. Spinny Lady.

'I knew Dav was too good to be true,' the bearded DJ fumed, pulling Lottie and Juanita down behind the DJ booth. He felt around his neck for a cloth respirator mask, its white surface covered in black dots and squiggles, and pulled it over his mouth and nose.

'He's fucked us, but he's got us what we need,' Lottie said, clutching Juanita's HeadBand hand tight. 'You really think the mask will scramble their sensors?'

'You two need to scram,' the bald DJ said, ducking his head back below the trestle table as a red circle of light grazed his polished dome. He stuffed a battered pair of black headphones into his own record crate and slammed the lid shut. The record on the turntable was still blowing up the room as a growing armada of collection drones set about picking off the ravers, one by one.

'We'll get the other important cargo to the recovery.' Peeling Lottie's fingers from her record crate's handle, he slipped a scuffed, silver mini Maglite in its place.

'Got mine, Scotty,' Lottie said, patting the front of her overalls as she pecked his clean-shaven cheek. 'And don't worry, Goo.' She stared the goateed DJ down. 'We're getting this shit done.'

Lottie leapt off the stage and scampered down the corridor towards the green room. Still paralysed by the unfolding horror, Juanita's foot felt around for the makeshift brick step behind her. Goo locked tired eyes with Scotty, decades of understanding passing between them as the crowd's terrified screams overpowered their epic climactic tune.

'Yeah, mate, I know,' Scotty said with a smile, gripping his friend's shoulder.

Juanita heard Lottie screaming her name from the corridor behind her. Scotty stretched the elastic of his own respirator around his ears. His mask, a hand-drawn cat's nose and whiskers, snapped onto his face.

Juanita could only just make out his parting words through the pandemonium. 'At least we smashed the place on our way out.'

| 4.08 |

Dead Eyes Opened

'Put the fucking thing on now!' screeched Lottie when Juanita finally bumbled her way into the green room. 'And switch to night-vision mode. Quickly!'

Lottie ferociously swatted through a stack of empty cardboard boxes to the left of the entryway, revealing the shreds of another white curtain over the entrance to a corridor running parallel to the one they'd been using. Juanita felt herself sway under a tidal wave of confusion and exhaustion. She longed to rid herself of Lottie and wash away this descent into madness in her steam room, then slip her helmet on, lie back in her recliner and let Love Buzz's warm caress swallow her whole.

'Juanita, *please,*' Lottie pleaded. She urgently waved Juanita towards their escape route. 'It's a long haul but I promise we'll be safe through here.'

Juanita slipped her HeadBand back over her eyes and zealously slapped her speaker cups into place. MIDI implants fused with metal frames. Connection to her brain's electricity-generating neurons established, Juanita's HeadBand powered itself back up.

HeadBand, engage night-vision mode.

Juanita grabbed Lottie's water canteen from the floor and swigged greedily as Lottie cast aside the tattered curtain. She gripped the back of Lottie's denim overalls, curiously sweat-free. Lottie veered them left down a walkway barely wide enough for the women to slide along sideways, then turned right into a wider passage. The beam of Lottie's Maglite bounced around Juanita's field of vision like a glowstaff being wielded by a drunk. Their surroundings otherwise gave off a grainy glow under night-vision mode, revealing brick walls, cement floors and a flat ceiling. Ahead, their escape path was clear.

Suddenly, the bottom-end thud from the adjacent chamber filtered down to a rumbling throb, before stuttering to a standstill like a system error.

'*This gathering is in direct contravention of the Public Order Act 2023,*' a scathing, robotic male voice, as intimidating as an army of Dr Who's Daleks, rattled out of the rave cave and down their escape route. '*Disperse immediately. Repeat: disperse immediately.*'

Once the echo of the drone faded, all Juanita could hear was their own shuffling footsteps, punctuated by shrill cries of pain, like rats climbing over each other to escape fire. She tried to ignore the chafing where her legs met the crotch of her overalls. *Thank fuck I ditched the catsuit.*

Lottie led them briskly to the left, then down a narrow shaft via a tradesman's ladder. 'Careful, it gets a little slippery from here.'

Five metres below, they reached a small platform with six pairs of black rubber gumboots neatly standing in a row along the closest wall. An additional pair, attached to bright yellow waders, lay crumpled beside them. Water steadily trickled along below.

'Put a pair on over your Volleys,' Lottie ordered, slipping into a too-large pair.

'I'm not setting foot in anyone's piss, shit or tampons,' Juanita protested. 'Not even if that fly-fishing get-up there has a built-in force-field.'

'These are drains not sewers, you silly woman,' Lottie barked. She plucked the noise-cancelling plugs from her ears and tossed them into the bubbling stream. 'And we're not the only ones who know this escape route – one of these pairs of boots was meant for your buddy, Dav.'

She took a step over the edge and landed ankle deep in the drain's water flow. 'Those System Seven collectors can get through any space we can,' Lottie said, walking upstream without turning to face Juanita. 'So unless you're okay with that pretty face of yours being chargrilled, I suggest we get a move on.'

Lottie navigated the drains with impressive dexterity, feet hopping either side of the gentle stream, while Juanita sloshed clumsily through. Earlier, night-vision mode had given her apartment the appearance of a psychedelic nightmare-scape. In the drains, it brought everything to life in glorious green monochrome. Clusters of limestone spikes jutted from the ceiling. Coral-like formations randomly sprouted from the walls. Sporadic patches of water glowed vivid green.

Lottie assured Juanita this wasn't radioactive waste but a form of plankton called *Noctiluca Scintillans*. Glowstick manufacturers had mimicked their bioluminescent chemistry, apparently, before Halcyon's pixel pushers replicated the planktons' light even more vividly inside the Ultraworld. Juanita hadn't seen such otherworldly beauty since she'd snorkelled in a small cove tucked in behind Phi Phi Ley's Maya Bay in 2015, years before her fellow '#blessed' Instatourists hashtagged the jewel in Thailand's tourism crown to the brink of death. ('About fucking time!' Tito had roared triumphantly in bed the morning the island's indefinite closure was announced, to prevent ecological disaster. 'Someone's finally put the planet above their bottom line.')

After what felt like kilometres of running at what now constituted her fastest pace, Juanita caught up to her guide. 'It's so clean down here,' she observed. 'And there's not even that much water.'

'It's been another dry summer Outside,' Lottie answered dismissively, annoyed at Juanita's slack pace. 'Alright, we've reached the hard bit.'

Lottie pointed to a flight of stairs rising above them. Each of the fifteen steps was two metres wide and close to a metre deep. Their immense span was dwarfed by the tunnel containing them, stretching out beyond the peripheral vision of Juanita's HeadBand.

The intimidating staircase reminded Juanita of the trio of escalators that used to carry weekend thrillseekers up from the innards of Kings Cross Station and back once their night was done, before most of central Sydney was legislated into a fun-free zone – unless it had a casino in it. The 3 am Lockout, the Public Order Act, the 9 pm Lockdown . . . if she didn't know firsthand the extent of Tito's wiles, the way he manipulated foolish minds so slyly they implemented his ideas in the belief they were theirs, Juanita would've been stunned his slice of the EDM scene had not only seen off every challenge but thrived.

'But the good news is we're nearly out of here. Just follow my lead.' Her energy seemingly boundless, Lottie sprinted at the steps. She leapt right onto a small foothold half a metre above ground, then banked left, setting down in the middle of the first step.

Juanita mirrored her gracelessly up the left-hand side. She landed on the first step with a clumsy thud, scouring a layer of skin from the heel of her right hand on the abrasive surface. The furious scowl of Ms Gillies, the gymnastics coach who'd mercilessly flogged Juanita until she'd cracked, aged thirteen, reared in her mind. Juanita leapt from step to step, the repressed memories of old training drills flooding back. By the time she reached the top step, her quads and glutes sang a two-part harmony of pain.

Juanita deactivated night-vision mode but still struggled to blink away the brightness of the well-lit chamber. A wall loomed twenty metres ahead, beneath another chamber emitting a dull, eerie light. Lottie had already scaled half the wall's height. She hung off an iron ladder cemented into the wall and beckoned Juanita to follow. From a foot-wide concrete channel to Lottie's right, a waterfall of wastewater spilled over the edge.

'Hurry, they're getting closer.'

Juanita could feel the hum of the collection drones echoing up the tunnel system behind her. They signalled to each other, like a chorus of cicadas operating cordless drills, as they bore down on their targets. She dragged her heavy legs across the platform and pulled herself up the ladder, her fingernails collecting crumbling concrete and moss and rust as she hauled herself up.

Lottie and Juanita were inside the base of an enormous cement cylinder, its ceiling at least twenty-five metres above them. The canal powering the waterfall bisected the room's ten-metre diameter, passing beyond the cylinder into another tunnel with no end in sight. To their left a spiral staircase wound around a thick metal support pole. It attached itself to the chamber's wall halfway up before continuing its spiral upwards to a footbridge hugging the wall opposite the fugitives. A rusted fireman's pole stood parallel to the stairs. Above the walkway, a fluorescent light tube highlighted the blemishes of the room: water stains dripped down roughly rendered concrete walls; the tags of previous visitors, sprayed loud and proud in aerosol paint – *'PREDATOR'* and *'LURKER'* and *'CAVE CLAN'*.

Juanita saw a gunmetal grey door at the end of the walkway. The hatch-wheel handle attached to the chamber's only exit appeared to be fastened tight.

'What is this place?'

'A water treatment plant, maybe,' Lottie said. Her slight shoulders heaved beneath her overalls' suspenders. 'Just gotta get up those stairs and we're out.'

Lottie pointed towards the door above them. Juanita doubled over, her shoulders burning as badly as her thighs. The insistent purr of their pursuers grew louder, until hundreds of miniscule red-dots shot out of the darkness below, darting across the abrasive concrete wall beside the spiral stairs.

'Hurry!' Lottie shrieked.

Juanita fell into step behind the shorter girl as she began climbing the circular metal staircase. Additional beams of angry crimson kept adding themselves to the array crisscrossing the cylinder's walls.

'Keep your chin tucked tight to your chest,' Lottie screamed above clattering footfalls. 'Don't let the scanners see your face.'

Sweat and thick, protruding seams shredded the already tender skin around the crotch of Juanita's overalls. Nausea snaked through her head and gut. As she rounded the sixth swivel of the spiral stairs, the sand-blasted railing tore chunks of flesh from her left palm. Then she was racing across the swaying footbridge, the room dozens of metres below. She felt the large blisters fermenting on both heels burst simultaneously. Lottie was five metres ahead, straining against the hatch-wheel handle. A tiny shark-like figure appeared over the waterfall's ledge below, then another.

'We made sure this thing opened, but it won't fucking budge!' Lottie screamed through tears. Juanita braced herself against the railing and gripped the wheel either side of Lottie's hands.

'*Juanita, darling,*' Matthias van Dijk's silky suave voice boomed out of the lead drone as it zoomed skywards. '*Are you sure your new friend has your best interests at heart?*'

'Fuck, fuck, fuck!' Lottie roared.

The hatch-wheel stuck solid.

'*Being seen at this protest is not a good look for the company, but come back to Halcyon Tower now and I promise you'll have my full support.*'

'Arrgghh!'

Juanita's primal scream stung Lottie's right ear as the Virtuoso threw her full weight behind her work. The hatch-wheel turned a full rotation counter-clockwise, then another. Red pinpricks of light danced across the pair's limbs, seeking a face-shaped target. Hovering above the far end of the walkway, the drone squadron leader oozed robophobia.

One more spin and the door creaked open just wide enough for the women to slip through. They scrambled into a short, pitch-black corridor, lit only by the drone's prying scanners. Lottie pulled the hatch shut, catching the edge of Juanita's backpack before she could get all the way through.

'*Get it off me, get if off me!*' Juanita shrieked, shaking her arms free of the straps and brushing them off like she'd just walked through cobwebs at the mouth of a giant spider's lair.

Lottie wrenched the wheel handle closed, spinning it hard left until it could be forced no further.

'*Fuck it!*' Lottie's voice hissed through the darkness. 'I've dropped my fucking torch.'

Crouching down on her haunches beside Lottie, Juanita braced herself against the escape hatch for impact, rough concrete grazing her knees. Once more with feeling, her throbbing ears and temples sang backup for her body's chorus of pain. A moment's silence, then the clunk of the drone's metal snout ramming the other side of the door.

Juanita screamed, and screamed again when claw-like fingers began scratching at the hatch-wheel handle. The clunking sound multiplied, like golf-ball sized hailstones hammering a tin roof. Lottie clutched the wheel. It held fast.

'They can't grip the handle,' Lottie gasped. She grabbed Juanita by her armpits and tugged her to her feet. 'There should be another door behind us. Can you see it?'

Night-vision engaged, Juanita edged cautiously towards a sliver of light creeping out from beneath a slatted timber door, while the metal hatch kept the battering-ram drones at bay. She grasped the brass handle and swung it towards them.

Juanita shrieked again as a wall of reeds fell into the door opening.

'What the fuck! Lottie, is that Outside?'

Lottie brushed past, ignoring the plant life. They were on a cement path, smooth and polished. It formed a one-metre perimeter around a curved wall of brown bricks and white mortar, which looked to Juanita like the base of a larger structure. They sidestepped a wrought-iron bench seat backed up against the brick structure and pushed ahead. To their right the wall of grass, at least six-feet tall, reached out for Juanita's face. She expected to be overcome by the early stages of grass itch but to her surprise felt nothing at all.

She was instead overwhelmed by the freshness, the invigorating daybreak smell – like a sporting field before anyone had disturbed the autumn dew. The agony wracking her body, the dank and the damp of the drains all over her, the discomfort of the rodents scurrying across her feet into the safety of the long grass; it was all absorbed by the taste of cool, crisp air.

'Lottie, where the fuck are we?'

Lottie pushed her past another bench seat and into a small clearing. Constant flashes of light again turned Juanita's viewfinder into an over-saturated, impenetrable white wall.

HeadBand, disengage night-vision mode.

Juanita's surroundings crackled a brilliant, fiery red, turning Lottie's face to molten liquid under her sky-blue viewfinder's glare. Thunder exploded through her speaker cups.

'Aren't you fucking done trying to kill us?!'

'Come on!'

Juanita couldn't believe what was happening. They'd escaped the drones only to land Outside, with no rat runs or spray-painter's suits or OxyPure units to protect them.

Lottie led them up a white and maroon timber staircase into a hexagonal rotunda. She brushed aside a thick covering of spiderwebs and strode confidently onto the fake lawn. Sucking in shallow breaths as she followed in Lottie's footsteps, Juanita involuntarily ducked at the sound of each lava-lightning strike, like she was retreating from a war-zone in a hail of crossfire. Juanita saw that they weren't the only ones seeking shelter – from the furthest railing, two possums glared at the interlopers with wide-eyed shock before taking turns scurrying up tim-ber uprights and onto the safety of the rotunda's roof. They galloped across its corrugated iron surface with the ferocity of Clydesdales and leapt into the gargantuan Moreton Bay fig tree, which hunched pro-tectively over three-quarters of the rotunda. Lottie dismissed another section of cobwebs on the railing opposite the stairs and grinned tri-umphantly at Juanita, whose jaw dropped at the view from the other side of their safe haven from the Storm.

A field of long grass swirled ferociously below Juanita, like a sea of small whirlpools, mirroring the violence of the storm-covered skies above. Thunderclouds erupted so constantly it was impossible to define single claps. Through bustling, low-flying clouds Juanita could just make out the crumbling ruins of apartment blocks on the other side of the water, choppy and completely covered in whitecaps. To her right, almost obscured by another of Observatory Hill's Moreton Bay fig population, the remains of Sydney Harbour Bridge were under sustained assault from several cloudbursts spewing lava lightning from above. The four brick pylons on either end of the coat hanger had all but crumbled to dust, while sections of the metal framework had evaporated out of existence. Inexplicably, the blacktop connecting Sydney's CBD with North Sydney and beyond was intact.

Juanita's HeadBand viewfinder filled with tears. 'How could we let this happen?'

'I ask myself this every time I come up here,' Lottie said from behind her. Juanita felt fiddling at the side of her head, then gasped as Lottie's palms smashed her speaker cups.

'Lottie wait—'

Lottie tore the HeadBand off. Juanita's words froze on the end of her tongue. The chill of the summer dawn's light felt like frost biting her eyes, which blinked disbelievingly at what they saw.

Juanita stared out across a vastly different parkland than what she'd seen from inside her HeadBand. Observatory Hill's grass was no longer tall and wildly undulating, but thick and green and closely cropped to the ground. Birdsong surrounded the rotunda, the gentle call-and-response of countless species soundtracking the butterflies fluttering gently above the windswept vista. To her right the Sydney Harbour Bridge stood in all its glory, its coat-hanger arch fully intact beneath streaks of little fluffy clouds in a magnificent deep blue sky, the horizon tinted with a red and gold sunrise.

In thirty-five years of life before the Storm, Juanita had seen this view dozens of times. In the thousand days since, she'd seen it behind Tito when he Vid-Linked her from his Halcyon Tower ready room. She'd assumed it was a screensaver. The wafting fresh of the grass and the leaves, the music twittering from the trees engaged senses she thought had vanished. The wondrous sight, the smells and sounds eased the dull ache of dread, which had consumed her like a fever forever.

Lottie flung Juanita's HeadBand into the Moreton Bay fig tree. One of the possums took the nose clip between its teeth and scurried towards the tree's uppermost branches.

'Feeling like a tourist in your home town – how good.' Lottie beamed. She filled her lungs with oxygen, then exhaled with a flourish.

Juanita felt a comforting arm wrap around her and squeeze her waist.

Virtuoso and DJ, star and disciple, looked out on Sydney Harbour, postcard-perfect and bereft of human activity, as if a landscape artist had frozen the deserted cityscape in time.

'Now doesn't *this* just change everything?'

THE DROP

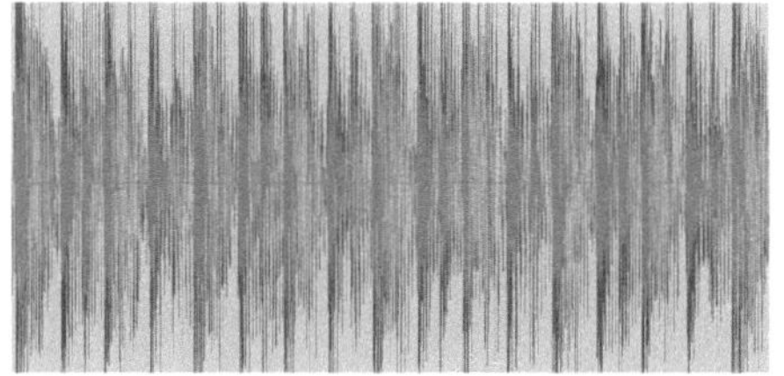

| 5.01 |

If Everybody Looked the Same

'Ken-tar-o!' Satoshi Ishii bellowed from the head of the dining table. He licked his right index finger and reached half a metre in front of his face then swatted to his left. Inside his viewfinder, a newspaper page visible only to him turned over. Though the damp finger wasn't strictly necessary, some pre-HeadBand habits had proven more difficult to shake than others.

'This isn't up for debate, *suekko*.'

Stefanie Ishii winced from behind the kitchen island to Satoshi's right. Even without his full force behind it, Satoshi's voice thundered through the apartment. And her husband was the only man alive who could make a pet word for 'youngest child' sound threatening.

Stefanie poured her blender's contents – a thick, yellowy orange sludge – into a tall glass. Its zesty tang overpowered every other smell in the room. It didn't look like much, but Stefanie swore by her 'world famous' (according to her) citrus protein shake to any Block 19 resident who'd listen. Whenever their monthly food ration from Halcyon was running low, Stefanie had confided in Mrs O'Flaherty downstairs, she would secretly skip meals to keep her children fed. Her world-famous shakes – Vitamin C tablets crushed into syntho milk and yoghurt, topped up with ice cubes then blended – then became the cornerstone of her diet. One alone was enough to sustain her through a ten-hour shift on the rice-cracker factory floor. And they tasted delicious – more satisfying than a month of syntho-cola spiders, no matter how much her twins argued otherwise.

'Had enough to eat, dear?'

Satoshi's breakfast plate was empty but for an assortment of crumbs and a corner of dark-brown bread, slathered thick with dairy-flavoured spread and black paste. Absentmindedly, his left hand felt around the plate until it closed in on the remaining morsel. His eyes never strayed from the newspaper, flickering like an apparition between his eyes and the rest of the apartment.

'Your mother and I slogged our guts out all week for this day off together,' Satoshi muttered. He stuffed the final piece of toast into his mouth and spoke while he chewed. 'So you either go to childcare like you're supposed to, or we lock your HeadBand out of Love Buzz while the rest of us watch Juanita tonight.'

'But, *Daaaaad!*'

Kentaro's whine was clearly audible from his station behind the closed bathroom door, across the apartment to Stefanie's right. *His father's son in every way.* She grinned. *And just as stubborn.*

Satoshi shook his head with dismay. 'If the eight-year-old's so grown up,' he grumbled to himself, 'he can take my place at the factory tomorrow and see how he likes it.'

On the other side of the apartment Toca stormed down the hallway with Kai in hot pursuit, past the bathroom door and into the lounge area towards the front door. Gone were the Sailor Moon wigs, shelved as soon as they'd beaten Lockdown with seconds to spare the previous night. The twins' haircuts were identical – clipped close to their neck and face, like army cadets – and their mother was determined they'd remain that way until the great Doonside Tech headlice scare of February 2028 was over. Unlike their Love Buzz outfits, today's uniforms were matching: form-fitting white business shirts buttoned up to the top, black polyester trousers and black canvas slip-on shoes, issued by Halcyon Industries to all teen workers at the start of each calendar year.

Each carried a blue nylon backpack, front pocket bearing the Halcyon logo, slung across opposing shoulders.

'Bye, Mum! Bye, Dad!' Toca cried, not daring to meet her mother's eye as she opened the front door and raced through it.

'What about your breakfast?' Satoshi brayed. He licked his finger and turned another page without looking over.

Stefanie's eyes narrowed suspiciously.

'No time,' Kai said breathlessly, colliding awkwardly with the back-rest of their bright-red three-seater sofa before following Toca through the front door. 'If we don't shuttle now, we'll be late for work.'

Kai slammed the door shut behind him. His sister leapt with fright.

'What'd you do that for?' Toca pushed frantically at the middle lift's down arrow.

'It was an accident!' Kai hissed.

The lift doors opened. 'Come on.' Kai grabbed the crook of Toca's elbow and dragged her inside.

The lift-bound sax player struck up his exuberant refrain. As the doors closed, an arm unexpectedly thrust itself through the gap.

'Not so fast, you two.'

The heavy doors screeched to a stop either side of the white terry-towel-clad limb, then whirred smoothly again once their trajectory reversed.

Stefanie Ishii stood outside the lift, fists on hips in her best *You've made your mother really mad this time* pose. Her left foot impatiently tapped the lift lobby's yellow and white tiles. Her eyes darted from twin to twin. There was no self-deprecation. She looked distinctly unimpressed.

Kai's favourite sax player continued his merry melody.

The twins' mother pulled her robe's belt tight around her waist and slowly, pointedly began tying a knot, exaggerating every movement so that each rustle of the old, rough fabric cut sharply through the silence. Satisfied with her handiwork, Stefanie fixed her eyes on Kai's left hand, clinging to his backpack's shoulder strap. She looked up. Target acquired.

'Do you have something you'd like to tell me, *Toca?*'

'No!' Kai said guiltily. He racked his brain for a retort worthy of his twin. 'Should I?'

'Mr Banerjee seems to think you spent half the night in the lift,' the twins' mother said sternly. 'So if you can't outsmart him, maybe you're not half as clever as you think you are.'

She really is going to wig out on us now, Toca thought.

Kai gulped. *Yep, this is over before it started.*

Stefanie's best attempt at a withering glare dissolved into a look of bemusement. She shook her head, as if to say *What am I going to do with you two?*

'I don't know what you pair are up to and I don't care to,' Stefanie said. She reached across the threshold and straightened Toca's tie. Kai's breathing returned to normal. 'As long as your father won't be reading about you when his newspaper arrives tomorrow.'

Once the doors slid shut, the twins hurriedly switched which shoulder they carried their backpacks over, completing the transformation into each other that had begun when Kai had switched their HeadBands in the lift the previous evening. Toca felt for Kai's hand and interlocked her fingers with his. The twins descended down the tower block in stark silence. Even Kai's sax-playing friend took his fingers off the valves, maintaining a respectful quiet until the ding of the lift reaching the car park set him off again.

'Are you sure you want to do this?' Toca asked her brother.

Kai was not sure. He'd followed Juanita through it all, dreamt of the day he'd be called up by Tito to join her. Now that day had finally come, he couldn't quite believe what he was going to do next.

'Too late to turn back now,' Kai said. 'Just try to look a little less cha-lant.'

'Nonchalant then?'

'Better.'

The twins exited the lift and walked briskly across the car park.

'Poor Mum,' Toca sighed. 'Dad is going to lose his shit.'

She dragged Kai into the tunnel towards the Three-Way. Sunday morning's foot traffic was typically dense and raucous. The twins were dressed identically to the other teenage boys and girls bustling past them on their way to work. Like their peers across the world, they'd been assigned to a work detail on their fourteenth birthday, pulling eight-hour shifts every Sunday at Doonside Tech's childcare centre – a compulsory initiation for all citizens at the start of their track into Halcyon's workforce. The one-day-a-week childcare assignment had been devised to give the adult population a day of respite from the mundanity of their working week. Whatever Satoshi and Stefanie Ishii got up to on their day off, they rarely shared the details with Kentaro and the twins.

Not that it mattered. After Tito's revelations the previous night that he'd been spying on him, Kai suspected the teen job initiative was just a front, another component of Halcyon's ruthless assessment of Survivors' teen progeny, dressed up as a reward for their unwitting adult workforce.

The twins had been among the earliest babysitters set to work. On September 1, exactly three months after the Storm struck on 1-6-25, the Ishiis had awoken to the news the world had reopened for business overnight. Matthias van Dijk announced that schools would teach again. Scientists, engineers, teachers and doctors were declared VIP citizens for life. Public servants filled the clerical roles: distributing monthly allowances, ensuring syntho rations were re-upped in a timely manner, all in the hope they'd be bumped up from purgatory to the VIP tier. The remaining adults, the Premiums, would find themselves in the lifelong employ of Halcyon's essential service industries – food processing, manufacturing, maintenance – until they could work no more.

A young man and woman Kai recognised as a former 'glamour couple' of Doonside Tech tromped disconsolately past, baby stroller rattling in front of them, trapped in a teenage wasteland of their own making. 'Peak time, all the time, is about more than just partying,' Satoshi rammed the point home repeatedly to the twins. 'It's the recipe for success in every part of your life.'

It was why he insisted they tackle their school and childcare assignments alike with equal diligence. Fail at both and you were consigned to a lifetime on the scrapheap of manual labour in the food factories or drone maintenance camps, he said. Only if you excelled in your schooling, selflessly cared for the next generation at childcare and fully absorbed the HeadBand's offerings, Satoshi preached, could you ever hope to rise above your station and enter the VIP academies. ('I feel ashamed that it's the best you and your brother can ever hope for,' Kai overheard Stefanie telling Toca one night, her voice breaking underneath a steady trickle of tears.)

Toca took Kai's hand, grounding him back in the present.

'What does this Martin—'

'*Maar*-ten,' Kai corrected her.

'Ungghh!' Toca groaned. 'What does this *Martin* look like anyway?'

'More kempt than anyone else here,' Kai said. 'You'll know him when you see him.'

Kai glided through the tunnel like it was only Toca's sweaty hand wrapped tight around his preventing him from floating away. Since 1-6-25, Stefanie had drummed into the twins that there was a world beyond Doonside and the towers and the production line that employed her and their father. If they pursued medicine or the sciences, they could land themselves an apartment in the Green Square Cluster or, even better, among the Upper VIP of Kings Cross or the CBD.

'The Love Inn will be right up the road, if you play your cards right,' Stefanie told Kai whenever he complained about suiting up for childcare. That task suited Toca's 'heal the world' ambitions, but Kai had grander desires – to earn his own room in Love Inn beside Juanita herself.

Kai could sense the sub-audible hum of Kam-E's EDM sermon, delivered from a Silo nestled somewhere deep in the wreckage of São Paulo. The hum wasn't confined to his speaker cups. The Halcyon logo-shaped speakers dotting the tunnel walls either side of him added some body to the synths and cymbals gently caressing his ears on the lowest volume setting. Kai imagined the speaker network would wrap itself around the planet several times over if every cable link of bass boxes and tweeters was ever laid out in a row.

For the first time since Kam-E's debut a year or so prior, Kai hadn't kept a viewfinder window open on her nimble avatar's routine. He was about to deviate from the only course he'd ever known. This was no time for distractions.

'He said he'd be waiting around here somewhere,' Kai said, tugging his twin away from the tributary tunnel that led to their school.

The collision of corridors outside Doonside Station entrance was more frenetic than usual. The Three-Way was drenched in the smell of stale synthesised canola oil, fired up in enormous woks by illegal street-food vendors, their small business endeavours ignored by Halcyon under the guise of 'community building'. Dozens of Love Buzz wannabes were already streaming through the turnstiles of Doonside Station, dressed in their most dazzling psychedelic finery. Even though Sydney's Lockdown had ended only two hours prior, almost thirteen hours had passed since Rakh-E's set kicked off Love Buzz 1000. Given the 'VIPs prioritised' warnings that had bombarded his HeadBand over the past month, Kai suspected many of Doonside's finest would return home on the Stadium Loop disappointed.

'Just imagine the most super nonchalant guy you've ever seen at the Three-Way, then double his hotness.'

Toca dragged her twin to a halt. 'Like him?'

| 5.02 |

The Man with the Red Face

Maarten van Dijk stepped into the darkness at the western extreme of Doonside Station platform one. Behind him, the ready room's door clicked gently closed and became one with the wall. Maarten peered through the gloom, towards the tunnel leading back to Sydney's CBD. As far as he could ascertain, no one on the platform had clocked his arrival. He smoothed out some imaginary wrinkles in his charcoal-grey jacket before setting off down the platform. If anyone could make out his cheeks through the thick beard, they would've seen that they burned scarlet.

On any other day Maarten would've appreciated the discretion of the ready room's automated door, but not since his teenage years had he received a savaging from his father as merciless as the one he'd endured minutes earlier. Slamming the door behind him would've been a poetic response – if only for the satisfaction of the clapback ricocheting across the Doonside Station platforms, temporarily shaking the pathetically compliant populace out of its collective stupor.

Just keep your cool and stay on target, Maarten reassured himself. *You've got this.*

Maarten tried to rearrange the broken fragments of the conversation in his head. He swerved past a Love Buzz-bound couple, both so overweight they looked like two enormous scoops of rainbow ice-cream balanced on pairs of crumpled green and gold straws.

The old man's finally lost control and you're the easiest one to blame.

'She's your fucking responsibility, son!'

Tito had raged at Maarten from his own ready room at Halcyon Tower, its backdrop a wall of glass looking north from the old observation deck. The usual view across Sydney Harbour behind him had been blacked out.

'Keeping her in line was critical if Love Buzz 1000 was to go off without a hitch and now she's gone rogue, completely off-grid.'

Maarten was seated on a stool in Doonside Station's ready room, identical in every way to the one situated below Trancentral Sydney. His father, angrily pacing the floor, worked every available inch of Maarten's HeadBand viewfinder, like a caner with no intention of holding in his gurn.

'Well, you said we've already got all the data we need for the new headline setlist,' Maarten said, hoping he'd struck a suitably deferential tone. Outright rebellion would have to wait. 'And the drones picked off everyone else that mattered in the underground, so what does it matter if she's on the run?'

'Did it occur to you there's a fucking good reason why she's not headlining Love Buzz 1000 tonight?' Tito fumed. His hands clutched the silver crown of his hair. His index fingers gently massaged his HeadBand's technofibre straps, as if trying to coax the MIDI implants out of his temples. 'The little bitch always did have a mind of her own.'

Maarten's lips scarcely twitched, but it was enough to fan the flames of Tito's rage.

'I'm glad you think it's funny, son,' Tito seethed. 'You'll be sitting there with your mouth full of teeth when this succession plan of ours goes down the drain.'

'I'm sorry, Dad, I just think it's ironic that a man who runs the world has met his match in a tiny little DJ from Tasmania,' Maarten said.

One of my best, he'd thought as the words left his mouth. That one gibe had been enough to set Tito off on a blistering tirade in which he questioned Maarten's commitment to the Halcyon cause, his inheritance, and whether fathering him had been the worst mistake of his life.

Maarten stopped and pretended to dust his jacket. Love Buzz wannabes congregated more densely around him. At times like these he wondered if his mother had had the right idea after all; a locked garage, a length of hose, the roof of her Mustang convertible closed as Los Angeles went about its business outside, oblivious to the Storm soon to come, oblivious to the V8 engine that idled until its petrol was gone and his mother's sorry existence with it. *Free yourself, mate.* Maarten shook off the memory, shook off Tito's barrage of barbs and got into character.

Pushing through a gaggle of teenage girls – slathered in make-up yet still not looking a day over sixteen, skipping childcare duties to get in early and try their luck at Trancentral Olympic – Maarten rounded a corner into a narrow brick walkway. In the distance, the scanner gates which separated Doonside Station from the rest of the tunnels glowed.

His viewfinder's identifiers danced across the milling throng, seeking his prey. Reams of data flooded his viewfinder. Whenever it scanned a five-foot-five person in the vicinity, his HeadBand received a brief profile: name, age, occupation, cluster. He pressed his thumbprints down on his HeadBand's speaker cups and passed through the scanner-gate sensors without being X-rayed, unlike every other oblivious Survivor passing through.

Maarten dodged adults blinded by the endless good times of Love Buzz, sidestepping toddlers who'd never known another normal. From one of the many street-food stalls his nostrils were assaulted by the smell of rotted chicken wings, soon to be marinated and barbecued to an unrecognisable state to mask the taste of bacteria-ridden flesh. Another car park storage area turned into a chook pen, Maarten surmised, given battery farms had been abolished on the pretext of being a 'safety hazard'. 'No worker under my care will risk their life Outside so people can eat meat' was how Tito had spun it, because trying to explain the carbon-intensive nature of meat production had always proven impossible, even for someone as persuasive as Tito. Yes, Maarten conceded, he had to hand it to the Premiums. They were steadfast in their ignorance, and they always found a way.

Maarten felt the crunch of a rat's ribs beneath his right foot. Rattled, the creature scurried as quickly as it could towards the marketplace. Two visits to this muck-hole in a twelve-hour window really was unacceptable. At least he hadn't had to slum it on the Doonside Express a second time.

He stopped in the centre of the Three-Way. He panned slowly across the plaza, his gaze stopping briefly at each tunnel to give his ID scanners time to do their work.

Maarten spotted Kai and Toca before his scanners did. Clad in the official Sunday dress of Halcyon's childcare workers, the identical teenagers appeared in the tunnel stretching diagonally to the left. The analogue clock face in his viewfinder ticked over to 9 am.

Punctual. Tito will approve. He fixed his gaze on the rake-thin Austra-Asian duo and let his HeadBand do its work.

Thank you, Daddy-o. Maarten flicked two fingers on his wrist, as if taking his pulse. *I couldn't have done it without you.*

The ID scanners in his HeadBand stood down and his viewfinder immediately decluttered. He strode confidently towards the twins, who only Stefanie Ishii and their own HeadBands' biometric profiles could tell apart.

| 5.03 |

You Don't Know Me

Kai considered himself the maestro of dishing out studied ambivalence to the rest of the Premium masses, yet he was being schooled by the man sashaying towards them. Matthias van Dijk's son and right-hand man looked immaculate, despite seemingly not having changed clothes since sliding, unnoticed, into Kai's life. He'd added a charcoal-grey jacket to his effortlessly cool ensemble of white Halcyon tee, stonewashed skinny jeans and navy-blue early-noughties Air Max joggers. His gait possessed the self-assuredness of one who knows more about the ways of the world – and the behind-the-scenes machinations that revolve it – than everyone around him combined. Behind his HeadBand's lime-green lens, his eyes oozed alpha confidence.

Most impressively, Maarten van Dijk's five o'clock shadow hadn't changed shape or density in the twelve hours since he'd escorted Kai back to Doonside on the final Stadium Loop before the 9 pm Lockdown. It was as if he'd pulled a matching beard out of the same closet as the suit jacket, slapped it onto his handsome jawline, then stepped out the front door fresher than ever. And he swaggered with a confidence which all but screamed, *I'm Maarten van Dijk, PhD – in zero fucks given.*

'Woah,' Toca gasped. She clasped Kai's elbow. 'He's kempt as fuck.'

Kai wrapped his arms around his sister, pushing the back of her head so her mouth and nose snuggled into the recess above his collarbone.

'Remember, stay in character,' he whispered. 'It all ends here if we don't make it out.'

Maarten stopped in front of the twins and cleared his throat. 'Good morning, young man,' he addressed Toca, confidently zeroing in on the twin identified as Kai by his HeadBand. He took Toca's backpack from her shoulder and slung it over his own. 'Ready to turn on, tune in and drop out?'

Toca nodded, before wrapping her arms around Kai's neck once again.

'I'll get you out of here soon, Tokes,' Toca whispered. Her gut bottomed out. Nervous energy rushed through her. She was the good twin, the self-proclaimed 'worst liar in the world'. ('You're only bad at lying because you never believe the lie enough to not get caught,' Kai had assured her the previous night in his bedroom, each with the other's HeadBand firmly in place, after he'd regaled their parents with a fabricated version of the evening's events.) She felt an unfamiliar guilt, not so much at telling the lie but for the ease with which it rolled off her tongue.

'Just look after Mum for me.'

'Do us proud, brotato,' Kai said. He'd never been so thankful his adult voice and growth spurt had yet to arrive. 'I've gotta shuttle or I'll be late for work.

Kai walked briskly in the direction of Doonside Technology School until he was swallowed up by the crowd, then cut left through the throng when he reached the mouth of the Doonside Tech tunnel. Skulking in the shadows, he watched Maarten lead Toca towards the station's scanner gates, where they queued without speaking behind the Love Buzz 1000 hopefuls. Once they'd cleared the gates, Maarten took them right, away from the masses surging towards the narrow walkway that emptied onto the northern platform.

Kai slunk back further behind the curving wall, so that only his left eye could see through the wire mesh fence surrounding the station. Toca walked timidly behind Maarten, her unease obvious to anyone actively watching for it. Maarten strode ahead, some disquiet of his own writ large in the worry lines of his forehead. Whatever was going on inside his HeadBand, or inside the mind behind that inscrutable beard, was enough to stop him from questioning the lie he'd just been served up by the twins.

At a gesture from Maarten, the green door in Doonside Station's outer brick wall sprung open. He waved Toca past and followed her inside without casting a backwards glance. The door closed.

This is happening.

'Are you sure it'll work?' Toca had asked Kai the previous night on one of their many return trips to the basement before they'd collapsed, so wired Kai's eyes could barely focus.

Once the twins' parents had briefly grilled them on the Love Buzz experience ('I never even left her side to hit the slasher,' Kai had assured Satoshi in one of his more credible half-truths), Satoshi and Stefanie had decamped to their bedroom, rinsed out by another six-day week on the rice-cracker factory floor. Within minutes, Satoshi's familiar snoring – so raucous it could only be bettered by his trademark early-morning hit parade of farts – began rattling the loose door handle of their parents' bedroom. With the place to themselves, the twins crept out of the apartment and into the lift, where not even little brother Kentaro could disturb them.

'I'm with you all the way but it's a bit far-fetched.'

'I've got no idea, Tokes,' Kai had responded, his eyes fixed on the lift panel display, watching the slow journey down from floor 11 to L2. 'It sounds like Maarten has to train me up for something big, which you've just got to fake your way through. You pretended Dad was better at soccer than you so he didn't feel bad, so I know you can do this too.'

Kai broke cover. He sprinted out into the Three-Way and veered right, where he joined the colour wheel of Doonside colonists lining up to enter the station. The scanner-gate's sensors locked onto Kai's

HeadBand. After freezing briefly, as if second-guessing itself, the display identified him – Toca, 16, student, Doonside Cluster – and deducted twenty-five credits from his sister's account as the hard-plastic gate slid open.

'And my part all comes down to whether Juanita still lives at the old Love Inn, where Mum said it was,' Kai had whispered, mindful of the car park's echo-chamber acoustics. He'd pressed the 11 button on the lift panel. The doors glided shut. Sax man started up. The lift lurched upwards. Kai gathered his thoughts. The course of action was clear, albeit based on a hunch – and a conversation with his mother long before the sky rained fire.

'If we're stuck in our apartment, surely she is too,' Kai reasoned.

'She'll know what to do,' Toca said. 'She always looks so beautiful and calm.'

Kai saw the Doonside Express pull up to the platform. He shimmied his slender frame past the dawdling hordes and pushed his way through the Stadium Loop's doors. Spotting a pocket of space, he edged towards the sliding door to the next carriage, even more packed than his, then backed himself into the recess. The carriage door snapped shut, with most of the mob trying to barge their way in left trapped on the platform. Screaming hysterically, a fat blonde woman slammed her fist on the door as the train pulled out. Kai realised it wasn't a woman but an elaborately made-up Doonside Tech student, three years below him but looking more adult than he'd ever felt.

'It's not her looks we need,' Kai had whispered to Toca shortly after midnight. The lift's ding silenced their sax-playing friend again. 'It's her love.'

Kai unzipped his backpack and removed Toca's favourite long-sleeved tie-dyed shirt. Ralf-E's Virtuoso set unfurled around his ears, crackling intermittently as Halcyon's servers struggled to connect his Berlin studio with the Doonside underground. The train jerked towards the CBD, almost sending Kai tumbling into the bodies behind him. He slipped the shirt over his head, turned Toca's HeadBand volume up with a flick of his wrist, and imagined himself tapping out 'One

More Time To Burn Saltwater' on his KeyRoll simulator – five seconds before the rest of the carriage's viewfinders flashed the message that Ralf-E, the blue-eyed blond Virtuoso, had started playing it.

| 5.04 |

Discopolis

'Kai, what language do you think in?'

'Huh?' Toca blurted, with the crudeness of one roused from a short slumber. She was, however, wide awake, and overwhelmed by the wondrous, appalling sight confronting her.

Swirling winds buffeted Maarten's 'Kite Car' – a streamlined, solar-panel-covered hover car introduced by Maarten as 'what everyone would be driving if they could be trusted with the truth'. Outside of her HeadBand, its dial locked on Love Buzz, the car zoomed through the air in silence.

'She is truly something special,' Maarten had declared proudly to Toca as she'd scaled a tube ladder from the depths of Doonside Station.

She'd emerged through a hatch at the end of the vacuum-sealed passage to find herself in a low-ceilinged cargo hold. Hunched over like one of the hermits who hung around the Three-Way hub, hounding the street-food vendors for scraps, she'd surveyed the interior: black rubber floor and hexagonal white tiles, crosshatching the walls and ceiling. No dividing wall separated the cargo hold from the Kite Car's cockpit, even more minimalist than Toca remembered that of the Mirage rusting away beneath Tower 19. Its wraparound windscreen tilted so acutely it was almost flat. Its two white bucket seats were raised barely a foot off the floor. What passed for a steering wheel was more like the one Kai used to play driving games with on their console, back when you still needed hardware.

'The first of her kind.'

From what Toca had seen in their brief time Outside, she could confirm it was, at the very least, the only Kite Car in Doonside. And likely the only sign that life existed there at all.

The Kite Car hovered along a road Toca had travelled a thousand times before, but hadn't seen since she and her father battled their way home on 1-6-25. On the other side of the windscreen, the Storm raged away as it had for every minute, every second since Toca was last Outside. Doonside was coated in a dense, golden haze, like some devious god had turned the planet into a snow dome, a twisted souvenir to commemorate her worst nightmare. The atmosphere looked like it should have been impenetrable, like Stefanie Ishii's misguided attempts at miso soup, yet this sepia-coated suburban diorama was clear as crystal. Balls of Styrofoam and fingernail-sized chunks of bitumen rock and countless other forms of debris hurtled towards them from the far end of Doonside Road and over the top of the surprisingly intact structures lining either side of it. Toca braced herself for impact, which never came. The flying objects didn't bounce off the front window – they simply evaporated, before resuming their collision course with the windscreen seconds later, like history repeating.

'Come now, Kai ji, a trick question this is not,' Maarten said. 'Unless you don't hear in English? In which case we can try this in Dutch.'

Even after several minutes of Maarten's attempts at idle banter, Toca was as thrown by his accent as being addressed by Mr Banerjee's pet name for her brother. Maarten's precise diction was being uttered in the most American-sounding voice she'd heard outside of Cosmo's Love Buzz sets, tinged with Aussie though it may have been, and certainly the only one she'd encountered in person.

Not just kempt but couth as fuck as well.

'In English, I guess,' Toca replied eventually. She was still wrapping her head around having to answer questions on Kai's behalf, despite spending much of her life fielding questions from her hopeless father meant for her twin. 'The only Japanese we ever learned was insults.'

It wasn't just the role-play making her nervous. Kai's HeadBand's signal had disappeared from Toca's viewfinder once his train-line intersected with three more beneath the old Olympic Stadium. ('They can broadcast this Love Buzz nonsense around the world,' Satoshi Ishii had blown his stack to his wife when he'd first read about the blackspot in his morning paper, 'but we can't even track our kids in a tunnel twenty minutes down the road.') And being in the Outside here was even creepier than the view of it from the eleventh floor of Nurragingy Block 19. The Doonside landscape Toca had grown up with appeared frozen in time, as if any growth or degradation had halted the minute mankind went Inside. The pristine road markings, the perfectly manicured front lawns and median strips, the sprawling behemoth that was the Mountain View Adventist College all appeared as impeccably clean as her crush Cosmo's avatar. She remembered the glitching view of Circular Quay out of the Stadium Loop's window on the way into Love Buzz last night: the Harbour Bridge immaculate, moments later in ruins.

Maarten guided his Kite Car effortlessly through Bungarribee Road's disabled traffic lights. There was no gearstick or handbrake, nor any other lever Toca recognised from the Ishiis' Mirage, for that matter. Whatever the dials on the dashboard were telling Maarten, Toca couldn't decipher their meaning. The only other car she'd ever known was now a rotting canvas for Doonside's graffers to decorate or defile before she'd even had a chance to learn to drive.

'But your father must think in Japanese though, right?' Maarten probed.

Toca detected sadistic glee in his voice, a tone she knew well. Kentaro's was much the same when he teased his siblings about looking identical, oblivious to the irony that being a spitting image of their father as a child meant a far worse fate awaited him in adulthood.

'Given that he was born and raised in Sapporo.'

'He doesn't really talk much about that.' Toca shrugged. 'We Vid-Link my grandparents sometimes, but I don't think he ever went back after coming here for uni.'

'That's a big sacrifice to make, though, isn't it?' Maarten pressed. His hands held the Kite Car's U-shaped control wheel loosely. He looked irritably down at the artery pulsing irregularly in the back of his left hand. 'Take a man's language away and you rob him of his processing time, his instinct, his sense of humour . . . I wonder if you dropped a Japanese dog off in Doonside whether the local street dogs would understand it?'

'Everyone out here used to own pit bulls and Rotties,' Toca said. 'If they ever saw a shiba inu they'd rip its throat out first and ask questions later.'

Laughter exploded from Maarten with the force of something that had been trapped in his chest for some time, patiently waiting for its window of escape.

'Is that your "evil henchman" laugh?' Toca quipped. 'You've really nailed the volume and velocity, but your pitch control is way off.'

Kai had never been one for scathing wit, but Toca couldn't resist such an open invitation to dazzle Maarten with some of her sass. Expected or not, it shut her suave chaperone down mid-cackle.

'That wouldn't even scare my little brother on a cold winter's night,' Toca continued. 'And since getting caught in the Storm, he's too afraid to take a piss without the light on.'

'I'm amazed there's a sense of humour lurking beneath that stoic little exterior of yours,' Maarten retorted. 'Tito said you were a little dynamo, but I thought he was putting far too much faith in you being the answer to our Juanita problem.'

Toca clamped up. What 'Juanita problem'? And would it affect Kai's plan?

Satisfied he'd landed a shot on his smart-mouthed passenger, Maarten let the journey continue in uneasy silence, broken only by the intermittent beeps and blips of his control panel. The Kite Car zoomed through an intersection Toca had long forgotten, past another gated community of indistinguishable Australian dream homes and into an industrial estate of dilapidated white warehouses. Toca recognised the hydraulics factory that had stripped their father of his position, turning the jovial man of her early childhood into a hotbed of simmering resentment by her teens.

Maarten pierced the thick silence. 'Do you really think we're evil?'

Squirming uneasily in her seat, Toca shook her head just enough for Maarten to see.

'Toca used to joke about Tito being our new overlord, not me,' Toca blurted out, confirming in the process that referring to yourself in the third person felt as ridiculous as it sounded. Moment of panic overcome, she settled on 'brooding teenager' mode as her safest tactical play. The less shade she put out there, the more likely her subterfuge would go undiscovered.

'My father is some sort of genius, you know,' Maarten continued.

Toca's eyes darted across from the passenger side, locking focus somewhere between Maarten's left elbow and knee.

'He sired me very early in his DJ career, at Coachella of all places.'

Maarten paused. *Sired?* Toca screwed up her nose. *What is he, a horse?*

'Not that you'd know what a Coachella is.'

But Kai probably would. Toca quickly banished the thought from her mind. She had bigger issues to contend with, not least of which being how hot she found this gorgeous, well-spoken creep.

'Anyway, the point is he's got a saying for people going through the motions – if you're too blind to see the real joy all around you, you're just holding on to whatever you can.'

Maarten put his index finger across Toca's pursed lips, poised and ready to deliver a sarcastic rebuke.

'Are you ready to see it, Kai?'

The Kite Car raced through a roundabout, passing an immense warehouse on their right. Drones of varying shapes and sizes buzzed along its hundreds of metres of length. *The rice-cracker factory?* It had to be. She never knew her parents' place of work was so far from home. *No wonder Dad's always so cranky.*

A cross-bridge overpass loomed in the distance. Bolts of lava lighting nipped down either side of the road. Maarten's Kite Car flew on through the Storm's vicious assault, its flight path through the monochrome fury of dust and debris still perfectly smooth.

'Ready to see what?'

'The joy that exists all around you, of course!'

'I guess,' Toca shrugged again. She focused on the looming overpass, unsure where Maarten's cryptic small talk was leading.

'On the count of three, you need to tear your HeadBand off and hold on tight.'

'Wh-wh-what?' Toca shrieked. There was no escape if Maarten had seen through the twins' deception. She cleared her throat, trying to rein her fear in. 'Why?'

'One.'

Releasing the steering console, Maarten showily popped his speaker cups with his palms and then tore the viewfinder off the front of his face, nonchalantly tossing his HeadBand in the hover car's centre console.

'Two.'

Maarten thrust his foot down on the accelerator. The Kite Car's speed doubled in an instant, pinning Toca's head and upper body to the sculpted rubber backrest. She clutched tight to the seatbelt beneath her right breast, which she and Kai had done their best to conceal with tightly wrapped bandages beneath her shirt.

'Three!'

The Kite Car shot straight up into the sky, perpendicular to the ground, its hull narrowly avoiding the concrete safety barrier of the Western Motorway overpass.

Toca's screams filled the cockpit.

'Stop being such a girl, Kai!' Maarten said. 'Take it off.'

Toca reached for her viewfinder, then the technofibre straps stretched across her temple's MIDI implants, but hesitated to move towards her ears.

'Take it off,' he repeated gently. 'Pop the speaker cups, just like I did.'

Frantic breathing wracked Toca's tiny body, her lungs too tight to emit another scream.

'Take it off so you can see what I see.'

The Kite Car levelled off as Maarten relaxed the force applied to the steering column. They'd veered left during their ascent and were now headed due east towards the CBD. Peeking above the surrounding skyscrapers, Halcyon Tower seemed to anger the lava-lightning clouds enough to focus their early-morning assault on its turret. The sky was a chilling whirlpool of red, yellow and grey that the Kite Car sliced through, undeterred.

Toca drew a deep breath and closed her eyes. She popped the cups covering her ears. Love Buzz fell silent. Her HeadBand's straps went limp as the MIDI connection released.

Cautiously, Toca peeled back her brother's viewfinder. When she opened her eyes the stark, fiery sky was gone. In its place was a blinding, equally vivid pale blue, extending towards the horizon without the interruption of a single cloud. The once-clogged arterial roads and smaller capillaries which had linked one self-contained community to the next were no longer visible below them. The cityscape had been overrun by a thick carpet of dark-green vegetation. Only Sydney's pair of Trancentral stadiums, the seemingly random clusters of apartment towers that made up the city's colonies and the handful of enormous solar-panel covered warehouses surrounding them were visible through the expanding jungle.

In the CBD Cluster, the lava lightning's endless assault on the skyscrapers was gone. The office towers' mirrored surfaces reflected the brilliant mid-morning sun soaring high above Sydney Harbour. At the city's apex, Halcyon Tower's glass-encased turret glittered like a disco ball, hanging idle over an empty outdoor dancefloor. Dominating the western side of the turret was a cog-shaped disc, hands forming the shape of a heart at its centre.

'You Aussies used to call days like this a "passport shredder",' Maarten said, surveying the scene like a proud parent at an end-of-year school recital. 'Don't forget to look down.'

Involuntarily, Toca lifted her feet off the Kite Car's floor and gasped. The dark floor had turned clear to reveal a vast body of water hundreds of metres below her seat.

'That's Prospect Reservoir, the city's main water supply.'

Prospect Reservoir appeared placid at first glance, but Toca noticed the dark blue-green surface was alive with activity. Scores of drones buzzed above the water like giant dragonflies, firing occasional laser bursts at unwelcome guests, organic or otherwise.

'I always thought it looked like a mutant maple leaf, or maybe Sideshow Bob's hair,' Maarten mused to himself, 'though I suppose a *Simpsons* reference is as lost on you as a Coachella one.'

Raging Waters Sydney, where Toca had almost drowned Kai when she barrelled down a kiddie slide too closely behind her brother and collected his right temple with her knee, was the only splash of colour breaking up the impenetrable green landscape below. Even then, the water slides' twisted plastic tubes, which once imposed themselves on their surroundings with the subtlety of rainbow-coloured spiral pasta, were a pale imitation of their former selves, left to fade in the sun.

'He knew,' Toca whispered, before remembering who she was supposed to be. She turned her gaze along the motorway, past Trancentral Olympic and the derelict satellite arenas forever in its shadow, fixing her gaze on Halcyon Tower's sky needle.

'I tried to tell Toca and she wouldn't believe me,' Toca said, the memory of Kai's impassioned pleas almost bringing her to tears. 'I told her the Storm was a front from the start.'

'Paranoid Jack, indeed,' Maarten said. His hand rested gently on Toca's right shoulder and gave it a tender, comforting squeeze. 'That's why Tito's chosen you, Kai ji.'

Ripples of heat danced across the distant cityscape. Halcyon Tower's disco turret looked set to spin.

'That's why you'll be the star of the most important Love Buzz yet.'

Dark & Long

The Stadium Loop's vestibule was a heady brew of body odour and anticipation. Trancentral Olympic Station had swallowed up hundreds of Love Buzz wannabes, but it seemed to Kai just as many more had climbed aboard at the interchange where Sydney's spaghetti junction of tunnels collided. Whatever the case, both decks of Kai's Premium carriage were filled beyond sensible capacity.

As the Stadium Loop pulled out of the station, Kai edged his way out of the inter-carriage recess. Each time his face brushed the acrid tang of an adult male armpit, he cursed his lack of height. Not that his own pungent aroma, marinating since the Ishii family's February shower rations ran dry three days early, was going to endear him to Juanita – if she was even at the Love Inn . . . if his plan even got him that far. Still, if Kai's frame were any broader, he'd likely still be trapped in the Doonside Station entryway, unable to worm his way onto the platform. And if he had been more obviously on the cusp of manhood, like his Polynesian peers at Doonside Tech, he and Toca's shot at a cunning plan would've required more actual cunning.

Kai wedged himself against the vertical handrail beside the vestibule's small row of cushioned seating. Even at the lowest available volume setting, Ralf-E's Virtuoso set was distorting its way out of Toca's busted speaker cups. How the hell did she put up with this mess in her ears all day? To Kai's hypersensitive ears, Toca's headphones were crackling so badly they made Love Buzz almost unlistenable. He toyed with the idea of exploring Halcyon's ambient sound libraries, layering up some wind, rain and whale song for respite, but thought better of drawing unnecessary attention to Toca's HeadBand. Instead, he cast a furtive glance around the cabin.

The glitz of Love Buzz, enhanced by the carriage's low lights, wove its magic spell across dozens of enchanted eyeballs. None of the faces appeared conscious of their surroundings. None of his fellow passengers paid any heed to the friends they'd boarded with. Not a word was spoken in the vestibule or the two decks of passengers it served. What had Ian called it? *Total Euphoria.* But this was somehow more frightening. Total ambivalence? Total compliance? The show inside their HeadBands went on, and not one of them smiled.

The Stadium Loop reached the CBD Cluster in a matter of minutes. Kai slid out of his carriage at Town Hall Station. No Love Buzz punters were massed outside any of the Premium carriages as they had been at earlier stops. All of the action was now centred on the far ends of the platform, where VIP carriages bookended the train. Orderly queues of Sydney's elite filed into the carriages.

'Sorry about that, little lady,' came a gruff voice behind Kai's shoulder after a minor collision. A stocky man, dressed in a form-fitting street-cleaner's suit, held up a hand in apology.

Kai rode the puffy white man's slipstream out through the Town Hall Station scanner gates against the CBD colonists surging in the opposite direction. Amid yesterday's excitement, he'd not noticed how different the people on the VIP Floor looked. Chinese and Korean and Japanese faces streaked past, in a brisk yet orderly fashion, in stark contrast to the rough and tumble of Kai's passage through Doonside Station today and his race towards the Three-Way the night before. Among Doonside's melange of Desi and Middle Eastern and Polynesian colonists, Kai's Asian features were the exception, but in the CBD Cluster he blended right in.

All roads except the one Kai was walking led to Love Buzz. All ears were locked on Ralf-E playing 'Don't You Worry, Slippy Children'. All eyes were locked in a thousand-mile stare. No one clocked Kai's presence, nor anyone else's.

'Go with the flow, Love Buzz!' the Virtuoso's voice crackled in Kai's ears, cutting through the distorted rave sirens. 'That's the only way to roll now the Outside is gone.'

Ten metres ahead of Kai, a T-junction funnelled a parade of bedazzled automatons – a rare bunch of Caucasians – into the rat run he was desperate to escape. The street-cleaner's suit veered right then vanished like a shimmering mirage. Kai stuttered to a stop and stood to the side. There were more people living in the CBD cluster than he'd counted on.

HeadBand, chart course to Love Inn and navigate.

'*Thirteen-minute journey,*' Toca's HeadBand replied, the low-frequency male voice in stark contrast to the warm, gentle female tone of Kai's own tutor bot. Kai was surprised Toca had opted for a northern Japanese accent reminiscent of their father's.

'*Forward one hundred metres, then sharp left.*'

Kai set off briskly down the rat run, its air cleaner and crisper to his lungs than the Doonside underground had ever been.

'*Journey time revised to eleven minutes.*'

The rat-run opened out before him – not quite as wide as the tunnel to Nurragingy, but comfortable enough to keep claustrophobia at bay. The foot traffic coming Kai's way thinned markedly, and then he was pushing into the uncertain near-darkness alone. To his right, an immense cement wall dotted with fluorescent light tubes and Halcyon's record-cog logo speakers spanned from what was once the gutter to an awning above. To his left even the apartment tower foyers, packed with people bedecked in psychedelic colours, were dimly lit. A pair of young women – *hāfus*, just like Toca and Kai, and barely a day older – sprinted out of one of the towers and bolted past Kai, hand in hand.

Their Love Buzz outfits were accessorised by twice as many Kandi bracelets as Toca had crammed onto her forearms the previous night.

'Shuttle, little *chibi!*' the taller girl screamed frantically.

Toca calling him a runt in Japanese was one thing, random strangers joining the party was an insult too far.

'Get to the train before the Brainfeeders get you!'

Looking back into the packed foyer, Kai realised the people's faces weren't plastered with excitement but a mix of disbelief and terror.

A blonde woman locked eyes with Kai. Her lips formed the shape of one word, screamed at him over and over: 'Run!'

Kai broke into a sprint in the direction of Love Inn, faster than he and Kentaro had Keisuke Honda'd their way out of danger on 1-6-25.

'Journey time revised to six minutes. In fifty metres, turn sharp right.'

On his left Kai streaked by eerie foyers filled with multicoloured human blobs, arms gesturing frantically. He fixed his gaze on a rectangle of light at the top of the slight incline he was climbing. Distant shrieks fused seamlessly with the sounds of Love Buzz, until it was impossible to tell which sound was which. Kai sensed he was being followed. He swiped his fingers from the front to the back of his speaker cups, focusing their receptors on the sounds to his rear. Sure enough, Kai's own pounding footsteps gained some company. *Shuttle!* At the top of the slope he cut hard-right and continued down another rat run, this one fully enclosed by three-metre-high concrete slabs. The lights lining the walls either side of the tunnel disappeared into the impenetrable darkness ahead.

HeadBand, engage night-vision mode.

Kai's polyester pants were too tight to let him really stretch his legs out. His work shoes were not only loud, but uncomfortable and clumsy. The backpack slapped his back.

'Werrr comin' fer ya, *boyyyyy!*'

A chorus of cackles followed the twisted war cry. *Brainfeeders!* Of all the days to meet an urban myth, Kai had to choose the one he was least appropriately dressed to escape them. He snuck as much of a peak over his shoulder as his pinched neck would allow and saw human figures, three of them, HeadBand torch rails at full brightness, barging into the walls and each other like their proximity sensors had short-circuited. And still they were closing the gap on him.

'*You are now three minutes from your destination. In 250 metres, veer left at Museum Station.*'

At last, a landmark Kai vaguely recognised. The tunnel stretched out before him like a trench from some ancient pre-HeadBand video game. Hope flowed through him, even though he hadn't sprinted 250 metres since primary school, and even then only under extreme duress. He hadn't done anything athletic since he'd become a teenager, unless dynamic knee slides down the hallway qualified. Adrenalin flowing, like last night's 'stomach feeling' had been turbocharged, Kai found some extra shuttle in his legs and prayed his predators were unprepared for a speed-burst. Light boxes blinked as he sprinted past them. The bass boxes of Love Buzz boomed.

'Yerrr nah gunna mek it, *boyyyyyy!*'

Brainfeeders or not, the voices made the distorted rhythm and stealth of Ralf-E's Virtuoso set sound positively uplifting. The chorus of cackles was closer now – too close. Kai dug deep to find another spurt of speed. At the end of the tunnel, a single overhead light source grew brighter.

'*In thirty metres, veer left at Museum Station and continue uphill to Oxford Street.*'

Uphill, fuck! Tokes, I'm done.

Keep going, brotato.

Tokes, is that you?

Kai reached the edge of the Museum Station entrance and attempted to take the corner tight, but his feet collided with an immovable object. Kai's head and torso continued at full speed while his legs flipped out behind him, sending his body cartwheeling through the air. The last thing Kai saw before his head connected with the brickwork floor – the last thing his terrified eyes thought they'd ever see – was a heavyset apparition, its all-white arms and body braced for combat, stepping out from under the Museum Station awning.

Shrieks of sadistic pleasure gave way to agonised screams.

Black light, white light, lights out.

| 5.06 |

Song of Life

Irritable squawks rang out through the manmade channels of what was once Sydney's central business district. All the commotion Toca remembered from the city visits of her childhood (in a parallel universe) had fallen silent; the repugnant beggars and the charity chuggers and the 'dick-measuring displays' (another Satoshi Ishii staple) of over-revved sports-car engines were long since gone. In their place, the sounds of nature restoring its kingdom.

Shading her eyes from the blazing sun, Toca squinted east across Hyde Park. Nature's bid to reclaim the Earth seemed more carefully managed here than across the rest of greater Sydney, which from above appeared to be consumed by wilderness. Lush grass, thick but freshly cut, spread from the rear of St James Station across the unpaved sections of Hyde Park. The edges of every footpath were neatly trimmed. And the entire parkland was brimming with flora and fauna – more than Toca could ever remember seeing in the Nurragingy Reserve before it was bulldozed to make way for their apartment tower and the rest of the complex eighteen months before the Storm.

Birdsong whistled down from the trees: the gentle call-and-response of eastern rosellas, the urgent squawks of a departing flock of galahs. Spooked by the rare sight of intruders, a trio of kangaroos hopped away along the fig-lined avenue towards the Anzac Memorial.

Toca stood in wonder. If only there was a grove of gum trees nearby so she could get up close to a koala as well.

Flower gardens flanking the empty wrought-iron park benches were in full bloom, petals spread wide in the knowledge summer's end had finally arrived. Packs of mongrel dogs roamed the Hyde Park grounds and surrounding streets, keeping all the other beasts on edge, bar a herd of five cows, grazing on lush grass and blissfully unaware. Beside the Archibald Fountain, a hexagonal granite pond appointed with bronze gods and minotaurs and a sextet of tortoises spitting water into the sky, another group of mutts playfully wrestled and yelped. In a bid to escape its foes, one of the smaller pooches – part Staffy, part dingo, a prize-winning Doonside bitzer if Toca had ever seen one – leapt into the water. The other three followed and they were friends again, their squabble washed away in a flurry of splashes and playful nips at each other's necks.

The barking dogs drew the ire of the dinosaur-like birds perched around the fountain's perimeter. All white except for their black legs, heads and long, skinny bills, they were clearly unimpressed their morning meditation had been interrupted.

'What are they?' Toca asked, a little too eagerly.

'What, the flowers?'

'The birds,' Toca said, pointing towards the fountain. Anything to divert Maarten's attention away from uncovering her secret identity. 'What are they?'

'You've never seen an ibis before?' Maarten asked, bemused. Unlike Toca, he found the eerie stillness reassuringly familiar.

'Come now,' he barked. Hand wrapped around Toca's elbow, he briskly paced them towards the St James Station entrance. 'Time is of the essence.'

A pair of silver sentry drones cruising Elizabeth Street from Circular Quay came to a sudden halt as Maarten and Toca approached. Maarten had landed the Kite Car on a patch of grass behind the station's brickwork, not five metres to Toca's right. She readied to make a run for it.

'Stay cool,' Maarten warned Toca.

The pair, still HeadBand-free, slowly continued along their course while the drones' LED eye slits took turns scanning each of them. Invisible waves of robophobia washed over them both. Toca felt queasy; Maarten, unruffled, tightened his grip on her elbow and urged her forward. As suddenly as they had started, the sinister emissions stopped. Apparently satisfied that these particular humans were harmless, the silver cylinders veered right and flew down Market Street, disappearing beneath the glass-encased walkway linking Halcyon Tower's base with the second floor of the old David Jones department store building. Further down Market Street stood an enormous concrete bunker, stretching across Pitt Street above the pedestrian crossing which had once led to Myer and the other fast-fashion boutiques in the mall. In the distance to Toca's left, a narrower rat run turned right off Bathurst Street and ran adjacent to the park towards Museum.

'I haven't been Outside in years, you know,' Toca snapped, craning her head for a final look at Hyde Park before Maarten dragged her under the station entrance's ornate Art Deco façade. 'We get excited if we see a stray cat in the tunnels more than once a month.'

'Those birds are as much survivors as your stray feline friends, if not more so,' Maarten said, leading Toca into the station's shadowy bowels.

Not only were none of the overhead lights switched on, but there were no Love Buzz speakers lining the walls.

'I'm letting you go now, but stay on track or those drones will be down here in a flash, right?'

Toca nodded. Maarten fished his HeadBand out of his jacket's inside pocket and reattached it to his face with a dramatic pop over his ears. In an instant, his light rail sprung to life.

Toca fought the urge to dry-retch as the smell of the station engulfed her. *Sharing a room with Kai at this time of month is bad enough.* She'd learned to love the musty odour of the Three-Way, even tolerated the foul aroma of animals crawling in to die under cars beneath their apartment tower, but she'd never encountered a smell of lingering death quite as wretched as this.

'Would you believe they farmed mushrooms down here for a time in the 1930s?' Maarten asked rhetorically, trying to divert his own attention from the vile smell as much as Toca's. 'The vegetable of our times, come to think of it – "Feed 'em shit and keep 'em in the dark", as they say.'

At the end of a hundred-metre stretch of tunnel, decorated immaculately with tiny squares of gloss-white tile, Maarten led Toca through the station gates. All of their automated yellow wings were locked in the open position – permanently, Toca suspected. Maarten grabbed her elbow again and broke into a jog down a narrow staircase. They emerged into a plaza, which felt to Toca like a more carefully planned, more inviting version of the Three-Way. Tiled walls were broken up regularly by green doors, leading to toilets and station offices and other unknown destinations. To their right, one door, its handle surrounded by deep scratch marks, had been blasted off its hinges. Their momentum slowed. For a split-second Toca thought she saw Maarten's brow crease.

'Come!' Maarten hissed, annoyed that his actions were being scrutinised.

He dragged Toca across the station's western platform and jumped down onto the tracks. Toca did likewise, grimacing to mask the sting of slightly rolling her right ankle upon landing. She followed Maarten unsteadily across the rocks and rails until they came to a nondescript access panel nestled deep in the retaining wall opposite. Down the tunnel to their right, a train rumbled in the distance.

'Anyway, the ibis could have died off in the 1970s, like some of their less resilient fellow natives, as developers went to town on their habitats in the interior wetlands,' Maarten said, casually rattling off factoids like he was narrating a documentary on those wretched creatures.

Toca watched his hands manipulate unseen control panels in front of him until the rusted aluminium door popped open. Maarten motioned her through the access panel doorway. She pivoted on her ankle. The sting had subsided. *I should pull through.*

'But they migrated towards the coast, reinvented themselves as scavengers and thrived.'

They inched their way down a narrow cement corridor, illuminated only by Maarten's flashlights and a light at its far end.

'The ibis were a running joke when Tito settled us down here in 2020, just after the first wave of the first pandemic passed, when the rest of the world was an utter shitshow.'

After forty metres the corridor opened onto another walkway, encircling what Toca guessed was Halcyon Tower's shaft. Maarten led them to a trio of stainless-steel lift doors. A pair of golden, statuesque guard-bots stood to attention against the bare walls between them.

'They called them "bin chickens" or "tip turkeys", or worse,' Maarten continued, panting between word bursts, before bringing the pair to a stop outside the central lift.

Scanner beams shot discreetly from where the guard-bots' eyes might have been, assessing Maarten's face, and then the door between them slid open. Maarten motioned Toca to step into a mirrored lift compartment.

'But the ibis had the last laugh, because it held onto the instinct that most of our leaders lost when they resorted to mankind's tired old "divide and conquer" ways.'

'What instinct is that?' Toca asked.

'Adapt and survive, baby.'

The lift doors slid shut.

'Adapt and survive.'

| 5.07 |

Love and Imitation

When Kai came to, the MIDI implant growing pains were gone along with the knot in his neck. In their place, his rattled brain pounded with an intensity he hadn't experienced since Toca's knees collected his temple at Raging Waters nine years earlier. He felt his face rhythmically rebounding off a body clothed in foul-smelling white fabric caked with saliva and blood and other unidentified filth. Another rush of blood surged through Kai's head, amplifying the vicious throb which, in this moment, was his entire world.

Rectangular dark-grey pavers scrolled past like a conveyer belt beneath running shoes urgently pounding the pavement. Kai was folded like a paperclip over someone's shoulder. With each step, the sharp point of the man's shoulder joint stabbed deeper into the flesh between where Kai's stomach met his hip. Instinctively, he kicked out, but his captor clamped the backs of Kai's knees tighter against his sizeable chest.

'Think about it, son,' said the man gruffly. 'Kick yourself free now and you just end up back where you started, knocked out cold with the Brainfeeders up your clacker.'

Kai's captor changed direction abruptly, sending Kai's slack upper body swinging wildly off course. The pavers grew brighter, then changed to different flooring entirely as the man paced through a pair of automated glass doors. Kai stared down at a puzzle board of mottled cream squares, broken up by a large oval of dirt-brown tiles. His HeadBand viewfinder, presumably damaged by his fall, refused to light up. The lens in front of his right eye had been shattered. No vital signs, no coordinates, no ID sensors. He was alone, helpless, and flying blind.

'Guard-bots, resume formation outside Love Inn entrance and stun any intruders on sight,' the man commanded unseen figures.

Kai had never heard an order issued so genially – his father would laugh this guy's politeness right back through the front door and march him directly to the lift. Nonetheless, the sound of metal feet promptly clattered across the ceramic tiles.

'Put me down, *sukebe*!' Kai yelled. His fists bashed the man's calves.

'Lech?' The man gasped in mock outrage. 'Well there's no need to be nasty, *noroma*.'

Kai's captor flung him forward over his shoulder onto the ice-cold tiles. His butt collided forcefully with the floor.

'Sorry about the rough landing,' said the man, patting Kai's head. 'And I don't really think you're a dunce, but my Japanese insults are a little rusty.'

They were in a foyer, as dimly lit as those Kai had seen from the rat runs while trying to outrun the Brainfeeders. According to a gaudy sign on the wall to Kai's right, affixed above a pair of heart-shaped sofas, he'd made it to the Love Inn – the 'o' in Love represented by a Halcyon cog logo, a heart pulsing gently at its centre. Two gold-plated guard-bots were positioned either side of the Love Inn's sliding glass entry, their gleaming chassis in stark contrast to the dark void outside. Behind Kai's captor were two more, either side of a red lift door.

Spooked, Kai slid closer to the concierge's desk behind him. He frantically scanned the room for a way out.

'Calm down, Kai,' the man in the cleaner's suit said. He pulled his hood back.

Kai recognised the face – the unusually deep olive complexion and the widow's peak of black hair framing it – but couldn't immediately place its owner. Toca's busted HeadBand sensors had no answer, but

Kai knew those eyes. At Love Buzz, they'd met his from over Maarten's shoulder.

'I told you I'd keep a lazy eye on you.'

'*Ian?*'

'As much as your name is Toca then sure, Ian from Chatswood at your service.' Ian smiled. 'But my friends call me Lawrence,' he added, extending his right hand to Kai as he lowered to sit cross-legged on the floor before him. 'And I was Juanita's biggest fan before you were even alive to challenge for the mantle.'

Lawrence's handshake was as gentle as the orders he'd issued to the guard-bots. Kai slumped against the Love Inn concierge's desk. Everything hurt. Exercise was overrated.

'What are you doing here?'

'I could ask you the same question,' the cleaner formerly known as Ian said. 'I'm not sure what you were hoping to find here, but the fact you're looking means you're ready to hear the truth.'

Kai was ready and he wanted to know everything – about Brainfeeders and Total Euphoria and exactly what Toca meant when she reached out to him after the Drop. It was all becoming too much to make any sense of. The brutal ache wracking his skull intensified.

'Come on, let's get you on your feet.'

Lawrence clamped his hand around Kai's wrist and lifted them both upright as he stood. Kai's right shoulder throbbed where he'd landed after being upended outside Museum Station. Blisters swelled on both heels from his flight through the rat runs. Sore head aside, he was otherwise unharmed. He shrugged off Lawrence's offer of support and limped towards the lift doors, rotating his shoulder as he walked, defiantly staring down Lawrence's golden bodyguards.

'So I guess you know now that Brainfeeders are the real deal,' Lawrence said. He shepherded Kai inside and pressed the button marked 15. 'That's what happens if you keep going back for Drop after Drop like our young friend at Love Buzz last night – you get so burnt out you can't feel the Buzz anymore and turn to sucking the life out of anyone who does. Very unpleasant if they ever catch up with you, but lucky for you, quite slow on their feet once their brains turn to gravy.'

'Are we going to see Juanita?'

'Juanita's not here, my little brotato,' Lawrence chuckled wryly. 'But even if she was, there's no way you would've found her apartment in this rabbit warren of a joint. And she'd be about as useful to you as that contraption on your head.'

'Top floor. Enjoy your stay at Love Inn.'

Bright light flooded the lift cabin as the doors opened. Kai's forearm instinctively shielded his eyes. His body felt a fierce heat, more intense even than his classroom's array of OxyPure units mustered in the depths of winter. Lawrence strode out of the shadows and into the brilliant sunlight of the last day of summer lording over Potts Point. He tossed his HeadBand carelessly onto a round plastic table, its white surface streaked grey and orange with water stains.

Kai edged past another pair of golden guard-bots, standing to attention outside the lift doors. Squinting, he cautiously traced Lawrence's steps across the terrace. Heat radiated from the off-white tiles beneath his black canvas shoes. He couldn't decide which aspect of the sensory overload fascinated him most – the invigorating smell of trees, the endless blue sky, the sound of pool water lapping against tiled coping, or the absolute silence, sporadically interrupted by the roar of Love Buzz wafting across from Trancentral Sydney in the distance beyond his right shoulder, its roof covered not in wind turbines like Halcyon History suggested but a shimmering solar farm.

The murmur of Halcyon drones overhead jolted Kai from his daze. He reached the middle of the Love Inn terrace's pool deck, which wasn't as empty as it had initially appeared.

At the terrace's cement guardrail, a silver-haired man climbed off his deck chair to greet Lawrence with a firm handshake. He was clothed in black sandals, white swimming trunks and a white robe, untied to reveal a bronzed torso rippled with muscle. The Speedo left much less to the imagination than Kai was comfortable with. The man's face was equal parts impressed and proud.

'Glad you could make it, Kai Ishii,' Matthias van Dijk said, raising a cocktail glass in salute. 'I told Lawrence you wouldn't let us down.'

| 5.08 |

Darkbeat

Toca and Maarten stepped out of Halcyon Tower's service lift into a dark, curved corridor, lit by long strips of recessed floor lighting. The walkway's continuous curve gave Toca the impression they were walking through a cave with no ending or beginning; no light at the end of the tunnel, no way to escape if the corridor before them collapsed under the weight of the floors above. Outside the lift, an elderly man and silver-streaked woman in business attire stared at Toca as Maarten guided her to the right through the darkness. The man, wrinkled and hunched over, nodded respectfully, his eyes twinkling kindly. Beside him, the woman stood on tiptoes to whisper excitedly into his ear. Maarten deferentially tipped his head in the pair's direction.

'Who *were* those weird people?' Toca whispered once they'd safely rounded the continuous corner.

'They're on the board of directors,' Maarten muttered distractedly.

Maarten stopped Toca in front of what at first looked like more wall. Recessed into it was the faintest outline of a concealed doorway.

'They've all flown in for Love Buzz 1000, and those two will be *very* surprised when they learn they've had a sneak peek at tonight's main attraction.'

Toca shuddered. *If they're expecting Kai they'll be more disappointed than surprised.*

The door before them would've been even better camouflaged than the one at the western end of Doonside Station if it weren't for the stylised heart-hands insignia etched into it. Maarten's hands mimicked the deep-red symbol. Instantly, the door slid open to the left.

A gigantic man, bigger and darker than any human Toca had ever seen in the flesh, looked up eagerly from his seat at the rear of the surprisingly spacious cylindrical room. From Toca's perspective its walls – again covered in hexagonal tiles, this time grill-textured in gunmetal grey – seemed to climb up forever to a distant ceiling of matte black, dwarfing even the inhabitant's colossal frame as he rose. The only other fittings inside the room were a pair of calf-high circular platforms, distributed evenly across the centre of the room. Panels of green light around the side of each platform gave the room its eerie, radioactive glow. Atop each platform, in its exact centre, sat a small metal briefcase no wider than a slice of bread.

'Kai, welcome to Dav's Cognition Chamber,' Maarten said, extending a hand to the room's occupant. 'Dav has worked side-by-side with your hero Juanita for many years now.'

Dav flashed his friendliest gap-toothed grin. His handshake engulfed Toca up to her wrist.

'He knows the tricks that'll have you shining like a star for the entire world later tonight.' Maarten rested his hands on Toca's shoulders. 'Are you sure you're up to this?' he asked. 'No pressure or anything, just the world's biggest party at stake.'

'Maar-ten, please,' Toca said drily, stretching out his name for good measure. Performing her best Kai impersonation – nose upturned, impatient, dismissive – she pushed past Dav's hulking frame towards the Silo platform. 'I've been preparing for this day my whole life.'

Beneath the bluster, Toca's entire body trembled. *What have you got me in to, brotato?*

Sorry Tokes. She hadn't expected a response. *But you don't know the half of it.*

| 5.09 |

Journey Agent

'Kai, come,' Tito said. He motioned towards a table beneath a giant umbrella printed like a rainbow lollipop. 'Let's discuss our business in the shade before you burn to a crisp.'

Kai struggled to absorb his surroundings. It wasn't just the scorching sun, which seemed to zero in on his broken HeadBand lens with enough fury to ignite his eyeballs, its warm rays sending nausea crashing across his body in waves. Nor was it the unexpected appearance of Tito, dressed more like a sleazy uncle on a cruise ship than the leader of the post-Storm world. Kai had hoped to find Juanita at Love Inn, refreshed and ready for Love Buzz 1000. In the plan he'd concocted with Toca, Juanita would listen attentively while he expounded his theory about HeadBands being behind the Storm, give the theory her blessing, then agree to lead his crusade to set the world free from Tito's tyranny before welcoming him into the Virtuoso fold.

What really bothered Kai was that he'd been so right for so long and let it slide. The Storm was a front and he'd known from the start, from the moment he and Kentaro had escaped the 'projectiles' buffeting Block 19 – the palm leaves, the plastic chairs, the green shopping bag that was there and gone in an instant – when the Storm rolled in from the golden west, just as the dust storms and bushfire haze had through years of summers before it. History's greatest lie (*Did Juanita know?*) had unfolded right before his eyes, yet he'd let society's apathy and his sister's taunts convince him to keep his selfish little mouth closed. His parents worked a factory to keep him fed. His kid brother had forgotten what it was like to see the sun. And he'd willingly succumbed, allowed his suspicions to be buried deep in the dopamine rush of HeadBand life, the instant gratification of Love Buzz and the Drop, of *Space* turning music into a conquest, into just another video game.

Kai shuffled uneasily towards the table, dazed and disoriented, brittle and broken. All he'd ever wanted was to be a Virtuoso, to help the world feel the love like Juanita and Cosmo and Usura did. The 'stomach feeling' of anticipation had become one of emptiness. Everything ached, then ached again; his dreams shattered like Toca's HeadBand, clinging to his face like its life depended on it. This wasn't how the plan was supposed to end. *How could Juanita do this?* How could she condone what Tito had done?

On each of the three seats surrounding the table sat a small briefcase, each matte-chrome surface refusing to reflect the sun's light. Lawrence, now disguised not as a Love Buzzer nor a street cleaner but a corporate raider, in white button-up shirt and navy-blue suit and paisley purple tie, took a seat at the far side of the table, his back to the sun. He flicked his briefcase's lid open and inspected its contents. Pursed lips. Raised eyebrows. An impressed nod of the head. He snapped the lid shut.

'Does it do what it says on the box?' Lawrence asked Tito.

Their host tied his robe's white belt and took a seat on the left, proudly tapping the briefcase he'd set down on the table before him. 'All that and more, my brother,' Tito said. 'Kai, please – sit down. Relax! Have a drink with me.'

Tito plonked a glass carafe of sparkling water down in the centre of the table. Beads of condensation slid down its sides. Parched Kai may have been, but he wasn't going to give Tito the satisfaction of knowing how scared he was, how susceptible to the power of suggestion – just yet.

'Come now, Kai, this is no time to be staunch,' Tito said, pouring Kai a glass. 'I know we've got some explaining to do but you're making this sit-down more intense than it needs to be.'

Kai placed the briefcase assigned to him on the table and flopped down in the shell cushion chair. Three generations of men regarded each other warily. Above, a swarm of drone propellers whirred just within earshot. The pool, crystal clear and sorely tempting to Kai – the heels of his hands grazed and aching, knuckles bruised and throbbing with the growing pains keeping time, again, in the sides of his skull – was all he'd ever imagined a CBD rooftop pool would be. He took a long, satisfying swig on the glass of water, cold as ice, to compose himself. It tasted fresh, invigorating, like a different drink altogether to the chemical-heavy substance that ran out of the taps in Doonside.

'The Storm is a front,' Kai said, pouring the last drops of water into his right hand and splashing it onto his mouth and cheeks. He wiped his face with the back of his sleeve. 'And I've known from the start.'

'You liked the little slogan we painted on the wall, then?' Tito asked, sounding pleased with himself. 'I wish I could claim the secret message from Toca after the Drop as mine as well, but planting that in your consciousness was all Lawrence here.'

'We've kept the underground resistance under such tight scrutiny they'd be caught the minute they even thought about raising a spray can,' Lawrence conceded. 'But we took a few liberties to get your attention, even if the tags on the cars in your building's car park only reached you subliminally. If you barely noticed, there's not much chance anyone else paid much attention either. And it's all thanks to HeadBands: the ultimate distraction.'

'And you and your sister took to the news exactly how I'd hoped,' Tito chimed in with pride. 'If you'd just gone off with Maarten this morning and left her behind, things would play out far differently from here. But you and Toca working together changes everything for the better. You're the partnership Love Buzz was supposed to have from the start.'

'But why?' Kai asked. He looked pleadingly at Tito. 'Why would you do this?'

'Where do I begin?' Tito slurped the final drops from his glass through a metal straw. 'I've never told a newcomer before but I guess there's no better place than the start.'

Another muffled roar burst out from beneath the Trancentral Sydney roof. Kai noticed the outside of the stairwell he and Toca had climbed on their way inside to Love Buzz glittered like his mother's old Glomesh purse. The whole stadium gleamed, like it was coated in precious metals, just as Kai had imagined the concourse would before the overwhelming disappointment of traipsing inside.

'I was just like Juanita and Cosmo and Usura once, did you know that?' Tito nodded over Kai's shoulder towards the stadium. 'Except they called us Superstar DJs, and we were placed up on ridiculously high pedestals considering we were just a group of men – and the occasional woman – playing other people's music to help people forget their shitty lives. There was skill involved, and I'd like to think I invested more in my craft than most, but like anything in this life the spoils didn't always go to the best. Sometimes falling with your nose in butter—'

Lawrence snorted. 'Or in plain English, being in the right place at the right time, or just being there first and loudest.'

'Unless you were like my old friend Lawrence here,' Tito said, nudging Lawrence's shoulder playfully. 'For him, "it's about the journey, not the destination" isn't just some hackneyed catchphrase but a way of life.'

'It's a little more substantial than "peak time, all the time",' Lawrence countered. The gentle warmth Kai had come to associate with the man who'd just saved his life returned to his face. 'But I guess my era is long gone.'

'Anyway, I remember flying into New Delhi—' Tito stopped short and fixed his gaze on Kai. 'Are you old enough to remember when Delhi still existed?'

'I guess,' Kai shrugged. Geography was of little interest to him given he thought he'd never leave Sydney, but Kai knew Delhi topped the long list of cities that fell off the map on 1-6-25.

'The first of the great megalopolis ghettos,' Tito went on. 'Though even before the Indian government admitted the capital was a lost cause and relocated to Gujarat, we hadn't factored its survival into our long-term plans. The point is, I was flown in to perform there just after the turn of the century in a particularly unmemorable superclub in the basement of a five-star hotel in the diplomatic area. You just had to look around to see Delhi was on its deathbed – smog so thick it was like breathing razor blades, squalor and sadness at every turn. One of the great cities of the world was drowning in its own filth, and its richest citizens were too busy trying to escape their own misery to care.'

Kai snuck a glance past Tito towards the Sydney city backdrop: clean, pristine, glorious. Halcyon Tower rose above it all, like a king's sceptre. Kai sensed both men's eyes narrowed in on him: Tito's expectant, Lawrence's probing more curiously. While Tito just wanted Kai to love the sound of his voice as much as he did, what Lawrence wanted was unclear. No matter. Kai's destiny hadn't changed, and he'd work either, or both, of these uneasy allies as required to get there.

'I knew right then what I had to do. I knew it'd be a long game, and impossible to pull off alone. And I knew there'd be collateral damage.' A single tear rolled down Tito's cheek.

And Kai thought Juanita could work a crowd. *What a performer.* He wasn't convinced the tear was real – that anything he'd ever believed in was real – let alone genuine.

'So, basically what you're trying to tell me,' Kai said, 'is that a DJ landed in Delhi, saw the city was dying, and decided to set off a fake apocalypse?'

Another derisive snort exploded out of Lawrence's nose. Except it wasn't derision, Kai realised. *He's laughing with me.*

'See, I told you this kid had some sass once you cut through that frosty veneer,' Tito said, nudging Lawrence again.

Wiping a hand across his face, Tito's disposition transformed as if at the flick of a switch. Gone was the warm welcome he'd rolled out for Kai's arrival. This was more like the man Kai had seen delivering impassioned sermons down his HeadBand in the months after the Storm struck.

'Kai, I need you to listen to me very carefully. It's going to be a lot for you to take in, but we're not talking about little cows and little calves here. Before I invite you and Toca into the fold, I need you to understand that the fate of the planet is at stake. All good?'

'All good.' Kai gulped, feeling chastened.

'Before Halcyon Industries came along, people listened to music in an entirely different way,' Tito continued, after a pause and lingering glare that made Kai's stomach plummet. 'You had to seek it out. It wasn't fed to you on a platter. It sounded nothing like the EDM people know and love today. And it was rarely consumed passively.'

'That was changing, though,' Lawrence interjected.

Tito shot Lawrence some side eye – playful, though, and far less fierce than the daggers he'd fired at Maarten in the Trancentral Sydney ready room. Kai sensed this one was just for show, and Lawrence knew it. He had Tito's unwavering trust.

'By the time I got out of the game, my DJ sets felt like background action for people's personal photo albums,' Lawrence continued. 'It was all about who you were seen with and who you were seen by. The music and the journey played second fiddle to the race to rack up the most Likes.'

'So you can either get off the train, like the Phat "with a P-H" Controller here' —Tito chuckled. Lawrence smiled a half-smile. Whatever the joke was mystified Kai—'or you can put yourself in the driver's seat. Streaming music on smartphones wasn't new when Halcyon got involved, but our platform did it better than anybody. Artificial intelligence was already telling you which shoes you should buy, how many steps you should take each day, which TV character you were – based on answers to a seemingly unrelated set of questions. We managed to flick the switch on something consumers actually wanted – telling them what music they'd like before they'd even heard of the people who'd made it. Soon after, our engineers found the magic formula and *voila!* EDM was born.

'The world was paying so much attention to so many frivolous things – politicians pushing belief systems that should've died in the dark ages, confected reality TV outrage, professional sporting teams who did nothing for you but eat up valuable time you'd never get back,' Tito scoffed. He reset the digits on his hands and began counting them off again. 'When the things that really mattered – microplastics in our bloodstreams, AI reaching a stage where it could've wiped out the manual labour workforce for good – were put in the "too-hard basket", as you Aussies called it.' He shook his head and spoke in a mocking, childish tone. 'It doesn't affect me. Show me another cat video.'

Kai had heard most of this before – from Satoshi, over breakfast most mornings, before his father had become as addicted to his Head-Band's everyday sugar hit as the rest of the family, as the rest of the world.

'So we used our AI to weaponise music,' Tito gestured towards the sky behind him. 'We weaponised the soundtrack of people's lives. EDM was the game changer because it's designed expressly for listeners who don't like to think. It pumps selfishly away until your body has no choice but to move in response, never mind the negative signals that your brain is sending, that this sound has no musical substance at all.'

Tito's anti-EDM screed had Kai simmering, but that was an argument for another time.

'The flipside was that lack of depth meant our AI team could program any subliminal messaging we wanted to hide between the rhythm and melody,' Lawrence added. 'Stream more EDM. You hate your smartphone. Enrol to vote – for whichever populist strongmen we could easiest manipulate to make HeadBands compulsory so we could reach our goal.'

Tito interrupted with a gentle hand on Lawrence's arm. 'People thought the heart-hands symbol Halcyon's DJs threw to the crowd was a show of PLUR – Peace, Love, Unity and Respect, the way it was back in the Second Summer of Love – but it was really just a trigger, like a hypnotist's pendulum.' He paused to look down at his watch as another roar from inside Trancentral Sydney wafted towards the city. '9:59 and here comes the Drop, regular as clockwork. Once you're in a state of euphoria we can make you believe anything we want, even something as implausible as the planet developing a single weather system, the changing of the seasons be damned. And in the end we didn't need any more messages than that. The AI became so good at writing EDM, so good at finding the recurring patterns that triggered euphoria and amplifying it to infinity, that people became addicted – addicted to how good this music made them feel. And when your world revolves around your own pleasure, nothing outside your HeadBand matters.'

'Eventually,' Lawrence added as Tito stopped to catch his breath, 'people loved our sound and our superstars so much that HeadBands wiping out smartphones barely caused a ripple, and stopping the spread of COVID-23 was the perfect cover story. Control the flow of information and you can eventually convince people that up is down, day is night. So when the time came to activate the perfect illusion, people trusted us so implicitly they accepted the Storm as truth.'

'That still doesn't explain why,' Kai said. 'Can't you control all that without keeping us Inside?'

'It's not about controlling anything, Kai,' Tito sighed. 'It's all around you, can't you see?'

Overwhelmed by the heat and Tito's revelations, Kai longed only to activate his KeyRoll, to chase comets and asteroids through the Watson Beat's *Space* . . . to forget.

'No smog, no noise pollution, no one abusing the Earth for their own personal gain,' Tito said. 'It's simple, really – the Storm has come to save humanity from itself.' He leaned in. 'But there are people who want Halcyon's power for their own ends,' Tito said. 'And I'm too old and tired to keep fighting the good fight alone, which is why I need your help.'

He motioned towards the clip of Kai's briefcase. 'Take the HeadBand off,' Tito ordered. 'I know you've worked out how.'

Kai popped the speaker cups, which released their grip with a wheeze. He manoeuvred Toca's battered HeadBand off his MIDI implants and discarded it on the floor.

Tito's eyes gestured down at the briefcase. 'Put it on.'

Inside the briefcase was a wedge-shaped piece of black plastic, barely more than an inch long on either side of the V and no more than five millimetres in diameter.

'What is it?'

'Our new ViZar-1000, as promised,' Tito said. 'No more MIDI headaches, no more cramped ears. Just clip it to the bridge of your nose and the nanotech will do the rest.'

Warily, Kai removed the ViZar from its foam cushioning.

'We've loaded it up with all your biometrics and other data,' Tito assured him. He opened his own briefcase and casually attached an identical ViZar to the bridge of his nose. 'Once I establish the wireless MIDI-Link, the place this journey began is right inside.'

Kai clipped the ViZar to his nose. Invisible machines sprang into action, whirring like a microscopic army of the drones circling overhead. Within seconds his eyes were covered, his ears encased. There was a brief sensation of being safe again, back in the comfort zone he called home.

And then it was gone. The lights went out. A wall of white engulfed him.

And then Kai was somewhere else.

| **5.10** |

Plastic Dreams

'I just know this is going to be something special.'

The voice is Lawrence's, though not as gravelly as Kai knows it. This younger incarnation of Lawrence sitting across from Kai brims with optimism, at the endless possibilities that life and the universe have in store. He looks leaner, too, though not necessarily fitter, and his face isn't adorned by a HeadBand lens and speaker cups. In his viewfinder's place sits a pair of what Kai's mother calls 'Harry Potter glasses', round lenses encircled by frames of thick black. His hair is the same length, cropped close to his head, sans the tell-tale widow's peak of middle age. Lawrence's olive complexion of February 2028 looks positively lacklustre in comparison to this luxurious tan, more English breakfast tea than kombucha. The desk planner laid out before Kai reveals the date to be April 2013. Which means Kai can't be Kai, unless he'd forgotten holding court with Lawrence as a one-year-old.

Kai, who suspects he's inhabiting this scene as Tito, sees that he and Lawrence are seated around a desk in a ramshackle office. (*We prefer the term 'shabby chic', my boy,* an elderly Tito chuckles in the depths of Kai's imagination.) Tito-Kai is seated on the visitor's side. Windowless cream plasterboard walls surround them. Standing lamps with vintage tapered shades stand sentinel in each corner of the room. Garish music-festival posters have claimed almost every spare centimetre of

269

wall, providing the only brightness in the low-lit room. In the middle of it all is an aerial photo looking down from above on Juanita – sprawled on her back, surfing a festival crowd on a body board.

Directly beneath is a cork noticeboard, covered with a large map of Sydney. It's marked out with drawing pins in three colours. Above it, a handwritten label reads '*PORTFOLIO*'. Pins with spherical tips of yellow and green dominate the board, though what stands out to Kai is a concentration of heart-shaped drawing pins at Green Square, Chatswood and Macarthur. On an inset map of the city's CBD, a similar cluster of hearts dominates Kings Cross and Darlinghurst and the streets immediately surrounding Town Hall. Suddenly, Tito cranes his neck behind him. Two locks and a deadbolt hold the room's only door secure. A small sliver of unnatural light slips through the narrow gap between door and floor.

Whatever Lawrence is up to here, two things are clear: he's keeping a low profile, and doing Tito's bidding in the process.

'I know you think you've seen it all, brother,' Tito says. 'But even I've not come across a festival after-movie as ridiculous as this.'

Tito and Lawrence gather around Tito's laptop. The video unfolding on screen pans across a modern city on an open harbour not unlike Sydney's, only substantially beachier. In the near distance, high-rise towers reach up to meet pristine blue skies. Passenger cruise ships in the deep foreground dwarf the nearby barrier islands. The camera trains itself on a boatload of bikini-clad beauties, being transported speedily across the harbour by a young, sunglasses-clad Latino – a DJ, if the headphones draped inconspicuously around his neck are any indication, and one who is familiar to Kai from the Halcyon History channel by face if not by name. The DJ pointedly moves the throttle forward to full speed, symbolising the inevitable march of progress.

Cut to another DJ, in a hotel room. More bikini beauties excitedly bounce in slow motion around him. Like his boat-piloting counterpart, this DJ is not so easily distracted – it's almost time to go to work, after all. He majestically removes a USB stick from a laptop and tucks it safely away in the front pocket of a backpack. Everything that is happening is earth-shatteringly profound because the orchestral backing track and endless tracking shots deem it so.

Cut to a lone monarch butterfly, fluttering high above the harbour.

'Dude, that is fucking nuts!'

Quickfire zoom to the skyscraper clusters, in front of which tens of thousands of beautiful young people assemble before outdoor stages.

'Waiiiit for it,' Tito says. He holds his whisky glass stationary at his lips for dramatic effect. 'And, *action!*'

Heart-hands form across the screen – a lone pair in silhouette at first, then rack focus to an ocean of heart-hands signalling back. The camera tracks further back, levitating over a dancefloor with no end in sight in any direction.

Back on stage to Juanita, who mouths: 'Are you feeling the love?'

The camera cuts to behind her, controlling the ecstatic crowd below. A single finger held aloft is the signal for euphoric EDM riffs to erupt. The portentous orchestra and its ensemble of unseen players are blasted into orbit. Fire and confetti shoots into the sky.

Juanita leaps up and down in time, her triumphant finger holding its line. Blue hair whips behind her in the sea breeze. The congregation before her willingly follows her every move.

A hedonistic orgy, not unlike the hundreds of One World clips Kai had studied religiously in the months before the Storm had struck – or hadn't, as he'd known all along.

Tito interrupts the scene, 'Meanwhile, back in Australia . . .'

Tito presses play on a different movie, inside Sydney's Olympic Stadium before it was roofed in and rebadged as Trancentral Olympic. On another stage, looking out on another ocean of bikini-topped girls perched atop bare masculine shoulders, behind another DJ – Cosmo, young and virtually unknown, more than a decade before the Chicago via Valencia player became Toca's Virtuoso heartthrob. His heart-hands reach for the sky. The same camera angles. The same quick cuts. The same crowd reaction. The same bassline drops. The same call-and-response dance-off plays out.

'Ex-*act*-ly the *fuck*-ing *same!*'

'Exactly how I planned it, brother.'

Kai can feel Tito beaming.

'We give the promoters the building blocks, they do all of the heavy lifting for us.' Tito raises his glass. 'It's happening.'

'And she's already bigger than we'd ever dreamed,' Lawrence says, clinking his glass against Tito's before swigging the remaining whisky.

'A little too big, to be honest,' Tito counters. 'If the scene keeps building like this it'll burn itself out before we're ready to act.'

'Which leaves us with two options, so far as I can tell,' Lawrence ponders.

He shakes his head and cracks a wry smile as a hulking black DJ wielding a microphone fills the laptop screen – 'Of course bloody Coxy is there' – before returning to his thought bubble.

'Pull back until our tech is up to speed, or let the bubble burst and naturally rebuild.'

'This all needs to evolve as naturally as possible,' Tito agrees. He finishes his drink. Kai enjoys the taste, especially the hint of spice on his tongue before his throat feels the burn.

'Let the bubble burst. Let the small events wither and die once we've done our local recruiting,' Tito says, spitting the words like venom. 'The timespan between pop-culture cycles is shortening as rapidly as smartphones are killing attention spans, so mark my words: EDM *will* crash and burn. For our plan to succeed, it must. We'll use the downtime to perfect our creation, and my Theory of Cycles will do the rest – our sound will be back in vogue sooner than you think.'

Lawrence pours another dram into his glass. Tito waves away his offer of a top-up.

'And on that note, I think it's time to let your girl Juanita roam free,' Tito adds.

Lawrence looks like someone's just shot his dog.

'Fear not, old friend, she'll be well looked after. And there'll be new blood in Sydney for you to monitor soon enough.'

OUTRO

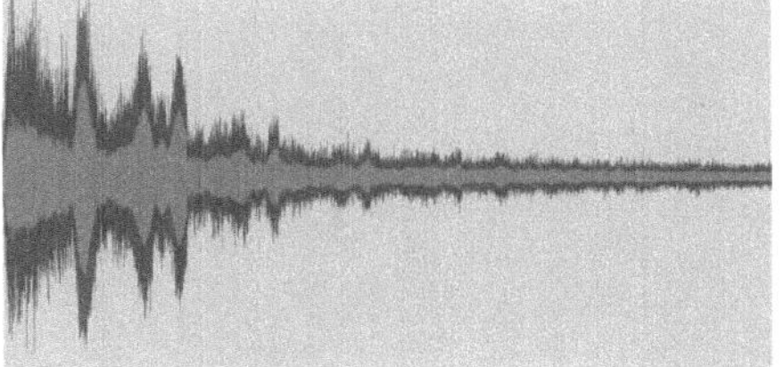

| 6.01 |

Silence

One hallucinatory dream fragment fused seamlessly with the next until Juanita crash-landed on a polished concrete floor, cool and soothing and reeking of spilt beer. Sticky and acrid, the surface clung to her right cheek like contact paper. The darkness around her was incredibly still. Her face felt flushed, naked. She groped around for her HeadBand, the comfort blanket she'd clung to when the scene that had made her the world's sweetheart began to rot her from the inside out. Then it hit her; a chilling wave of realisation; one she hadn't felt since waking up the morning after Danny Lawler had dumped her for Alex Ko, the Korean exchange student with the biggest boobs in the eighth grade. There was no point pinching herself – it was real. In the hours between the Drop and the disturbed, disturbing sleep cycle she'd just crawled out of, everything had changed.

Juanita's HeadBand was gone, flung into the fig tree protecting the Observatory Hill rotunda. The leafy branches swallowed up Juanita's mask, and with it, the final crumbling remnants of her Virtuoso façade. After the big reveal, Lottie had led them to the top of Observatory Hill and down into a different system of tunnels. Several minutes deep, in blackness more profound than Juanita had ever encountered, Lottie had guided her towards a small hole in the wall. Over her Day-Glo overalls, saturated with sweat and stormwater, Juanita slipped on a white street-cleaner's coverall Lottie fished out of the crawl space as a second layer against the underground chill. Though she'd kicked off her gumboots when they'd reached their rendezvous point, the water-logged Volleys remained in place, her toes inside as shrivelled as her fingertips had been the night before.

'Might as well own up to it, sister,' Lottie had said to her with a wry smile. 'You've run away from home and there's no going back.'

Juanita feebly felt around in front of her head, latching onto a brick pillar rising up from the cold concrete floor. Her fingers scratched at the grout until they found a grip in the cracks. She dragged herself into a seated position, feeling the sciatic nerve in her lower back twinge as she approached a right angle. It all hit her at once. The floodgates opened.

'What have I done?' she sobbed into her hands. Snot and tears poured down her face, forming a slippery membrane across her palms. 'What the fuck have I done?'

'You really shouldn't be so hard on yourself, you know.'

Juanita shrieked. The shadows to her left in the darkest corner of the room came to life – a human-shaped spectre of white fabric and Day-Glo floral motifs. Lottie wiped the sleep from her eyes as she backed herself into the corner, then pulled her bent knees towards her chest and clutched them tight against the cold.

'You know when you used to get your period and suddenly Insta was serving you ads about menstrual cups or blood-proof panties or what-ever the latest gimmick to separate us from our cash was? Most of us just fobbed it off, had a laugh about how creepy it was and went about our distracted little lives, like we'd seen the tip of the iceberg and de-cided the best way to avoid it was sticking our heads underwater and closing our eyes tight.'

Juanita's tinnitus raged like a chorus of Tibetan singing bowls crying her name.

'Tito fooled all of the so-called leaders of the free world with his little stunt,' Lottie continued. 'It's bloody impressive when you think about it – the guy won an AI arms race that most of the planet didn't even know was happening, let alone that they were participants in. And the other Big Tech giants didn't even see him on the game board until he'd wiped them right off it.'

Juanita swung to catch a glimpse at whatever Lottie was squinting at in the emptiness behind her. All she could see was more of their hiding place's deep, dark void, only darker.

'I still don't get it, though,' Juanita said. 'What does Tito possibly gain from all this?'

'Honey, that should be as obvious as the reason Tito took you on as his "protégée",' Lottie replied brusquely. 'It's why he got every person on the planet hooked on his mind-numbing tech. It's why he'd only put that enormous cock of his in the arse of any teenage girl or boy he recruited to the cause. And it's why he became a DJ in the first place.'

Juanita thought of that first long, lost weekend. Of how talking about music made Tito's arm hair stand on end. Of how talking about the state of the world made him cry.

'*Control*, sweetie,' Lottie asserted. 'Control our entertainment and you control us all.' Her eyebrows gestured behind Juanita. 'We've got company.'

Juanita bear-crawled across the floor and huddled beside Lottie.

'Relax, relax,' Lottie said, resting a hand on Juanita's polypropylene sleeve. 'If they're coming to the rendezvous point, they're one of us.'

Cautious footsteps crept through the adjoining room.

'Lottie?' a man's voice whispered, his voice impossible to disguise.

'Robbie!' Juanita cried. Leaping to her feet, she teetered across the room and leapt upon her giant play toy, again kitted out in a spray-painter's suit of his own. Robbie ducked his head to prevent his tight, bleached curls scraping the low ceiling.

'S'alright, s'alright,' he whispered, gently patting Juanita's backside while he walked. He unwrapped her legs from his waist and lowered her to the ground. 'Those fuckers ain't rounded me up yet, so I wasn't going to give them the satisfaction this time 'round neither.'

Lottie joined the reunion beside Juanita's pillar. 'The others?'

Robbie shook his head gravely. 'It was a fucking massacre, miss,' he stammered. 'Don't know if anyone else got out. Never seen collection drones so cold-blooded brutal.'

'And all because your mate Dav sold his soul for a taste of Tito's honey,' Lottie spat.

Juanita looked up at Robbie hopefully.

'What about the boys?' Juanita asked. 'The DJs.'

'Dropping bombs, to the last,' Roberto smiled ruefully. 'And out with a bang.'

'Well, that settles it.' Lottie paced back towards her corner.

Eyes finally adjusted to the lack of light, Juanita felt a jolt of recognition at the narrow timber ledge wrapped around her brick pillar. She spun her gaze towards a derelict DJ booth, buried in the corner at the other end of Lottie's wall. Its clear Perspex barrier was riven with cracks. The empty surface that had once housed DJ equipment was piled high with garbage. They were in the Slip Inn's stony bowels, back in the Cave.

'Always the Cave,' Juanita murmured to herself, grimacing.

Robbie ferreted around behind the DJ booth and emerged with a bowl overflowing with fresh fruit. 'The real stuff, miss.'

Moving specks of black dotted the bananas and green apples he offered her. Fruit flies.

'Better for you than that Alphabetti you stuff your face with.'

Juanita shook her head. Robbie pushed a Granny Smith apple into her hand and closed her fingers around it.

She grabbed Lottie's upper arm. 'Settles what?' she demanded, fighting to stay afloat amid cresting waves of nausea.

'Everything,' Lottie said, despondent. 'Years of work finding the music that would bring all those people together for the love of the music itself, without all the mind-fucking trickery. Couldn't you feel it, Neets? That indefinable special something? What we had in the rave cave was real, not just pixels bouncing around some fantasy land. Now Tito's stolen our sound and crushed us in the process.'

'We can't just give up!' Juanita cried, tightening her grip.

'This isn't just about you and your endless pursuit of glory!' Lottie snapped, tearing herself from Juanita's grasp. 'The underground resistance is dead, Juanita. It needs more than just us.'

'If it's just us, then it's up to us to stop him.'

'Have you ever tried to get into Halcyon Tower without permission?' Lottie asked, exasperated. 'You don't just rock up and skip the queue because your name's on the guest list.'

They locked eyes, taking stock before the next parry and thrust.

'Actually,' Robbie interjected. Both women looked at him. His deep baritone echoed off the walls. 'I think I can get us in the back door.'

| 6.02 |

Impact (The Earth is Burning)

Halcyon Tower's boardroom appeared to exist permanently on the brink of nightfall. Darkness fell across every crevice of the low-lit, cog-shaped space, entirely fitted out in black. It was the only room in Halcyon's entire property portfolio that wasn't austere white from base to apex. (The white theme was another Ken Loi innovation that Tito signed off on once he'd heard the rationale: 'No distractions. Nowhere to hide.') Tito had always believed, however, that some business was best conducted in the gathering shadows, where the worst of intentions could be cannily concealed. If it worked in the underground nooks and crannies he'd slithered through before he was famous, he saw no reason why it wouldn't hold true when the world's big fish finally began to circle.

Tito sat at the head of an irregular hexagonal table, ten metres long from his seat to Lawrence's position at the other end and five metres in diameter at the point the four longer sides intersected. Lawrence was struggling to make himself comfortable in an original Ovalia Egg Chair, its black fibreglass shell lined with deep-red velvet. Smiling at his friend's discomfort, Tito sunk into his own seat – an apricot, high-backed Arper Aston Direction, the most majestic chair Halcyon's goons could loot from the nearby office towers – while the room brought itself to order.

Maarten took his place in a black leather executive chair on the section to Tito's immediate right. Fifteen other directors followed suit, seated four to a side. Gently pulsing red hearts housed in cog-shaped Halcyon logos lined the walls. The greying hair atop Halcyon's eight female directors glowed forebodingly under the love lamps, as if lit up by lava lightning and not the sun's rays being piped down through pneumatic tubes from Halcyon Tower's turret. What little hair remained on the heads of his male directors, who'd already seemed ancient to Tito when he'd recruited them to the cause, was overpowered by their lustrous red scalps. If he was entering this boardroom as an intruder, Tito couldn't have told one wrinkly venture capitalist from the next if he didn't know them better than he knew his own son.

Gentle murmurs dissolved into reverent silence. Tito smoothed the creases out of the arms of his favourite black and white hooped tee. Satisfied all was in readiness, Tito rose to his feet.

'First, let me extend a warm welcome to you all,' he began, 'and a sincere thank you for joining me at this extraordinary general meeting on that rarest of occasions – a Leap Day.'

He cast the room and the directors from his mind, visualising himself in his happy place: inside a DJ booth sharing his truth, his vision of a better world, with a rapt crowd.

'I appreciate how reluctant you must have been to squander airtravel quota on this trip, particularly considering this year's reduced allowance after last year's alarming CO_2 projections report. As Halcyon's foundation shareholders, you've all sacrificed much to be here today – we've all sacrificed far too much, to be fair. But, considering what's at stake, this sacrifice is a small one. And there are still many more years of sacrifice to come.'

Beside him, Maarten stifled a yawn. *Your time will come, my boy.*

Tito pushed on. 'Our history together speaks for itself, so I will keep this brief. As our AI continues to learn more about what our audience wants, each new track – now churned out at the remarkable rate of 200-plus per day, across countless genres and moods on top of our flagship EDM content – propels us closer to our journey's end: Singularity, and the point just beyond where our consciousness can live on in our Prodigies forever.'

Lawrence led the room in a spontaneous round of applause. Reluctantly, Maarten joined in. Satisfied his recalcitrant son had suffered enough, Tito held up his hands. The room fell silent.

'And there's more to come,' Tito added. 'For on the final leg of this voyage, just a few short years from now if our current trajectory continues, everyone tuned into Love Buzz will be hearing whatever genre of music they love, composed in real time just for them. Our Virtuosos – which very soon won't have to be human, as Kayce-E, Rakh-E and the other newcomers have ably demonstrated – will continue as the conduits that keep the Survivors marching behind us, all as one. And no one outside of this boardroom will be any the wiser.'

Maarten couldn't mask his surprise at this revelation. Tito was pleased by the confirmation his son didn't know nearly as much of his masterplan as he thought.

'Which brings us to tonight, and the new sound we're premiering for the climax of Love Buzz 1000,' Tito's voice boomed across the room, emboldened. 'Thanks to your support, EDM has been the dominant sound across an unprecedented fifteen-year stretch. But we've reached a critical juncture, at which Survivors need something more. Tonight, we take Love Buzz to the next level, pushing a new sound with real substance. And we'll be launching it as I'd always intended Love Buzz to be – with a Virtuoso team, who share an unspoken connection they're yet to realise they have, as our headline act.

'On this exciting note, I'd like to announce that I'm reversing my decision to step down as executive chairman of Halcyon Industries next year,' Tito said to shocked exclamations from around the table. Maarten looked up at Tito as if he'd shot Comet, the van Dijk family's dog. At the far end of the table, Lawrence sank into the depths of his chair, like a chick who'd been hatched but didn't like what they'd seen outside their shell.

'Maarten has grown into a magnificent young man in his own right,' Tito motioned to his son, forcing a mask of pride onto his face. 'And tonight's activation marks the culmination of a project he's been overseeing for nearly three years now. I trust that when the time is right for me to step down, your belief in his vision of the future will be as unwavering as your faith has been in mine.

'But for now, thank you again for joining me Down Under to celebrate this momentous occasion. Please find the Cognition Chamber assigned to you in the old restaurant space on the floor below us and strap yourself in to your ViZar by 7 pm sharp for our headline set. Your journey into the biggest quantum leap in virtual raving history awaits.'

Tito strode out of the room, soaking up the adulation as Lawrence, shit-eating grin plastered unnaturally across his dial, led the room in another round of rapturous applause.

Maarten scurried behind Tito, who strode with purpose along Halcyon Tower's crescent-moon corridor to nowhere.

'I think that went down smoothly.'

'Of course it did, my boy,' Tito said with a dismissive wave. 'This poker face has worked bigger miracles with far poorer hands than what we've currently been dealt.'

Tito stopped outside his private lift. 'Have you tracked them down yet?' he asked, scanning for human shapes in the gloom.

'The drones found Juanita's HeadBand at Observatory Hill, but the trail is cold,' Maarten said, avoiding eye contact.

Tito clutched Maarten's chin and fixed his son with a glare, boring as deep into his son's being as the laws of physics would allow. 'Do not fuck me on this, son,' he hissed.

Maarten wrenched his head from Tito's grasp and met his glare.

'There's nothing more unpredictable than an escaped slave gone haywire,' Tito spluttered. 'If Juanita stays at large and the public gets wind of it, Halcyon is finished and us along with it.'

| 6.03 |

Hey Boy Hey Girl

The music wrapping its arms around Toca was unlike anything Love Buzz had previously subjected her to. No matter how good the music, and especially Cosmo's, made her feel, listening to it was like cleaning her ears with barbed wire, thrust in and out at 160 beats per minute and above, so fast her ears didn't have time to bleed. This new music – the music that Dav said 'he' (meaning Kai) would be debuting in the Love Buzz 1000 headline slot, with no mention of what Juanita would be playing, nor when – was deeper, slower, more spacious than any EDM she'd heard before. More organic than clinically precise, with more room to get lost inside each track's grooves. Replicating Juanita's rapid-fire moves had been easy. Now that the BPM had been reined in Toca felt herself flailing out of her depth, cast adrift and treading water inside her ViZar-1000 as the Ultraworld's perpetual zoom expanded around her like a digital Atlantis.

I'm just not Kai I'm just not good don't stop don't stop they'll find you out.

'Slow, slowww,' came Dav's words of encouragement, as if sensing her internal distress. 'This new sound is all about sitting back inside the groove, not racing out front of it.'

Toca swivelled to face off with Dav's avatar, dressed in skin-tight red and blue with iridescent highlights around his pecs and abdomen. It was a perfect facsimile of his human form – right down to the gap

284

between his teeth – boosted by an even more athletic frame, wiry and agile, effortlessly moving around the Ultraworld as if the additional muscle was only painted on.

Can't stop won't stop don't stop.

Toca's own avatar was a black catsuit-style interpretation of her brother's favoured white bodysuit, with a thick white collar. Rivulets of light pulsed through grooves lining Toca's limbs and body.

'Like you can feel the blood running through your veins!' Toca exclaimed when they'd entered the Ultraworld. Dav smiled.

'Just the way Juanita likes it.'

Only now, hours later, had Toca made the connection. Her outfit wasn't a tribute to Juanita; it was the genuine article.

'The Virtuoso interface is designed so simply that anyone can use it, but you need to *hear* the music to control it,' Davide explained. 'Get down real deep in the pocket.' He offered a knowing smile. 'It's EDM, not rocket science. Once you hear, you'll understand.'

Toca's ViZar readout told her they'd been at work in the Ultraworld for seven hours now, yet her teacher's patience seemed boundless.

'Let's start over, again,' he said. 'Just relax and remember to breathe.'

Toca reset, dialling down the *Can't stop won't stop* chorus in her head. The beat drove on.

Tilting her head downwards, Toca focused on her avatar's feet keeping the beat. She listened and listened until she finally heard. Dav was right. Now that she knew where to search, there was enough space between the rivers of bass for her to swim between. Her slender frame began to shimmy and shake.

'Get lost in all that space,' Dav said. 'Feel the different elements blend together until they meld, hear the subtle movement buried deep in the background where the real magic lies. The beat stays king, but in the end it's the spaces between the layers that matter.'

Toca's minutes became hours became days as she lost herself on the dancefloor at the centre of the Ultraworld. Her console lit up with an endless array of bliss bubbles and confetti cannons, sonic sabres and cosmic firecrackers. Toca deployed them all, randomly at first, then tactically, then, finally, in perfect service to the songscapes she was soaring through. Pulsing away at the centre of her Virtuoso console, teasing and tempting her as she defied gravity with every turn, a little drawing of a heart beat ever brighter until Toca could no longer resist.

Another build-up of white-noise sweeps reached its peak.

Toca reached for the heart.

'No, no, no! *Not the Drop!*' Dav roared.

Toca's neck whipped back sharply. Her ViZar clip was ripped from the bridge of her nose. A pair of firm hands spun her around in a half-circle. She was back in Dav's Cognition Chamber. Residual flashes of the Ultraworld bounced about her retinas, until they found a point of reference – a dark-skinned hand holding a disfigured nose clip, which was being investigated closely by a proud, beaming face.

'Congratulations, young miss,' Dav said. He passed her the charcoal-grey wedge, all that remained of her disabled ViZar. 'You're ready.'

'I know.' Toca beamed.

'And so am I,' Kai said, stepping out from behind Dav.

Kai looked different to the brother Toca had farewelled at Doonside only hours earlier, and not just because his childcare uniform had been swapped for a white bodysuit, specced up with light grooves of its own. The difference was nestled somewhere below the surface of his eyes, as if he were weighed down by the burdens of a man twice his age.

'You and me, Tokes,' Kai said. Even his voice had dropped a couple of semi-tones.

Toca stepped off the platform. 'Together at last.'

'Sorry to spoil the reunion, young miss,' Davide said, keeping the twins separate as they tried to hug. 'But we can't get this party started until we're sure you can play back-to-back.

Out of The Blue

'And to think you wanted to admit defeat,' Juanita hissed.

She took a final bite of her Granny Smith apple and tossed it in the direction of an ibis on the footpath to her right. Wings flapping frantically, it honked its approval.

Lottie was the last to emerge from beneath a rectangular metal grill, barely wide enough for Robbie's shoulders to slide through, just beyond the concrete walls of the Pitt Street Mall rat run. Brand names adorned the surrounding buildings – Swarovski; Florsheim; Rip Curl, the hippest surf brand in Penrith during Juanita's early teens – but the showrooms behind the glass shopfronts were empty, looted long ago to clothe the uppermost echelons of Halcyon's VIPs. Above the group, a crisscross of tense steel-cable wound around Halcyon Tower's shaft, its diameter narrowing halfway up the narrow central pole before widening to greet the base of the golden turret at its summit. The western windows of its observation deck glittered gold, reflecting the setting sun.

'Getting across town was always going to be the easy part,' Lottie retorted.

Despite visibly shivering in the city's cold shadows, she unzipped her street-cleaner disguise and stepped out of it with obvious distaste.

'Are you sure that's a good idea, miss?' Robbie asked.

Lottie waved him away dismissively. 'Think about it, Robbie – if we're on the Outside we're clearly not cleaners.' Wide-eyed and frazzled, she turned on Juanita. 'So, Virtuoso, do you have a plan once Robbie gets us in, other than getting us all killed?'

Clank! Robbie clumsily dropped the grill back into place, shattering the uneasy silence.

Lottie backhanded his shoulder. 'Especially now the element of surprise is gone.'

'I don't know,' Juanita snapped. She finished shimmying out of her white coverall and tossed it aside. Shredded thighs aside, the sports bra/overalls combo was one she could get used to, even if it left her pungent underarms exposed. 'Robbie, which way do we go?'

He pointed towards an Art Deco sandstone archway at the top of the street ahead. 'There's an access point hidden off the main St James Station platform,' he said.

Their gateway to safety stood at the top of a slight incline. Two more blocks, under the David Jones footbridge, and they were home. Wearily, the trio set off.

'I thought this tunnel would've brought us out a lot closer,' Robbie said sheepishly, looking to Lottie. 'Should've listened to you after all, miss.'

'I'm up for another dash for survival if your old legs can take it, Neets,' Lottie sneered at Juanita. 'On your mark—'

'*HeadBand removal is prohibited under the 2023 Public Order Act, addendum 2025a,*' screeched the shrill robotic voice of a sentry drone.

Fifty metres ahead, three collection drones lowered themselves in reverse arrowhead formation behind a silver-bodied sentry, hovering above the intersection like a giant pepper grinder. Juanita quickly ran the numbers in her head. The drone quartet blocked off the intersection of Market and Castlereagh Streets. Even if they got past the drones, it was at least another hundred metres uphill just to get inside the St James Station gates. Without their HeadBands, they'd be running blind the second they stepped inside.

'Fuck, fuck, fuck—'

'*Surrender immediately.*'

'Shut the fuck up, Bonnie!' Lottie hissed. 'We can get out of this.' Lottie clasped Roberto's shoulder. 'Robbie, we need you to take one for the team right up the middle.'

'Yes miss,' Robbie replied, resigned to his fate. He took Juanita's hand in his and kissed it. 'I always hoped we'd be together forever.'

'*Repeat: surrender at once or the collection drones will shoot to kill.*'

'Run *at* them, are you crazy?' Juanita shrieked.

'We're not going to outrun them so let's outfox them instead,' Lottie said. 'You and I need to split up and take the flanks. And keep your fucking head down!'

'How will we get inside without Robbie?'

'Just shut the fuck up and *go*!'

Robbie unleashed a guttural roar, like a war cry, as he launched himself towards the drones. Sprinting straight up the centre of Market Street, his footfalls barely made a sound as his joggers streaked over the bitumen.

Lottie jinked left towards the Swarovski side of the road, almost as exposed as Robbie without an awning to protect her from above.

There was little Juanita could do but break right and run for it. At least her side of the street had some semblance of protection overhead.

'*HeadBand removal is banned under the 2023 Public Order Act, addendum 2025a.*'

Robbie's roar was suddenly strangled silent. Juanita snuck a glance to her left to see his body rise limply into the air. Like a ghost, he glided towards the intersection under the command of a collection drone's red tractor beam. Smoke poured from the grid of laser pointers pinpricking his face. Blood and brains squirted from his ears like a fine mist.

'*Surrender is no longer an option.*'

The sentry drone's body shook vigorously until it emitted a sonic boom. Soundwaves tore across the streetscape in every direction.

Shopfront windows shattered. Shrapnel sprayed into Juanita's face and body. Glass littered the footpath under her stormwater-sodden shoes.

The other two collection drones broke formation. When Juanita risked an upwards glance, one was awaiting her just beyond the point where the footpath met the Castlereagh Street kerb, thirty metres ahead.

'Collection drones will shoot to kill.'

Millions of red laser sensors locked onto Juanita's face. Across her limbs, hundreds of tiny glass cuts stung at the salty touch of her sweat. Juanita readied one of her honey-coated roars.

'Now babe now!' Lottie screamed from the opposite side of the road.

When Mary from the rave-cave cloakroom had asked 'Where will you be at the end?' the previous evening, Juanita had no concept of her own mortality. Now, she had her answer: on an abandoned city street, running headlong into the face of evil, waiting for the moment her pain was permanently scorched away.

She closed her eyes and let it go. *'Arrgghh!'*

Except when the burning sensation on her face stopped, she was still running. The clatter and clank of metal on bitumen snapped her out of her kamikaze charge. Juanita opened her eyes just as her feet stepped off the kerb. She pulled up just short of the fallen collection drone, which had crashed to the ground in sync with the rest of its formation. The smell of Robbie's chargrilled flesh lingered thick in the afternoon air. The only sound Juanita heard was her own frantic breathing. What happened? How was she still alive?

A rapid-fire burst of footsteps rang out from the opposite side of Market Street. Lottie ran towards the far side of the intersection and flung herself upon their saviour.

Maarten van Dijk's hands tweaked invisible dials from inside his HeadBand for a moment longer before he warmly returned Lottie's embrace.

'I knew you'd make it,' Lottie sobbed into his shoulder.

He breathed Lottie in deep, from her hair to her left shoulder, before turning towards Juanita with an exhausted smile.

| 6.05 |

Sweet Harmony

From the open-air deck of Halcyon Tower's Skywalk, Matthias van Dijk gazed out upon his kingdom as he had countless times before. The VIPs looking out of the penthouse on the other side of King Street hadn't clocked his presence – how could they, when all they saw through their HeadBands was lava lightning and clouds of dust, a city shrouded in despair. Through the glass-bottomed platform beneath his navy-blue shoes, not a living creature stirred on the abandoned roads and pavements some 300 metres below. Narrower cement tunnels split off from the vast enclosure of the Pitt Street Mall rat run, making the CBD look less like a grid than a maze. The deserted city's soundtrack was as lush as any of the dreamy breakdowns of the progressive house classics of yore: a swirling sea breeze whistling around the turret, steadily growing in intensity as if in anticipation of a build and drop to come. Only a trio of collection drones upset the serenity, breaking from their patrol route along King Street to dart across the former shopping mall at the tower's base.

Before the Storm, Tito found himself troubled by this view of the world going about its business. *So much self-important bustling done by so many for the benefit of so few.* It had all changed on 1-6-25, at the flick of the switch in an operations room on another continent. As soon as he'd successfully cleared the city's streets, ridding them of the petty thoughts and pointless squabbles of the financial elites, standing astride this platform gave him a sense of peace that to this day eluded him elsewhere. Even the gentle sway of the tower itself, when buffeted by winter's breeze during what amounted to a Sydney cold snap (decidedly mild compared to what Tito's Dutch genes were accustomed to), felt more like the gentle rock of a baby's cradle than a safety risk.

Home at last, Tito reminded himself. *Job almost done.*

With a satisfied smile, he turned from the view and leaned against the guardrail.

ViZar, connect David Lieb.

Frown lines formed across Tito's forehead above the top of his viewfinder until he got the desired response.

'Yes, Mr van Dijk, sir.'

'Just Tito is fine, Mr Lieb,' Tito said, smiling. 'It's time, Dav. Lawrence will bring up the twins.'

A single crack, like a fighter jet breaking the sound barrier, echoed through the deserted cityscape below.

| 6.06 |

Son of A Gun

Adrenalin pumped through Juanita's limbs in a way Love Buzz hadn't roused her in years. Her suicide sprint at the collection drone had revived a competitive spirit she hadn't experienced since her final gymnastics meet, twenty-five years ago, leaving everything on the spring floor to prove that old hag Gillies wrong, once and for all.

In Halcyon Tower's service lift the unlikely trio hurtled towards their destination, the only sound their fevered breathing. Though Lottie's face showed signs of wear and tear after the encounter with the collection drones – her left eye socket, riddled with glass by the sentry's sonic-boom strike, was caked with blood and swollen shut – she, like Juanita, was a picture of intense focus, as was Maarten.

'So.' Juanita, having processed the events on Market Street as Maarten escorted her and Lottie through yet another secret passage in St James Station, turned to Tito's son. 'You two have been working together to overthrow Tito all along and you've only now thought to invite me along?'

'Deep down he's a great man, my father, you know this too,' Maarten said. 'But he's more concerned with keeping the Outside world to himself than he is with making it fit for Survivors, which is why this charade must stop.'

'And Survivors will believe you when you tell them what he's done,' Lottie said to Juanita. 'But if we don't stop him now, he'll cling to power forever, or at least until he can put a Prodigy in his place.'

The lift doors opened.

'A Prodigy?'

'Like Kam-E and Ralf-E and your blonde friend—'

'Abb-E,' Juanita gasped.

'Exactly,' Lottie muttered. 'So annoyingly human you'd never think she wasn't real. And if you load one of these humanoids up with your own consciousness, you're as good as immortal.'

Maarten led Juanita and Lottie into a dusty alcove. The doors slid shut, leaving Juanita clutching for a safety hold in the darkness. *They were all bots?*

'Can you give us some torch, Maarten?' she asked.

'Negative,' Maarten whispered. 'If Tito's wearing his ViZar, he'll pick up my signature as it is, so I don't want to draw any unnecessary attention to us.'

'Right.'

Ambient light snuck through horizontal louvres at the top of the wall panels – not enough for Juanita to move confidently through the gloom, but enough for her to assess her surrounds. They were inside the Halcyon Tower turret's fifth floor, surrounded on all sides by the derelict Skywalk. If Maarten's hunch was correct, Tito would be admiring the setting sun from the northern deck, as was his tradition whenever he returned to Sydney. He'd be alone, Maarten said, although a drone squadron would be hovering nearby, just out of view, in case their services were required. A successful strike hinged on the element of surprise.

'We came in through the south entrance, didn't we?' Juanita asked Maarten rhetorically. She ran her fingers across a schematic of the fifth floor affixed to the wall opposite the goods lift. 'So we should just follow the path through the plant room here until we get to the window-cleaning equipment garage on the opposite side.'

'Theoretically, yes,' Maarten said. 'Tito never allows anyone else up here, but that's where the main Skywalk deck is, so there must be a doorway there.'

'C'mon then.' Juanita brushed Lottie aside and tiptoed sideways to her left. She pushed through a creaking door into a small equipment room. Blinking lights from control panels mounted on the external wall danced across her face. Juanita led the group confidently past a pair of control panels. Her right elbow collected a rusted metal locker door. It clattered to a close. Juanita's heart sank.

'Careful!' Lottie hissed.

Taking short, deliberate steps, Juanita moved into another sub-sector of the plant room. Tears welled in her eyes as she clutched her smarting funny bone. Two telescopic window-cleaning poles rested against the wall beside an electrical distribution board, its rust-flecked blue door sitting ajar. The fuse boxes and cables inside were a confusion of colours. Juanita's eyes were hollowed out and dry. She pined for her HeadBand's warm embrace.

'Sooooo,' Juanita began, waiting for Maarten and Lottie to join her. Turning away from the control panel, she looked hopefully at Lottie. She tried to shake the pain in her elbow away. 'What should I do?'

'You've always been Tito's number one,' Lottie said.

Maarten nodded his agreement.

Juanita's tear ducts opened, the full weight of the day's events finally hitting home.

'We'll give him a chance to surrender,' Lottie said. 'If anything's going to make him see reason it's an appeal from his one true love.'

'And if that doesn't work,' Maarten said, staring dead ahead, determined. 'I'll seize control of his drones and we'll watch him burn.'

Juanita nodded through gritted teeth. She sucked the mucus filling her nose back down her throat. With the backs of her hands, she brushed the tears from her face. She pulled her ponytail tighter through Tito's scrunchie. For once, she was thankful there wasn't a mirror in sight.

Ignoring the cavalcade of conflicting thoughts thrashing about in her frantic, fragile mind, Juniata picked up the pair of aluminium cleaning poles and started towards the Skywalk door.

| 6.07 |

Setting Sun

'It's wonderful, Kai, Toca, isn't it?' Matthias van Dijk said.

Tito's arm beckoned the twins to admire the vista. The waters of Sydney Harbour appeared immaculate in the slow-moving late afternoon air, broken only by the occasional white cap. Halcyon's flag fluttered gently atop the Sydney Harbour Bridge, flanked either side by the Australian Aboriginal flag's black sky, red soil and golden sun.

Beneath his new ViZar's untinted lens, the glare of the fading sun stung Kai's eyes. In his speaker cups, 'Don't You Worry, Slippy Children' kicked off Cosmo's warm-up set – the penultimate set of Love Buzz 1000, the final hour of power before Kai and Toca's headline debut. He looked beyond Darling Harbour towards the west, where Trancentral Olympic was little more than a long shadow and Doonside just a blip. The sun's dying light shone through long strands of altocumulus clouds, colouring the city in a magnificent collision of purple, yellow and blue – a far cry from the fake blood raining down on the city from Halcyon's pyrocumulus clouds since 1-6-25.

'I didn't realise the world really could be this beautiful,' Kai observed. The angle was different, but the scene was identical to the one he'd seen when the twins' carriage window had malfunctioned at Circular Quay station – not a 'malfunction' exposing Premiums to the VIP carriage's screen saver, but the view that had been there all along. Just as he'd suspected; as Toca, too, had finally accepted.

'A real passport shredder,' Toca agreed, wondering if she'd ever see Maarten again.

'Can you believe people once threw themselves from this golden basket into the abyss below?' Tito enquired of the twins. He motioned through the glass squares of the terrace beneath him towards the streets 280 metres below. 'Unspeakable, really, the desperate lengths our civilisation pushed its people to if they felt they'd failed in their pursuit of some elusive, perfect life.'

Toca, wincing, tried to imagine the sensation of hurtling headlong towards her own demise.

'If only all of man's monstrosities turned out like this,' Tito said wistfully, setting his gaze past Toca towards Sydney Heads. He wrapped his right hand around Toca's left.

Trembling slightly at his touch, cold and wrinkled and creepy, she gripped the viewing platform's railing tighter still. Her acid tongue had abandoned her.

'I've seen this city at its best and its worst, when its nightlife was locked up so prime real estate could be packaged up and sold off, slowly sucking away at its soul one square metre at a time. And the ruling class governed by the politics of fear, which built a wall between people, here and everywhere else, and their most powerful weapon against megalomania – each other.'

Kai looked across the guardrail as Tito uttered 'each other' to find Toca's eyes seeking his.

'But Sydney's back to its best and so am I, right back where it all began with Juanita all those years ago.' A warm breeze whistled through cracks in the glass safety barrier. Tito's fingers squeezed Toca's tiny paw, still trembling. He put his other hand on Kai's shoulder. 'Forget Lennon and McCartney, forget Kylie and Jason – it's time to introduce Kai and Toca to the world.'

'*Tito!*'

Juanita strode up the metal steps to the Skywalk platform. Lottie and Maarten flanked her, two steps behind on either side. A conspiratorial grin edged across Lottie's freckled face.

'Juanita, my darling, we've been expecting you,' Tito said, releasing his grip on the twins, palms held out to show he meant no harm.

'What have you done to these children?' Juanita demanded.

Tito prodded Toca towards the eastward railing to his left. He patted Kai's shoulder, reassuringly, as if to say, *I've got this, my boy.* Toca's heart soared at the sight of Maarten, eyes fixed on Tito, as if Kai and Toca weren't there. Kai was frozen. He almost didn't recognise his idol, dressed in a getup fit for a child, face bearing the scars of the years that her Love Buzz avatar stripped away, her hair – not blue but two-toned brown and blonde – littered with shards of glass, her body covered in scratches and bruises, her left hand caked with blood. This wasn't the benevolent Juanita, plastered across the Three-Way's countdown ticker, nor the bewildered one who'd alerted Kai and the world to the coming Storm. This Juanita looked fierce, determined. This Juanita was near enough to touch.

'What have you done?!' Juanita's shrill scream reverberated off the nearby skyscrapers.

'Nothing untoward, I assure you,' Tito replied indignantly.

'That would be a first,' Lottie seethed at him from over Juanita's left shoulder.

'A bit rich coming from you, Lottie – weren't *you* controlling *me?*' Tito countered. 'But I guess playing victim helped manipulate my son into joining your little power grab.'

'It's not about power,' Maarten retorted. 'I love her, Dad.'

'Then you're even more soft-headed than I was, son,' Tito said. 'But this he-said, she-said routine is already boring me.'

Flamboyantly, Tito clicked his right thumb and middle finger in the air. Three collection drones rose up from behind the Skywalk guardrail, lining up opposite Tito's adversaries. Maarten motioned in the air before his eyes, frantically working his fingers across knobs and sliders in an attempt to wrest control of the drones from their master.

'No, no, no,' he muttered. 'Someone's overriding me!'

Red light streamed from the eyes of the drones on the flanks. Juanita shielded her face.

'Maarten, quick—' Lottie's words became a scream of abject terror.

'Lotts, I—' Maarten's dancing fingers froze like claws, forever clutching at thin air.

Hundreds of red pinpricks of light formed two thick shafts that gripped Lottie and Maarten's faces, then lifted their petrified bodies off the deck. Three metres above the platform they suddenly rocketed towards the collection drones, bodies trailing their faces at a forty-five-degree angle. Maarten's head collided viciously with the collection drone's nose cone. When Lottie's head did likewise her right eye burst from its socket, splattering her Day-Glo overalls with blood. Droplets of thick claret fell from her canvas Volleys into the grand abyss below.

Juanita's scream echoed across the top of the city.

The drones continued to hover ominously.

Kai army-crawled across the floor in front of Tito to reach Toca, who cowered against the guardrail, covering her face.

Juanita stared down her own metallic shark. If she was going to get through this alive, tears for her fallen companions would have to wait.

'Juanita, this can end now,' Tito pleaded.

Juanita broke free of the collection drone's dead-eyed gaze and stared Tito down.

'Let me show you to your private Cognition Chamber downstairs, where you'll never have to worry about any of this again,' Tito said softly.

'Until you drop a Prodigy in my place, huh?' Juanita spat. 'Bonn-E? I think I'll pass.'

'Don't believe everything those traitors told you,' Tito barked defiantly, though his guilty expression told Juanita this was information she shouldn't know.

'How could you take all of this from us?' The words escaped Juanita's throat with such ferocity they threatened to loosen strips of flesh. She waved her arms across a cityscape frozen in time. Bodies moved inside the apartment tower to Tito's right, but they only had eyes for the Storm.

'Oh, Juanita.' Tito's kindly face turned cruel. 'You still can't see it, can you, you silly little moppet,' he said. 'Stuck inside Bonnie Stapleton's "International Party Girl" fantasy for so long you can't see the difference between the world's end and its salvation.'

Expecting Juanita's resolve to crumble as it had every other time he'd manipulated her over the decades, Tito's lips pursed in a rueful smile. 'Yours was the generation that turned inwards, resigned to its supposedly inevitable fate,' he asserted. He held out a hand of invitation. 'Come with me now and you can retire safely in the knowledge that when the dust finally settles, your face won't be recast as a symbol of humanity's demise—'

'*Oh* would you *please* just shut the fuck up?!' Juanita interrupted. 'I never want to hear your voice again you fucking self-righteous fuck.'

Juanita assumed her signature starting position: left foot and body turned outwards; right leg forward, knee bent, foot on pointed toes. Her hands came out from behind her back, each holding a cleaner's pole extended to one metre in length.

Kai shook his sister. *Tokes, you've gotta see this.*

Toca warily spread her fingers and peeked through the gaps.

Juanita held the left staff across her face; the right was by her side, ready to strike.

The briefest flash of uncertainty zapped across Tito's usually implacable blue-eyed calm. The fear disappeared with a twitch of his jaw, uncharacteristically covered in the patchy silver stubble he'd forgotten to shave off as the previous 24 hours had gotten away from him. He took a single step away from the guardrail and stood his ground.

'*Arrgghh!*' A primal scream, stripped of any honey coating, exploded from Juanita as she charged across the platform.

Three steps into her run-up she cartwheeled forward on her knuckles, reproducing the Ms Gillies training drill that had finally made her quit gymnastics for good. She landed the move without releasing her grip on the poles, three metres from Tito, who was taken aback at Juanita's sudden turn of speed.

Spinning the poles like giant glowstaffs in the Ultraworld, Juanita sprung back into the air in the one movement. This stag leap, once her signature move – and designed to be performed in figure-hugging fabric, not loose-fitting denim – was too lacking in grace to satisfy the bitter old hag who'd taught her, but its shock value had the desired effect.

'Drones!' Tito cried.

The collection drone behind him kept a respectful distance, its eye sockets refusing to light up. Tito wasn't sure whether to block the squared-off knee pointed at his chest or the foot kicked up behind Juanita's ponytail. Juanita's spinning staff smashed into his forehead and sent his ViZar crashing to the glass terrace. Doubled over, Tito saw the nanotech lens and speaker cups disappear back into its nose clip before the other pole uppercut him, flush on the cheek, as Juanita's feet landed the manoeuvre a metre in front of him. The force of the blow sent him back into the guardrail, bruising his lower back and knocking every molecule of carbon dioxide from his lungs.

Momentum flung his feet over his head, his hands clutching for a secure grip they couldn't find. Matthias van Dijk's body reverse somersaulted into the depths below, on and on and on until he was swallowed by the shadows beneath Sydney's perfect sunset.

Juanita stared in shock through the Skywalk's glass-bottom floor. Kai and Toca moved to Juanita, stunned as much by being in her presence as by what they'd witnessed. The lead collection drone and its companions hung silently, unmoved by the gentle breeze buffeting Lottie and Maarten's dangling bodies.

From somewhere above the Skydeck bloodshed, a pair of hands slowly clapped.

'Brava, Juanita!'

Juanita spun towards the turret's centre, impromptu quarterstaffs instinctively raised to protect her and the twins. Through tear-filled eyes, she frantically searched for the source of the voice.

'That's a perfect ten from this judge.'

Kai's hand directed her gaze upwards, towards a balcony built into the walls two levels above. Tucked in behind two communications dishes stood a lone figure, bedecked in a smart two-piece suit and a ViZar nose clip much like Tito's. The olive-skinned face peering down at her from beneath the Halcyon Tower spire was a distant ghost of kick-ons past.

'L . . . Lawrence?' Juanita stuttered.

'Thanks to you, Neets,' Lawrence yelled down at her, 'the journey's over.'

Juanita's 'stomach feeling' of fear and uncertainty returned, swinging samurai swords instead of quarterstaffs.

'I've finally arrived.'

Don't Give Up

Love Buzz 1000's global dancefloor was threatening to flatline as its twenty-fourth hour of power neared its zenith. Staccato hand claps, trailed by layers of syncopated delay, weren't enough to rouse Kai and Toca from their energy-sapped torpor. Waning enthusiasm radiated out of the twins, Love Buzz's new life source, and into the hungry hearts of Survivors.

'*L . . . l-l-l . . .*'

The disembodied voice, already deeper than the deepest depths Dav had plumbed with Toca in his Cognition Chamber three hours earlier, sunk an octave deeper.

'*. . . is for love.*'

A flurry of snare drums burst through the gentle atmos. Looking across the vastness of the Ultraworld, the twins saw three billion pairs of hands rise to herald their arrival. Survivors clamoured for the traditional farewell salute from their newly anointed king and queen. This was the momentum boost the fledgling Virtuoso team needed, as if they'd been hoisted upon the shoulders of the world, victorious, energised for the final run home.

Ghost-like archival footage of Juanita, from her teen prodigy beginnings to her incendiary One World performances, danced in the spaces between and either side of Kai and Toca's avatars. Juanita's array of catsuits from across the decades glistened as brightly as the twins' contrasting black and white bodysuits. Kai and Toca swivelled and pulsed in perfect sync, as they had throughout the preceding fifty-nine minutes.

Following Kai's lead, Toca dismissed the control panels framing the left and right of her ViZar's screen with karate-like flourishes of each arm. She pictured Satoshi Ishii, tuned in for Juanita but unwittingly seeing his progeny's Love Buzz debut instead, beaming with pride at each swipe, more powerful than Sailor Moon, Sailor Mars and Sailor Mercury combined.

Toca shook her father from her thoughts and focused on the bright-red icon pulsing atop her otherwise empty console.

'A . . . B . . . C . . .'

'Love Buzz 1000, thank you for making us so welcome tonight!' Toca cried.

The shapeless mass of every voice on the planet roaring as one filled her ears.

'A . . . B . . . C . . .'

'Are you ready to slow down gravity with us?' Kai challenged. A second wave of exaltation galvanised Kai, like a citrus-shake shot into his limbs.

'C is for consciousness-s-s-s-s . . .'

From atop a raised platform not far from the Trancentral Sydney main stage, Juanita watched the twins' avatars effortlessly run through the playbook she'd formulated over twenty-two years. Her vantage point was a small life raft of calm in the middle of a raging sea of Silo platforms. Love Buzzed limbs flailed around the old SFS's playing surface, bodies thrashing as if at the mercy of a faith healer, pulling their strings, speaking in tongues. Juanita's head bobbed up and down of its own accord, even as she wept for Lottie, Bonnie Stapleton, Tito, the twins, the unsuspecting world.

A fresh assault of snares snaked its way towards the ultimate crescendo. She felt the firm squeeze of a hand on her shoulder.

'Raise your hands, Neets, and strap yourself in,' Lawrence said, thrusting a ViZar-1000 nose clip towards her. 'After everything you've been through, you don't want to miss the finale.'

Reluctantly, Juanita nodded. For the second time in twenty-four hours, her hips shook to the melting bassline she'd never heard until visiting the St James Lake rave cave; the music of the underground, reheated by Halcyon's robots and served up as something new. Tito's Theory of Cycles at work, even in death. She clipped the ViZar to the bridge of her nose and a translucent viewfinder sprung from its sides. Lens complete, the ViZar generated a custom-fit fibre casing, which wrapped around the back of her head to keep the nanospeakers firmly fastened to her ears.

'*L . . . l-l-l . . .*'

From his aching sides, Kai's hands began a slow arc to the juncture above his head, echoing the stance of the expectant, adoring legion of new disciples willing the beat back from its hibernation.

'No more empty platitudes,' Kai breathlessly declared.

'No more senseless white noise,' Toca added.

'*Only the true sound of the underground!*' the twins cried in unison.

Dav nodded approvingly from Juanita's velour recliner chair. It was the only original fixture that remained in her apartment aside from her Silo platform, which Kai had stepped up to and made his own. Toca stood atop a companion platform to Kai's left.

One metre in front of each of their faces hovered a collection drone, poised to strike if the twins went off script.

Satisfied, Dav attached his own ViZar to his nose. Nanotech robots worked their magic across his eye sockets. Sinking his fingers into the plush armrests, Davide rocked the chair back as far as it would go.

'*. . . is for love.*'

Each of the twins' fingertips met above their head at full stretch, forming the unmistakeable ideogram of a human heart. The dancefloor sent billions of heart-hands right back. The empathy rush of the Drop surged through them all, twice as powerful as it ever had before.

The Storm is a front. Toca reached out to Kai. *You were right from the start.*

And when Lawrence drops his guard. Kai braced himself for impact. *We'll make it stop!*

The twins' bodies fell limp and then they were gone, engulfed by a sphere of blinding white light as a shock wave of euphoria blanketed Earth and the Ultraworld.

ACKNOWLEDGEMENTS

To Rakhi, my amazing (dare I say, 'loving and devoted'?) wife, thank you for tolerating a relentless barrage of blank looks when I was lost adrift in the Ultraworld, and just tolerating me in general, really. To Liz Galinovic, for red-penning all the rubbish that got me to this point, and for red-penning this, twice, and for everything else. To Andrew Mast, for not batting an eyelid when a blog piece entitled 'Is EDM just a new form of MK-Ultra mind control?' landed in your inbox all those years ago.

To my editor Gemma Dean-Furlong, for demanding both less *and* more at every turn, asking 'Really?' when it really needed to be asked, and mercilessly striking 'whom' and 'whence' as required. And from the top and all the way through, thanks to David Ryan for your peerless perspective on all things geek, and Jaymis Loveday for the early tech advice.

To the original Drop cronies, Scott Walker and Damian Wheeler (whose design work, along with the amazing Juanita illustration by Pete Georgiou, also adorns the book you hold in your hands), thanks for soundtracking some of the best times of my life – and a shout-out to all the honorary cronies who have aided and abetted them along the way. Thanks also to every producer whose track I've trainspotted across *The Drop* (legend has it that if you successfully ID every one of them, a mint original edition of Charanjit Singh's *Ten Ragas To A Disco Beat* will materialise on your Expedit), particularly Drax, Gooding and

Taariq for bequeathing 'ABC' on the world and allowing me to use it as my centrepiece. And at the business end of proceedings, thanks to Ryan Dickinson for capturing the sound and essence of *The Drop* for the promotional video, and to Jase Percy-Spiller for his wise counsel around how to launch the book into the world – or more importantly, how not to.

Finally, thank you to Mum and Dad for buying me a drum kit, surely the most insane hobby any parent can voluntarily inflict on their household, and for encouraging my creative endeavours all the way through.

Around the same time, my high school English teachers, Mr Yeabsley and Mr Caldwell, encouraged me to open my mind and speak it honestly when most of their peers just wanted that half-smart teenager to recite the script.

The journey to here started there. Like my girl Juanita, I guess I finally arrived as well.

Last but not least, let's see some hands in the air for all of the Kickstarter backers who helped me get this book into your hands, particularly my Cronies, Randoms, Virtuosos and Double Droppers: Scott & Lisa Robertson, David Appleseed, Cosmo Cater, Leo Hede, Mary Myers, Carl Sullivan, Fergus Seppanen, Daniel Crichton-Rouse, KC, Cam Swales, Ralphie, Rob Swales, Aditi Chaudhuri, Vikram Chaudhuri, Scott Walker, Chris Walker, Danielle Evans, Aimee Bynon-Powell & Christopher Robinson, Mike Redfern, Trent Allen, Renee Moynihan, NATO2042, Erin Doyle, Robert Angi, Ruby Angi, Amber Stocks, Natasha Lewis Honeyman (MC), Clarissa Esteller, Steph Porrino, Stu Robinson, Shanel Catasti, Frankie Hart, Arjun Rao, Uma Nair, Simon Maher, Jane Hincksman, Jase and LP, Old Dog and Uncle Mich and the boy cousins.

Kris Swales is an Australian writer and lapsed musician who works as a home-page editor at *The Australian Financial Review*. He was the final editor of Sydney's weekly dance music bible *3D World*, wrote extensively for *Inthemix*, and has performed at events like the Big Day Out, Earthcore, Parklife and Future Music Festival. *The Drop* is his first novel. www.krisswales.com | @KrisSwales